Swords and Scoundrels

Vocho's right hand found his blade where he'd put it, on a bracket under the chunky table where it was hidden but easy to reach. Even as he got it, his left hand was reaching out for the chest. Jewels, had to be. Jewels, gold, a king's ransom, his and Kacha's way out of this hovel and back where they belonged.

"Don't be an idiot," Kacha hissed and whacked his hand with the flat of her blade. "Whatever it is, it's still out there."

"You've really lost your sense of humour lately, you know that?" But Vocho withdrew his hand and faced the door.

Outside, it should have been sunshine through rain clouds, a yellow and green spring, but that was the opposite of what Vocho saw through the shattered doorway. Blackness, dim and swirling like fog. Silent too, as though it was sucking up all sound. Hard to not to let the first thought into his head unnerve him: the magician was back for his chest. How in seven hells had he found them? Quickly followed by: could a magician really vaporise him?

He didn't want to find out. Something moved in the fog, and Vocho moved too. No thought behind it except get out alive, preferably with the contents of the chest. He launched himself forward into a roll, bounced up to his feet, sword at the ready . . .

Swords and Scoundrels

The Duellists: Book One

Julia Knight

www.orbitbooks.net

ORBIT

First published in Great Britain in 2015 by Orbit

1 3 5 7 9 10 8 6 4 2

A CIP catalogue record for this book is available from the British Library.

ISBN 978-0-356-50407-0

Typeset in Apollo MT by Palimpsest Book Production Limited,
Falkirk, Stirlingshire
Printed and bound in Great Britain by CPI Group (UK) Ltd, Croydon CR0 4YY

Papers used by Orbit are from well-managed forests and other responsible sources.

MIX
Paper from
responsible sources
FSC
FSC® C104740

Chapter One

They say that an ounce of blood is worth more than a pound of friendship. Vocho wasn't so sure about that. Probably depended on whose blood you were talking about, because blood seemed to have got him into nothing but trouble.

The wood Vocho and Kacha lurked in was a mean little thing, a straggle of trees and stunted bushes that fringed the muddy track between some two-cow town in the province of Reyes and a different two-cow, perhaps even three-cow town up towards the mountains and the border with Ikaras. A desolate and rain-sodden spot in the back of beyond, a far cry from the city of Reyes itself. Vocho sat and shivered and dripped as he watched his sister, atop her restless horse, wrestle with the clockwork gun.

"Are you certain you know what you're doing with that thing?" he said at last. In retrospect, it wasn't the best thing Vocho could have said to her just then.

Kacha stopped scowling at the gun and scowled at him instead before she raised a cool eyebrow and blew a drip of water off the end of her nose. "Of course. Pretty sure I know where I went wrong last time."

"You shot my horse's ear off."

A curl of her lip from under her dripping tricorne. She

was indistinct in the darkness under the sodden trees, her heavy black coat and that ridiculous hat fading into the shadows, leaving only the pale blur of her face.

"Anyone could have made that mistake," she said airily. "It's not like, oh, I don't know, killing the priest we were supposed to be guarding, right?"

"That was an accident!" Vocho was pretty sure anyway – the memories of that night were vague, and though they seemed vivid enough in his dreams, they soon faded to guesswork and ghosts when he woke up. Sadly the duellists' guild hadn't seen it as an accident when said priest had turned up with a sword hole in him. Worse, it was Vocho's sword, the hilt still in his hand. The guild, not to mention the prelate and his guards, tended to take a dim view of that sort of thing. Very dim.

"He was only a priest, and a bad one at that, and that was a good horse." Vocho still smarted at the fact they'd had to sell the horse – for some reason it had got very nervy after that accident, and nervy horses weren't good in his new profession of highwayman.

"Maybe only a priest," Kacha said. "But he was the prelate's favourite. He was paying our wages, and the prelate's department and the guild get very upset about people killing priests they're being paid to guard." Kacha hefted the gun, prodded the clockwork mechanism and scowled at it some more, like that would make it work properly. "At least in the guild we didn't have to deal with these sodding things."

Vocho subtly tried to edge his horse backwards, out of line of sight of the gun, but instead the beast barged sideways and knocked into Kacha's horse, making it shy and snap at the air, narrowly missing the feather stuck in the brim of Vocho's hat.

"Careful," Kacha muttered, "or it'll be your ear I take off, and not by accident."

Vocho knew when it was time to stay quiet, and now was

such a time. His older sister was mercurial in nature and never more so than when waiting in a dark and rain-drenched wood on the edge of cold mountains for some clocker or ex-noble to drive by so they could rob him, instead of being in a nice dry guild house in a nice hot city down by the coast. Especially when it was because of that dead priest they weren't in said dry guild house or hot city. Even more especially when Kacha had a new-fangled gun that was difficult to shoot right at best, and an accident waiting to happen at worst. Oh, how the mighty are fallen.

The rain intensified, bouncing from leaf to sodden leaf, shivering from cloud to ground in a constant litany of sound. Confounded northern mountain weather. Vocho would have given a lot of money to be back in Reyes city. It'd be full-blown spring down there by now, and a Reyes spring tended not to include bucketloads of rain, but featured long hot lazy afternoons with a cool breeze coming in off the sea. The nightlife tended to be a little more refined than getting soaked to the skin in the muddy arse-end of nowhere as well.

Raindrops plastered the jaunty feather on Vocho's hat into a tangled mess, ran down his neck, soaked through his heavy cloak and his fancy trousers, was utterly ruining the finish on his best coat and made his hands slip on the little crossbow. He didn't like crossbows any more than he liked guns, but they had a tendency to backfire less and sometimes you needed one, even if it was a coward's weapon. Not so long ago they'd have been drummed out of the guild for using one, or the gun, if they hadn't already been drummed out. He could hear his old sword master now. *A projectile weapon is only for those with no class or no balls.*

Three months ago he wouldn't have gone out on a night like this for any money. Three months ago he'd have had that choice. Now he had no money and no choice, so here he was, shrivelling in the rain like a sodding prune. He might be poor, more than poor now, but a man had to make an impression and right now all he was good for was looking like a rat drowned in a water butt.

One insignificant little mistake, and they never let you forget it.

Kacha sat up straight beside him, listening. The rain had soaked through her hat, turning it into a sopping mess, and her blonde hair was dark and lank, but she didn't seem to mind. Over the whisper of the wind and the rush of the rain came the faintest jingle, as of a horse harness. A vague splashing rumble, as of carriage wheels negotiating a muddy road.

"Kacha . . ."

She shot him a lopsided grin, but it was wound tight as a bowstring. She always got twitchy before a fight, and always hid it with a grin.

"Mask," she whispered. He pulled his soaking scarf over his chin and nose and she did the same, making sure it was pulled up far enough to cover the telltale puckered scar under her eye. Between the scarf and hat, he'd have been hard pushed to recognise her if he didn't know her.

A carriage came in to view around the corner, mud splashing from its wheels. A lumbering coach and four, it looked promising – well kept with fancy harness, and the horses were all matched too, which boded well. The driver was a huddle of clothes bundled up in an overlarge shapeless hat and an oilskin cloak against the weather. One armed and lightly armoured man in front on a springy bay horse that looked like it'd jump out of its skin at the slightest provocation, one to the side on a steadier-looking grey. Both men looked thoroughly miserable even under large hooded cloaks. Vocho could sympathise.

A lamp either side of the driver gave Vocho and Kacha light to work with. They waited till the coach was almost on them, then Kacha dug her heels in and her horse leaped from behind the screen of bushes and in front of the carriage. Vocho wasn't far behind, aiming his horse to the rear of the carriage to stop it backing up. The bodyguard on the side didn't have a chance to do more than draw his sword before Vocho's bolt had his hand pinned to the side of the coach. Which was embarrassing because he'd been aiming somewhere else, but he'd take what he could get.

In the hazy darkness at the front of the carriage the driver swore a blue streak and yanked on the horses, which protested at the treatment and managed to get themselves tangled in the traces. The carriage slewed to a stop, making the pinned bodyguard scream before his hand, bolt and all, came free. He knocked his head on the way down into the mud and slumped unconscious. Which at least saved Vocho a job.

By the time the horses had stopped, the fore bodyguard was down and out in the mud thanks to Kacha's bad-tempered horse lashing out at the bay and an expertly aimed smack in the head from the butt of Kacha's gun. The bay horse dumped its suddenly unresponsive rider and shot up the road, reins and stirrups flapping, like as not never to be seen again.

Like a well oiled machine, the two of them. When they worked together, nothing and no one could stop them. They hadn't been the best in the guild for nothing. At least it was earning them some money.

Muffled voices from inside the carriage, most with a hint of moneyed education about them, expressed varying amounts of surprise or drunken annoyance. Vocho heard a faint, "I say! That was bit harsh. Need to discipline your driver, Eggy old lad, I almost spilt my wine."

Kacha might have been wearing a mask, but her brother could see the flinch around her eyes at the name. Good and not so good. Ex-Lord Petri Egimont, ex-noble who liked to let everyone know it, first-rate duellist, currently a lowly clerk in the prelate's office, a pet, a symbol of the revolution the prelate liked to parade in front of his admirers more than anything, and yet of more than solvent means. He also knew both Vocho and Kacha, very well indeed in Kacha's case. Their little spy at the inn on the edge of the woods had neglected to mention who the owner of the carriage was, instead telling them how the man thought tales of highwaymen lately come to the woods were a crock of bollocks and how he was determined to reach his destination by morning. Not to mention how he didn't bother with many bodyguards, thinking he was above being robbed, or if he was, could beat them in a fair fight.

Sounded just like the pompous Eggy. More fool him.

A pale-haired head poked out of the carriage window. Not Egimont, but certainly once aristocratic if the quality of the chin, or lack thereof, was anything to go by. "Driver? Driver!" His voice was strident and slurred. "What the blazes do you think you're—"

Kacha shoved the barrel of the gun into the side of his nose. She made her voice a couple of octaves lower than it already was and slipped into a guttersnipe accent to avoid giving herself away to Eggy in the coach. "Good evening. If it's all the same to you, I'd like to divest you of all your valuables, trinkets and trifles. Money or a hole in the head. I like to do things properly."

"We'd prefer the money," Vocho added from his end, affecting a noble accent. "But sometimes a hole in the head is so satisfying, don't you think? And we haven't shot anyone for *days*."

A click as Kacha did something menacing with the gun. A whispered conversation inside the carriage. Vocho caught sight of the driver, who waggled his eyebrows as though trying to say something. Sadly, Vocho didn't speak eyebrow.

"Oh," said the pale-haired man, going cross-eyed as he tried to look at the barrel of the gun while not moving his head. "Well. I'm sure we can come to some arrangement. Perhaps twenty bulls? I'm sure I've got enough change. That would seem fair . . . Oh."

Kacha had nudged her horse up parallel to the carriage, and the evil-minded beast knew exactly what was wanted. It grabbed the pale man's hat off his head with a great show of teeth and for good measure at a signal from Kacha kicked hard enough to hole the carriage. That horse was more a highwayman than Vocho was, and made him mourn once again the loss of his old horse with its one ear. This new one was dancing under him like a ballerina.

"I think . . ." Kacha said with an air of contemplation. If she hadn't been wearing her mask, Vocho knew he'd see that lopsided grin again. "I think everything you have would be fair. Those are our usual terms. I wouldn't like it said that we had favourites. As it's cold, I'll let you keep your underwear. Can't say fairer than that, can we?"

Just to underline her words, the horse snapped its teeth a hair's breadth from the pale man's nose. Between that and the gun barrel, it was looking like he'd have no nose left come sunup.

"Um, well yes, you have a point." The pale man retreated into the carriage to a hurried and whispered conversation. Vocho caught, "Damned cheek of it!" "They've got a gun," "So have I, somewhere . . ." "You can't even see straight, never mind shoot straight," "Being robbed by highwaymen is an extra, my lord" in a woman's voice and "God's cogs, I was just starting to enjoy myself," followed by a boozy-sounding burp.

Another head poked out. Dark rather than fair this time, long hair done in the latest foppish style, bound at the base of the neck so that it curled across one shoulder. The face less vacuous, with more of a chin. A trim little beard, a long haughty nose, sharp dark eyes and apparently at least slightly less drunk than Pale Hair. Egimont. Vocho had his sword out and ready, just in case. Just in case Kacha shot the ear off a horse by mistake, or Egimont in the face. Given their recent history, it wouldn't have surprised him. If she didn't, he might very well give it a try himself. He sneaked a look at her and was troubled to see her look stricken just for a moment. Like she was ready to drag down her mask and let the world know who they were. Let Eggy know who they were, which would be a disaster.

Time for action. "Could we hurry this up?" Vocho asked. "I'm getting sodding wet here."

It was enough to get Kacha to pull herself together, and she gave him a brief nod to let him know.

"I'm sure we can negotiate, my good sir," Egimont said to Kacha in the sort of deadpan drawl that made Vocho's shoulders itch. He said everything like that – when he spoke at all, which was rare enough – as though all was beneath his notice. He was just so effortlessly bloody *suave*, which was only the start of the things Vocho had against him.

He braced himself for Kacha's reply but she kept herself reined in. For now. Only the Clockwork God knew how long it would last.

"No, we may not," she said in a voice thick with suppressed fury. "Instead, I will shoot your gormless face off if I have to. We're good with cash though. And jewels, we like jewels, rings, necklaces, trinkets, trifles, baubles and bibelots. How much have you got?"

Egimont raised his eyebrows. Kacha had never got the hang of courtly manners though she could pretend well enough when she needed to. "Not a lot as it happens. Temporarily embarrassed. You know how it is." Egimont sounded odd – Vocho could only assume he was playing to the drunk ex-nobles in the carriage – which begged the question of why.

"Not really," Kacha said. Vocho didn't like the way her finger was twitching on the what-d'you-call-it – trigger, was it? The thing that made the gun go bang anyway. "Everything, that's what we're going for. Now out, all of you. And anyone looks like they're trying anything, this gun tends to go off at a moment's notice. So do I. And blood is such a trial to get out of silk, isn't it?"

Egimont sighed as though he was suffering a great trial for a mere triviality and feigned defeat, though knowing the preening mountebank Vocho didn't believe it for a moment. The door opened and they trooped out. Three men, one so drunk he could hardly stand, but not so drunk he couldn't be sick, which he managed to do all over the pale-haired fellow, who was pretty damned drunk himself. Two women not, how could Vocho put this? Not of the same class. Underfed, underdressed. Women who were most certainly of his own original station – wretched and plebeian, just trying to earn enough to eat the only way they could. Vocho leaned over the pommel of his saddle, sword out and ready in case these fools weren't as drunk as they looked.

"You ladies may go. If you're quick, the inn'll still be open."

They didn't need telling twice – a quick glance of agreement between them and they hared up the muddy road without a backwards glance. Pale Hair looked after them forlornly. "But I already *paid*!" he wailed to no one, or no one who cared anyway.

Kacha looked up at the driver, who silently spread his hands as if to say, *These posh sods deserve everything they get*. He was still waggling his eyebrows and mouthing something, but what with the dark and the rain, Vocho couldn't catch it.

"You keep an eye on him," Kacha said to Vocho with a nod to the driver. Her horse grabbed at the ruffles on the front of Egimont's shirt and started to munch with much apparent delight and flashing of big teeth. Vocho would have sworn it understood the concept of intimidation, though good luck to it trying to get a rise out of the imperturbable Eggy.

"And now, gentlemen, if you'd like to empty your pockets." Kacha was enjoying this, Vocho could tell by the undertone in her voice even as she tried to disguise it. Payback for whatever had happened between her and Eggy, which had left her bad-tempered or alternately silent and dreaming for weeks.

A gun waved in front of them seemed to get them going. Eggy threw two purses into the mud, both clinking heavily. "Go on, Berie," he said. "And get Flashy's too."

Three more purses, all full. Not bad, not bad at all. At a signal from Kacha, Vocho leaped down from his horse, and that's where it all went wrong.

Kacha's evil sod of a horse took exception to Eggy's face and made a grab for it. Eggy wasn't as drunk as he looked, jumped back half a pace and snatched at the sword at his waist. Kacha wasn't drunk at all, but the horse's sudden lunge caught her off guard. The gun fired, there was a bang that seemed like it might take Vocho's ears off, followed by a brief, gurgling moan. Flashy held up a hand with a hole in it, and promptly stopped being drunk and started being passed out at about the same time he fell into the mud.

"Aw, shit," Kacha said but she didn't get any further. Eggy had his sword out – despite the rest of his foppish appearance, it was a good if plain sword, well used – and went for her, smooth as well oiled gears, looking as effortless as ever. Berie tried the same with his flash and glitter sword, got it tangled up in his scabbard, tripped over his own feet and ended up face first in the mud next to Flashy, only less passed out.

Then things got really bad. A tinny feel to the air. The smell of burned blood. The two things together seemed very familiar, but Vocho couldn't place from where. The hairs on his neck and arms rose. Burned blood . . . what did that remind him of? And then it came to him that he was deep in the shit. Who burned blood? Magicians, that's who. What the hells was one doing here? There hadn't been one in the kingdom for years, not since the prelate gained power and had them killed or chased out for being against his careful, orderly new clockwork plan for the country. Which didn't explain why the smell seemed familiar.

Time for that later. He had to take out these men before the suspected magician still in the carriage caused carnage. He planted one foot on Berie's prone back, with a softish kick to the head to keep him there, and swivelled.

Kacha was off the horse by now – was it Vocho or was that evil thing grinning? – and stood, ready and waiting for Eggy to come on. The stupid gun was still in her off hand, and as Vocho turned she flung it at Eggy, catching him a great crack across the forehead that made him stagger back, feet slipping in the mud.

Even Vocho had to admit that Egimont was a fine duellist, but Kacha had the measure of him and a grudge besides. Vocho took half a heartbeat to see her slip under his guard and then left her to it. If there was one thing he was sure of, it was that his sister could take care of herself.

He wasn't so sure he could, not against a magician. About as rare as rocking-horse shit they were, or had been. Now they were non-existent in Reyes. Just about all he knew was that they were as powerful as kings, which is perhaps why the prelate hated them so much. He'd heard of a man fried where he stood, turned to ash with not even the chance to flinch. Time to be seriously careful, but Vocho had never been a careful man. When he won, which was always, however he could, he did it with speed and above all *style*.

Only he'd never actually faced a magician. He'd never even seen one, only heard tales. Fuck it, you only lived once.

The inside of the carriage smelled of burned blood and

infamy. It was no wonder Kacha hadn't seen the man, magician or not – he was in the far corner, dressed in flowing midnight blue, cloak, robe and hood fading into the shifting shadows of a dark and rainy night. His face was a pale, scarred smudge against the window and naggingly familiar. The faint suggestion of blood on his hands was the only new clue to what he was. Vocho's scant consolation was that if he was a magician, he needed blood to draw on to power his spells and there wasn't any handy. Except his own or Vocho's, but he had no intention of letting anyone get blood on his clothes.

During all the business outside – Vocho could hear the click and clang of blades, and Kacha flinging barbed insults that the stoic and ever-so-noble Egimont wouldn't deign to answer – the magician would have had time to prepare. He didn't seem drunk like the rest, in fact he seemed distressingly alert.

Vocho approached, blade ready in the Icthian style. Free form and ready for anything seemed best at this point, and besides it was his favourite. He advanced slowly but not especially carefully – his forte was the sudden, impulsive move that was frowned on in the guild but would also catch his opponent off guard.

The magician, if that's what he truly was, held up his bloodstained hands in a gesture that looked like a yield. Vocho didn't trust it for a second. Another step forward and his blade hovered over the man's throat.

"My money or a hole in my head, I understand," the man said. Odd sort of accent, sort of hard and sibilant at the same time, the voice soft but with a crackling undertone that shivered all the hairs on Vocho's neck.

"That's the idea," Vocho said and arranged his feet so he'd have the perfect balance should he need to thrust. He'd never been one for killing for killing's sake, but he'd not shy away if it was necessary. And a magician – it could be *very* necessary, if he wanted to live out the night. "What have you got? No, no dipping in your own pockets, thanks. I'm a thief not an idiot."

The magician inclined his head in agreement. "So I see. I have nothing that would be any value to you, I assure you. A few papers, the clothes I wear. Quills and pens and scalpels for my work, you understand."

A quick movement of his hand that drew Vocho's eye, a hand scarred beyond belief but in a bizarrely beautiful sort of way. Dark patterns flowed across knuckles, symbols etched there by who-knew-what sorcery. They seemed to move on their own, those patterns, a flow that took the eye and caught the brain, made him follow them like a starving dog following its master. An itch started between Vocho's shoulder blades, familiar and yet not, and turned to a burn.

"Nothing for you," the magician said. "Except I may have to kill you. With the utmost regret, of course."

"Of course." The patterns shifted, became scenes of blood and murder, of headless bodies and sightless skulls, of days of glory in the guild sparring arena that led Vocho's head off into odd, dark dreams. The voice sounded more and more familiar but he was past caring, too wrapped up in what the hands were showing him. The burning on his back grew worse, made sweat pop up all along his lip and his hand slick on the hilt of his blade. Frighteningly familiar, yet he couldn't remember – and did it matter, when those patterns were drawing him in?

A shout from outside, a curse from Kacha and then Eggy calling out an odd word, a name perhaps? A plea for help, certainly. The sounds snapped Vocho back to himself, just in time to see the magician dip a pen into a pot of . . . *of blood. Let's not be shy here, that's blood* . . . and begin a new pattern on his outstretched palm.

The magician was quick, but Vocho had made his name being the quickest man in the duelling guild, so fast he could stab a man and put away his sword before anyone had seen him move. Well, almost that quick. Maybe the magician wasn't expecting him to be so fast, maybe he thought Vocho was still hypnotised by the flowing patterns, maybe he didn't expect anyone to attack him at all – magicians were renowned for their arrogance. Whichever, he wasn't expecting a sword to run him through. Even so, he surprised Vocho by almost getting out of the way – so fast he blurred, but the point still caught him. Just not in the neck. Instead, the sword went straight through the meaty top part of the man's shoulder and pinned him to the side of the carriage.

The magician let lose a stream of words in a language Vocho didn't have a hope of understanding. Blood bubbled from the wound – Vocho needed to finish this and quick, before the magician used the blood to finish Vocho. Another thrust, quick as the first, and the magician was too busy grabbing something out of a pocket to move. The blade slid in, right into his windpipe. *Cast a spell now, bastard.* The magician's eyes flew wide and one hand scrabbled at his neck, at the blade. The other had hold of . . . *Oh shit.*

Vocho knew less than bugger all about magicians, but even he knew the scrap of paper with bloody shifting patterns on it wasn't good. A stored spell, that was all it could be, blood marking the paper like written death. There were tales of them that Vocho had never believed, but he did now. A spell to do what? He'd heard of some men vaporised . . .

He knew enough to get the fuck out of the way. He whipped his sword free of the man's neck in a gurgle of breath and blood and dived out of a window head first, rolling as he landed, screaming when the burning on his back caught on his shirt. Straight into the mud, but even he didn't care about getting mud on his nice coat now.

When nothing obvious happened, no explosions and he

was still all in one piece, he dared a look up. The carriage door flapped open. Inside, the only sign of the mage was blood on the seat and side of the carriage and a now burned and shrivelled piece of paper fluttering to the floor.

A lucky escape. *You're sitting in the mud, looking like an idiot while Kacha gets all the glory again.* He shoved himself up and took stock. He'd ended up on the other side of the carriage from where Kacha and Egimont were fighting. Hadn't she finished him off by now? When he thought on it, he realised how little time had elapsed from getting into the carriage and his rather ignoble exit.

He wriggled his shoulders – the burning had subsided as suddenly as it started – and made his way around the carriage to watch the show, maybe butt in and finish the job in case Kacha was having second thoughts. Flashy was still flat out in the mud, Berie either out cold next to him or pretending to be. Vocho rather thought the latter, but he wasn't fighting so that was all right.

Kacha had Egimont on the back foot – quicker even than Vocho when she was at her best, and against Egimont she would make damn sure she was at her best.

"Can we hurry up?" Vocho called. "I'm freezing, soaked and pissed off, and the rest are all dealt with. Stop playing with him and get on with it."

Egimont was good, but he was never going to be good enough to beat Kacha, who could thrash every man and woman in the duelling guild except Vocho. And it was that "except" that made her so deadly – she was always trying to up her game so she could beat him. Not to mention they weren't in the guild any more so no guild rules.

A wink from Kacha above her mask, a thrust that would have killed a lesser duellist. Egimont was quick though, Vocho had to give him that. He slipped in the mud as he parried, recovered like a guildsman, used the movement to come up under Kacha's guard in a classic action in the Ruffelo style that caught her off guard and made Vocho wonder whether she was going easy on him, then startled them both by not going for the thrust. He hesitated just a fraction, staring at Kacha like he'd never see her again, like all he wanted to see was her.

"Please, Kass."

This was not good. Nor was the way Kacha hesitated at that "please", the way she shook her head as though trying to shake some traitorous notion out of it. She'd lost her head over Petri bloody Egimont once before and got burned. Vocho wasn't going to let it happen again.

"Kass, we need to finish this. *Right now*."

"Yes," she said slowly. "Yes, we do."

With that, she spun behind Eggy, so quick he hadn't a hope. Took him out with a well practised wallop to the base of the neck that rolled his eyes up into his head before her other arm came up between his legs with an audible *whump*, a move that the gallant Ruffelo probably never even considered. Vocho caught Eggy before he fell into the mud with the rest – he'd some nice clothes on him, no sense ruining them.

Kacha blew out a ragged breath, wiped a hand across what he could see of her face and picked up the gun. "Bloody things. Never will get the hang of them. Coward's thing, really. A good blade is where it's at, right?"

She threw the gun into the bushes by the side of the road. And good riddance.

"Better off sticking with swords," Vocho agreed, knowing exactly why the subject had changed. "Know where you are with a sword. Guns have no style anyway. No, no *panache*."

She rolled her eyes but laughed anyway, a bit shaky but back to herself again. For now.

A peculiar noise reminded them of the driver, still up on his seat. Only just though, because he was bent over and wheezing like an old man, oilskin cloak flapping in the sodden wind like bat wings. On closer inspection, it seemed he was laughing fit to piss himself.

"Oh, that was a good one. Nice shot there." He went off into gales of more laughter.

Kacha raised an eyebrow his way. "Oh, do be quiet, Cospel. I didn't want to kill the stupid sod, just rob him. Now come and help me get his boots off."

"Only good nob is a dead one, I always say, so it's all good to me." Cospel wiped at his eyes, allowed himself one last chuckle and jumped down from the seat.

"You might have mentioned Petri was in the coach," Kacha said.

"You might have mentioned the magician as well." Vocho kept his voice light, but he could still feel the pained thud of his heart at the sight of that piece of paper, still remember the way the markings on the man's hands had tried to lead his brain astray.

"Magician?" Kacha asked in a weak voice.

"I tried!" Cospel said. "Only couldn't *say* anything, could I? Not unless I want everyone to know I'm helping the robbers of Fusta Wood. Only turned up last minute. Didn't have a chance to let you know. Knew you two could deal with them though."

Vocho yanked Eggy's boots off. A good make, soft leather to the knee, polished to a high shine under the mud. Probably even the right size. "That's what the eyebrows were all about? Maybe you should teach them to do semaphore, then next time I'll have a hope of understanding. Though I don't want there to be a next time, not to meet a magician." Vocho shuddered.

Kacha looked down thoughtfully at Egimont and if there was a wistful look it soon vanished. "What's *he* doing with a magician? He's only a clerk at the prelate's office. Not even a very important one. He's got some money as ex-nobles go, but not enough for that. Above that, his family has no power any more, and that's what I hear magicians crave. When I hear of them, which is just about never. Are you sure he was one?"

"Good question." No, he wasn't sure, in fact he really hoped he was wrong, but if there was even a hint that it had been a magician they could all be very dead. It was probably just him being paranoid. He'd been twitchy ever since the whole thing with the priest. That must be it. Magicians were long gone. Paranoid. "The answer is, I don't care as long as he isn't *here*. Now come on. Time we were on our way. Time to get paid."

Between the three of them, they soon had everything of value off the men. Not a bad haul as things went. As well as the five purses, each of which would keep them fed and warm and drunk for a week or more, Vocho had a fine new pair of boots that didn't pinch too much, a splendid crimson silk jacket and matching short cape from Flashy that he would probably never wear, not in that crap sack of a village they were living in, and Berie's gilt and glitter sword, which looked good but on closer inspection bent like tallow when pressure was applied. Ah well, he could sell it anyway. Kacha made sure she got Eggy's sword – far better than Flashy's for all it was gilt-free – and stripped them of all their jewels.

They took all the clothes they didn't want and bundled them into a sack, leaving three almost naked gentlemen and two nearly naked guards. Who wouldn't care nearly so much as the gentlemen when they all arrived wherever they were headed, wearing nothing but underwear, with some rather suspicious damp staining around the crotch area in Berie's case.

On to the carriage, and their spy – Cospel – had been right. Under a seat was a trunk big enough to stash a dead body in, secured with no less than five impressive locks.

Vocho almost drooled just looking at it. Whatever was in this chest, it was very valuable to someone – bodyguards, locks *and* a possible magician to guard it, a thought that made sweat prickle on Vocho's scalp. But they'd made it out of the debacle alive, the winners, and they had this too. That was the important thing.

He could hardly wait to open it. If they got away before that magician recovered from a sword through the throat, whoever owned it would never find it.

It took the three of them to get the chest up onto the back of Vocho's horse, which sank into the mud and groaned under the weight. Vocho gave him a pat and decided that seeing as his boots were covered in mud already, he could probably walk back. It wasn't like he wasn't already soaked.

Once they were done, Cospel too stripped off. Vocho tied him up on the driver's seat and left him to a shivering wet drive, with a "We'll leave your share in the usual place." He thought for a moment. "Where were you headed anyway?"

Cospel shrugged. "A town just along the valley – that's as far as this coach goes."

Hmm. A long way from Reyes and Egimont's usual stamping grounds. Never mind, he could think on that later. Vocho and Kacha manhandled the limp and muddy men into the carriage and Cospel clucked the horses on.

They watched the carriage until it disappeared around a bend and all they could make out was a faint light through the rain. Kacha forced a laugh and took Vocho's arm as they led the horses off the road and into the darkness of the woods. Vocho wasn't fooled. Her hand shook, ever so slightly. He knew why too – she'd almost killed Flashy, and it had been a miracle she hadn't. She'd never say it, but she didn't like the killing part. Things happened in the heat of the moment, it was true – a slip, a stray thrust, an unexpected movement and she couldn't avoid that – but she avoided killing if she could. Too merciful, without that ruthless instinct. It was her one weakness as a duellist, as far as Vocho could make out, which meant obviously it was the one he ragged her about as often as he could. A duellist might have to kill, to protect whoever he was guarding, to finish the job, though they were expected to refrain whenever possible. Just as well he managed for them both when it was necessary, mostly.

That's what was making her edgy perhaps; not that Petri had popped up, like a bloody jack-in-the-box, just at the worst possible moment.

He sidled a look her way. No, it was Petri that had her rattled with that "please", damn the suave bastard.

They stopped to watch the carriage light disappear behind another line of trees.

"The respected Egimont sent off in his drawers, displaying the only jewels he has left," she said with a satisfied smile. "Well, if that doesn't make you your precious new name, nothing will."

"Bugger."

"What?"

"I forgot to tell him our new names."

Chapter Two

The next morning was cold still, though the rain had let up. This was small comfort to Vocho as he squelched across the yard.

Nights out robbing were all well and good, but the days were grey and boring lately. Ever since that accident with the priest, after which no one wanted to employ them. Not to mention the arrest warrant. He supposed they would have been unemployed sooner or later anyway – guns were the coming thing, no matter how long the guild tried to hold out against them. It'd taken a while for them to gain popularity because for a long time only the very rich or the clockers, men and women who owned the clockwork factories, could afford them. Then something – he didn't know what because he didn't pay much attention – had happened, and all of a sudden almost everyone in the capital, Reyes, had one. He'd heard all the guards, employed by the prelate's council and otherwise, used them now. Mostly they were cheap things, liable to spring apart into a thousand pieces the moment anyone tried to fire them, probably knocked up by some clocker looking to make a quick bull or ten, but still.

As Kacha had amply demonstrated last night, they were

not cut out for guns. At least out here in the arse end of nowhere guns weren't so common. Yet they would be, and then he and Kacha would probably have to live like this, as *farmers* for fuck's sake, all the time. Unless they could start getting to grips with guns. Or get back into the guild. Or grow bloody wings, which had about the same probability.

Vocho hated farms. He hated the mud, the shit, the smell of pig pens, the beady little eyes of the chickens. He hated the hours too – up at the crack of sodding dawn, when any right-minded duellist should just be thinking of going to bed. Especially a world-famous duellist like himself. Bloody priests getting mysteriously dead, buggering up his perfectly good life.

He and Kacha should practise, really. How hard could guns be if even the city watch – a band of men known more for their ability to be bribed than intellectual thought – could figure them out? But that would be like admitting defeat. Twenty years he'd trained at the blade, twenty years man and boy. And he was the *best*. He'd not been beaten since he was eighteen, and everyone knew his name, which was a byword for being fucking good with a sword. Only Kacha could come close. Privately he knew she was better at technique than he was, was certainly craftier, quicker at times, but, God's cogs, he had more style, more élan, more . . . well OK, more height and weight. But it was him they sang about, his name they called. He'd made bloody sure of it, and it rankled to have all that hard work thrown away.

Because everyone *had* called his name. Bards had sung of how he and Kacha had pulled themselves up by their bootstraps, out of the gutter and into the employ of kings and prelates and great men. They both had, but his was always the name that was sung the loudest. Because he paid the bards to, mostly, but even so. They'd sung of duels he'd fought and won, of great feats of heroism while guarding whoever was paying his wages via the guild that week.

Most of it was a load of bollocks, naturally, but there had been one or two occasions where he'd been mildly heroic, like when he'd saved that child from falling out of a window at the change o' the clock, or he'd foiled that heist on the bank and the resulting swordplay had spread into the market before he'd nailed the ringleader, to a wall as it happened. Mostly it had just seemed like fun at the time, and a great way of showing everyone, particularly Kacha, how great he was.

The bards had sung about the romance of a guild that no one outside it really understood, about its history as sworn defenders of the old emperors before the Great Fall. They'd sung about how afterwards, when there were no emperors, the guildsmen had changed to swearing their lives to each other and how no man could break them from that swearing. They'd sung about how the empire had fractured into a thousand little kingdoms, and how the guild served them all on its own terms, and they'd sung about the nostalgia for a long-lost age it represented with Vocho as its most powerful icon, and how dashing he looked, which was only to be expected. And then . . . and then an evening that was vague in his mind, too much wine probably, and that priest. Now they sang about Vocho the priest murderer, who stabbed holy men in the back – only the second person, after the reviled Jokin, ever to be exiled from the guild after he'd taken his master's test and sworn his oath to be true.

He stamped across the yard and glared at the chickens. A fucking *farmer*. What style did a farmer have? Sackcloth trousers and perfume of pig shit. Vocho opened the gate to the coop and flung in the grain, not caring how it bounced off the heads of the hungry birds. The only bright spot in his day was going to be later, when he and Kacha would go through their haul from last night. Silks and jewels and bulls, lots of lovely bulls. Not enough to stop him being a farmer, though he had high hopes of the chest, which had been satisfyingly heavy. The locks looked tough but would yield with time. He'd always been good with locks.

The chest had been guarded by a magician too. Magicians were so rare they were almost legends, and they could command the ransom of kings as payment, or so the stories went. And what was anyone doing going to those lengths if what was inside wasn't worth a fortune? Our lad Eggy was an idiot only having the two bodyguards, even if he did have magic on his side. Not that it would have made much difference. They'd still have the chest; there'd just be more dead, or at least denuded, men.

Muffled exhortations to "Stand! Stand, you ruddy horse," leaked out of the stable, followed by a massive *thunk*, a *crack*, and a puff of splinters exploding into the yard as the horse took exception to Kacha's tone of voice or perhaps just the world being what it was, it was hard to tell.

Vocho finished his chores moodily and sloshed back across the yard to the house. To the chest. It sat on the table like the world's biggest birthday present. He itched to get started on the locks, but Kacha had stropped and fretted and pulled the older sister trick, which made him even more determined to open the damned thing. She was the cautious one, comparatively, and she'd said that if a magician had guarded it then they had to make sure there was no magic on the thing before they opened it. Which was all very well, but Vocho was dreaming of the things they could do with whatever money or precious items were inside. It was heavy enough to hold a bloody fortune in gold. Maybe . . . maybe enough to buy a pardon, get their old lives back. Maybe. Enough money and the good folks of Reyes would forget everything. The prelate's palace probably would, if he bribed the right person. Then perhaps Kacha would forgive him too. His life wasn't the only one he'd buggered up. He had things to make up for.

She caught him just as he was about to try the first of the locks.

"What in the hells are you doing?"

He jumped back, red faced and ready with a lie. "Just looking. To see if I could find any magic on it."

She snorted disbelief and came to the table, her recently cut ragged blonde hair bouncing indignantly. "And I'm the queen of the pig people. Honestly, Voch, do you think I can't tell when you're lying? Your left eye always twitches."

"Does not!"

She narrowed her eyes at him. "See, it's doing it again."

He studied her for a moment and wondered how far he could push it. Not far – he never could. She always saw through his bullshit, and it was why he loved her and why she drove him insane too. Kacha the wonderful, Kacha the perfect, Kacha, who could see when he was lying. Kacha, who always believed in him anyway, when no one else would.

To look at them you'd be hard pressed to say they were related. She was fair-haired and paler-skinned like their mother, and he was dark everywhere. He was taller than most, hulking at the shoulders like their docker father. She only came up to his shoulder – southerner blood, his father always said, like it was a good thing. But there were things that made them the same – the brown eyes, the straight, sharp nose. A grace and speed that showed in every movement, and a quick and ready grin. Her grin had faded just lately though.

"Fine," he said at last. "I was trying to open the lock."

"Idiot. What if there's magic on it?" She frowned at the chest. "What if he can trace it? I don't want to deal with a magician. Who knows what they're capable of?"

"You won't have to deal with one. I got him right in the windpipe. I'd be surprised if he lasted the hour. And if a magician was guarding it, it *has* to be valuable."

"We dump it," Kacha said, weary from repeating herself.

Vocho stared out at the mud and shit in the yard, wishing she'd actually listen to him for once. "We dump it, we're stuck here for . . . for . . . for ever. I'm not a fucking *farmer*. This could be our way back in. Back to what we were meant for, where we belong."

"Voch, enough."

"Please." He screwed himself up to say it, because it didn't come anywhere near naturally, but he owed her. A lot, more than she knew, and he was determined to pay the debt. "Look, I got us into this shitty situation. I admit it. I lost us our jobs, our reputation, our everything. Our lives if they catch us. Let me get it all back. For both of us. Please?"

She was weakening, he could see it, so he pressed his advantage. He'd always been able to wheedle his way around her if he tried.

"Look, Kass, with enough money we can pay the right people, get our names restored or at least cleared. You won't have to wear that fucking rag of a dress any more, just because you're a 'farmer's sister' and that's what they wear. I'll even get you your blades back."

She raised an eyebrow, and he made a note to lay it on less thick.

"You know who has my blades?"

"I do. And I'll buy them back just as soon as I have the money. And of course there's Egimont—"

"You just shut up about him." The ice in her voice made him shiver.

She wouldn't look at him but played with her hair, hiding her eyes behind a loose lock, considering. Vocho wondered what had happened between her and Eggy. One minute the two of them were a mismatched pair, and he'd never seen her happier. Even if he thought Eggy was too smooth for words, a stuck-up pompous mountebank, too damned quiet, sneaky and devious with it, he'd never have said so to Kacha. He'd had words with Eggy, but he wouldn't say so to Kacha, because she was happy and under it all he did love her, when he remembered to. The next minute, well it seemed like the next minute Kacha was cursing Eggy like a sailor and then wouldn't have his name spoken. Vocho had revelled in that for a while, glad that he'd been right about sneaky old Eggy, but Kass was constantly in a bad mood lately, and he was the one getting it in the neck.

"OK, I'll shut up about him. But your blades, our lives, we can get them back. Or go somewhere else and live like kings and queens. If we get this chest open and find out what it is someone wants so much. Aren't you even a *little* bit curious? And with a pardon maybe you could—"

"Don't even suggest it."

He held up his hands in mock surrender. "Just a thought. I mean, with you restored to the guild, maybe he'd—"

"I *said*, don't even suggest it. I'm well rid of him, if that's where his priorities lie."

What the hells had happened there? He didn't dare ask. "Fine, fine, don't say I didn't offer. But your blades. With money, we could get them back, get our guild places back, everything we had. Everything. If we open this chest."

She cocked an eyebrow his way, but he could see the distaste no matter how she tried to hide it. "Still. How can we find out if he's done something to it?"

Vocho shrugged – he didn't know much more than she did. "Blood on it, probably. They use blood for their spells."

"That is creepy as hell."

"Isn't it?" A voice from the doorway startled Vocho so much he tried to pull a sword that wasn't there. Kacha groaned quietly.

The man that Kacha referred to as the "gibbering ninny" stood in the doorway. Vocho couldn't agree with her – simpering was a much better word for him. A vain, twittering fool in the best fashion of high-society Reyes. Only they weren't *in* Reyes, and he stood out like a chorus girl in a hen house among the local farmers, wheelwrights and blacksmiths. Still, he had his uses.

His full name, often repeated by him, probably because it was the only way he could remember it, was Narcis Donat Chimo Ne Farina es Domenech, though in an effort to appear friendly to the locals he had asked them to call him Dom. Mostly they called him Ninny, only not to his face — his father, a prominent clocker, had bought the local manse after the revolt and was a lot of people's landlord. He was also a controlling tyrant and no better or worse than the previous noble landlord. He'd lately developed a penchant for having his employees, of whom there were many, flogged for minor transgressions. So no one was willing to say openly the slightest thing against him or his son. Sadly for Kacha and Vocho, Dom had taken a liking to Kacha despite the fact she was supposedly just a farmer's sister and as such not good marriage material for someone like him. The revolt may have demoted a hells-ton of nobles, but old habits died hard and in effect they'd been replaced by clockers with no titles but lots of money. Supposedly this was fine by the prelate, because a self-made man showed merit and the good blessings of the Clockwork God, who rewarded truth and industry. Or so all the newspapers and storytellers said.

Kacha seemed to have an odd effect on men, though Vocho could never really see why. Five years ago the fashion had been for stick-thin ethereal women strapped into plain black dresses that went straight up and down, with deathly pale faces and long lank ringlets. Thanks to a new artist who'd painted portraits of the prelate's wife and others, the fashion was now for plumply voluptuous women, hair piled up and puffed out to the size of a small pumpkin, in ridiculous dresses that swept the floor behind them, usually with lots of frilly things around the neck and wrists that Vocho couldn't name.

Kacha had managed to never quite fit into either category, being what Vocho thought of as sturdy and not giving a fig about fashion anyway, except in a "Can I fight in it, or will it just get in the way?" manner. Not skinny, not plump, but somewhere in between where her muscles tended to show a little through whatever shirt – or farmer's sister's dress – she wore. Above all, she was his sister. All he usually saw was a pain in the arse – too ruddy perfect. But while even in a poor light after a couple of beers only a compulsive liar would call her beautiful, he grudgingly supposed there was *something* about her. He just had no idea what attracted men like flies. If he'd known, or if he hadn't been her brother, perhaps everything would have been different, he supposed.

"What's he doing here?" Kacha hissed under her breath.

"I, er, I asked him to come – sent a message as soon as we got back," Vocho whispered back.

"You *what*?" She didn't have time for more than that so contented herself with trying to kill Vocho by glaring at him.

Dom came in, a soft-looking little man with a pale, watery sort of face, a handkerchief often pressed to his nose and washed-out brown hair dressed in the latest style – a loose pigtail worn pretend-carelessly over one shoulder and powdered to make the hardiest man sneeze. Maybe that explained the handkerchief. He was dressed for a ball, not a trek across a muddy farmyard, but to Vocho's annoyance he didn't seem to have a splash of mud anywhere on his exquisitely made shoes, and his breeches were a pristine white. His clothes were worth more than this all-but-derelict farm and everything in it – silk, more silk than Vocho had seen this side of a Reyes whorehouse, embroidered and studded with sequins, feathers, tinkling trinkets and who knew what else until the man fair rattled when he walked. Vocho itched to turf him out on his ear, maybe liberating some of those clothes in the process, but this was their disguise and he had to keep to it. Besides, having a rich friend with a powerful father couldn't hurt, and Vocho had invited him for a very specific purpose. He just hoped he wasn't going to regret it later, when Kacha said all the words that by the looks of her mouth, clamped so thin it had almost disappeared, were demanding to be said. Vocho was pretty sure his ears would be bleeding by the end of it.

Dom fluttered the hand with the handkerchief Vocho's way, took Kacha's hand with the other and bent low over it. "My dearest Kassinda."

They'd had to come up with new names, as the old ones were so hotly sought after, but had managed it so that they could still call each other Kass and Voch, as they always had. Saved on unintentional slip-ups. Only now those were short for Kassinda and Ranvoschan.

By the way Kacha's nose wrinkled, it was taking all her control not to whip her hand away or cuff Dom around the ear. This was *not* how you treated a lady of the guild, if you liked your face the same way it started. People had been thrown in the Shrive for less. Dom didn't seem to notice – he never did, not the looks and glares, not the whispers behind his back or the occasional plain words. Instead he smiled his watery smile and turned to the chest.

A look of mild interest, the closest he ever got to an actual expression, crossed his face, and Vocho wondered how much he'd heard of what they'd said. Not that it mattered – a lot of things seemed to pass straight through Dom's skull without pausing.

"Is this what you were asking about, Ranvoschan?" he asked, peering more closely at the chest. Vocho belatedly hoped like hells Egimont didn't have any identifying crest on it.

"My . . . er . . . my mother's chest," Kacha said. "She always said to be careful opening it."

He took that well enough. Considering he believed every-thing Vocho told him, it was a fair bet he couldn't tell a lie from a hole in the ground.

"Well, I can't see any magic on it. And if it's been sitting around a while, any magic would have faded a long time ago in any case." He looked up at Kacha like a dog hoping for a bone. "My father made me study all this sort of thing, you see. Sent me to Ikaras University. Such an interesting country. Do you know the thirteen provinces each used to be the private estate of one family, before the Great Fall? There are a few records left, you see, in Ikaras. The families used to compete, and built each capital after their own expertise. So not much clockwork in Ikaras – that family were more scholars than engineers – but they actually still have magicians, if only a few. Scary sorts, to be honest. Need to be careful of looking at the patterns on their hands. Anyway, I think my father always sort of hoped the prelate would get around to making a few new nobles out of the clockers, and wanted me to be prepared. Old stories, histories, why the old empire fell, the war to establish the city-states and the lines of kings, famous magicians, he had me study everything. Total bore, but some of it stuck. Magic uses blood, for example. A magician can store a spell, such as a ward for this chest, but once the blood is dry it doesn't last long. Not unless they permanently mark it into skin, like a tattoo. That's the only way it lasts, you see? Constant blood supply. And the skin ones tend to be very limited, and specific, unless they're actually on a magician. Anyway, without a blood supply, this wood wouldn't hold a spell for long." Dom stopped to take a breath – the man could talk for Reyes when he had a mind.

Vocho thought back to the magician's hands with their weird moving pictures, and the paper with the bloody patterns on it. That's what the magician had been doing before Vocho got in the carriage, just in case. Probably he'd meant to take the chest with him when he went, but a sword in the throat will change a man's priorities somewhat.

"So, just the locks then?" Vocho asked.

Dom's watery smile broadened. "Yes, should be. Did I help?"

Kacha caught Vocho's eye with an implied promise of violence later, smiled sweetly and took Dom by the arm. "You did, very much. Now if you'd—"

"I, I was wondering," Dom said before he cast a glance Vocho's way. "Um, Kassinda, I was wondering if you'd do me the honour of coming to the spring dance with me? That's why I said I'd come today, you see. An ulterior motive."

"Well I'm not sure . . ." Kacha sighed at the sudden crest-fallen look. "I'll consider it, Dom, definitely."

That perked him up. "Excellent! Oh, and one other thing. You might want to be a bit careful. I brought you these."

He patted himself down, muttering under his breath for a minute or two, brought out a box of snuff, two more handkerchiefs and a small exquisitely decorated box before he found what he wanted. "Actually, these brownies are for you as well. I baked them myself. My speciality. Real fudge pieces. But here. A lot of trouble out in Fusta Wood. Cut-throat robbers on the road. So, please be careful."

He pulled out two sheets of paper and put them on the table, smiled his watery smile, bowed low to Kacha and left with a spring in his step and a flutter in his handkerchief.

The newspaper wasn't much of a thing – in the capital they ran to a dozen sheets or more and often had pictures for those that couldn't read – but that didn't matter. What mattered was the headline: EX-LORD AND PRELATE'S MAN EGIMONT ROBBED IN FUSTA WOOD! Followed by a report that included: *"these robbers are now fast becoming notorious for their audacity, cunning and banter"*.

"I *knew* I should have told them the names we wanted to use."

"But we're notorious anyway," Kacha said. "And look, they've given us names."

Vocho scanned down further. So they had, and better ones than he'd thought of as well: the Dread Swordsmen of Fusta Wood.

And under that a bit of a shock. "Ten thousand bulls reward? Ten *thousand*?"

"Only if they get back what we stole."

The pair of them looked at the chest. It seemed so innocuous. Plain wood stained a deep blue, brass bound. A chest like a hundred others. Except for those locks, that reward and knowing who had previously either been guarding it or owned it.

Vocho was now even more desperate to find out what was in it. If they were offering ten thousand, it was probably worth ten times that. Never mind getting their names back, he could buy half of Reyes with that much money.

"Right, I say we open it and see why they want it back so much."

Chapter Three

Petri Egimont made his way through the tiny little town dressed in borrowed breeches likely to fall down if he didn't hold them up with one hand, and a shirt that was two sizes too small and ten years out of date. Over it all a cloak that was more a loose collection of patches and what looked like mould.

Stares and whispers followed him, but he ignored them. There had never been a time when he hadn't been whispered about. He did what he usually did, and sank into the background. Berie and Flashy were making enough noise for ten men anyway, and soon all eyes were on them as they made raucous demands for ale and food and women and some decent clothes, right now, damn it. Petri slid down a small side alley and found the curtained carriage at the other end, ready and waiting. No one saw him get in or saw him leave the little town. Just as it should be. What wasn't as it should be was the lack of chest.

Past the square with its new clock tower, its shrine to the reborn Clockwork God. Past the temple, where the worshippers weren't certain whether they believed in the reborn Clockwork God or were hanging on to the gods that had replaced him when he fell. A punishment, men had called it when Castan empire fell to pieces. A punishment for turning away from the Clockwork God and leaving him to rust as they concentrated on their work, on making clockwork in his image. Blasphemy and heresy had brought down the empire and killed their god, leaving the good people to turn away from both him and what engineering the Castans had left. Until Bakar had brought the Clockwork God back to life.

Out here in the country though, people didn't trust this reborn god yet, so were hedging their bets by displaying icons of all of them, interim and reborn. Back in the city of Reyes the prelate would have had a fit if he'd known. At last something made Petri smile. Out of the city changes took a lot longer to take root, and here the other gods, even the old way of looking to the Clockwork God, were still in people's minds and superstitions.

It didn't take long to get out of town, and then the carriage took a broad unpaved road up into the twisting mountains. Mud clogged the wheels, but the way was smooth enough. Before long his destination came into view, white towers against the black bare stone of the mountains, all wreathed in cloud and rain today so the buildings looked insubstantial, as though they might blow away at any moment.

Petri had never been to the king's palace before. Once it had been his summer residence, a retreat from the heat and fug of summer Reyes, a place to lie cool and comfortable by the waterfalls that glittered in every available tree-swagged nook. Now it was the king's only palace, and Petri came not in triumph or summer, but in rags and in a cold and blustery spring with snow still on the upper slopes of the mountains.

The road narrowed as they climbed, and the palace played hide and seek among the crags and clouds until a last turn and the carriage rumbled to a stop before the main gates.

"Can't take the carriage through, sir," the driver said as he opened the door. "Sets off the clockwork, see?"

"I'm afraid I don't see," Petri said as he got down from the coach. The palace lay on a break in the slope of the mountains, white stone walls and black slate roofs arching far above him, little turrets that looked back down over the road at every corner. Behind the high wall, more white towers, seeming almost as tall as the mountains. It didn't seem like a palace as much as a town.

A man ran up, whispered into the driver's ear and ran off again.

"Looks like you'll be getting the full treatment, sir. If you'll just get back in? It's a marvel and no mistake."

The clockwork, of course. Since the rebirth of the Clockwork God, anyone who had a scrap of clockwork on their property was proud of it, and the king's summer palace was renowned, second only to Reyes in the complexity of its mechanisms. It was all the Castans had left behind in Reyes when their empire fell – clockwork everywhere, a few names and a tendency for children in the northern areas to be born with springy black hair and burned-copper skin. That and a dead god.

The carriage rattled through the now open main gates, and a warning bell followed by a series of clacking thuds had Petri looking out of the window. They'd entered a wide courtyard paved in black stone. At each corner a turret wound upwards – the clockwork sent them slowly spinning, growing taller with every turn. Each turn also brought arrow slits into view, along with strange markings and pictures burned into the stone. Below them, other things turned and moved, some hidden, some plain. Windows slid away or came into view. Alleys disappeared and reappeared, paving slabs slipped up and over to the other side of the palace, making the courtyard treacherous in many places and the horses snort and prance and roll their eyes.

No one knew why, or how exactly, most of the old clock-work worked in the province. No one knew anything except it was all old, from the time of the Castans and part of their glory. People had forgotten the hows and whys, and just accepted it, tried to ignore it. But things had changed since Bakar brought the dead god back to life, and people's curiosity had grown with his rise. Most of the clockwork was hidden, or dangerous to play about with without risking the buildings that moved along on it, so no one knew much about the really old mechanisms, the huge ones that twisted palace and city into new shapes. No one except prelate Bakar, and that rankled the king no end because, after all, knowledge was power.

The king had been trying to find his own power in knowledge by the looks of it. Most of Reyes's clockwork ran on water power, they knew that – waterwheels lined the banks of the river for miles after it entered the city, and those powered the lesser, newer clockworks. Rumour was strong that it was something similar that drove the greater mechanisms like the changing o' the clock, when all Reyes moved along hidden rails and twisted itself into new combinations. Yet the palace here had barely a stream across the valley and a well in the courtyard for water. But *something* powered the clockwork, and piles of crumbling earth and shattered stones lay at intervals around the courtyard by the walls.

Three mud-covered men stood by a new hole, looking into it uncertainly with spades at the ready. Petri wondered if the king had found out how it worked yet, and thought not – if he had, no doubt he'd have made use of that knowledge the first chance he got.

A footman trotted out to greet Petri and turned not a single wigged hair at how he was dressed. Instead he inclined his head and led Petri inside.

The inside was no less a wonder than outside. A great atrium fronted the palace, filled with clockwork that had been dismantled – automatons in a hundred pieces, a clock set into the floor that had been carefully pulled up, all the cogs numbered and set in sequence along one wall. An orrery, a mechanical model of the sun and planets and stars, twin to one the prelate kept in splendour, lay in a different kind of pieces. Cogs lay bent and broken, gears scattered carelessly across the floor like petals. The model sun winked from within the leaves of a glossy plant; planets lurked together in corners. Petri grinned savagely and went on with a renewed vigour in his step. He had to show the king he was worthy, despite this setback. He *had* to. Had to know too that the orreries and what they represented under Bakar could be broken.

He stood as tall as he could while the king paced his anger away before he flopped into his chair, and Petri wondered if he'd get the chance to show anyone anything.

"How the hells did they know? If anyone was going to rob a coach, you'd have thought it would have been the one leaving Reyes, carrying my quarterly allowance." King Licio spat that last word. An allowance, like a wayward teen not a grown descendant of kings. "I made sure it had fewer guards than usual. Your coach would seem slim pickings by comparison, low key, just a group of ex-nobles on a little spree. So how did they know *that* was the coach we didn't want robbed? That the chest was what I can't afford to lose? How did they know? Petri, how did they beat you? You were trained by the duelling guild; you should be able to beat off some bloody peasant thieves. And really, Petri, almost naked?"

Egimont gritted his teeth — it would take a long time to live *that* down. He could be sure the tale would have reached Reyes by the next available coach. A source of endless amusement for his supervisor in his pathetic job at the prelate's office. Intentional too, he thought. Kacha knew, none better, how to hurt him by wounding his pride. He just didn't know why.

"Not just common robbers, your highness. These were

highly skilled swordsmen." And one a woman, though he kept that part to himself for now. He'd recognised Kacha instantly. How could he not? Kacha had never gone for Ruffelo's techniques and instead preferred her own, at least when not officially duelling at the guild. He almost smiled at the thought of their duel, of watching her fence like she was born to it, and then squashed the smile. That part of his life was over.

"Highly skilled?" The king leaped back up from his ornate chair at the head of the room. The hall was a whitewashed affair with rich hangings, plush carpets, bright windows and no clockwork – it had all been ripped out, and recently by the look of things, leaving odd gaping holes that seemed to make the rest of the room look even finer. A glazed case ran the length of one wall, filled with more precious things than Egimont had ever seen anywhere together. A hall far fairer than almost any other in both the city and country of Reyes. And that was the trouble. It was the almost that rubbed King Licio raw. He was no longer king in anything but name, and the only other palace finer than this used to be his, but now, nearly two decades after the revolution against the old king when Licio was a baby, belonged to the prelate and his departments. All Licio had was a useless and meaningless title, a seat on the council, a few concessions which meant little in practice, and the *second*-finest hall in the country. And now a magician, a fact which unnerved Egimont.

It'd been a long time, but he'd had as much cause as any to celebrate when the prelate got rid of them after the revolt. If bringing the king back meant a magician . . . No, he'd sworn loyalty to his king for good or ill, and that was everything. His father had been a faithless man, and Egimont had no intention of following in his footsteps. In any regard.

Licio stalked over to Egimont. Even in anger – especially in anger – he looked like a king. Tall, golden-haired, loose limbed, with the sort of face that could charm angels into sin. He smiled easily, his eyes shining with courage and honesty. All he needed was a crown and a fanfare to complete the image. He looked the part and Egimont had begun to wonder whether it was that which had seduced him into this plot, or his own greed and pride. Yet he sounded the part too, and Petri sympathised with his frustrations with the prelate, with the reborn Clockwork God he said they must pray to now, the notion that all their lives were laid out ahead of them on rails, and they couldn't turn from what the clockwork had planned for them. Each of their frustrations was nearly the same as the other's.

"*You're* highly skilled, or so you claim, and yet you ended up with no clothes. I need that chest back." Licio blew out his cheeks and relented as quickly as he'd exploded, as usual, his temper like a brief summer storm that's soon spent. "That chest is vital, do you see? Contracts, agreements, negotiations. Not to mention a lot of gold. A *lot*. The whole treaty with Ikaras depends on those papers. They were our guarantee that Ikaras would help with armed might when the time came, in return for a few concessions about the mines on the border. Without that treaty and their army we've no chance of toppling the prelate; without the gold, no chance of getting a few councillors on side before we strike. Without that chest, I have nothing to offer anyone, and a new treaty might take months – those Ikaran weasels will take every opportunity to get more from us in return for their help. And if that chest falls into the wrong hands . . ."

Egimont kept his mouth shut. He wasn't much of a man of words to start with, but the presence of the magician, Sabates, over the last weeks had kept him even quieter. Months ago now Egimont had sworn to Licio he would help restore him to the throne in return for his father's old duchy and revenge on the guild that had given him up so easily.

Also, there had been plans for true justice. Plans to rid the kingdom of wastrels while helping the deserving find work. Many plans to undo what had been done in the prelate's name and under his supposed ideals of democracy, which had ended up more a brawl for power, more corrupt than any of the worst brutalities the previous kings and nobles had managed.

When Petri had joined him a few months ago, it had been Licio's high ideals that Egimont had supported, especially the plan about reinstating all the nobles, giving them back their land, titles, and most particularly the part where he was made guild master. No more scribbling away in that dank little box in the prelate's office for Egimont, drafting increasingly ludicrous edicts. No more believing all the prelate's lies of a new and brighter future at Egimont's expense. No more being tied to the predetermined fate that the prelate, or rather the clockwork, had outlined for him.

Licio's loose ideals had changed with Sabates, had become firm plans. The magician sat there now, though the Clockwork God alone knew how he'd survived the stab in the throat. Magic, Petri supposed. Even before the magicians were massacred or run off after the revolution they'd been secretive so no one knew much of what they were capable of, or how they did it, bar a few gruesome details and stories that had twisted in the telling over time.

Yet Sabates had survived, and had been there in the shadows with his sneer and his scarred face as Egimont and the rest had staggered out of the carriage, numb from being tied up for hours, and stinking from being too close to Berie and his stained underwear. Egimont had been livid too, but one look at the crawling bloody patterns across the man's hands, and he'd kept quiet and done as he was told. It was all he did since the magician came. And when Sabates had come to Reyes, that's when Licio had changed from a young man of even temper and high ideals, wanting only the best for the country, into a man possessed by the need to right the wrongs he'd been dealt before he was old enough to walk.

Sabates smiled at Egimont now, cold and impersonal, like he was inspecting an insect before he squashed it.

Licio put an arm around Egimont's shoulder. "So, how are we going to get that chest back? I'm sure you'll think of something, Petri. Won't you?" A squeeze of the shoulder, a glance to Sabates and back. An implied "or else". Oh, he looked like a king, all right, but it was only now that he was starting to act all too much like the last king. That hadn't ended well for both the king and many of his nobles, whose blood now haunted the square outside the Shrive.

"Of course, your highness. Upon my honour." Egimont risked a look at Sabates and got a smirk in return.

"Ah yes," Sabates said in a grating whisper. "Honour above all, isn't that your family motto?" Yet it wasn't honour that stung Egimont to action, but the cool look on Sabates' face as he stared down his nose and the soft words, spoken past the miraculously healed wound in the man's throat. "See that it's so, Egimont."

Something about that cool voice, the dark eyes, chilled Egimont to the bone and yet drew him in. Licio may have been a young idealistic fool, but he was a fool with money, the only realistic claim to any resurrected throne and some vestige of honour. Sabates wasn't a fool of any sort, of that Egimont was sure. Maybe he was the only hope Egimont had now that he'd sworn.

He bowed to his king, nodded to the magician and took his leave. They'd given him his orders, and no one could say he wasn't an obedient man. His footsteps sounded loud on the tiles as he left in silence. He made his way to the stables and wasn't unduly surprised to see Sabates there before him. The man had a propensity for appearing just where and when you thought he couldn't be.

Sabates didn't look his way at first, but stroked the nose of the nearest horse. "Strange things, horses," he said. "Seemingly intelligent, full of blind courage, a good sense of self-preservation but ultimately brainless, if easily trainable. It makes them the perfect beasts to put to our own uses, don't you think?"

Egimont said nothing. There didn't seem much to say. Sabates took his hand from the horse – the beast seemed grateful the touch was brief – and turned to Egimont.

"Your king is like this horse. I think, with training, he'll become the perfect beast. Let me be frank, Egimont. The country needs us. The clockers are worse than the nobles ever were. They need to go, and you know it. Reinstate the better nobles – like yourself – and leave the idiots to it. The prelate's dream was equality for all, for positions to be given on merit. But that hasn't happened, has it? Instead of idiot nobles, we get clockers whose only virtue is making money. And the more money they get, the more they want. They're more corrupt than the nobles, maybe even more grasping because they don't have the titles and history to fall back on, to guide them. Some are more equal than others, and those with power use it only to squabble. That's why you swore to Licio, wasn't it, because you saw it needed to change? Because you saw the good in him?"

Egimont stared at him. Was the man reading his mind? Egimont couldn't take his eyes from the swirling patterns on the magician's hands. They seemed . . . There, yes. A ducal crest, the one his father had proudly worn until the day the king was stripped of power. Two stags rutting on a blue field. A crest his father had soiled, but Egimont could clean it, given the chance. The crest dissolved and changed into a sigil of two crossed swords – the guild, and didn't that burn in him more? The guild that had let him down, cast him adrift, and for what? For nothing. More than anything else he wanted Eneko the guild master's head on a pike and himself to lead the guild, to mould it as he wanted. The guild had only barely scraped by in the last revolution, spared because nominally it wasn't controlled by anyone but its guildmaster, though in practice it had mostly served the nobles. This time it would not be spared, would be brought under the wing of the monarchy, and Egimont would lead it after the fires had cooled. Only Licio would, or could, give him that.

"Perhaps," he said at last. No perhaps about it. He'd done what was asked of him for a long time, believed what the prelate had told him. And then he and Kacha – she'd opened his eyes. Even as an ex-noble, he still had privilege, money, a position that paid even while it demeaned. He'd thought the prelate had done a fine job with Reyes, had been brainwashed to think it perhaps, and then Kacha had shown him. Shown him poverty, hopelessness, the deep grinding apathy that only the end of hope can bring. It hadn't been deliberate on her part; she'd just taken him to where she'd come from, shown him who she was or had been. And open his eyes it had. He'd sworn to himself he'd do something about it, convinced that a few ex-nobles like himself could do it better. He'd been undecided until her and the truth of what she'd shown him. He'd sworn in order to make things better, for her and those like her, and then . . . They needed someone to gather behind, and Licio was perfect. Young, idealistic, impressionable.

"To do all you want, we need Licio," Sabates said. "But he needs help. I can't be everywhere. I need a helping hand, one who's good with a sword and yet doesn't hold outdated notions about guns either. Someone with a shred of honour and some brains. And you know who stole that chest, don't you?"

Egimont's head was whirling. Sabates was a magician, and even now Egimont was sure that the ban on magicians had been the right thing to do. They'd run the country before – Licio's father had been ruled by them whether he'd admitted it or not. They'd run it, and look how that turned out. But Sabates seemed to know what Egimont wanted and to want the same himself. Egimont wanted to trust him, but trust hadn't worked out so well lately.

"Perhaps," he allowed.

"Perhaps." A smile from Sabates. "Very well. And perhaps you already have two masters, the prelate and your king. One open, one secret. How about a third? A third who can actually make what you want happen rather than just talk about it. One who will give you what you want most. Tell me, why did you swear to the king?"

The patterns flowed across the magician's hands, now two-headed snakes, now a noose, now a duelling sword, now two armies battling and neither winning. They flowed and swam and brought strange thoughts to mind.

Egimont couldn't have not answered if his life depended on it. "The prelate . . . I believed in him. I believed in what he set out to do, in a way. He *made* me believe it. And then I saw. She showed me. What he'd really done. But if – when – he falls, his council will turn on each other like starving wolves, all trying to own the whole carcass. The only one of that council with enough support to take over without a full-scale civil war is Licio, but he needs money to do it. He was, *is*, the king. Enough royalists still keep the faith, enough only pay lip service to Bakar's new Clockwork God. Enough of the rest will support Licio when it's clear he'll win. He was never tested; the revolt was against his father. There are whispers that he isn't his father's child, that a sane king is better than an insane prelate. Many don't agree with the prelate's new laws, the taxes, the unending dispute with Ikaras. I can't blame them."

Egimont managed to drag his gaze away from Sabates' hands, frowned and shook his head. He hadn't meant to say that much. And yet none of it was untrue.

"And now that you know the king better?"

"We'd replace a madman with a young fool." The words seemed ripped out of him and wrong somehow — Licio hadn't seemed foolish, not until Sabates had come. Before that he'd seemed full of ideas, and ideals, naïve perhaps but no fool.

"Unless the man who truly rules isn't Licio." Sabates moved his hands, and the patterns faded to nothing as he stroked the horse again. "And that man will need a reliable lieutenant. One who will be amply rewarded for his trouble. With, say, a duchy? And a duchess to go with it?"

Egimont glanced up sharply. Did he mean . . .? No.

Still, Egimont was tempted. For all his misgivings about the magician, Egimont had begun to despair. A fool who was perhaps a touch mad or a different fool? Neither appealed; either would destroy this country given half a chance. The prelate had already started. Yet Egimont wavered. Working for a magician wasn't an honourable position.

"Unless that's the only way to save a country," Sabates murmured. "A duellist serves their country first, isn't that what they say? What you were taught at the guild before you were so rudely ripped from it? Over and above the prelate or any temporary hiring, they serve their country, their guild, ultimately their own conscience. They do what seems good to them. You're no longer a duellist in name, but you are one by training and heart, aren't you? Why not do both? Work for me, and the king and prelate too. Do my bidding when it seems good to you, for your country. I will not fail to reward you."

What did he have to lose? Nothing, not any more, not since Kacha . . . Enough of that. It was done and gone, and it was all he'd had left to lose. Other than a pathetic job he'd taken because the prelate had convinced him, he had nothing but some money, and not enough to do him any good if the country fell to war. Instead perhaps he had a chance to avert that. Sabates wanted the king on the throne again, and with sound men to advise him, men like himself, perhaps the country might not fall. Perhaps Egimont might even get to be the hero he'd always dreamed about being.

His head felt foggy and his thoughts indistinct, except one – that denying a magician wasn't a good idea. Whispers at the back of his head telling him what would happen if he refused. The pictures on Sabates' hands seemed to dance in front of his eyes.

"All right," he said at last. "When it seems good to me."

"A wise choice," Sabates said. "Licio wants the chest back, and so do I for more reasons than he knows. But not just that – I want the people who stole it. You know who they are, as do I."

"Kacha and Vocho." The words seemed yanked out of him.

"Indeed. Find the chest but inform me before you do anything. I think I may have plans for those two. A suitable revenge for you, I think? As the prelate's fall will be for me. I have a very personal grudge against him. I believe you saw some of the magicians die during the revolt. Too many died, too many, and one in particular. My son, killed by the prelate's own hand. Oh, I have as much or more reason for revenge than you do. Let us exact it together and for the good of your country."

Revenge. On Vocho for being an insufferable pumped-up little tit, for always beating Egimont in duels no matter what he did, what tricks he tried. For being such a bastard to Kacha. On the guild for abandoning him to his present miserable fate. On Kacha, yes maybe even a little on Kacha, for cruelly leaving him for no reason that he could see, for humiliating him.

Egimont found he was smiling.

Interlude

Nineteen years earlier

Vocho couldn't recall being quite as excited about anything. Not even the sword swallower at the fair in the summer, or the fire breather, or even when his da said he was old enough to go out with Kacha onto the jetties, docks and wharves that surrounded the one broken-down room they called home. He could barely contain himself as he, Kacha and her friend sneaked past the dead statue of the Clockwork God and into one of the smithies that overlooked the big square.

The vast rooms inside echoed with the sound of hammering, of water hissing as metal was cooled, the huff-puff of giant bellows it took three men to work.

Up a rickety set of stairs rife with cobwebs and rat droppings and out into the air. The roof wasn't empty – far from it. Vocho's da said it was all because the city was growing, finally recovering from the Great Fall, when the old Castan empire had cracked apart like an egg into all the city states and petty kingdoms, taking knowledge with it. A long time ago, Da had said, people had known more than they did – known how to make a city click and clank every three days as it turned on its axis, how to make the city spin and turn and change, how to make great clocks that were the symbol of Reyes and rang out every quarter in a helter-skelter of bells that echoed along different streets depending on what change o' the clock it was. How to make a whole clockwork city that was the envy of all the other provinces, even though the Castans had left different marvels elsewhere. They must have been dead smart, Vocho thought, to do all that.

The old empire had died because the Castans got too arrogant, Da said, tried to make clockwork to rival the god himself, tried to make their own gods. Now Reyes was moving ahead, relearning smithing tricks, making better swords, better ploughshares, remembering old things or inventing new things, like metal crossbows with winches on to pull the string bit. Not much clockwork though, only little bits, because otherwise the priests got all fussy about heresy and burning in the hells, in case Reyes fell prey again to what had destroyed the Castans.

As the city got back to its feet, more and more people looking for work had arrived till it was nearly bursting. No one wanted to live outside the walls – bears, wolves and lions and such lived out there, he'd heard, and he'd been disappointed when Da had strictly forbidden him to hunt them, and given him a smack around the ear for being stupid to boot. Then there was the row with the neighbouring kingdom of Ikaras – all the sailors talked about it – and the water meadows that swallowed huge bits of land for months at a time this end of the Reyes river. Inside was safer, easier. So they'd built shacks wherever they could, taking over cellars, cramming in as many as could fit into a house. Vocho lived in one room in a falling-down house and had more neighbours in that house than he could count. Lots, anyway; you could always hear someone moving about. The nobles who owned all the property were . . . what had Da called them? Vocho couldn't remember, because his da

had whispered it and still earned himself a sharp look from
Ma for saying such words. Vocho had got the gist anyway.
They'd had to move three times in the last three months as
the rents got higher and the work got scarcer.

Maybe soon they'd be living in one of these places. Not
even a room, just a shack on a roof, cobbled together from
rotting planks of wood and string. A gaunt man in a flapping rag of grease-stained tunic lurched out of the nearest,
making Vocho jump. He snarled at the three of them until
Kacha's friend Andoni threw a few pennies his way "to rent
the parapet for an hour". The way the man scrabbled for
them turned Vocho's stomach, though he wasn't quite sure
why. Because the man was beyond pride, perhaps. Vocho's
family were poor, more than poor, but Ma and Da had their
pride. Their clothes were ragged but scrubbed to within an
inch of their lives, and Ma would rather die than have a
flick of mud on the doorstep of whatever room they were
renting. He couldn't imagine Da ever scrabbling in a pile of
stinking rubbish for a few pennies, no matter how poor
they got. *Pride and dignity. Not even the nobles can take those
from us. If it's all you have, you hold on to it with everything
you got*, Da was fond of saying when he was in his cups.

Kacha pulled Vocho on, and he let her, glad not to watch
the man any more.

The day was golden like apples and seemed full of sunlight,
as though he could squeeze it and light would fall out, drip
down his hands. A breeze from the sea drifted across, ruffled
hair and took the worst of the heat, blew away the clouds
of smoke over Soot Town and beyond. A crowd had gathered
in the square below them, shoving for position near the big
clock left over from the empire before it fell, which chimed
out the warning for the midnight change o' the clock so
everyone could get ready. A funny-looking contraption sat
next to it that Vocho couldn't figure out, so he ignored it.
Instead he looked at the crowd, watched them gossip and

elbow and laugh. An old lady who'd got a prime position near the contraption had even brought a rickety chair and a picnic. Something was going on, something exciting or something dreadful, he couldn't tell which – it fizzed through the crowd so even Vocho could feel it from up here. He didn't know what was exciting though, only that Kacha was jittery and kept laughing and twisting her hair around her finger like she did when she was nervous. All he knew was it was some kind of dare that her friend had said she didn't have the guts to do. Even at his age Vocho thought the friend was an idiot. Kacha *always* took the dare.

They settled down near the edge of the roof. Kacha gave him a funny look and said, "You got to promise not to tell Da. He let you come cos I told him we was playing duellists down on the jetty and he and Ma had to work. If he'd a known where we was going, he wouldn't a let you come with me."

Vocho scrunched a glare onto his face, like he saw Da do whenever he did something wrong, which was all the time. Kacha never got the glare, so maybe that was why she ignored it.

"You're only a baby, really, but we got to let Ma and Da work when they can, so I'm in charge. And if you cry, I'll push you over the edge meself."

Andoni laughed, a sticky sound because he'd been stuffing himself with sweets all the way here – *his* da had a steady job and no gimp knee that kept him out of work for days at a time. *His* da could afford to buy him sweets, and toys, proper good new ones with clockwork innards so the soldiers marched all on their own, which the priests said would make him burn in any one of the hells. Not like all the old toys, the boring ones the priests didn't mind, which just stood there. Whenever they went to temple, that's what Vocho prayed for – a little clockwork duellist with a waving sword and everything, which would cost his da three months' wages. Maybe he was praying to the wrong one, or maybe he'd burn in hells for wanting clockwork. There were lots of gods and goddesses, one for every little thing, it seemed like, and Vocho could never get them all straight in his head. They all seemed to believe in his burning in hells for wanting a clockwork toy though.

"I bet," Andoni said. "I bet you one of my toys that he doesn't just cry, he widdles himself."

"I bet you he won't," Kacha said hotly, and Vocho kind of loved her at that moment, even if she was annoying as hells most of the time. "Bet you anything you like."

Andoni curled a lip. "You haven't got anything I want."

"I bet you . . ." Kacha screwed up her eyes. "I bet you half a bull."

"You haven't *got* half a bull. Your da doesn't make half a bull in a month!"

"Half a bull," Kacha repeated firmly. "You want a bet or not?"

Andoni laughed again. "Your money you're throwing away. Bet." With that he spat on his hand, Kacha spat on hers, and they shook on it.

Andoni went back to stuffing sweets in his mouth – too stingy to share, of course – and Vocho whispered to Kacha, "Half a bull? Where are you—"

"Just don't widdle. All right?"

Vocho was about to answer when things started happening down in the square. On one side there was a squat grey building that gave Vocho the shivers. He didn't know why, only that the windows were too small and barred and . . . hopeless. The windows looked dead. It sounded stupid in his head even as he thought it, but he couldn't shake the feeling. He wasn't sure, but he thought maybe this building was what they called the Shrive, where his da kept threatening to send him if he misbehaved, which was a lot. It was where they put all the bad men, Ma said, but plenty of good men too, and none ever came out again till they was dead. Just the mention of the place was enough to make all the grown-ups twitch. It looked like that sort of building, sure enough.

To one side and below the grand staircase a door opened and the crowd fell briefly silent. It was the first time Vocho had seen a crowd so together, so *intense* – he'd learned that word from one of the priests and liked it lots.

Five men and two women came up a smaller, meaner set of steps. One of the men had a hood over his face so you couldn't see it, though it had eyeholes cut in it. The women and one man had their hands tied; the other three men carried pikes. Somewhere someone started banging a drum in a slow beat that made all the hairs stand up on the back of Vocho's neck. The crowd fell silent, and all he could hear was the drum.

"Kass . . ."

"Shh!"

On the other side of the square a tall man, a fair-skinned southerner, broad shouldered and with a mane of blond hair that went every which way in the breeze, shoved his way through the crowd, his face all twisted. He shouted something Vocho couldn't catch, but it stirred the crowd. Other people began shouting, anger swirling through them like ink in water.

The little procession of men and women came on. Only now they were being buffeted by the crowd. Not the people with their hands tied, but the others, the man with the hood and the other three. Someone reached out and tried to drag the hood off and got a pike in the face for his trouble.

It was like the crowd had been wound up like clockwork toys, and now someone had pressed the button to release the mechanism. They surged forward, and someone threw something, a rock perhaps, which hit the hooded man right in the face. The tall man whose shouts had started it shoved closer and closer, and he threw something too, which brought a wash of blood to the face of one of the pikemen.

Kacha grabbed Vocho's hand tight, too tight. She was white lipped as she stared down, so was her friend. *He* looked like he might widdle himself, which helped Vocho take his mind off his own pressing need to pee.

The crowd howled. The little old lady crammed another pie into her face and gummed it happily. Next to her a couple of children a few years older than Kacha were scrabbling around for more rocks to throw. A woman reached into a bag, fished out what looked suspiciously like a tomato and threw that.

A hollow boom echoed around the square, and the crowd stopped, unsure, nervous. The main door to the squat grey building had slammed open, and through it came a tight wedge of king's guards. They had their swords out and the crowd fell back before them. One lad wasn't quick enough, and blood splashed the cobblestones.

At the back of the square a horse whinnied and there were another two dozen king's guards, mounted and forcing their way through the crush, laying about them with long sticks. A woman fell trying to get away and was crushed by stamping hooves.

The crowd wasn't howling any more; it was screaming, crying, trying to escape, caught between guards on two sides and by walls on the others.

Through it all the drum kept beating, the hooded man kept going, the tied-up women and man kept getting shoved on. Towards the contraption in the centre. Suddenly to Vocho it didn't look as harmless as he'd first thought.

This thing on a pedestal was tall, and black except for the silvery-blue of a piece of metal near the top and a flapping rope. It looked kind of like a doorway with no door in it, and it was scaring Vocho stupid. He *really* needed to pee.

The guards fought for control and several minutes later won. One of them climbed the pedestal and surveyed the now-subdued crowd – the big blond who'd started it all was crumpled and bloody, a guard on each arm as they dragged him towards the steps of the grey building.

"I'm the captain of the king's guard." The man on the pedestal glared around at the crowd. "This is the legal execution of three convicted criminals, and you *will* stand by and let it go ahead, unless you want to go into the Shrive as well."

"Murderers!" the blond man shouted. "It's not a crime to—" He broke off as a guard smacked him in the mouth, and then he was gone into the blackness of the doorway. Vocho had the feeling that doorway was the gate to the hells. Hells were where the bad men went, the priests said, and Ma had said bad men went into the Shrive, so it stood to reason.

The captain ignored the southerner, gave the crowd a last meaningful glare and stepped down.

"Execution?" Vocho whispered. He really needed to widdle. Really, right *now*. But he daren't. Kacha had bet he wouldn't and she'd no way to pay the debt. He jiggled up and down and tried to think of something else.

"He's a . . . a . . . herry-something," Kacha said.

"Heretic," Andoni said in a hushed voice. "My da says he reckons that the world is all like clockwork or something."

"It needs winding up?" Vocho was rapidly starting to think Andoni was an idiot. The world would need ever such a big winder.

"No, Voch, you plank," Kacha said. "That it all . . . I don't know, runs the same all the time, on rails or something. Like those toys that always do the same thing every time. Everything we do is already done, or pre . . . something. You know, like we got no choice in what we do because we're like clockwork too. He says that the Clockwork God isn't dead, only sleeping, that we're the herry-things for using his old temples to pray to the gods. He says we just made them up because the Clockwork God turned away from the Castans, from us. An' that all that talk from the priests about using clockwork being a sin, that their gods will save us an' all, well that talk is the sin, cos the Clockwork God says it ain't true."

"Oh." Vocho spent a minute thinking about that as the group closed in on the contraption. "But why—"

"Because the king is supposed to be blessed by the gods, right?" Andoni said knowledgeably, looking like he was welcoming the distraction from what was going on in the square. "That's why he gets to be king. But if there aren't any gods, or the world is made of clockwork, then, well, who's to say he gets to be king? My da says this un's been spouting about it all over, him and his mates. Saying the Clockwork God will rise again. Them's the ones making the clockwork toys and selling 'em, secret like, because them's prayers to wake the Clockwork God back up. Fermenting trouble or something, my da says – like beer, I reckon, you know when it goes all frothy. People're listening and all, getting all stirred up. King don't like that, so he has 'em done for heresy. Man who's getting chopped said that him being chucked off the throne is what's bound to happen. Cogs said so. Or something."

"But what if the gods made the clockwork?" Vocho asked. All he got was a "Don't be daft" look. "Seems a funny reason to kill someone anyway."

They all looked down at the contraption.

"Da says the king *is* funny, in the head," Andoni said at last. "Lots of people getting arrested and shoved in the Shrive for all sorts, and lots of times they ain't even done nothing! Excepting be poor. Lots go in, more every day. No one comes back neither. That bloke they took away, I reckon he was one of them heretics and all, cos my da, he took me to see 'em speak down in Soot Town, and I reckon it was him that did the speaking. He made it sound all proper, like the world made sense if you only looked at it right, and if you did, then everyone could have a nice life and everything and you don't need no king, 'specially not one that won't look at the world right and goes around arresting people for nothing. Bet they'll kill him too, soon enough. Bet you a bull. Man said it had to happen, and he made it sound sensible, my da said."

Oh gods, oh gods. Vocho really had to widdle now. Kacha was scaring him the way she looked, the story Andoni told him, and so was everything else. He wanted to go home, he wanted his ma. He wanted to widdle something *bad*.

A low moan from the crowd brought his gaze back to the square. There, in the shadow of the ancient, barely understood clock that ruled the city, the man with tied hands stepped up onto the pedestal. Vocho didn't want to look, but he had to. Something about the man made Vocho want to look away but made him look too. The man was crying, and Vocho had never seen a man cry before. He wasn't crying because he was scared, even Vocho knew that, or that wasn't all of it, or even most of it. The man turned once to the woman behind him, and they shared a look, and Vocho *knew* that look. It was the look his da gave his ma when they had to move again, or when they could only afford food for one meal a day and that fish-head soup was more water than anything, when Ma scrubbed that step till her hands were raw, when Da talked about pride and dignity in his cups.

The man turned back, straightened his shoulders, knelt down and put his head through the gap in the door thing. The hooded man pressed a lever, there was a whirr of ropes and metal in runners that echoed around the square, a chunk sound, and the man's head rolled away into the crowd. Blood painted the flagstones, and the little old lady grinned and shoved another pie in her face.

Vocho never needed a widdle more, before or after, as he did right then, but Kacha had believed in him so he managed to hold on until all three were dead and Andoni had handed over the clockwork duellist, the toy that was a prayer to the dead Clockwork God on the one hand and might send him to burn in hells on the other.

Vocho took his spoils home and put it on a shelf. A reminder of the first bet he ever won, but he never played with it.

Chapter Four

Petri Egimont sauntered into the guild wearing a chilly little smile and with revenge in his heart. Not so long ago the guild master, Eneko, would have had a conniption at the thought of Petri entering. Now, with his two most notorious duellists wanted for the murder of the prelate's favourite priest, he didn't have much choice but to let the prelate's man in.

The guild was just as Petri remembered it. Walls built from huge blocks of mellow ochre stone, rough at the edges, terracotta tiles on the roof, channels worn in the places where rain ran off. The great gatehouse, imposing and dour, the gates always open – they'd been shut only once in living memory, a day that was burned into Petri's head with fire and blood. The courtyard-cum-sparring arena inside, echoing with the sound of swordplay and the ticking of the clockwork duellist who watched over the yard. She was bronze and brass, wielding a rapier so fine it looked as ephemeral as a lightning bolt in the sun. She ticked and watched, watched and ticked, until the next time someone switched the lever and set her into her motion of whirling sword and flashing eyes. A stern face, keeping all the lessers and journeymen in line, with a hint of compassion, of sadness, for those the guild lost to war, to jobs, to death on a sword. She was the heart of the guild, that nameless duellist.

The aspiring duellists knew better than to stop their practice as Petri strode through the cloister on the south side, but they turned as they fought so they could watch him, and he could hear the rumour of whispers. He clenched his teeth and carried on.

The young lesser who was supposed to be guiding him couldn't keep up, and he knew the way well enough. Through the cloisters, up stairs, around twists that changed with the change o' the clock, until he came to Eneko's door. He didn't bother to knock but opened the door and went straight in. Eneko wasn't surprised. Petri thought it would take a lot more than someone barging in to do that.

The guild master sat back in his chair and looked up at Petri from under lidded eyes, hands clasped across a belly that was just now running to fat. The eyes were warier than they had been, the jowls looser, the long dark hair in its neat ponytail more sprinkled with grey, but he'd lost none of his poise.

"Again, Petri?"

A tight smile from Petri as he took a chair he knew would never be offered. "Again, Eneko. And again, and again, until the prelate is sure." Not that he came from the prelate today, but the questions would be similar. "I *know* you've got some idea where they are. The prelate knows it too, and I'll keep on coming until he gets what he wants. It's not like you've never betrayed your duellists before now, is it? When you need to, as you will no doubt say. I think you're going to need to before the prelate loses what little patience he has with you."

Eneko shifted in his chair but didn't seem unduly perturbed as he spread his hands in a gesture of innocence that Petri didn't believe for a second. Eneko hadn't got to be guild master by being open and honest, or naïve.

"And what will he do about it? What *can* he? Nothing, or he'd have done it by now, and razed this guild to the ground. But he can't, not unless he wants a revolt against him. Isn't that so? Who really rules Reyes? That was always the old question, after the Fall. The king ruled their bodies, and now the prelate does. He gives them their god to believe in, and they do, mostly, but it takes longer than a few years to dim people's memories that much, and you know it. Old ways live on, not openly perhaps, but in peoples' minds. A superstition here, a chalked rune that was once a call to the old gods, a half-forgotten tale of how the world was made there, and us, right where they can see us. We're legendary, and worshipped, and *real*, Petri. The guild has protected this city for hundreds of years, maybe longer, and its people know it in their blood and bones. We don't tell them who to worship or how to live. We just are. We are the city, and the city is us, and yet we are not *of* the city, and the prelate has no claim on us, cannot rule us and can compel me to say nothing. So tell me, what will the prelate do when his patience runs out? The same as he has all these past years – nothing of any consequence. He can make our lives more difficult perhaps, but not by much, and we'll weather it as we weathered much worse before now."

Petri sat blandly. This was Eneko's standard response, and while true enough, he'd heard it too many times before. But what came next startled him.

"I told her, you know. Told her that you were using her. Because you were, weren't you? Using her to try to winkle information for the prelate. Spying on her, and me, the guild."

He smiled at the look of shock that must be written all over Petri's face. It explained everything – why Petri's note offering Kacha comfort after that idiot Vocho had killed the priest had been returned so vehemently with his ring, why she'd taken such a delight in their duel by the carriage. Why she seemed to hate him when once she'd said she loved him. She'd found out the truth he'd worked so hard to hide, a truth that had rapidly become false as he'd got to know her, but how would he ever make her believe that? He couldn't, and not just because she'd probably skewer him if he got too close. He'd betrayed her even before they knew each other.

"You think I didn't guess? That I wouldn't tell her, make her see?" Eneko said into these thoughts. "A prelate's man cosying up to my personal apprentice? A blind man could see what you were about, but you blinded her well enough. Did you find anything out?"

Petri pulled himself together, but all thoughts of trying to get Eneko to tell him something, anything, fled. It had been a faint hope at best, but one that had to be tried. "I found out enough."

Eneko laughed. "I rather doubt that, or not from Kacha. Vocho on the other hand . . . You may as well leave now. The prelate can set his men to watch me all he likes, open my messages – no don't deny it, he has – do whatever he feels he needs to. I don't *know* where they are. If I did, I'd hardly hand them over to you for execution, no matter what they've done. They're no longer part of the guild, which is punishment enough for both of them, and no longer my responsibility."

Eneko turned away to some papers on his desk, effectively dismissing Petri, as he'd always done. Dismiss, disown, destroy. It was Eneko who had made his life the misery it was.

Petri swept the papers off Eneko's desk and was gratified to see a crack in the calm façade. "Soon enough," he said. "Soon enough this won't be your guild. I look forward to the day I can return the favour you once did me, and shut the gates on you."

They stared at each other for long moments before Petri straightened up smartly and left. His boots clicked on the stone floor in a staccato rhythm that echoed in his head. Not long now, and this guild would be his, and Eneko would be the one staring at a guild that had betrayed him.

Not long, provided he could find Kacha and Vocho and the damned chest.

Egimont rode into the horse dealer's yard with ten good men behind him. It was a ramshackle place with falling-down fences, a barn with more holes than roof and what seemed like acres of mud. One of the early clockwork combination hay scyther/stookers lay in pieces in the shade of the barn, straggles of grass growing through it as though in mockery. The horses dealt here didn't seem much better – a group of underfed nags fetlock deep in mud looked up dully as they rode in.

A woman came out of the hovel that seemed to pass for a house, though she was spruce enough in a homely kind of way. She gave them an appraising glance and perked up instantly at the flash of colour on the lapels of Egimont's men.

"Prelate's guard, eh? Well, if you're looking, I've got some fine horses for sale. Not that sorry lot over there, I keep the best in the stables around the back. How many do you want?"

"None." Egimont slid down from his horse and tried – and failed – not to step in any shit. "You have a horse with one ear?"

Once he'd ascertained from Eneko that he'd get no help there, it hadn't taken too long to find the previous victims of Kacha and Vocho since they started their new life of crime. Half a dozen men and women had told him everything they could, happy to help the prelate's man apprehend the vicious highwaymen of Fusta Wood. One of the women had told him how, during the robbery, one of her attackers had shot the ear off the other's horse. Egimont was certain both horses had the full complement of ears when the siblings had ambushed him, and so a trip to all the horse traders in the area seemed a good place to start.

The woman raised an eyebrow. "Not a lot of call for them. But yes, as it happens, I do. Can do you a good price too."

"Oh, I don't want to buy it," Egimont said. "I want to know who you bought it from."

The woman's mouth twitched as she looked him over, noted the way his hand rested on his sword, went on over his men and back to him. "Don't suppose I got much choice, then? A bloke from up the way there. New to the area, he said. Bit of a dandy, seemed to be, in his manner, but he reckoned he were a farmer. Didn't look like no farmer to me, excepting his clothes. He looked like someone playing dress-up."

"Did he say anything else?"

The woman hesitated with a greedy smile on her face, so Egimont took two bulls out of his purse and bounced them in his palm.

"Oh, aye, he did. Talkative bugger, he was. From Reyes, I reckon, accent sounded about right. Bit posh and all, for all he said he was a farmer. Reckon him and his sister are the ones renting the old place up past the Domenech manor. Said the beast had got too nervy, so I swapped him. Managed to beat him down, and all he got was a carthorse that's seen better days."

Egimont turned on his heel and mounted.

"The money?"

Once he'd have given her the money. Once he'd been an honourable duellist who wanted only to be the best there was. Once he'd had a heart that wasn't dull and dead to anything except what he wanted, but money and a duchy and revenge were all that he wanted now.

"I'll give you a tip instead. Always take the money up front."

With that, he kicked his horse into a canter and led his men towards the Domenech place.

It took Vocho most of two days to get the first four locks off. He wasn't too shabby at locks – the guild made sure the men and women they supplied for clients were well versed in whatever skills they might need, even if they looked down on them, and being able to pick a lock was very handy for certain jobs. But these locks were a make he'd never encountered before and none of his usual tricks worked, so it was down to brute force. At one point, covered in sweat and sporting a fine set of skinned knuckles, he'd considered putting the damned thing in with Kacha's horse and letting him kick it to splinters, but the wood was harder than anything he'd encountered too. An axe barely even scratched it, and he no longer had the funds to buy a clockwork hammer that would have smashed the thing to bits in minutes. Fancy clockwork like that was for the rich; all most farmers had was one or two plainer pieces of machinery that they swapped about so everyone got a turn. Reyes city might be the clockwork wonder of the provinces, but the rural poor didn't see a hell of a lot of it.

The thought of what the final lock must be protecting, and of the reward – ten thousand? It *must* be worth ten times that then – spurred him on. With Kacha out, taking Cospel's share to the appointed place, he dragged the thing to the top of the yard, all the better to get a damned good swing at it, but each blow did almost nothing. The last lock was proving to be a bastard and a half, and despite the early spring chill he was sweating worse than the pigs. He took off his shirt, fetched a crowbar from the shed and tried again, and succeeded in doing nothing more than bust a gut, or that's what it felt like.

His mood wasn't much improved by the sight of Dom at the gate, waving a handkerchief and calling "Halloo!" up the hill.

Clockwork God preserve me, I've not been granted great reserves of patience. Please save me from this . . . man who will surely make what little I possess snap.

His prayers, as so often, went completely unanswered, in fact seemed to have the opposite effect as Dom picked his way across the mud and shit. And still none got on him. How in hells did he do that?

"Good morning!" Dom was one of those eternally cheerful people who would try the serenity of the Clockwork God himself. He dabbed at his eyes with his handkerchief and held it delicately over his nose against the smell of the pigs behind the barn. "A turn in the weather, do you think?"

Vocho grunted in return, and Dom carried on with a whole spiel of twitterings that hurt Vocho's ears. Kacha appeared on horseback at the far end of the lane, and Dom stopped his ramblings for a pace. Then, "Could we talk, somewhere privately, do you think?"

It seemed pretty private in the yard with only the chickens to overhear, but Vocho was intrigued despite himself, so led Dom to the gate of the first field. He was sort of proud of the field. Sort of because, well, who gave a crap about fields when you could be fencing? But if he had to farm, then he was proud of it. He'd had to make do without a clockwork plough, or even much of a plough horse, because Kacha's devil beast had taken one look at the rig and tried to destroy it, and Vocho's new horse was permanently exhausted, or at least looked like it every time it saw the plough. But he'd got there in the end. The wheat was just coming up, little streaks of green against the brown of the earth. It wasn't exactly neat or anything, because it was just a field. But stuff was growing, and that was the important thing, right?

Dom gaped at the field in horror, twittered a bit and then became all business. "Vocho, you are no farmer."

"Well, I farm so—"

A wave of Dom's hand shut Vocho up. "No, it was clear to me the day you rented this croft. Do you think I'd try to court a common farmer's sister? Make a fine mistress perhaps, but marriages are made of more, especially mine, if my father has any say in the matter. I think you catch my drift. Of course, my natural courtesy prevented me from saying anything, though now it becomes pertinent. You, sir, and I think you are a sir, are no farmer, and this field proves it. If I was in any doubt, seeing those sword scars on your chest would have clinched it. The sign of a guild education, if I'm not mistaken."

Bugger. The silly sod was sharper than he looked, which wasn't hard, in fairness. Time for the story they'd worked out in advance, though a new twist occurred to Vocho. He tried on a thoroughly abashed face, which didn't sit naturally but it seemed to work. "It's a little delicate. I mean . . ." He leaned in, going for open trustworthiness. Had to be worth a stab. "Can I rely on you not to say anything?"

Dom bridled at that, pulled himself up to his not very tall best height and puffed out his chubby soft chest. "Naturally. We're both gentlemen, aren't we? I shall give you my word."

Vocho was hard pressed not to laugh, but let his acquired accent, honed from years of insulting gentlemen, slip through. "A slight problem with an arranged marriage."

Dom squinted as he thought about this. "She *is* your sister? I mean, you aren't, well, married to her yourself?"

Vocho's grimace was genuine enough. "She's my sister, that's for sure. No, our father had some marriage all lined up, but she didn't take very well to the idea, or the intended groom. So we left. If he finds us . . ."

"Oh, rest assured, your secret is safe with me. Not a word shall cross my lips, on my honour as a gentleman."

Most of whom had about as much honour as chickens, in Vocho's experience, at least when it came to getting what they wanted. But Vocho had caught glimpses here and there that Dom was a closet royalist – plenty still about, most of them dreaming about the romance of nobles and ladies and balls and a gentleman's or woman's honour and all that tripe. Mostly these were the new nobility-without-titles. The self-made clockers' sons and daughters, who didn't remember what the gentry had really been like, read the old – and frankly made up – stories romanticising them, only saw the grand houses their parents had bought, saw the paintings and fine things that had come with them and thought the people surely must have matched. Gentlemen and -women they hadn't been, his guild education had made that abundantly clear, though to Vocho's mind the clockers were little better. When he'd been in the guild it hadn't mattered – its members were something apart from clockers or nobles alike. It was starting to matter now though.

"I'm glad to hear it," he said. "Such a trial for my sister, living like this, you know. But worth it. And of course we'd never have met you otherwise, and I know my sister thinks of you often." Vocho mentally added *in extremely uncomplimentary terms*. "I do wonder, now that you've guessed our secret, whether you might do me a small favour. It would certainly help Kass look upon you even more favourably."

Dom's eyes lit up and positively glowed at the request. He gave a stiff, formal bow that had his hat skimming the mud. "Certainly, if I can."

God's cogs, he was almost too easy. Vocho looked around as though afraid someone might overhear them. "Our father is an odd man. Rather old-fashioned – you know what fathers are like."

Dom nodded eagerly. His own father was nothing short

of a tyrant, and a bit of sympathy would only help Vocho here.

"*Extremely* old-fashioned, and so was the intended groom as well as just being plain old. So when Kass got betrothed, they tricked her into having a magician put wards on them both, tattoos like you said."

Dom took an aghast step back, handkerchief to his mouth. "May the Clockwork God preserve our gears, how barbaric!"

"You see why we had to get away? Why we wanted to know about magicians? The chest — sort of a ruse. Kass knew you'd know, because you're so educated and worldly wise." Vocho wondered if he might be laying it on a bit thick, but Dom looked tickled pink. "To tell you the real reason seemed imprudent. And of course, if you want me to help press your suit with Kass . . ."

Really, when it came down to it, Dom was quite decisive. Perhaps the thought of those tattoos — the only magic Vocho was sure about and that because of him — had sharpened his mind.

Dom waved his hand, as though the thought of Vocho's favour in the matter of Kass had never crossed his mind. "Even if I didn't, I thought those wards hadn't been used in years! Not since the prelate killed all the mages, at least. I'm surprised your father could find a magician to do it. Turning up all over, all of a sudden. What do you need me to do?"

"Outlawed, yes, but there are still people prepared to use them, and magicians prepared to draw them, if you know where to find them. It's not far to Ikaras, and a few people might slip past the guards, might go to your old university to find a magician. What I need is a magician to *un*draw them. Someone we can trust, and someone within the borders if I can, because my father'll have them watched, you can be sure." Vocho wanted to know who this magician was. There wouldn't be two in Reyes, couldn't be, but if there was one . . . Dom would perhaps know or could find out without suspicion falling on Vocho. Dom might be a ninny but he was a well connected ninny.

"I quite understand," Dom said. "And rest assured, I'll breathe not a word! Poor Kassinda would be ruined if anyone were to find out. Especially around here. The capital is much more tolerant of such things, so I've heard. A magician, yes, perhaps I might be able to help. Perhaps. I've heard a rumour about a magician just lately. Didn't think to believe it of course, but now, yes, maybe it's true after all. Perhaps I can help. But he'll cost."

Vocho looked down forlornly at his sackcloth trousers. "That's a shame, really. My sister would so *love* to know you better, I'm sure, but with the tattoo she's embarrassed, you see?"

Dom seemed to struggle with himself for a while, opening his mouth, closing it, going pink about the ears. Finally he said, "If I can persuade my father that you two really aren't farmers . . . and he has been on at me to finally chose a wife . . . Who was your father, did you say?"

"I didn't, and I won't just yet. Not until those wards are off. With them on, he still controls her, in a way. He's looking for us, I know. My cousin is helping him. He has a big place up to the north, in the mountains – perhaps you've been there?" A smile and a knowing wink.

Dom's mouth flopped open at the word "cousin" and the hint at the palace in the mountains, the only big place for miles. A subtle little misdirection always worked wonders – the king had the gods knew how many cousins, so Dom would hardly know them all. Or indeed Vocho's actual cousin, who wasn't a king but a knacker's man with a big yard in the next town.

"I'm certain I can arrange a loan to cover the fee," Dom gasped out eventually. Vocho could almost see the visions he was having: of living in a palace in the capital, of reflected if banned rank, of making his father bow to him even if it was strictly outlawed.

"And I certainly won't forget it, on my honour as a gentleman," Vocho said. Down the lane Kacha was nearing the house. "Now, would you like to see Kass while you're here?"

Chapter Five

Kacha spotted Dom following Vocho as he dragged the chest across the mud-splattered yard, swore and reined her horse in. It didn't take kindly to being told what to do – it rarely did – and tried to bite her foot. She swatted its mouth away absent-mindedly and it settled for terrorising a nearby bush.

She knew what her brother was about, damn his eyes. Trying to make up for it, for the whole debacle with the priest. Trying to make sure she got another good match, even if as a duellist she'd never marry – all duellists swore never to hold anything above the guild, so no marrying, no children.

Screw good matches; it hadn't been that she'd been after. She'd not been after any kind of match, good or otherwise, before Petri.

What *had* it been? She couldn't say, not with any sureness. Because Petri and Vocho were opposites, because they balanced each other in her life perhaps. Petri was everything that her brother wasn't; all the things that annoyed her about Vocho found their reverse in Petri.

He'd taken her as he'd taken everything – seriously, demanding nothing of her but her time. His affection hadn't depended on her being obedient, diligent, perfect, not like with Eneko and her da before him. Petri had been the Pole Star in her life, a constant antidote to the streaking comet that was Vocho.

Until he'd stopped being constant in the blink of an eye.

But *Dom* instead? Sometimes she thought the whole thing with the priest had broken something in her brother's head. He'd been odd ever since, through the whole nightmare of their inglorious run from Reyes. Past the note from Petri. In his handwriting, with his seal, which had said only *"Renounce your brother, or return my ring, forthwith."* Her note back had been somewhat more acerbic – she'd described exactly what he could do with his bloody ring. She'd even drawn a little picture, in case he had trouble.

Petri hadn't asked her whether it was true about the priest. Just the note, and the implication that Vocho was, naturally, guilty. What did he expect her to do? Blood was thicker than water, so they said, and hers and Vocho's was thick with everything they'd been through together, even if she was tempted to throttle him occasionally. OK, quite often.

Seeing Petri again had been a shock, and that *"please"* – that had almost undone her. But robbing him, and beating him into the bargain, had been so very, very satisfying. She wanted to do it again, and this time without a mask. She wanted him to say that maybe Vocho was innocent. She wanted to prove that was true, and perhaps that was the only thing that overrode the hate. Vocho was innocent, she had to believe that, that this whole farce was one they could fight back from. Not with money either, no matter what Vocho thought.

Vocho was trying, she knew that. Trying to get their standing back, their place in the guild. He didn't seem to understand she wanted nothing from Petri, not any more. She'd stay and be a farmer shovelling pig shit for the rest of her life before she took a single thing from Petri, except perhaps his dignity, his honour, his pride, all those things that he'd taken from her with a few strokes of a pen. That was what she was going to do. Prove Vocho was innocent. Then she was going to parade that in front of Petri like a flag.

Maybe then she could lay that ghost to rest, stop dreaming of the note, of his face, half in darkness, half in light, just staring at her with those sharp dark eyes, kissing her silent and reproachful till she woke up with a cry on her lips.

Maybe.

So, Vocho was trying to make it up to her, trying to make up for what he thought she'd lost. But hell's teeth, Dom instead? Yes, something had clearly broken in her brother's mind. She urged the horse on and its ears pricked up when she promised it that it could eat Dom's hat.

Vocho tried a grin as Kacha shut the door on Dom and whirled to face him.

"And just what was that all about? Are you *trying* to encourage the gibbering idiot?"

Vocho held up his hands in a plea for peace. "Hey, a friend among the clockers can only help us right now. And if he's sweet on you, all the better, as is the fact he's prepared to get us a loan from his father. If I'd wanted to annoy you, and I accept that usually I do, I'd have accepted his proposal of marriage to you."

"It seems he thinks that's on the cards anyway. What, exactly, did you say to him?"

So Vocho told her, ending with, "And then we'll leave with his money – without him, I promise," and she calmed down, a bit.

"Thievery? I thought the highwayman stuff was bad enough. But we need to go if he knows we aren't who we've been telling him. All right. But if it comes to it, you're the one telling him we're not getting married. Because I am *not* getting married, to him or anyone."

"Fair enough."

Vocho's eyes kept going to the chest. He had to get the damned thing open. It was going to be the answer to everything. Weird though, that every time he got too close that itching started between his shoulder blades. It worried him. He'd spent hours trying to look in the mirror to see what it was and couldn't see a damned thing. For reasons he couldn't quite fathom, he didn't want to ask Kacha to look either.

"You were born to be a highwayman. Always did have itchy fingers," Kacha said now.

When he turned round she was grinning at him. Funny how she could do that, just throw away her anger like it was yesterday's bathwater. He wished he could be so easy with his. Probably just as well he didn't have much, because when he did, it tended to fester.

"I wasn't born for the hiding part. What good is it being a great robber if you don't get to brag about it? Or have to play at being farmer?"

"Yes, but—"

That was as far as she got. The light coming in the window disappeared: blackness seemed to flow in from it, under the door, everywhere. The chest began to rattle, blue and green sparks arcing from the lid and earthing on the floor, bright in the sudden darkness. The itching on Vocho's back turned to a burn that made him yelp. Kacha grabbed him and threw him to the floor just as the door blew in, flying across the room and cracking into the chest, smashing the lid off with a sound like someone was bowling at mountains.

Sudden silence, broken only by the lights on the chest crackling and flickering in vivid blues and greens before they died.

"What the fuck was that?" Vocho whispered from down in the straw.

"No idea." Kacha drew Egimont's blade from where she'd hidden it in her ragged skirts. "But I think it wants the chest. I *told* you to dump it."

Vocho scrabbled about for his own sword. He felt lost without it at his waist, but his disguise had demanded it. Kacha was right too – whatever the blast had been, it had definitely targeted the chest. The thing rocked gently in the straw, loose locks flapping. He would be able to see inside now, see what it was that was so very valuable.

His right hand found his blade where he'd put it, on a bracket under the chunky table where it was hidden but easy to reach. Even as he got it, his left hand was reaching out for the chest. Jewels, had to be. Jewels, gold, a king's ransom, his and Kacha's way out of this fucking hovel and back where they belonged.

"Don't be an idiot," Kacha hissed and whacked his hand with the flat of her blade. "Whatever it is, it's still out there."

"You've really lost your sense of humour lately, you know that?" But Vocho withdrew his hand and faced the door. She might not be much fun of late, but she was usually, and annoyingly, right about when to be careful.

Outside, it should have been sunshine through rain clouds, a yellow and green spring, but that was the opposite of what Vocho saw through the shattered doorway. Blackness, dim and swirling like fog. Silent too, as though it was sucking up all sound. Vocho gripped his sword harder and then wondered why – hard to duel a fog.

Hard not to let the first thought into his head unnerve him: the magician was back for his chest. How in seven hells had he found them? Quickly followed by: could a magician really vaporise him?

He didn't want to find out. Something moved in the fog, and Vocho moved too. No thought behind it except get out alive, preferably with the contents of the chest. He launched himself forward into a roll, bounced up to his feet, sword at the ready and just piercing the blackness.

"It's not going to work," a voice said. One he recognised. The cultured deadpan drawl of Petri bloody Egimont. The blackness lifted, and Vocho wished it hadn't, because it revealed not just Egimont with a cruel little smile on his lips, but a cohort of men behind him too. All with swords at waist or in hand, some with guns ready. It also revealed a disturbing piece of paper dangling from Egimont's left hand. Funny how a scrap like that could instil a sense of deep dread, but it wasn't the paper itself; it was the markings on it, in blood still damp. Still active, if Dom was right.

"Whatever you think you might do," Egimont said, "it won't work. All I have to do is say a word and boom, you're dead. If you kill me before I get the chance –" he shrugged as if that was a minor detail "– then while you're doing that, one of my men will shoot you dead. Both of you."

His gaze flickered over to Kacha, hesitated for long ticks of the clock on the mantel while he licked a lip as though wanting to say something and then reluctantly came back to Vocho. "So, perhaps you'd prefer to hand over the chest and live. However briefly before you're executed for murder, and your sister for aiding you."

Vocho made to strike anyway – strike first, ask later, always his motto – when Kacha's voiced snaked out from behind him and stayed his hand: "Get screwed, sideways."

"I rather got that impression from your note." Egimont's voice had turned ice cold, clipped with scorn, but he didn't seem able to take his eyes from Kacha, and there was heat there even if there was none in his voice. "The diagram was very instructional."

"Shame you didn't take me up on my suggestion."

Vocho was lost – what note? What diagram? Still Egimont was looking at Kacha, looking like he wanted to forget everything except her. Vocho took advantage of the fact no one was taking any notice of him.

Strictly speaking, it wasn't a move he should have used. Strictly speaking. But then he wasn't a member of the guild any more, and besides rules were for fools. His sword whipped towards Egimont's eyes, almost got the bastard too, but he saw it just in time and bent back out of the way. Still, it left him unbalanced and concentrating on Vocho instead of mooning over Kacha.

Egimont's right hand came up, sword ready to beat back Vocho, while his left still held the paper. A word, *the* word, the one that would unleash whatever was on that paper, formed on his lips with a smile. "Des—"

That was as far as he got before Kacha launched herself into him, leading with a kick to the groin that removed his ability to speak. She always did love that move.

A familiar voice shouted, "Down!" and on instinct Vocho ducked, just in time for a bullet to whizz over his head and carry on to smash a china jug on the mantel that had miraculously survived the initial assault but now succumbed to a bullet to the heart. Outside, someone else was fighting, bringing grunts and yowls of pain from Egimont's men and cries of "I'm terribly sorry about that," "Pardon, I'm sure" and "Would you mind? Oh, I see. Perhaps not, my mistake." Inside, Egimont had recovered enough to stand up, but he had both Kacha and Vocho against him. He still had the scrap of paper with its disturbing patterns on it, but Vocho thought maybe they'd gone past that.

Egimont growled low in his throat at Kacha, lunged, turned it into a feint and caught Vocho off guard with a move he would never have expected of honourable stick-in-the-mud Egimont — an elbow to his face that knocked him flying.

Looked like all bets were off, and anything went. No guild rules, which from Egimont was surprising but suited Vocho just fine. He and Eggy had a score to settle. All his blood was pumping as he sprang back to his feet. He could beat Egimont standing on his head.

Three swift cuts, and none of them legal – to the face, the balls and back to the face in less time than it took to blink twice. Old Eggy caught the first two, but the last got him and whipped a triangle out of his cheek. Keep him on the hop, don't give him the chance to say a damned word, any word. Three more slashes, and a line of blood appeared on Eggy's arm, seeping through the silk.

Outside was chaos from the sounds of it – at least two men were screaming, and the clash and clang of metal told Vocho there was going to be more screaming by the end of it. Inside, Kacha hefted her sword, itching to join in, but Vocho had the bastard now.

Or so he thought. All that blood pumping, all the glorious excitement had made him forget the stupid bit of paper. Cool-headed Egimont hadn't though. He flung the paper down and leaped back, away from Vocho's sword, away from the paper, and stumbled into the yard, saying the nonsense word he needed.

Vocho barely had time to do anything except duck as the paper caught fire. Blackness descended again, so total he might have gone blind, and then something lifted him off his feet and thrust him into the wall, hard enough to knock him out for a moment or two. It couldn't have been longer because when he opened his eyes again the blackness was shredding, revealing the mess it had made of their hovel. Half the table was splintered around the room, including several pieces buried in Vocho's arm and one that was causing a dribble of blood to trickle down his face. The rest of the table wobbled in the centre of the room as though surprised it was still there. The straw that had graced the floor now floated in drifting eddies, lit by the bright sunlight that pierced the ruined roof. One wall had a new hole in it big enough to fit a cow through. The only thing that remained virtually undamaged was the damned chest.

Vocho couldn't see Egimont as he struggled up, his eyes going every which way from the knock to the head. His first thought was Kacha, but she'd ducked down behind the chest, which seemed to have saved her from any lasting damage, but she was white faced and shaking as hard as he was. Explosions were not a usual occurrence.

A quick glance to the doorway showed Egimont advancing again, three of his men behind him. Kacha grabbed Vocho's arm and pointed at the hole in the wall. "Time to go, right now."

Vocho was in complete agreement, until he caught sight of the contents of the chest. A slew of papers, each headed with an official crest, each covered with the sort of swirly writing that meant Something Important. Something Important, and something someone might want to pay for. He was determined not to walk away from this without something to show for it, and grabbed a handful. Underneath the papers was the tantalising glint of gold. Lots of gold.

"Come *on*," Kacha said from the hole.

But there was gold . . .

He scrabbled in the chest but only came up with more papers. One of Egimont's men fired. The bang was deafening inside the hovel, and something scored a hot line along Vocho's arm, almost making him drop the papers. A sword ran Egimont's man through from behind. As the man fell with a look of terminal surprise, Vocho caught sight of Dom, idiot face bemused as though startled he'd got hold of the right end of the sword. Vocho was certainly surprised.

Dom saw Vocho with his mouth hanging open, sketched a wave and called, "This is quite fun, isn't it? You go, I'll catch up! Get the horses ready."

"What in hells . . ." Vocho said before he lost any words he might have said.

"Don't know, but getting the horses seems a bloody good idea," Kacha said. "Come *on*."

Vocho hesitated. Getting out seemed like a good plan, but . . . but *gold*.

Egimont roared towards them, but Dom was either craftier than he looked or, more likely, too clumsy to have much hope of living very long or impressing Kacha. He tried a dashing swish of his blade, got it caught up in his own cloak with the point sticking straight up and staggered in front of Egimont, forcing him to stop, or stop having a face.

"Go!" Dom called again. He got his sword untangled and despite everything looked as though he was enjoying himself immensely, but there were more of Egimont's men on the way. Vocho didn't need telling again – he might be reckless but always tried to make sure he wasn't entirely stupid. Still, it only took a second to grab two bars of gold and shove them inside his shirt, where they bulged and swayed alarmingly and made him run like a hunchback.

He grabbed Kacha's arm and dived through the hole. It led to part of what had once been a kitchen garden but was now a jungle of raspberry canes and blackcurrant bushes gone wild. Vocho crashed through, Kacha right behind, cursing her dress, which kept getting caught on twigs. In the end she ripped the skirt off and to hells with it. At least she was wearing a decent set of bloomers.

They reached the corner of the hovel and peered around. Three men lay groaning in the mud. Two more weren't groaning. Another sat propped against the wall with a silly smile on his face – concussed if Vocho was any kind of judge. No sign of more, though by the sounds coming from the ruined doorway, at least two were still inside backing up Egimont.

"Dom did this?" Kacha whispered.

"I think so. I'm not sure it was entirely on purpose though. Come on."

They drifted across the muddy yard, keeping to the

shadows of the barn and sty before nipping inside the stable. Kacha's horse greeted them with a whicker and a kick to the door of his stall that would have broken bones.

"Have you still got those stupid papers?" Kacha asked as she grabbed for the bridles. "Just leave them, and let's concentrate on getting out of here. I've got half the bulls anyway, and some of the rings."

Vocho looked down at his hands and was startled to see that yes, he did still have the papers. Ten thousand bulls reward, and whatever was in the chest must be worth ten times that. He'd left behind maybe five thousand bulls in gold and a whole mess of papers, but he wasn't about to throw perhaps a fortune away. He shoved them inside his shirt with the gold. Time enough to look later.

They hurriedly bridled the horses but didn't bother with saddles – not enough time. Kacha's evil-tempered bastard tried for Vocho's leg with its teeth as he went past, but missed, and they kicked out into the yard just in time to see Dom strolling out of the farmhouse like he was looking forward to a picnic. Vocho was bloody annoyed to notice that he didn't have a speck of muck or blood on him anywhere. He hadn't even broken a sweat.

With a clumsy flourish Dom saluted Kacha with his blade, sheathed it and whistled for his own horse, which sauntered out from behind a blackcurrant bush, as indolent-seeming as its master.

He swung up into the saddle. "I think we should be going about now."

"But—" Vocho said.

"Oh, they aren't dead. Egimont in particular will be . . . Oh, look, here he comes. Shall we?"

Egimont staggered through the doorway, looking like he'd survived a fight with a big cat, but only barely. His fine clothes were in tatters and a bloody line sprang from a nasty-looking cut in his scalp.

He also had a gun, and was winding it up, pointing it their way.

"Yes, now's good." Kacha kicked her horse into a canter, leaped the wall of the yard and out of Egimont's sight. Dom's horse seemed to amble along like it had all the time in the world, but still somehow managed to beat Vocho's tired beast over the wall. A shot smacked into the stones, and then all that was left of the ambush was the lonely sound of Egimont swearing while the three of them galloped up the lane.

Chapter Six

Egimont paced up and down on the rug that graced the floor of the magician's rooms in the king's palace, the ruined chest on a table by the fire. Every so often he'd stop by the chest, glare inside and then carry on his pacing.

He'd almost worn a groove in the rug by the time Sabates glided in like a swan crossing a still pond – calm and serene on the surface. His eyes were hooded, his face implacable, and Egimont stopped pacing. Sabates might seem calm, but Egimont knew what boiled beneath the surface.

The king didn't even pretend to be calm. He burst into the room behind Sabates, arms waving and eyes alight, and launched straight into Egimont.

"The chest! Excellent. You recovered all its contents? The thieves? Dead or waiting for it, I assume."

Egimont hesitated. Sabates knew some papers and gold were missing, that Kacha and Vocho had escaped, but gave no sign to Egimont of whether he expected him to lie or tell it true. Start with the truth and lie if necessary – one of the prelate's first lessons. Egimont held himself straight and tall, eyes forward, looking at a vast painting on the far side of the room and barely seeing its colours. "The chest, yes, your highness. Some papers are missing though, and some small amount of the gold."

"Missing?" Licio started pulling papers out of the chest onto the polished golden wood of the table. "What do you mean, missing? And the thieves?"

Egimont cast a glance at Sabates, but the magician seemed to be examining his reflection in the mirror over the mantel in minute detail.

"Managed to escape, your highness. I've a dozen good men—"

"Pfft, good men. You took ten with you and couldn't apprehend two peasant thieves." Licio glared at Egimont, and there was the whiff of alcohol on his breath, even this early in the day. The man fairly reeked of it, as he often did since Sabates had come. Egimont took a moment to wonder if Licio wasn't as naïve as he'd thought, whether it was fear of the magician that was driving him to drink. "Tell me again, why am I employing you?"

Egimont bristled at "employing", as though he was some lowly gardener or skivvy instead of the son of one of the king's old dukes. Noble blood, if no longer noble by title. If now only the prelate's pet.

Sabates turned smoothly from the mirror. "Because *Lord* Egimont here has a plan. One which involves knowing who it is that conspires against you, highness. Isn't that right, *Lord* Egimont?"

"I—"

"Because," Sabates went on, "I fear there's undoubtedly a plot. When isn't there? It's unthinkable that your plans wouldn't become known at some point and that someone wouldn't try to counter them. Now we know who, and where they're going. We follow them and see where they lead. Use a little fish to catch a bigger fish."

"Fish?" Licio's brows furrowed. He'd never got the hang of metaphors.

Sabates pursed his lips. "The prelate, highness. If we can prove he's moved maliciously – and illegally – against you . . ." He let the rest hang in the air.

Licio's lips moved while he tried to think it through, until Egimont almost screamed at him in frustration, and at Sabates for throwing him into this with no preparation. Yet that "Lord" – he could forgive the magician a lot for that one little thing.

Finally, Licio came out with, "Then I could have the council move against the prelate?"

Sabates spread his hands as though blessing the room. "Indeed, highness. Use his democracy against him, then no suspicion falls on you."

"But the army I've negotiated, the alliances, the loans. The Ikaras bank was very insistent on certain terms being met, you see and—"

"All those things will still be needed, and the terms met. There's enough of the gold left to, ahem, persuade a councillor or two to side with you. But with the prelate weakened, your position becomes stronger, our plans less risky. Far better than hanging the culprits and losing any clue to what the prelate is planning against you. A brilliant plan of Lord Egimont's, don't you agree?"

Licio looked like he was still trying to work it all out but managed a compliment, watching Sabates for his reaction all the while. "Yes, yes, I think so. Maybe next time, Egimont, I could be informed beforehand though? Your king would appreciate it."

This last was said in the sort of patronising tone most people reserve for pets and small children. If any other man had used that manner with him, Egimont would have called him out, taken him to the duelling guild and settled it like gentlemen. Not something one could do with a king who'd seemed fair and generous and turned out to be naïve at best. Not something you could do with a king at all, if you wanted to keep your head.

Sabates interrupted smoothly before Egimont could make any comment he might later regret.

"But of course, your highness. We just don't want to bother you with little details."

Licio settled down a little. "Good. Well, maybe you can go through the papers and find out what's missing, Sabates. And Egimont, shouldn't you be off chasing your little peasant thieves?"

With that the king turned on his heel and left. When the door had shut behind him, Sabates said, as though to the air, "What an insufferable prick. Sort through his papers – I'm a magician, not a filing clerk!"

He turned to Egimont and they shared a look. "Neither are you," Sabates said. "Or you shouldn't be. Why *are* you working at the prelate's office?"

"Because my father thought it would be beneficial to show willing with the new government." A small lie, but one that might suffice.

Sabates tapped his fingers on the table and narrowed his eyes. Egimont wondered if he knew how much of a lie it was. "Ah yes, your dear departed father. An interesting case. I'm surprised he had time to say anything, considering. And do you regret following his advice?"

Odd, the look on Sabates' face. He seemed as implacable and unreadable as ever, but there was something else there. Some eagerness behind the eyes. And his hands – Egimont found his gaze drawn ever more to the hands, to the patterns on them, ever changing, ever shifting in trails of blood red. The patterns moved from a noose to a crown to crossed swords.

Egimont frowned, perturbed, but couldn't take his eyes from them. Didn't *want* to. They made him want to spill his soul, and he couldn't muster a glib lie. "Yes. Not at first, of course. Not for a long time. I believed in the prelate, utterly. He saved my life once, promised me everything if only I would do as he asked, showed the whole country that he was fair to ex-nobles, that his new regime was fair to everyone."

"And then?"

The crossed swords in Sabates' hands faded away to nothing, but still Egimont couldn't seem to stop.

"The guild. He promised it to me, promised that one day I would be the guild master and run it for him, the way he wanted, orderly, like clockwork. An anachronism, he called the guild, a throwback to the old, chaotic ways, and he hated it as much as I did. And then . . ." He trailed off – it was all still too raw and complicated, even with the patterned hands drawing him on. "He betrayed me, he betrayed everyone," he finished at last. No need for details – for a man like Egimont, brought up to believe in honour and duty, betrayal was enough. Bakar had forgotten his promise of the guild, had meant it as no more than a throwaway remark perhaps, but Petri hadn't forgotten. Petri couldn't forget.

"And then Licio offered you a way to get the revenge you craved? You didn't care what sort of man he was, as long as you got that revenge. You're very similar to me in many ways, Lord Egimont. Many ways." Sabates'' glance was sharper than knives.

"And what about you?" Egimont wasn't sure where the question had come from, only that it burned in his head along with other, more traitorous notions. "Why are you here, doing what he asks?"

A smile from Sabates, a cool thing barely twitching his lips, but so different from his usual bland mask it seemed like a belly laugh. "Because I want not just revenge of my own, as I told you; I've plans of my own too." He held up a hand when Egimont opened his mouth to protest. "Not on your kingdom. Or not much. But this kingdom is the key to many. The *right* man behind the king . . . and for that I need men I can trust."

Again their eyes met.

"I need men of their word, men that other people, royalists and workers alike, will trust. Like you. True and noble men, sadly deceived by the prelate's lies and willing to help me redress the balance even if it means following, or appearing to follow, a fool. In the meantime I've other work for you to do — on behalf of the king, naturally."

Chapter Seven

Kacha watched Vocho pacing up and down, wearing a groove in the threadbare rag rug that was just about the only colour other than mud grey in Cospel's one-room shack.

"They must say *something*," Vocho kept saying. "And be worth something. But if we don't know what they say, how can we get the money?"

They'd ridden here like the hounds of every hell were after them, until even Kacha's bloody-minded horse drooped with fatigue. Finally they'd had to slow, but Vocho seemed gripped with some fever and nothing like the easy-going brother Kacha thought she had. They hadn't spoken much, even as they rubbed the spent horses down and got them settled in a mean patch of grass around the back. Not even to ask Dom how he'd beaten all those men.

Dom sat in the room's only chair, a broken thing that might dump him on the floor any second. Yet he sat there like he was a king and it was a throne, one hand wafting a lace handkerchief in front of his nose, and looking as pin neat as though he'd just got dressed for a society ball. He watched Vocho's pacing and arm-waving with a faint grin. Kacha couldn't shake the impression he was enjoying himself immensely. Possibly because he didn't realise just how much shit they were in.

Cospel, after finding grain and hay for the horses and seeing to the riders' various minor wounds, sat bewildered and silent. He'd known Kacha and Vocho long enough. Once they'd passed their final tests, the guild had assigned him to them as their valet and general person who got things done. Duellists weren't much noted or trained for real life outside the walls of the guild except in execution of their clients' desires, mainly because most were nobles. Cospel had been with them through a lot, but Vocho's sudden passion seemed to unnerve him.

"There must be some way we can find out what these say," Vocho said.

"I'd rather discover how Egimont found us, and what he'll do to find us again." The sight of Egimont at their door looking ready to kill them, and particularly her, had shaken Kacha more than she wanted to admit. She hated the fact that her first thought had been that he'd come to apologise, beg forgiveness. The realisation it was the chest he was after had been a crushing blow but one that sharpened her loathing.

Vocho threw her a look, and she knew what he was about to say but wasn't quick enough to stop him.

"Why is Egimont after us? You, dear sister. Perhaps the chest was just his excuse to track you down. I saw how he looked at you."

"Like he wanted to kill me. No, it was the chest he was after. But why? Why Egimont of all people?"

Vocho shrugged. "That was *not* a killing look, Kass, more like a kissing one. Maybe if we find out what the papers say, we'll find out your why, and then we'll know what to do."

Kacha wanted him to be right about Petri, and she'd seen the look, but she didn't want to hope. Far, far safer to hate instead. "Or perhaps we could just dump them and get out of whatever mess this chest has got us into. Petri looked pretty bloody serious to me, and he's not a man to stop when he's set his mind on a thing. Let's get out now, while we still can."

"Where's the fun in that?" Vocho struck one of his poses – the one he thought made him appear noble of purpose and full of derring-do, but actually made him look like he had a squint.

"I wasn't thinking about fun, Voch."

He finally stopped pacing and stood in front of her, face serious for once. "You never do, lately. You used to be daring and reckless – not as much as me, but good enough – and above all *fun*. Pompous old Eggy sucked it out of you, bit by tiny bit, turned you into a . . . a . . . clockwork mannequin of what he thought a woman should be. I miss the *old* you, the *real* you. So, time to get some fun back in our lives! And some Kass back in my sister. Maybe get her a few other things back too."

It was the first time in months she'd seen him with anything approaching a bit of life in him, wearing the grin that always meant a world of trouble for everyone else. Maybe he was right – she was tired of being angry, but it was her only defence against Petri, against the tangle inside her when she thought of him. Against the thought that she'd fucked up, this once, hadn't been perfect like Eneko had always expected her to be. She'd been wrong about Petri, which rankled, and maybe Vocho was actually right about him, which rankled even more. She'd wanted to please Petri, be perfect for him as she was driven to be for everyone else, and so, bit by tiny little bit, she'd changed.

Now she wanted to go back to being the sort of woman who laughed loudly and often, who swore and cussed and went her own way. Maybe she could get back there, and maybe she couldn't, but it had to be worth a try. Besides, even if they dumped the papers, Petri wouldn't know they had. If they were that important, that valuable, then Petri wouldn't stop. He never did, once he set his cap at something. Constant to the end, one of the things that had drawn her to him in the first place. It seemed like less of a virtue now. First things first: they had to get out of here before he found them again, that was certain.

"All right," she said at last, then wiped her face after Vocho planted a great big kiss on her cheek. But she was laughing too, at the sudden change in Vocho and the unexpected and just as sudden change to herself. *Fun. It's going to be fun, like it used to be; just keep hold of that thought.* Of course there was the part Vocho wasn't mentioning, the bit about if they got caught they were up for the block. But there was no going back, not to the farm. They had to keep moving or die. Much as she hated to admit it, Vocho was right about finding out what the papers were. They could maybe use them to bargain for their lives. At the very least they might be able to return them. It was that or spending their lives robbing people, always hoping no one recognised them. Petri had, and look how that had turned out.

"Excellent!" Vocho said, expansive now. "So, first things first. Cospel, we need a translator. A good one. No idea what language we need translated. Off you go."

Cospel's face fell. "But—"

"What?" Vocho had the papers all laid out in front of him now and was looking them over as though he could already understand them.

"I think," Dom murmured from his chair, "that Cospel, while undoubtedly a servant of much initiative, would struggle to find a translator of anything in this region."

Vocho cocked an eyebrow his way, and Kacha could see her own thoughts mirrored on his face. There was something different about Dom now, though she couldn't quite put her finger on what it was.

"I suggest therefore," Dom carried on with a flick of his

handkerchief, ridding himself of some imaginary speck of dirt on his knee, "perhaps Reyes. I've never been, you know."

"Ah well," Vocho began. His left eye was twitching. What lie he was going to spout now? "You remember what I said about our father?"

Dom smiled, and Kacha wondered how she'd ever thought him an idiot. "Oh yes, I suspect Reyes is difficult for you. For me, however, it's not a problem. I could take the papers, get them translated and return them."

Vocho's eyes narrowed. "Strange how you were there just as Egimont turned up."

"It would be strange if I hadn't then helped you to escape him, hmm?"

Vocho and Kacha exchanged a glance.

"All right, so why did you help us?" Kacha asked. Dom seemed less, well, less a bumbling pillock than he had been. Perhaps he'd just lost the silly manners that were all the rage lately. He'd certainly bumbled the swordplay. It was a miracle he hadn't stabbed himself.

Dom shrugged, but the nonchalance fell flat as he turned pink about the ears. "Oh, well, you know. I mean, um, well. I saw them as I got to my horse, and thought perhaps it meant trouble for you, that your father had found you. If I can help in any small way, it would be my pleasure." He stood up and smoothed out an imaginary crease in his jacket. "You'll want to discuss it, obviously. I'll leave you to it while I see to my horse."

He left the hovel like a king leaving an audience.

Vocho blew out his cheeks. "There's something very odd about him. I mean, he's a bumbling idiot, with a sword or without, only . . . is he even who he says he is? There's something more to him than he's letting on."

"I don't think we can claim the moral high ground there," Kacha said. She looked after Dom thoughtfully. "But we could use someone who can get into Reyes without being arrested. He's right there — probably nowhere else to get those pages translated, except perhaps the king's palace. Either is going to be dodgy as hells for us to get into, and even if we did manage it, well, having a man on our side with some ready money and an influential father could be a big advantage. And he didn't have to help us, but he did. I say we bring him along. But keep an eye on him." If they had to go to Reyes — and they did — then taking Dom seemed like it might be worth it. And if they got into Reyes without being spotted they had a hope of disappearing into the crowds in Soot Town or the docks, where Petri would never find them. Probably. That thought shouldn't give her a shaft of regret.

"You're grinning," Vocho said. "You're enjoying yourself already, aren't you?"

"Maybe." Enjoyment might be a bit strong for what she was feeling.

"Maybe, my arse. I haven't been this excited since that time we stopped the heist on the bank. Duels in the streets, down back alleys, across rooftops. Now *that* was fun. This is going to be even better, I can feel it in my water."

Kacha rolled her eyes, but she was grinning like a fool. This *could* be fun, something to take her mind off her old life, and a way back in for them. Best to think that and forget the death bit. Whatever was in those papers, it was important enough for Egimont to come after them with ten men. Something didn't smell right, and if there was one thing she couldn't stand, it was not knowing the answer to a riddle.

"OK," Vocho said, rubbing his hands together gleefully. "Cospel, tell Dom he's in. Then go see what you can find out about him. Here." He threw a few bulls in Cospel's direction. "Buy a few men a few pints and see what you can dredge up. Buy a few women some too. Rumours and hearsay have been the downfall of many a good man, even more so when they're true. Oh, and get some decent breeches for Kass while you're out. No man should have to see his sister in her bloomers."

By the time Dom came back in, Kacha had joined Vocho in poring over the papers, trying to glean what they could from the smudged and charred crests that headed the parchments.

Interlude

Eighteen years earlier
Springtime on the docks was the best time Vocho could remember. The smell of salt and fish guts, the newly minted sun warming the jetties, the screech of the gulls and, best of all, the traders from every corner of the world – or so they said.

The dolorous tolling of the bell on the god-buoy out in the harbour warded away the deep-sea creatures and gave safe passage to any and every craft who wanted in. That day the harbour was crowded with traders, nut brown and white as fish bellies and everything in between, loading, unloading, shouting their wares to the shopkeepers and merchants onshore. Spices from Five Islands offloaded in barrels that leaked their fragrant dust. Silk from far Beroa, where they said it was hot enough to send men mad, furs from the myriad of tiny valley kingdoms in the far south, where it was under snow for half the year, shark meat from the Vergon Islands, where great trees like giants ruled, beef, elk, whale meat and all that went with it, blubber and oil and bones, funny little crabs the size of his hand that held barely a shred of meat, but which when you tasted it was good enough to make your eyes cross.

Vocho trailed Kacha, as he always did, dogged her, annoyed her because a reaction was better than being ignored, which is what she aimed for when she was with her friends.

They dawdled by the spice trader, inhaling the scents of a different world. The sailors would tell them stories of vast deserts that would dry a man up, of searing heat and burning cold, of the strange spirits that wandered there that would lure a man to his death. Sailors from other boats joined in, told them about the hairy man-like beasts that roamed the frozen snows of the south and preyed on anyone stupid enough to leave their village at night, or the trickster spirit-gods from sweltering jungles who stole naughty children. Dock rats like Vocho and the rest were good luck to super-stitious sailors, who wouldn't set foot in Reyes proper because they thought the clockwork was cursed, the Reyens and their dead god with it. So they were tolerated, given odd little treats like the crabs. Further on was a small sturdy ship from the south with rugged-looking men unloading grey and brown and the brightest white furs. The men sang a sad song as they worked. Vocho didn't understand the words, but he didn't have to; it was in the melody, in the way they sang – of home, of a far port, of the people and lands left behind.

The group of dock rats wandered and scampered and ran shrieking through it all, until the spring sun lowered and it was almost time to go home. Then at the head of a jetty they spotted a crowd, more people than Vocho thought he'd ever seen before, excepting the time in the square, but he tried never to think of that. They hurried towards the press of people, not wanting to miss a spectacle. Maybe it'd be the fire-eaters again – Vocho had loved those and almost given Ma a stroke and earned himself a scalping from Da when he tried it at home.

No fire-eaters today, which had Vocho sulking until he saw what it actually was. In the midst of the crowd stood a tall and stocky man, his skin a dark dusty colour like some of the northerners, his springy black hair just turning to grey around the temples, worn long and tied back. Dressed in a flamboyant shirt with ruffled cuffs that almost hid his hands, high boots that shone like stars and, best of all for Vocho, a tabard in green and gold, with an emblem of two crossed swords. A duellist.

The guild was a myth, and also very, very real. There'd always been a guild in Reyes, so they said, since before the Great Fall, since before the Castans even, since for ever, the only thing apart from the Shrive and the change o' the clocks to survive intact through all the centuries. Once they'd protected kings and the old empire, until it fell. When the Castans had gone – died or just left, Vocho wasn't sure – the guild became its own master. Now they protected whoever paid them enough, although there was some promise that they would protect the city for free, if ever it needed it. In the centre of the city, but not part of it, its buildings were set on an island in the great river, overlooking the harbour and separated from Reyes by a narrow strip of land and a short bridge. Every third morning, with the change o' the clock and the change of the city's landscape, people would get their bearings by where the guild stood.

The guild was the last gasp of the old days, with its own rules and codes. Each master duellist was sworn to protect the others, sworn to a code that none would break – none except Jokin, of course, and they told tales of him, of his fall from grace and exile in hushed tones around the fire in the tavern Vocho's father drank in.

The guild was funny, Vocho thought, because they didn't use crossbows and all the other new weapons people were making. An anachro . . . something, Vocho's da once called them, but still everyone loved the guild. They recalled the old stories, of the men and women with nothing but their swords and hearts and guts, who'd beaten people from far to the north and south, and lions and dragons and gods. They said that the guild had been the ones to fight against the Great Fall, the last line against the blackness of ignorance that followed, and that this was the only battle they'd lost, but they at least remembered what had caused it even while everyone else forgot. Some things changed, but not the guild, and not the men and women in it. Kingdoms were won or lost by duellists. Vocho knew every one of the stories by heart.

This duellist had a bundle of wooden swords at his feet and was handing them out to every child old enough to hold one and young enough not to have started sprouting new hairs in funny places. Vocho almost fainted with excitement. Apprentice Day – how had he not remembered? Every year the guild sent a few men into the city looking for recruits, for raw, natural talent. Most unsworn duellists – the lessers and journeymen – were nobles, and their parents paid through the nose for the honour of their children getting a duelling education, which involved rubbish food, longer hours than most labourers worked and a good chance of getting hurt or worse, or so Da said. A few stayed on to become masters, swearing their lives away to the service of the guild, just as they had once sworn their lives to protect the Castan emperors. But those who ran the guild knew that money couldn't buy talent with a blade or loyalty, and so, one day a year, Apprentice Day.

Kacha was getting in Vocho's way so he used his elbows, but too late – the man had given her a sword with a smile and a wink. "Show me how good you are."

She gave it a practice swish and dinged Vocho around the back of the head, knocking him to the dust. "Teach you to stop following me around like a dog."

"That any good?" she said to the duellist.

He grinned down at the pair of them. "Not really fair if he's not got a sword of his own. First rule of duelling, never go for an unarmed man. Or boy." He pulled Vocho up off his arse. "You going to let her get away with that?"

"Not ruddy likely!" The boy next to him had a sword, and Vocho wrenched it off him, kicked him in the shins when he howled about it and went after a suddenly fleet Kacha.

It was a game and not a game; even at six he was dimly aware of that. A game they played most days, him annoying her till she snapped, and then the chase, though it was her chasing him. Jumping bollards, scooting around long-shoremen, onto ships, off again, swinging on a rope here or through a man's legs there, ignoring the good-natured shouts that followed them.

As usual, he couldn't catch Kacha by speed alone – two years older than him meant her legs were longer. Instead he had to outwit her, but she had two years on him in canniness too. Today the game ended with her atop a mast he couldn't climb – the spar he needed was just out of reach – laughing at him. It burned in his gut, that laugh, brought with it all the little looks he endured at home, and worse. Perfect Kacha, couldn't you be more like her? Why can't you tie your laces as well as she does, read as well, be as kind, as obedient, as clever? Why are you so stupid, Vocho, when she's so smart?

He swallowed it and taunted her down, said the things he knew would have her fit to burst and off that mast in moments. "So, afraid of me then? Afraid of your little brother?" The real kicker. "Afraid I'll be better than you? Afraid they won't want you in the guild?"

She was down the ropes almost faster than he took his next breath, wooden sword coming for him, and he laughed, knowing that he'd got her riled up.

Then the game changed, as it always did, all teasing put to the side, and they were brother and sister. Now they were pirates, they were bandits, they were highwaymen who held up laughing sailors and got thrown a few copper pennies. They were duellists. They fought halfway along the dock before the old duellist grabbed them both by the scruff of the neck, and laughed like all his name days had come at once.

"Knew I'd find me some good uns down by the docks. It's all the salt in the air, see, hardens the bones and quickens the blood. Now, let's go and give your parents the good news, eh?"

So they did, though once the duellist – Eneko he introduced himself as – discovered they were brother and sister he tried to back off. "I'll take one from you," he said to Vocho's da. "But not even the guild would be so cruel as to take two, and your only two at that. I'll take the girl. She's the quickest I've seen in a long time; she's got enough heart for two men, and the guts of a few more. The boy will get another chance another year, if he's still willing, perhaps. He's a cunning little devil. A bit too cunning perhaps."

"But . . ." Vocho protested. Kacha always got to do the fun stuff, while he only got to watch because he was "too young" or "too stupid" or "too useless". A look from his father silenced him, but not for long. "But I want to go too!"

Kacha glared at him from under her blonde curls. "Can't I go anywhere on my own for once? Da, please! Ma, tell him."

Their father had sat down in the rickety chair that was his by the mean fire. Not only did someone want to take his precious Kacha away from him, she wanted to go. It seemed to squeeze all the air out of him, like the balloons down at the market that went all saggy after a bit. For the first time Vocho realised how old he was, noticed that the grey in his hair was no longer a sprinkle but a blanket. The lines in his face seemed gouged there by age and regret. Vocho looked over at Ma, and while she was younger, he saw the same weariness born of long work for too little reward, the toll of too little money and too much pride perhaps.

Finally, Ma said, "We'll talk it over. An hour?"

Eneko inclined his head, winked at Kacha and said, "An hour it is, but no more. I'm to have my recruits in the guildhall by sunset. We like to get them settled before the change o' the clock."

When he'd gone, their parents had talked together in low voices for a while. Neither Kacha nor Vocho dared to interrupt, though Kacha had given Vocho a look that could wither stones. "Why can't you never let me do nothing on my own? Why do I always have to take you too?"

There was a lot Vocho wanted to say to that, but he didn't have the words for it then.

A few choice phrases leaped out from their parents' whispered conversation. Da saying, "They can take the boy off our hands – won't need to feed him then," and, "I suppose they'll send him back when they realise what he's like." Vocho gritted his teeth – it wasn't anything he'd not heard a hundred times. Da tried to put his foot down, but Ma's face was the one that meant no one argued, not even Da. Vocho never knew what it was she said but Da agreed in the end. Finally they turned to the two of them.

"Well, then. It's a chance most don't get. A chance to get out of this place." Their father waved a hand at the shack they currently called home. "Chance to better yourselves. Earn a decent living. Honest work too. No matter what the king's like, the duellists stick to their code and their honour. They're their own masters even if they work for the king at times. Fearful hard though, I hear. Fearful hard."

Kacha stood up straight. "I'm not afraid, Da."

"I know you're not, Kacha, I know." Da beamed at her, pride oozing from every creased wrinkle, the kind of smile he only ever gave Kacha.

"Neither am I," Vocho chimed in, earning a glare from his sister.

Da gave him a sour look – the only kind Vocho ever got from him, like he was something nasty his father had stepped in, but the words weren't so bad this time. "Aye, lad, and maybe that's the problem. Neither of you are afraid of anything, and that's not bravery; that's not knowing how bad things can be. You'll learn, whatever you do, whichever path you take, that's my thought. Here or in the guild, you'll learn just how bad things can be. A shame, but there it is."

"But the guild, the guild is different," Ma said. "It's part of the city, and not, and has its own laws and customs. It's seen kings and empires come and go, and it stays the same. If things go bad – and they've been going bad a while and'll only get worse, I'm thinking – the guild can protect you better than we can, and the bad things will be maybe not as bad. Do you understand?"

Vocho didn't, though he nodded as though he did when Kacha said, "Here it's no food and how little we got. The threat of the block. Nobles being blood-sucking bastards." Ma gasped at that but said nothing – Kacha was only repeating what Da said ten times a day. If Vocho had said it, he'd have got the belt, but Kacha was perfect so Da looked at her with a fond eye and an encouraging smile. "With the guild, it'll be that pol . . . poli . . . politics thing."

"Ah, you do listen when your old Da talks then. Aye. Down on the docks it's keeping a roof over your head, your family fed and with you, keeping away from the guards and out of the Shrive. Hard at the best of times, and times are about to be harder, I'm thinking. There's trouble brewing all over. More and more taken to the Shrive, and blood on the square more days than not. Maybe even war brewing with them heathen Ikaran devils if them sailors are telling the truth. The guild will be all right. They'll be paid handsome to protect the city, and they's always all right. Rich people'll get richer, and we'll get poorer, that's always how it goes, and that's not counting being press-ganged into the actual fighting. But if you're at that guild, being fed whether I got work or not, with all them rich people's sons and daughters, making friends, good steady job at the end of it then you'll be all right. Besides, they'd not arrest a guildsman without fearful good cause. When chance comes knocking, you'd be a fool not to open the door. So that's why you're both going."

Kacha opened her mouth, no doubt to protest about her stupid younger brother coming too, but she didn't get the chance.

"That, and because together you can look out for each other," their mother said. "There's still plenty bad out there that ain't starving down here on the docks. And plenty bad is coming, you mark my words. One or other on their own, they's on their own. Together you got each other."

Kacha still looked ready to argue the point – she always was – but Ma's word was final.

"You're both going. And you're to look out for each other, always. Now get going and pack what you got to pack. Won't take but a minute, I reckon."

Kacha had stomped off, though Vocho was sure he caught the glimpse of a smile. At least she was going, and she'd dreamed of being a duellist at least as often as Vocho had. All the dock children did. It was that, sailoring – whether freebooting or trading – or a lifetime of drudging on the docks with nothing but gnarled hands and sad eyes to show for it.

When they'd packed, Da spent the rest of the time until Eneko came back with Kacha on his lap, telling her how great she'd be, what a marvellous duellist she'd make, how proud he was, while Vocho sat in a corner. His corner, where he always sat while Da serenaded perfect Kacha. It was safer in the shadows, unnoticed and out of range of Da's long belt.

The goodbye for Kacha was long, heartfelt and full of tears, at least on their parents' part – Kacha seemed oblivious, excitement leaking out of her in waves.

His da's pinching hand on his shoulder stopped Vocho as he was about to follow his sister. "Now, you listen good, boy. I ain't sad to see you go, and you know it. Maybe the guild can knock some sense into that head of yours, maybe some brains too, though I doubt it. But I know Kacha will look after you, because she's a good girl – the best." It didn't escape Vocho's notice that he managed to get in a dig even now. "She always does look after you even when you drive her round the twist. But you're not like her, and more's the pity. Still, you and her share blood, so I'm asking. I need you to promise me, son to father, that you'll look after her too. You watch out for her, or I'll be up that guild sooner'n you can blink so you can feel the lash of my belt, and make no mistake it'll be the buckle end. And try to stay out of trouble. Try not to be stupid, eh?"

Vocho looked up at the man he idolised and who always seemed to prefer Kacha, always listened to her, applauded her, admired her, told Vocho to be more like her and cuffed and lashed him when he couldn't manage it. A long-birthed coil of jealousy stirred in his gut, but, as always, he squashed it and wouldn't let it show.

"I will, Da, I promise."

"Good lad, Vocho. Good lad."

It was the first time he could recall his father ever saying that to him – and the last.

Chapter Eight

It was more than a week after they had left Cospel's when Vocho looked down from the low ridge and saw Reyes for the first time since the city had spat him out. It'd been a long week too, with Dom chattering all the way, Kacha silent and thoughtful, and Cospel's gloomy face bringing up the rear. Even now Dom didn't stop talking.

"Doesn't look like much from the outside, does it?" he said. "Not like Ikaras and its glass spires, all red in the dawn. Or Barring and its gardens, even Entos – did you know you can see its waterwheels from three leagues away?"

Kacha shared a secret grin with Vocho and rolled her eyes. Dom might be a fountain of knowledge, but it would help if he ever shut up about it.

"Have you ever been?" he asked them. "To any of the other provinces, I mean, the other cities?"

"Had a job in Ikaras once," Kacha said with a distracted frown. "Delivery of something or other, had to make sure it got there safe. Was only there a day. That was enough – all that sunlight reflecting on glass gave me a headache. Surprised it didn't all get broken in the Fall."

"A headache?" Dom looked aghast. "That glass is the most sophisticated . . . The whole *city* is run on that glass, did you know that? Something to do with the sun, they tell me."

"The sun?"

Dom shrugged and peered down the hill towards Reyes. "Well, yes. Before the Great Fall, the family that owned Ikaras province were known for their love of astronomy. They figured out a little gadget that told you where you were on the open ocean only using stars and magnets or something. Saved countless sailors. That survived the Fall too, that and the glass. No one really knows how the glass works, of course, not any more, though there's some interesting theories at the university. Bit like Reyes and its clockwork really, or used to be. Engineers in this province, so I'm told. I understand the prelate found out how it all worked, with a little help from Ikaras."

"Something like that." Vocho wasn't really paying much attention; he was too busy looking at Reyes. Always seemed strange from the outside, when he'd spent so long on the inside.

It lay sprawled under the setting southern sun like a cat. Dun-coloured walls, houses topped with red and black roofs, the odd green cloud as some tree made it through a crack between buildings towards the sky. The great river that wound slow and brown across the plains and into the city, the river that ran all the old clockwork – the ancient mechanisms that had been rediscovered, relearned and changed everything. Vocho could have sworn he heard the ticking from here. Reyes, city of wonders, just like all the other cities of wonder along this coast. All different and all the same, barely understood relics of a different time, a different people, so old that people just accepted what they were without a second thought. But mostly Reyes was home, familiar, even a bit boring perhaps.

The fields below Vocho and the others were dry and turning brown, even this early in the year. Little plumes of dust moved along the road hiding horses, wagons, whole caravans. Beyond the road lay the city, and beyond that lay the sea. A natural harbour off the main river channel butted up to the city, deep enough for the greatest ships, protected from the storms the north trade winds brought in the autumn by a high bluff of crumbling cliffs. To the south were the wetlands and delta of the Reyes river, haven of birds and mosquitoes and the shivering sickness. In the centre of the city, its top just visible from here on a high rocky island in the river, the guild watched over everything, while across a bridge, hidden from here but lurking always in the heart and mind of Reyes folk, was the Shrive, squat and grey and full of dread and old spilled blood. The two buildings that never changed with the clock, too ancient even for that. Eneko swore that the guild records went back even before the Castans had come and built their empire here.

But that was long ago, and Reyes had changed. Now it was a haven for honest merchants and more disreputable freebooters alike. Reyes didn't care, as long as no one stole from the city, each ship paid the berthing tax and the clock-work ran. Vocho could almost hear the toll of the god-buoy and the clack of ropes on masts from the flotilla berthed there today. Warships, trading ships, pleasure craft.

Kacha reined in her horse next to him and looked down. Was that a sneer on her lips? Sometimes Vocho wondered if he knew his sister at all. Dom nudged his horse up on the other side, looking earnest and vacant at the same time but at least mercifully silent, while Cospel brought up the rear on his dogged little pony.

Cospel hadn't managed to find out much about the mysterious Dom – far too little for the supposed son of the local landlord, which tweaked Vocho's interest. Dom didn't seem to do much of anything at all except spend money. The only information Cospel had obtained was that he'd gone away "to be educated" a deal of years ago – no one could agree quite when because that was before his father had bought the local manse, but Dom was a good few years older than Vocho, so it must have been a fair while ago. He'd come back when his father moved in and had flitted about, playing at being rich ever since, sometimes in the country, sometimes off travelling in a vast coach that supposedly had all manner of clockwork gizmos for the comfort of the traveller. All in all, there was nothing to indicate they couldn't trust him, but then again nothing to indicate they could.

"I've heard a lot about Reyes," Dom said now. "Is it all true?"

"Depends which bit," Vocho said when Kacha didn't seem inclined.

"Do the streets really move? On clockwork?"

Vocho chuckled — no one ever believed it till they saw it — but said only, "Best just to come at it with an open mind and a steady pair of legs." One of the joys of being a native of the city was watching what happened when a newcomer experienced the change o' the clock for the first time. Vocho was prepared to bet quite a bit that Dom would fall flat on his face.

"So, what's the plan?" Dom asked.

Vocho cursed the hot spring sun. Even in the wane of the day it was too hot for hood and hat, but how else to wander the city streets without anyone recognising him or Kacha? Not that their faces were known everywhere, but it would only take one person to spot them and they'd be back where they started, running from the executioner's blade as well as trying to dodge Egimont and his magician. More than once Vocho had been tempted to stop at a magistrate's or a church, anonymously hand over the parchments and ask that they be sent to Eggy at the prelate's palace in the hope that him and his magician would leave them alone. He'd been tempted, but the lure of his old life back was too strong to ignore. Better dead than some poor bloody farmer, dressed in sackcloth and smelling of pigs. At least Cospel had found the tools to chop up the gold bars into something more manageable, and had spent a few days travelling to various villages to change a bit here, a bit there so they had plenty of actual bulls. Which meant Vocho was no longer wearing sackcloth but a fine new set of breeches with his pilfered coat and matching cloak in scarlet and gold.

Kacha gave him a sideways look and a little hooked grin, a look he knew from old. It said, "Dare you."

Neither of them could ever resist a dare. He flipped up the hood of his cloak and put the hat on top. At least the feather made him feel a bit jauntier. Kacha followed suit, though her hat was more restrained than his. Still, it shadowed her face well enough, and he could barely make out the giveaway scar under her eye. Maybe they'd get away with it. Maybe they'd live long enough to see tomorrow. Reyes was their only hope of that, if they didn't fancy living in a cave for the rest of their lives. And Vocho most certainly didn't.

He sat up straight and looked Reyes right in the eye. "The plan is, Dom, my old friend, that we get in and settled well before midnight and the change o' the clock. Then we go and find ourselves a nice discreet translator. First lodgings, nothing too flashy, and then Cospel can go and see who he can find."

"We could try down by the docks," Kacha said. Then, in a wistful voice, "No, I suppose not."

No. Not because someone down on the docks would be sure to know them, though that would have been the reason Vocho gave. More because he'd have to face the spectre of his dead father, when Vocho could ignore him anywhere else. At the docks he'd see him, hear the echo of him tell Vocho he'd broken his promise, just as his father had expected him to. It'd taken a while, but he'd broken it just the same, when he'd dragged Kacha into being wanted for murder and now this. The thought of the disappointment in his da's voice made Vocho shiver worse than the thought of being vaporised. Worse was the thought of what would come after – that it was no more than Da had expected of him, because he was only stupid, clumsy, imperfect Vocho, after all.

"Anywhere but the docks," he muttered and kicked his horse on.

It took a little while to get down onto the main road into Reyes. The dust there was worse, made a sticky choking in the back of Vocho's throat that he'd forgotten about in his wistful daydreamings. They slid in behind a trade caravan and caused no raised eyebrows. So far, so good.

The guards on the gate looked bored and thirsty in the heat and waved them through without a second glance. Just inside the gate lay the first indication that they were home: two turrets, ticking as they spun in place. A guard held up a warning hand, and the caravan stopped, Vocho and his companions with them. The guard nodded as he counted the ticks, a final clonk and a flurry of spears shot out of each turret right into the centre of the roadway. Three more ticks, the spears withdrew and the guard waved them on. Vocho didn't hang about – they might have fifty ticks to get through or fifteen. Turret guard was a specialised job, and there'd been more than one accident at the gates when a guard had counted wrong, or misremembered what part of the sequence the turrets were in. Vocho had always assumed that's why the cobbles beneath were painted red, so as not to show the stains and alarm visitors, and said as much to Dom.

"Stains?" he said faintly.

"Oh, didn't they teach you that at university? The clockwork isn't just a wonder – it's a damned good defence mechanism too, especially the seemingly random parts. Just be careful when you hear ticking."

They made it through Turret Alley without staining

anything, out into a square lined with smoothly whirring mannequins going through their motions, and then the city swallowed them whole.

Narrow cobbled streets ran higgledy-piggledy away from the square. Each was filled to bursting with traders, riders, hawkers, gawkers, buyers and beggars, storytellers and thieves. Houses leaned over the way and at points met in the middle, holding each other up like drunken lovers. Kacha and Vocho's hats were a decent disguise but also handy for fending off what got thrown out of the windows.

The horses moved slowly in the crush, with the exception of Kacha's, which cleared a path with teeth and feet, until the street opened up and the crowds spread out. It was market day in Bescan Square beneath the slowly spinning arches. Stalls made of wood and draped with silk and wool or sun-bleached furs. Corrals full of horses or pigs or sheep, stinking the place up, with another pen in a corner for hired bodyguards – men and women dressed in leather and dripping weapons who wished they were in the guild but instead took on petty jobs that no duellist would look twice at, protecting a sausage stall from thieves or some cargo for coppers.

Reyes took in trade from everywhere in the world, or so they said, and while the sailors never made it further into Reyes than the dockside bars, the traders and more wealthy merchants were less superstitious, or at least more likely to put that aside for a sale.

The market brought it home to Vocho that he really was home – the mishmash of faces, of colours and languages. Copper-haired bronze-skinned Nurre, whose women, tall and regal and looking like the world belonged to them, walked two paces ahead of their bowed silent men, and sold amethyst and opal and agate set in cunning twists of silver and gold. Doe-eyed little spice men and women from Five Islands, hands dyed red by their wares. Hulking great men and women from away inland, who seemed born bearing arms and mostly ended up in the bodyguard pen hiring themselves out by the hour. Tall and rangy men from the deserts away east, with old eyes, solemn smiles and golden rings, whose Castan ancestors had ruled Reyes and the rest of the provinces before the Great Fall. Men from far to the south, from the frozen valley kingdoms, selling furs and oils, little bone trinkets and curses written in pictures scratched onto wooden sticks. Their sailors wore their white-blond hair and reddish beards in braids and sang sad songs, but they only sent their shamans ashore to trade – half a head taller than most Reyes men with legs like tree trunks, shaved heads, bones through their noses and sweat-drenched fur across their shoulders even in the heat, holding poles with beads and dried skulls on they'd rattle at anyone who got close. A very young Vocho had once believed the laughing Nurre woman who'd told him they were ghosts, that's why they were so pale and strange, and he'd believed it right up until Kacha dared him to touch one and find out for sure. He'd been chased halfway back to the docks by a roaring giant of a man with red whorls painted on his face, and had steered clear of them since.

There were plenty of Reyes traders there too, haggling and hawking, selling little clockwork trinkets or purple flags, pots and pans or spicy sausages whose aroma filled the square. Men and women of the villages around Reyes, mostly swarthy like Vocho himself, with one or two from the south with paler but still golden skin and hair that bleached in the sun, selling fish, squid and whatever else had turned up in their nets. Soothsayers and fortune-tellers, doctors and dentists with their downcast queues who looked on the instruments with a quiet dread. Wood turners with lathes they operated with their feet, carving exquisite bowls and furniture. Bards and storytellers in every aisle, and so many tales of the guild sung or told Vocho often wondered if Eneko paid them. They hurried past those men and women with their heads down.

At the other end of the square, when Kacha took a left towards the more solid, permanent artisans' shops full of clockwork and swords, Vocho knew where she had in mind to take them and nodded in satisfaction. It might give Dom a bit of a fright, and Cospel would have a fit, but the Hammer and Tongs was just the place for people who didn't want to be seen and had business they didn't want anyone to know about. The inn was the centre of Soot Town, inland from the docks and just as seedy but without the benefits of a breeze. What wind Soot Town did get was stained by the reek of the coal fires of blacksmiths and armourers, and lately gunsmiths.

The coal fires were what gave the area its name. Everything was covered in soot. Houses, streets, clothes, horses, people. Smoke curled along the alleys like a browser at a market, looking for things it hadn't tainted yet. Dom held his handkerchief over his nose, and bleated faintly when it turned sludge grey in minutes.

"I'm sure I could find us somewhere *much* nicer to stay," he twittered as his horse splashed through some sewage. "It's so very basic here."

Vocho laughed at the look on his face. "At least your father won't think to look for you here."

Dom had a minor conniption about that. His father liked to control everything, and Dom wandering off was, apparently, "akin to murdering my mother". But he had been determined to come with them and hadn't mentioned any of that until they were three days out and a cohort of men had come sniffing around the inn they were staying at. He'd also refused to elaborate further.

"He might find me wherever I am," Dom said now. "He owns about half the smithies in Reyes, three clocker factories and a fair few houses in Soot Town. I never thought I'd have to stay in one."

"Think of it as an addition to your education."

"They never taught choking to death at Ikaras University, it's true," Dom muttered.

By the time they made the inn, Vocho was covered in a fine layer of sticky soot. Cospel looked like he was wearing a mask and Kacha had two white circles around her eyes where the smoke had made her eyes water. Dom, incredibly, had only a grey hanky to show for his trip through Soot Town. The rest of him looked as pristine as ever and as out of place as a diamond in a dung heap, earning him a few looks that seemed to be weighing up how much he'd be worth if they rolled him, versus how much trouble they'd get into for mugging a clocker.

Vocho coaxed his horse under the broken sign and into the mean courtyard at the rear. "Dom, it might be prudent to, well, to look the part a bit. You know, less rich."

"Whatever do you mean? I'm wearing my oldest clothes and I've tucked all my jewellery away. I—"

"Look like a clocker's son wearing his old clothes." Despite himself, Vocho found he quite liked Dom, at least when he wasn't chattering too much. "Come on, let's get some rooms and we'll get you looking right."

Chapter Nine

Egimont rode into Reyes alone as the last of the light left the sky. Alone because in Reyes at least he was the prelate's man and a lowly one at that, and for now he had to act like it.

He entered by the south gate and made his way to the back of what had once been the king's palace and was now little more than a huge office for the paperwork the prelate seemed determined to drown everyone in. A guard with a long-barrelled rifle barred the way, but subsided as soon as he recognised Egimont. "Beg pardon. Prelate's orders. Not letting anyone in or out, excepting as we knows them."

Egimont raised an eyebrow. "Why's that?"

"Couldn't say." The man's face spoke volumes though – it was common knowledge within the palace that the prelate was getting a little eccentric lately. Maybe more than a little.

The guard checked the sequence of the mechanism above the way, let him through and fastened the stout gate behind him. Interesting, Egimont thought, but not unexpected. He rode on past empty marble plinths that had once held statues of great kings and princes towards the main building.

It was the most magnificent in the country, a huge thing that loomed over this half of the city on a hill that currently looked out over the harbour to one side and the coastal road to the other. It seemed to stare across at the guild, as though they were challenging each other – who ran the city, really? Who had the love of the population? A rivalry born in the Great Fall, and still ongoing even past the age of kings, an enmity that might never end. Bakar was aware, none better, that any man can be deposed.

The front façade of the palace must have had half a hundred windows on each floor, each of which now spilled light out onto the formal gardens, all neat and orderly how the prelate liked it, a symbol of his rational universe. A glimpse through the window showed Petri lines of clerks bent over their desks in what used to be the ballroom. Its great windows showed no dancing ladies and gentlemen now, no glittering gowns or frock coats. No music had graced that room for long years, unless you thought that the rhythmic rattle-chunk-whirr of counting machines was music. Egimont sometimes wondered if the prelate did. Music certainly didn't move the man's soul, but money did, *accountability* did.

Something soulless about the whole palace now. Egimont had been young when the last king had finally handed over his rule, his crown, his palace and ultimately his head. But Egimont had been old enough to witness some of the balls both here and at his father's estate. Great, glittering magical things they'd been, full of beautiful women and dashing men dancing, drinking, laughing. Now they were just ghosts flitting among the grey little men behind their grey little desks. Him included. He'd been born for great things. Not to be the duke – that had been his older brother until he'd died of the bleeding sickness – but to be great nonetheless. A master duellist he'd once thought and hoped he'd be, but his brother's death had put paid to that. After that he was heir to a noble title, destined to be the first duke of the realm, to lead men and win victories for his king, to oversee estates, rally armies, spend money and hold balls of his own. He'd barely had time to get used to the idea before his title no longer existed and the prelate had filled his head with notions of equality, of predetermination and the reborn Clockwork God.

It had taken time and Kacha to shake off those notions, to realise that the prelate's vision was a crock of lies. Now he was nothing, less than nothing. Worth no more than the hundred other men, the thousand, who worked here looking at numbers, and for what? For the prelate's vision of equality for all, a vision that had merely turned great men into clerks, and turned clerks into pompous windbags like his overseer. A sneering, snide little blob of a man who liked nothing better than to remind Egimont that he might have been born to a duchy, but he, the overseer, had been born to a fish gutter and now gave him orders. The realisation he'd been taken for a fool had festered, and had led Egimont to swearing to the king and regretting it later.

In a sour mood Egimont stabled his horse and made for the entrance to the palace.

Some splendour still remained – a bit of gilding around the mouldings, the geometric pattern in the gold and red tiles. The prelate had added one thing to the grandeur though: a mural of the Clockwork God at the moment of his rebirth, casting aside the lesser gods people had made for themselves and taking his rightful place in their hearts again. That and an orrery that moved and bent and ran on clockwork, as the world did, as the universe did, so the prelate preached. The sun sat at the centre, a glowing ball of glass lit up from within. Moons and planets moved on rails around it, each on its prescribed course. Everything predictable, or so he said. No room for free will or dissention, no room for being anything other than what the clockwork said you were. Egimont felt like shoving it off its pedestal, watching its cogs and gears spill out across the floor so he could stamp on them.

And there, waiting across an echoing hall, half in shadow, she stood, the lady he'd come to meet. Alicia was a vision in blue. Somehow, after everything that had happened, her family had managed to keep their money if not their titles, and now the money was all hers. A fortune she was said to have, owning warehouses and factories, a clocker at heart, and she dressed like it, in silk and pearls and powdered hair. None of that was quite as entrancing as her face. She looked like an innocent with the face of a goddess. Yet underneath . . .

"Ma'am." He doffed his hat and bowed, old-style manners which his father had insisted upon and he now used mostly cynically.

Alicia smiled at him, and had he been a weaker-willed man, he'd have been lost. "My lord." She held out her hand and he took it, rested it on his arm as though he was an old-fashioned suitor and she his lady love. It was as close as he wanted to get. Sabates had warned him that a snake's heart lay hidden beneath that pale breast.

He led her out through the back of the hall, past an array of glazed doors that in daylight would show a panorama of the guild, the harbour, the cliffs on the other side and further. Nearer to hand lay what was left of the formal gardens. No more vast rows of flowers, beds of roses, arbours under honeysuckle and hidden fountains. The prelate had ordered them all uprooted, replaced with a clicking clanking version of the planetaria, objects moving smoothly along their pre-described courses, unable to do anything else. Only one arbour remained, in a prime position to watch the world as it sailed past the sun on its preset course, and Egimont steered them that way.

There, finally hidden from any prying eyes, he dropped her hand and the act. She smiled, wry and teasing, put the hand back and leaned towards him. "My lord, do we need such distance?"

Hell's teeth. "I think so. You have what Sabates wanted?"

Because she was employed by Sabates, not the king; indeed Licio had no knowledge of her. The magician had warned him, not too subtly, not to fall for her charms, because "She's buried two husbands to my knowledge, and I'm not sure they were dead first." He'd added, "But she's the best winkler of information I've ever known. Even I can't match her when she sets herself to a task."

"Be still, my beating heart," she said with a laugh now, and a delicate gloved hand went to her pale throat. "Such a charmer you are. Of course."

She delved into a little bag and brought out a packet of papers. "A copy of the prelate's plans. More taxes to fund the coming war with Ikaras, which seems inevitable now. More guns ordered. But I think Sabates has overlooked something."

"Which is?"

Her mouth twitched into a cruel smile. "You make a poor spy, Petri. All that time trying to discover what was going on inside the guild, and you didn't see what was under your nose."

"I never pretended, or wanted, to be a good spy."

"No, Sabates said. That you were blinded by many things: revenge, desire, Kacha."

The way she said the name, like Kacha was some sort of disease – Egimont had never struck a woman, not outside a duel at least, but he was sorely tempted to strike the word from this one's mouth.

"All that time, and you never realised, did you? Or perhaps you did but never told anyone."

"Realised what, precisely?"

It was the sort of tinkling little laugh that would be right at home in an intimate soirée, and it sent shivers down Egimont's spine.

"Whether you'd got it right, about who the assassin was.

We know all the past ones, don't we? All the most renowned men of the guild, who did dark jobs, assassinations when they must. Biken, until he died during one such job, and of course Jokin."

"But he—"

"Was exiled from the guild, yes. Not for what Eneko told everyone, not for failing his sworn duty. Another matter entirely." She laughed again, as though at some secret joke. "Such a poor spy you are, never to find out for sure about Vocho, but he did the job anyway. They think they're doing it for the right reasons, you know, Eneko's assassins, but instead they're fed lies and half-truths and are cast off or killed when they no longer believe it, when they find out the truth, as they often do. Still, if we knew who Eneko had ordered to be killed, perhaps we'd know more about what it is he's planning. Maybe you could ask your lovely Kacha?"

A barb in that last. She knew that wasn't an option, and she knew why. If only Egimont did. Why Kacha doted on her wastrel of a brother, why she trusted Eneko. Why she'd sent him that note out of the blue. Why Egimont cared when he should have been just gathering information about her wretched brother, as this woman said.

"I suppose not," she said now. "But Eneko has plans of his own, I don't doubt it. Tell Sabates I'll arrange to find out, though I may need assistance, if you will provide it."

"Very well." He rose to leave, but her soft hand stopped him.

"Take care. You've been out of Reyes for a time. Things are not what they were. But they will be, and better than before, if you follow Sabates' orders to the letter."

Egimont took his leave and the papers she'd given him, and headed for his mean lodgings up in the cramped and rat-infested roof of the palace to contemplate many things – grey drudging jobs for the prelate, youthful dreams crushed and ideals betrayed. Revenge on Eneko, for thrusting him here in the first place. Kacha . . . Kacha. Revenge on the guild would be revenge on her too, and that could only come about through Licio returning to power.

Whatever it took, the return of the king couldn't come soon enough for him.

Interlude

Seventeen years earlier

Kacha sat on the parapet that spiralled around the duellists' guild and looked out over the docks as the sun rose. Stupid, she knew. Stupid to think she might spot Ma or Da down there in among the people who looked like beetles scuttling over the yellow stone of the docks and jetties, weaving among the warehouses or just loitering on the shore looking longingly at those who had work. She hoped to anyway. Her ninth birthday, and the first without either of them. No being woken before dawn so Da could give her a present before he left for the docks, if he had any work. No special cup of chocolate – the yearly treat that he saved up for, for months sometimes. No sitting on his lap and soaking up his adoration, no one to be perfect for.

All she had to look forward to were drills, drills, more drills, Vocho trailing her every move like an annoying puppy that was her only link to home, and endless lessons on the history of the guild, interminable lectures on ethics and doing the right thing, the good thing. Vocho lapped all that up, loving the romance of the guildsmen and -women from long ago, before the empire when the guild had been a loose union of mercenary warriors looking to have a bit of security.

When the Castans had come, and brought all their fantastic engineering with them, they'd been smart, Eneko said. Kacha loved listening to him more than she loved the history. There was something reassuring about the guild master at a time when everything was strange and new. He always had a smile for her, an encouraging word, a comforting hand on her shoulder, a trick or hint on how to do better at sword-play. He was the closest she had to Da here, and already thoughts of Da and Eneko were getting confused, mixed together.

Instead of fighting the duellists, Eneko said, who even then were seen as figures worthy of respect, the Castans had hired them wholesale as bodyguards, given them this stronghold and autonomy, and set up the codes she now had to live by. They'd become so strong that when the empire fell, the guild stood. The guild always stood, solid and invincible, which is why Da had sent them here.

She didn't care. Homesick, that was the trouble. However much she'd thought she'd wanted this, she wanted to be home. Vocho being around helped. They had turned to each other a lot in the first weeks, and he wasn't *always* annoying, but he wasn't enough. She wanted home, all of it. Listening to Ma and Da, smelling his pipe smoke, telling him every-thing she'd done that day, and he always put aside everything to listen. Freed his lap from whatever job from around the house he had to do, scooped her up and listened. Here no one listened, not really. Not even Eneko, though he was better than most. No, here she was the one listening – do this, do that, mind your footwork, keep your guard up. Her only consolation was she was getting pretty good. She could beat half the boys in her year in a free fight, and the other half she'd get to a draw. She had to be good. There had to be something instead of Da and his listening and his pipe smoke; she had to make leaving him behind worth it. When she won a duel, even if it was with wooden practice swords, she got a bit of praise from her tutor, sometimes Eneko's hand on her shoulder and a "Well done." She had to make Da proud too, Eneko proud. Anyone proud. That "Well done" was what she lived for, the fuel to her fire. Some of the others, especially Vocho, teased her about being Eneko's little pet, but she didn't care. She needed something, someone instead of Da, and Eneko was it.

Why couldn't she see Da down there? His face was starting to get hazy in her memory – every time she thought of him, his eyes would be overlaid with Eneko's twinkling ones, his nose would morph into Eneko's, his hair would lengthen, become less grey so she had no clear picture of him any more, and she hated that. Just one more glimpse. That's all she wanted for her birthday, a chance to burn his face back into her treacherous memory. She wiped her eyes and looked around to see if anyone had noticed – she'd learned quick enough not to cry where anyone could see, especially in front of Vocho, who would rib her about it for days, but she was on her own up here.

Down on the docks the familiar start to the day. Calls floated up on the breeze, sailors shouting to longshoremen, faint curses, the toll of the god-buoy and the measured tick of the duellist automaton in the arena behind her.

Then other noises, less familiar. An unusual crowd around the harbourmaster's office, where the king's men oversaw everything, made sure all the taxes – and maybe a few more – were paid. A tax for berthing, a tax for hiring a long-shoreman, a tax for having blue sails. Things had always been tight, but she'd heard Da muttering about taxes late at night, when he thought she was asleep. She wasn't *exactly* sure what taxes were, only you had to pay something or else you ended up in the Shrive.

She had no worries about that here. No muttering about taxes, or seeing executions, or those politics things Da had told her about. Here she just had training and making it through another day. Down on the docks, though, it looked as though a lot of people were worried about them. A lot seemed to be complaining to the harbourmaster anyway. A southerner longshoreman – easy to spot because he was a blond head taller than everyone else – shoved his way forward to confront a man dressed in bright red. Kacha could picture the gold braid on the harbourmaster's uniform and remember the smug look on his face when he told everyone he was a king's man. The dock rats had all kept their distance as he'd a reputation for using a switch on any child he thought getting too big for their boots.

Hard to tell from this far away, but by the way the southerner picked him up, she thought it a safe bet he didn't give a rat's tail whether the harbourmaster was a king's man or not. She couldn't quite see what happened next, but she saw well enough when the southerner heaved the harbourmaster into the foul water at this end of the jetty. Even from where she was, Kacha could hear a ragged cheer.

"Well, that's put the fox among the chickens." Eneko's voice startled Kacha enough, she almost fell off the parapet. He looked down towards where she was watching. The crowd had changed now. Before it had been loose, nervous, unsure. Now men strode with purpose under the direction of the tall southerner. Gathering things together, blocking off the docks with carts and crates, collecting long billhooks and gaffs. What were they doing?

"Gods damn it, I knew it was coming, it had to come, but I didn't think it'd be this soon. How did Bakar get out of the Shrive again anyway, the shit-stirring bastard? I thought he'd be there for good after all that crap at Novatonas's execution. His followers have been muttering away while he was gone, making little clockworks in secret where they think the priests can't see, but now things are really going to go tits up."

Kacha squinted down at the docks again – yes, the big

blond. She'd thought he looked familiar. She'd last seen him with a mouth full of blood being dragged up the steps to the Shrive. No one ever got out of there, excepting to meet the guillotine, or so all the bards sang anyway. But this one had managed to from the sounds of it.

They watched for long moments as the barricades grew, and so did the shouts and the waving of makeshift weapons. Someone got hold of a Reyes flag and set it alight to much cheering. Someone else rolled a barrel out of one of the inns along the dockside, and the cheers grew louder.

The roar died down when the clatter of horses came along the narrow streets from the palace. King's men, a whole street full of them, swords out and ready, a few of the new windlass crossbows in among them – the priests had muttered that they were a touch too close to blasphemous clockwork, but had allowed themselves to be persuaded eventually. The king's captain pushed his horse forward to address the long-shoremen and got a fish in the face for his trouble.

Eneko looked down at her, as though he'd only just noticed she was still there. "Kacha, go. No, wait. First go and tell the sergeant-at-arms to get up here right now. She needs to see this before I can make a plan. Then go and wake the rest of your dorm, and the others. I want everyone dressed and ready for anything in half a bell. All right?"

"Eneko? What's happening?"

He smiled down at her, laid a comforting hand on her shoulder and squeezed. "It'll be fine. What's happening is what has to happen, I think. But you'll be safe enough here, I hope. We've been preparing for this a while. The guild has always been here, from before the empire, and it'll go on being here whatever happens today."

"My da's down there, I think. He usually is."

He cocked an eyebrow at her. "Ah yes. You're a dock rat, I recall." He bent down so they were eye to eye. "And because of that, you might come out of this a lot better than a few of the others here, all those noble sons who might be slightly less noble come sundown. Things are changing, girl. We need to change with them. And we will because we always do. How else did the guild survive the Great Fall? Flexibility, ruthlessness and a steady hand or fifty with a sword. Your da'll be safe enough, if the gods will it. Even if you were down there, what could you do to help him?"

She stood up straight, glared him right in the eye and put a hand on the hilt of the practice sword that went everywhere with her. "I could fight, if it came to it. Fight better than some of them too."

He laughed at that, caught her frown and smothered it. "I shouldn't laugh. Maybe it's true enough because you've got the knack of it and enough determination to see it through. You're going to go far in this guild. Very far indeed, and I'm glad it was me that found you. But right now you're here and your da is down there. And your duty is here, not there, not any more. What has a duellist got above all?"

She shuffled her feet, for once not liking the answer. "Honour."

"And that means?"

"Doing my duty to the guild, to my sword master, my fellow duellists and myself."

"Remember we're your family now, and for always. The biggest family and the best, and you have no other claim on your loyalty. Your da would expect no less, would want you to do right by your new life. Wouldn't he?"

She nodded sullenly. He would, true enough, only . . . only it didn't *feel* right. She looked back down over the docks, half hoping to catch a glimpse of Da's dark hair streaked with grey, a wisp of his pipe smoke, anything. They kept telling her that the guild was her family now, but that felt like betraying the family she already had. Even the annoying Vocho. Felt worse because she was having trouble remembering what her own father looked like, kept thinking of Eneko when she should be thinking of him.

"Well then. Get going, quick! Oh, before you do – here. Happy birthday."

He pressed something into her palm and shooed her off the walkway. It was only later, after she'd taken his message to the sergeant-at-arms, had woken all the students and got ready herself, ready for she didn't know what, when she was looking out of the windows with all the rest, her mouth open at the carnage in the streets, at the older duellists who waited behind the gates of the guild, swords sharp and eyes hard, that she remembered to look at it.

A pip for the lapel of her tunic, to show she'd passed the first test. Passed her first milestone, first of many, with luck. A pip to say she was on her way in the guild. Da would have been proud.

Chapter Ten

By the time Kacha had haggled over rooms, had the long-suffering Cospel take what little luggage they had up and cleaned up to only slightly grey, it was dark.

She slipped along the creaky corridor and knocked at the warped door to the room Vocho and Dom were sharing. No answer. She knocked again, and still nothing. They couldn't have – they wouldn't have – but this was Vocho. Of *course* he'd gone down to the bar. He'd be wanting to see if everyone was still talking about him. He was such an idiot at times. Scrap that, all the time – maybe Da had been right. Voch always did things first and thought about them – or how they'd got him into trouble – afterwards. All the brains of a week-dead fish, Da had always said even when Ma chided him for it. Looked like she was going to have to be the sensible one again, a thought that made her grind her teeth.

Kacha grabbed her cloak so she could flip up the hood and at least partially hide her face, and made her way downstairs.

The main bar was packed to bursting – Third Threeday, last day of the working week and payday, so all the smiths and tanners and night-soil carters were busy spending what they'd earned before the city reset itself at the change o' the clock. She scanned the room, fended off a casual grope from some drunken artisan with a cheery elbow to the face but couldn't see Vocho or Dom anywhere. Maybe that meant he was being careful, but it seemed unlikely. Careful wasn't in his vocabulary, not when he could be boasting.

Or maybe that racket coming from the end of the bar, the one that sounded very much like a brawl about to spark off, was Vocho putting his large foot into it, again. She made her way through the press of bodies, past grimy chunk-armed smiths, tanners with their whiff of ammonia and the boys who pumped the bellows and looked after the clock hammers, their faces slick and shiny from the constant heat of fires. It didn't take long to find the pair of them, but to her surprise it wasn't Vocho arguing – it was Dom. He was pink cheeked with indignation, his twittering voice almost a stammer as peevishness took hold. Kacha couldn't make out much against the background of a couple of hundred drunks enjoying themselves, but she could see the way Dom was jabbing his finger at someone, his handkerchief wilting in the fuggy atmosphere. This wasn't going to go well.

Worse, Vocho looked like he was doing nothing to stop it. He seemed a bit bemused, if truth were told, and the empty jug in his hand might have had something to do with that. Vocho sober was impulsive, reckless in a way that mostly had her grinning even when she was grinding her teeth; Vocho drunk was . . .

She used her elbows to force her way through the crowd, all eagerly pressing to see what the fuss was about. The usual Third Threeday fight, only there was something more to it perhaps. Some extra undercurrent that seemed to swirl through the room like blood in water, luring in the sharks. A few men at the edges seemed apart from the rest – hard-eyed, sober, watching. One or two looked . . . odd. Their arms were as rope-muscled as the rest, they were dressed as smiths or clockworkers, but there was something about them. The way they held themselves, as though used to favouring the weight of a sword or gun at one hip, as though just waiting for something to happen. They were wound tight as any spring.

Nothing very unusual about them even so, except that, like her and Vocho and Dom, the grime of Soot Town hadn't ground its way into every line and wrinkle on their faces yet. What was more unusual was the way they were looking at the *other* hard-eyed watchful men. The ones with the prelate's badge and the gold flash on their tunics.

Something about the whole room felt like a gun about to go off, and who knew what it would shoot? Kacha loosened Egimont's sword in its scabbard at her waist and pushed forward just as Vocho put out a hand to stop Dom and said into a sudden silence, "*What* did you just say about the duellists' guild?"

"I *said*," the burly man across from Dom replied in the careful tones of a drunk trying not to slur, "I *said* that they're all a bunch of arselicks and sellouts."

Oh, shit on a stick. Any hope of saving the situation had just flown out of the window. Vocho had his sword out before the man had finished speaking, the point of it making a delicate tracery of cuts in the man's shirt without spilling a drop of blood – Vocho's favourite party trick and threat.

He grinned brightly at the drunk. "I'm a generous man. Want to try that again?"

The drunk eyed Vocho's sword, and Kacha suddenly realised that apart from the prelate's men in the corner, this was the only sword out in the open. Of course the rest of the crowd had plenty of weapons, but the swords were a bit of a giveaway down in Soot Town, where they made them for their clocker employers but couldn't afford to own one, not when a sword could feed and house a family for a week or more, and a good sword for a month.

"Arselicks, sellouts . . . and murderers," the drunk sneered.

"You one?"

The silence that followed the word echoed around Kacha's skull. *Vocho, please don't. Just this once? Be sensible just this one time?*

Fat chance. Vocho leaned forward, his eyes on the drunk's face as he reached around him and yanked the man's long knife out of the sheath where he kept it at his back. He handed it, haft first, to the drunk. A challenge and a get-out. A duel wasn't murder, even if someone ended up dead. Just as long as the challenge was accepted in front of witnesses, and there were about a hundred, more pushing into the back bar all the time as word raced around the inn. There were plenty on Vocho's side from the murmurs – the guild was an institution and no man not ten sheets to the wind would say a word against it, not openly. But this man was that drunk, and besides it wasn't a proper Third Threeday in Soot Town without at least one bar fight. Half the crowd were probably looking for an excuse to punch someone; the rest, well, a bar fight was a gold mine for a decent pickpocket.

Kacha stepped forward in a last-ditch attempt to keep a bit of sanity in the evening. "Hey, now, I don't think—"

Too late. The drunk grabbed the knife and in the same movement lunged at Vocho, narrowly missing Kacha as his swing went wild.

As if this was the cue, the room erupted. Kacha, mainly by dint of being the soberest one there, ducked away from a wobbling punch and came up behind Dom, who looked more confused than ever.

Out of the corner of her eye she spotted the odd-looking "smiths" drawing together into one knot, drawing hidden swords from beneath their cloaks too. Not just cheapjack swords either; these were good ones, she could see that from here. Nothing fancy, but workmanlike, sharp and well used. These men ignored the brawl that had broken out with

Vocho, atop a table and grinning like an idiot, at its centre. Instead they made straight for the prelate's men, who were waiting for them, their own swords out.

The brawl was one thing – normal, expected, banal even. Her da had always said that brawls were what inns were *for*, a bit of roughhousing to let out pent-up tension, nothing worse than a few bruises, maybe a broken bone to show at the end of it usually. This was something else, something that made the hairs on the back of Kacha's neck prickle. The prelate's men should be trying to break up the brawl, not squaring up to a bunch who looked intent on murdering them. This wasn't an ordinary fight. This looked planned.

She was briefly distracted by a scar-faced sweating lump of a man and his fist aiming for her face. She sidestepped, waited for him to stagger past as the resistance he was expecting disappeared, and smacked him on the back of the head with a random mug. Dom had joined in the brawl, his sword still in his scabbard. Instead he deftly avoided being wherever his attackers expected him to be, luring them into other knots of men, who would then take over where he'd left off. He seemed to be hampered by the need to apologise to everyone, and she could track him through the crowd by following the trail of "I'm so dreadfully sorry," "Excuse me," "Pardon, I'm sure," "Could I just cut through here . . . " The ever-enterprising Cospel, aware that he'd only get bawled out for trying to help either Kacha or Vocho, was instead making himself useful by grabbing a tray and whacking anyone who looked like they were getting too close to Dom.

When she looked back, it wasn't just the nape of her neck that prickled – every hair on her body stood up. Two of the prelate's men were down, and they didn't look like they were getting back up again, ever. The remaining two wouldn't last long. They were hard pressed, their backs against a wall as three "smiths" toyed with them. Only no smith or clockworker would be stupid enough to take on prelate's men, or councillors' men, not unless they wanted a one-way trip to the Shrive. The prelate didn't chop off so many heads as the king had done, but he wasn't shy about imposing law and order. Blood didn't splatter the square very often, but the Shrive was still full enough. The only difference was, the prelate let some out again after they'd done their time.

She didn't know what was going on here, only that it shouldn't be this, and two prelate's men were dead already. An attack on the prelate or his men was an attack on the city that the guild was sworn to protect, that *she* was sworn to protect. She didn't even think before she launched herself at the back of the nearest swordsman – she'd been brought up a duellist, and this was all part of that, part of what it meant. That the guild no longer wanted her made no difference at all.

She kicked at the back of the man's knee. He staggered forward and turned as he did so. His eyebrows shot up as he noted she wasn't wearing anyone's colours, nor a duellist's tabard, but that didn't stop him defending himself when she leaped to the attack.

He wasn't bad, but he wasn't that good either – no duellist, that was for certain, and she was hard put not to just get to it and beat him soundly, but no sense giving herself away. It didn't take long before she had his sword out of his hand, and he'd have a nice new scar to show off along one arm in a few days. She had him cornered just about the time his friends joined in.

They didn't join in for long – one did his best to hold her off while the other two made for the door. She let them. All she wanted was to stop this, stop them killing men in this inn. Because sure as shit was shit, the lowly city guards would be down here before long, blaming it on the poor sods who lived in Soot Town. More prelate's men would come too, maybe other councillors' men with them, and then people would be hauled off to the Shrive, like as not. So she let them go and turned to the prelate's men.

The two on the floor were as dead as you could get. The ones standing up didn't seem much better. One had blood pouring out of a gash across his stomach – the waft of a midden told her this was a killing wound, if not now then later when it got infected, and it would. The other's eyes were screwy, like he'd taken a good blow to the head. He'd have had a good chance of surviving if not for the dagger thrust into his ribs that made blood bubble out of his mouth in a macabre fountain.

She made sure her hood was still firmly up – these were men who might recognise her, even if not for long.

"What the hells is going on?" she asked the one with the gash.

"King's men," he gasped.

"What?" Surely Licio wouldn't be so stupid? If the prelate discovered this, Licio would go the way of his father. Had things changed so much since she'd left? Then again they hadn't been dressed as anyone's men. "Are you cert—"

"King's men."

There was a possibility they were in more shit than she'd thought.

Interlude

Seventeen years earlier

Petri Egimont held his breath as the mob came down the street past the guild. It had been bad enough when the king's men had ridden the other way towards the docks, intent on stamping out the insurrection. Bad enough when men and women had started running back this way, past the narrow bridge that led to the guild. Panicked, some of them bloody and silent, others screaming. Worse when the sounds of the screaming down by the docks had stopped.

He waited with the rest of the duellists, those who'd passed at least the journeyman's tests. He'd passed his last week, at thirteen one of the youngest ever to do so. Now he stood with older men, and wiser, better with their swords, and took a bit of comfort from their stoical faces. Though not everyone was so steady, especially when the horses of the king's men started coming back riderless, or with dead men dragging from stirrups, their heads thumping rhythmically on the cobbles.

Egimont gripped his sword. A duellist is constant and neutral. No favouritism to anyone, except towards those who've paid for their services. Even then, a duellist had to believe in his client, in the job. *Do what seems good to you.*

But Egimont wasn't the only one there with a noble father. At least three full master duellists were second sons of nobles, and two should have been barons, even if they no longer had the lands and money to go with the titles, had given them up along with everything else to pass the final test and take the oath. Some others, the journeymen, were earls' children, or like Egimont dukes' children. Sent to the guild to become better men, to learn honour and duty, to get some legitimacy – all nobles' children came to the guild. Some left early, spending just enough time to say they'd been there. Firstborns would leave before the final test, before the last duel that would cement their place as a permanent member of the duelling family. Most would anyway.

Egimont had wanted to take that last test, swear everything away. His father would have let him too – he bore no love for his second son. Egimont would have done it and been happy had his brother not died, leaving him sole heir. Now his father had forbidden it, would send men to drag him away when the time came if need be. Egimont was no minor noble, but would be the Duke of Elona in time, second only in rank to the king. His father admired the duellists for their code, for what they could teach his son, admired the free-minded guildsmen because it was expedient to keep them happy, but not enough to lose his last heir to them. The guild and the nobles were locked in a constant, if subtle, jostling for power and popularity, and the heir to Elona joining the guild as a master would shift that power too far one way for his father's liking.

Enough of the men, women and youths here had plenty to worry on when the king's captain came back minus his head. Egimont tried not to listen to the murmurs around him, and not just from the nobles' sons. Plenty here were born into poverty and they'd lost none of their hatred of those who'd beaten their families down.

Revolt. Revolution. Had to happen. Long time coming.

The king would put it down; the streets would run with insubordinate blood. Or they'd drag the king kicking and screaming from his throne to his own guillotine, and good riddance. Eneko, standing right behind the open gates at the head of the narrow strip of rock and grass that joined the guild to the city as though daring anyone to come through, turned a baleful eye on them, and the murmurs stopped. He conferred a moment with his sergeant-at-arms, an older woman, stocky and as grey as Eneko and as wily, who'd seen more duels than probably half the guildsmen put together.

"All sword masters, shut your traps. No loyalty but to the family, right? You fought for it, you swore it, now live it. The rest of you —" Petri couldn't be sure whether Eneko's eye sought him out or not, whether it was just the man's usual unfathomable disdain for him "— you've sworn little as yet. For the nobles, if the king's men win through, you're safe enough. If they don't . . . if they don't, even I can't keep you safe if it comes to it. Not once you go outside these wa—"

A noise interrupted him. Petri had never heard anything like it, except perhaps the sea when it crashed against the cliffs. A swelling sound, rising and falling like waves, only the noise wasn't made of water on rock, but voices. Shouting, screaming bloody murder. Through the noise Petri was sure he heard someone singing an old song, one he remembered his nurse singing to him when he was very small, before he'd been shipped off to the guild. He couldn't make out the words now, but he remembered them – a song they used to sing on the battlefields of long ago, to stir the men up, give them courage for the fight.

Eneko licked his lips. "Maybe too late for anything," he said and turned back to the open gates, to the short narrow walk with nothing but a sheer drop to either side. They wouldn't come, surely? Madness if they did. Madness . . .

But Petri couldn't be sure they wouldn't. The air over the city had been thick with anger these last months, and what was anger but another form of insanity?

Half the docks had to be striding up the streets towards the dead Clockwork God, which stood at the end of the strip and reminded everyone how the Castans had fallen in their arrogance and had killed a god when they did. Maybe half of Soot Town was coming the other way. Heading for the statue and the broad avenue that currently wound away up to the palace. Down the avenue were more of the king's men. But not enough. Nowhere near enough. Not for this.

The dockers turned at the god and reached the guild first. The smell of the sea came with them, of fish and seaweed and a poverty so deep Petri thought he could taste it – a solid wall of people bearing fishing gaffs and billhooks and long wicked knives. They were led by a man a head taller than all the rest, his blond hair bound back but coming free now, smears of blood on his ragged shirt, on his hands, on his trousers where he'd wiped those hands on them. His face was paler than a fish belly – the Shrive, that pallor said, the colour of all the men and women dragged out to the block after maybe years inside, but that was stupid because no one ever got out of the Shrive. All the flesh seemed to have melted away from his bones, along with any mercy. The billhook in his hand dripped with gore as he cast a hard eye towards the guild and signalled the dockers to stop.

For long moments Petri thought they'd ignore him and the guild, that no one led this mob, that perhaps it would all fizzle out and he'd be safe, they all would. The first men from Soot Town reached the god, armed with hammers and the swords they'd forged themselves. Behind came younger men, poorer men, armed with nothing but stones, though the gleam of a knuckleduster here, a half-hidden blade there, made him wonder.

The tall man at the head of the dockers stepped forward,

and everyone else stopped as if by unspoken agreement. Whoever this was, he was in charge. It was in the way he stood, the way he stared around as though the guild was already his, his gaze ending on the open gates and Eneko.

Eneko walked to meet them, drew his sword and rested it point down in the dirt on the bridge. The tall docker towered over him, billhook dripping.

"And where does the guild stand, old man? With us or with them?" He raised his voice so all could hear.

Eneko stared straight back up at him, easy and loose limbed. Petri wished he could be as nonchalant, but his hand was shaking so badly he had to take it off the hilt of his sword in case the jangling gave him away.

"Same place as always, Bakar. With ourselves and whoever has money and morals enough to pay for us. I have no quarrel with you, you know that. Not yet anyway. That can change."

The docker shifted his weight, and Eneko's grip tightened on his sword. Petri wouldn't have liked to bet which way it would go, if it came to it. The docker was a big man, and for all his flesh was melted away, under his skin snaked a thin whipcord of muscle, the muscle of someone using it whether he's fed or not. The billhook was a good weapon too for anyone used to it, but Eneko hadn't become guild leader by failing at his swordplay.

"Seems to me you work more for the king and his nobles than anyone else," Bakar said.

"Seems to me they've got more money than anyone else. You know, well as I do, most master duellists aren't nobles or rich, and we'll even work for free if the cause seems good to us. You've got no quarrel with that, have you?"

Bakar snorted in disgust. "Mercenaries, and in the king's pocket too, his little favourites, and you think that gives you power. It gives you nothing, as I intend to show you. Just money-grubbing mercenaries."

The sword point came up out of the dirt and was a blink away from Bakar's stomach before Petri realised what was going on. "Don't use that word in my hearing. Duellists is what we are. We got our own codes we stick to, and you know it. If you want a fight you'll have one, but this is my guild and you're not coming in. Tell you what: if you win, I'll work for you all you like, because you'll have the money then. Even throw in a free job. But this guild is mine, is all of ours, and we go our own way. Always have, all these centuries since the empire fell, all these years of false gods and dead gods and preening kings. Always our own way. Right?"

Bakar eyed the sudden forest of swords pointing his way, smiled and held up his hands. "A free job? I may take you up on it earlier than you think. This is no bloody revolution, Eneko." He looked up at the billhook dripping blood down his arm. "Or no more than it needs to be. They attack us, we'll defend, but I want no more heads on the block than I must for change to happen. Maybe the nobles' or king's. Not yours, if you don't hinder us, but if you do you can join your paymasters. What we want is fairness. For everyone. An orderly place in an orderly universe, everything happening as it should. Like clockwork."

Eneko chuckled. "Hah, you listened to that Novatonas too much. I heard about him and his clockwork universe, and it's a crock of shit. Didn't he teach you too that life ain't fair, or that clockwork breaks, or that people make choices all the time that make that movement jump its rails? Well, you go on and give it a go, fight the king and all his men for what you want. We'll be here waiting when it's all done."

A thought seemed to strike him then, and he turned to the duellists ranged behind him. "Unless any of you want to take on a very low-paying job and help these people out? I won't stop you. Nor if you want to work on the side of the king. You're your own men and women, and you know your hearts best; you make your own choices, you all know that. I'll be here waiting for you too, when you come back."

Lots of shuffling of feet and staring at the dirt before one or two made their way through the gates. Eneko nodded each one past, seeming to bear them no ill will. A duellist took whatever job he saw fit, what seemed good to him, as long as he acted within the honour set out by the guild. Once a job was taken on, it was an oath to see it through, but those who paid didn't always get *exactly* what they asked for, if the duellist decided there was another, more honourable way.

Bakar turned to the assembled workers, dockers, thieves and shirkers and spread his arms wide.

"I have a gift for all of you, for all of *us*. They put me in the Shrive for heresy, for talking against the gods that men made after this, our Clockwork God, epitome of our city, died. They put me in the Shrive for saying those false gods couldn't grant the gift of kingship, couldn't answer prayers. That, despite what the king and his nobles say, there is no shame in clockwork, no sin in it, as some of the priests preach. Clockwork is not blasphemy, it is *prayer*. Because I said the Clockwork God died not for arrogance, for ignorance. Because we did not see his true message and the true beauty of him. Some of you kept that faith even when I was in the Shrive, after Novotonas was executed for his beliefs, and I thank you for that. But I was wrong."

A gasp from the crowd. They were giving him all their attention now. Petri couldn't blame them – the way Bakar's voice rolled around the space was mesmerising, forcing you to listen to his words. Even Eneko was rapt.

Bakar's voice dropped, but was still enough to be heard in every corner. "I was wrong, because the Clockwork God is not dead, merely sleeping, waiting for us to understand his true purpose. I found my way out of my cell in the

Shrive and down under the city where no man dares to go if he wants to live. There are cogs down there the size of houses that will chew a man to pieces at the change. Axles the size of trees, movements the size of this guild. It is truly a thing of beauty and a sight to inspire the lowliest of men. The priests tell us it was their arrogance that made him strike them – us – down, his sorrow for doing so that killed him, that no man should look upon it in case he is tempted to follow that pride, that arrogance. The priests lie. They tell us one thing from one side of their mouths, and yet they aren't just priests. They go into the bowels of the movement to tempt themselves against wanting it, to test themselves, oil the gears and clear the debris and prove that even though the city moves, the old god is dead. So they *say*. But I know the truth. A hundred days and nights I spent in the workings of the city, feeding on the scraps that fell through at the change. A hundred days and nights contemplating the truth of the cogs and the beauty of that truth. I know, because I found the secret. The Clockwork God gave it to me in my hour of need because it was written in the movement."

He beckoned to a youth at the front of the mob, who looked up at him with adoration and handed him a bag. Bakar spread his arms again, the billhook in one hand, and the crowd roared like a lion, deafened Petri with its intensity.

"*This* is how I know that the king is not gods blessed. *This* is how I know the Clockwork God is not dead."

He stepped forward, and all the crowd fell back before him, some bending to one knee. Petri found he was holding his breath, found also that he wanted to believe this, needed to. Needed something more to believe in.

Bakar opened the bag with a flourish and brought out something complicated made of what looked like gold and silver and rubies. A pretty thing to be sure, but not something to make a revolution over. Then Bakar stepped up to the dead Clockwork God and opened – to a scandalised gasp – the plate on his chest with a little silver key.

Where? How? Petri could feel the questions flow around him. No one could get into the dead god. Many had tried and all had failed. Except the golden-haired Bakar. He turned an eye Petri's way and smiled, a smile that would burn in Petri's memory for years. No matter how he turned it over in his mind, that smile always came back to utter belief and serenity. And serenity, that was what Petri had never had, what he craved.

The gold and silver contraption went into the god, the door closed, the key turned. For long minutes nothing happened, and murmurs grew in the crowd and in Petri's heart. His father had forbidden him the new gods and the old dead god, everything that might have given him some semblance of belief. But now the Clockwork God moved. Its head came up, its arm came around, fingers pinching as though trying to grab something.

There was silence broken only by the clicks and clanks of the god as he moved. Bakar stepped forward and laid something on his plinth. The god bent down to pick it up, seemed to read the scrap of paper before solemnly opening the compartment in his chest and putting it inside.

Bakar turned back to the crowd, his face alight, arms raised. "The only comfort is truth! And only the clockwork can show us the truth, if we learn to read it right. *That's* what the Clockwork God means, that's what the Castans lost, why their empire fell. They forgot about the truth behind the world, the clockwork that runs us all, and sought only fancies and lies, sought only to imitate. All our futures are written in the movement, and he has given it to me to see it. The king will fall, and we will rise, all according to our gifts, according to what the god has planned for us in his workings."

The crowd came to life slowly, men and women creeping forward to touch the god, to look at Bakar with wonder.

"Clever trick," Eneko growled, his voice sounding harsh after Bakar's smooth tones.

"No trick, Eneko. No trick. Now where do you stand?"

"Same place as always, Bakar. Right here. Perhaps now you'll go?"

"Perhaps," Bakar replied. "There's just a small matter. While the god tells me all, no harm in making sure we have the advantage in the coming hours and days. Besides, I've seen it in the movement."

Petri's stomach coiled in on itself as Eneko turned to stare straight at him. Later, he'd wonder why, whether this was something cooked up between Bakar and Eneko, that his guild leader had sacrificed him days ago and was only now telling him.

"Just a small matter of leverage, of making sure the movement doesn't break, as you say, Eneko." Bakar smiled, serene like a priest who knows he basks in the glow of the god's good regard. "There are no choices. There is only what must happen. And right now what will happen is you, Eneko, will give me a hostage for your good behaviour. For your guild's good behaviour, and with that I will leave you the goodwill of the people of Reyes, because know this: if you go against me you will see how fleeting that love is. Pick one. Whoever you like. It will be the right one because that is how things are meant to be. The clockwork moves along its rails and you can't stop it because you too are just one of the cogs that make up the universe. One hostage out of these here. Choose, and the guild may yet stand a while. You are merely turning like the cog you are because today we rule this city, and you."

Eneko couldn't hide the sneer or the twitch of his hand. Wanting to use his blade or fear? Or both? Petri couldn't decide.

More men and women were congregating around the reanimated god, offering it their truths. Eneko seemed as made of brass as the god, but he took in the crowds, the surge of people cheering, the tide of them welling up behind Bakar and muttering, more than muttering some of them.

The guild was something apart in Reyes, and that was its strength and right now maybe a weakness. Because it wasn't just apart, it was above, or at least above the crowd of people that glared at it now. It took in dock rats and smiths' children sure enough, but it then kept them for itself. It had what these people didn't – food and money enough. Petri hadn't seen much of what life was like down in the docks or Soot Town, but he'd seen some of the new recruits come in on Apprentice Day. Thinner than whips, all sharp knees and elbows and eyes too big in their faces as they were herded down to the mess and promptly fell on the food like the half-starved waifs they were. Later he'd shared dorms with some of them, and his eyes had begun to open.

Add to that the certainty of being fed, a certain position and, most importantly, those who passed the initial weeding-out process had a near immunity to being arrested and having their heads chopped off. Even the king wasn't stupid enough to antagonise the guild. The guild was revered for the link to the past it was, but it was something else too, a reminder of what all the rest of Reyes didn't have. It was a force to be reckoned with because of the people's goodwill, but it also existed only because of their goodwill. Now Bakar was telling the people they could have everything because it was all going to be *fair*, because he'd woken the old god, and that god had told him so. Even Petri could see how that had fired them up. It stirred something in him too, if he was honest, because being noble or having money didn't mean you had a good life. Just made it easier to cope with.

He thought he understood this, and he wanted to understand more, but that wasn't enough to prepare him.

Eneko eyed the glowering crowds and their makeshift weapons. Bakar gave his serene smile again, a smile that held secrets behind it, and pulled out an odd-looking contraption. Petri couldn't make it out – it looked like a pipe with a winding mechanism attached – but it meant something to Eneko, that was plain. He looked back at the duellists behind him and licked his lips. Maybe the guild could survive an attack and maybe not, but Petri was sure that Eneko would fight. The guild was everything to him, as it had become to Petri. A family, his family, who'd loved him more than his real family had ever done.

Which is why Eneko's next words came like knives in the dark.

"Petri, come here."

Bakar nodded as though this was the only outcome that could ever have been, and waved Petri over using the pipe contraption.

Petri didn't move. He *couldn't* move. All around him duellists muttered under their breath, but the sergeant-at-arms shut them up, though she didn't look as though she liked it any better than they did.

"Petri!" Eneko's voice sounded odd, stretched, but it got Petri moving, along with a prod in the back from someone – the sergeant, he thought.

He stood between Bakar and Eneko, his head whirling. What was Eneko doing? Wasn't he going to fight for the guild?

"Do I have your assurance that the guild will stand?" Eneko said to Bakar.

Bakar shrugged. "I suppose we can make use of you. There'll be changes, of course. More taxes and more control. None of your more, ahem, irregular activities, which we will discuss at great length at a later date. But the guild will stay. We can haggle on the details later, but rest assured you will be brought to heel. Maybe we can give you a looser leash once I'm sure you'll behave."

"But—" Petri began.

"Your sword," Eneko snapped, "and your tabard."

He didn't give them up; they had to take them, rip the sword from his hand, the tabard from his back. With them went every fragile certainty in Petri's life. He felt awkward without the weight of the sword at his side, naked without the guild colours covering him. Bakar planted a hand on his shoulder and turned him. Petri looked back at Eneko, saw him blank and implacable.

"Why?" was all Petri could think to say.

Eneko shifted as though guilt was stirring in him, but his voice was hard and cold. "You're the price."

A master surged forward from behind Eneko, sword out, driving for them. Petri never did work out what he was trying to do, whether to attack Bakar, pull Petri back into the guild or somehow try to take on the whole crowd. Bakar didn't hesitate a second but raised the pipe contraption and pulled a lever. The noise was tremendous, deafening Petri. When he could hear again, the master was on the floor with blood leaking from him, and the contraption was pointed at Eneko.

"I will shoot you, if I have to," Bakar said. "And if I do, your guild will be the first thing I take down, piece by piece, stone by stone. Your masters will work for me or die."

Eneko ground his teeth, twitched his hand on his sword and cast a glance over his shoulder at the masters waiting for his command, for the chance to draw their swords. *Do what seems good to you*, that's what he always said, the motto of the guild, but here on their land he was the voice of the guild. He chose, for good or ill, how the guild would respond.

One last glare at Petri as though this was all his fault, another look at his masters, and he turned on his heel, put up his sword and bellowed, "You heard the man!"

Things grew dim after that. Men and women swirled around him; the guild gates were shut for the first time Petri could ever recall, and Bakar pulled him across the bridge to the reborn god.

"How does it feel," Bakar said softly in his ear, "to be betrayed by a person you looked to as a father? To be used to buy the guild's safety? Is it a consolation that this is the only way your life could turn out? That you were destined to come with me?"

The words seemed to swim in front of Petri's eyes. "Destined? That's—"

"Predetermined then. Everything is clear to one who can see the clockwork behind the world. The world is as it is, and can be no other way, and neither can we be other than the clockwork makes us. Past, future, present: all run like clockwork and our paths are decided for us. It is written in that clockwork for you to come with me, and to become mine not Eneko's. Do you want to stay with a man who'd sell you out so easily? It was written that I would start this." He raised his voice so that the whole crowd could hear. "Written that we will all overthrow the king. The clockwork behind the world is clear."

He looked up at the solid incarnation of the god, his representative here in the world, gleaming in a sudden burst of sunshine as though the god had arranged the clouds just so. "It's time it was clear to everyone. I think after today, after the king is gone, that we'll show the whole world the clockwork that runs it. Only I know, but I'm not greedy. I'll share. They threw me in the Shrive to try to find out what I knew. Kept me there in the dark, worse than dark, but I never told them. Never told them how I found the great clockwork under the river, the waterwheels that power all the clocks, your mechanical duellist, power the change o' the clock. Found all its gears and levers and cogs, found out how it works. How everything works."

"But, my father and the king, they'll kill you. Men tried before, my father said, and they were no match for the gods-blessed king." Petri didn't know who he was trying to convince.

"Pfft to the king. He says he's gods-blessed, gods-chosen, but we know the truth, that there is only one god and he doesn't choose the king. Wheels turn, that is all, and now they're turning for us. We have these guns – not many, but enough. All your training, Petri, all your mastery, and I can snuff it out just like that, like I did with that master, like Eneko knew I could do to him. This –" he waved the pipe thing around, causing more than one man to duck, "– *this* is revolt. *This* is revolution. This is ours. We made it, and we're going to use it.

"Listen, Petri, we aren't the king, killing good men with bad, or the nobles, bleeding the poor for every drop of blood and sweat. Today this city, this country, starts afresh. We will all be one, both great and free. Free of a demented king *and* his magicians."

Petri didn't know much about magicians except that his father, a man who as far as he knew was frightened of nothing and no one, hesitated to say their names and had actually flinched when told one of the king's pets had turned up at his estate. The sword masters talked about them, but not openly and in whispers. Everyone was afraid of magicians.

Bakar slung an arm around Petri's shoulders and gave him the news that changed his life. "I'd thought you of all people, young Petri, would understand what a tyrant the king is, after he hanged your brother."

"My brother? No, he died of the bleeding sickness . . ."

"The bleeding sickness, Kemen?" A low chuckle. "Yes, I can see they'd tell you that. But sadly a lie. A lie your father colluded in, and so did the guild you revere so highly, the guild that handed you to me without a qualm. Betrayed you. Strange no one's mentioned it to you, hmm? They *said* Kemen committed a heinous crime. But no, not at all. We shared a cell for a time, he and I. Do you know what he did? What earned him a hemp necklace? He found that your father, the king and Eneko were colluding in slavery. Not all the runts picked on Apprentice Day come to the guild. No, not all, not even most. Eneko sells them — to your father, to other nobles, to work on their farms, in their sweatshops, in dark little boxes where no one will ever see them. Some go to the magicians, to be bled dry and tossed out like night soil from a chamberpot. Some go to Ikaras, worked to death on their plantations. No one misses them because lessers don't leave the guild for years. If no one ever sees them again, that's why. Illegal, naturally, but the laws don't apply to them, do they? Then your brother found out, and Eneko thinks you know too. Your brother was hung, and you — you needed to be silenced, and I think he hopes I'll do it for him, or perhaps you'll handily die in this uprising."

Petri stared at him in horror. Lies. All of it. He was tempted to tell Bakar he was wrong, that it couldn't be . . . but that look Eneko had given him. The sort of person he knew his father was. The cogs spun round and moved everything into place with a click that was final.

Petri turned his face forward and refused to listen, refused to give this man even a hint that he might believe him, but all the while he was thinking, *It's true*. His father had been strange all the week before they got the news of Kemen, as though grieving in advance — and almost, almost *relieved* afterwards. There had been no tears, no wails, no grief, just a cool blank numbness. For a man who showed no emotion if he could help it, this was maybe not so strange, but with Kemen he'd always been different. He was uninterested in Petri's mother, leaving her to her causes and balls, and to Petri he'd been like a far-off god, moving when he needed to, saying the right things, lecturing on proper behaviour, on the need for honour always, but with no heart, nothing but logic and gears. But with Kemen he'd come alive. He'd laughed and clapped at his every accomplishment. If he could have cried for anyone, could have grieved, it would have been for Kemen. Yet he never showed a thing. Not a tear or a white lip or a clenched fist. Except the week *before* they'd heard of his inglorious death aboard a ship, and nothing after.

Bakar's hand gripped his shoulder, and he looked Egimont in the eye like the most honest of men. "I saved your life today, Petri Egimont."

A deep breath signalled the end of all he'd thought was true. Still, some things were hard to give up. Truth, duty, honour. All the things they'd instilled in him while flouting them in secret. He wasn't going to be that man. Not ever. "You won't regret it."

Chapter Eleven

Vocho wasn't quite sure how he'd ended up on a roof with Dom at his back, only that it had seemed like a good idea at the time. They'd managed to shake off the original drunks in the inn but had then managed to pick up some more. The roofs were a great way to escape, and a good place to watch from.

What the hells had happened in Reyes since he'd left? Before, there'd been some mumblings among the clockworkers and others, but when wasn't there? People were poor but they always had been, and at least most seemed to be getting fed. People always grumbled about whoever was in charge too, but it hadn't been more than grumbles as far as he knew. Then again he didn't really pay much attention to what went on outside the guild.

Behind him the great clock in the square rang out in warning. He looked about quickly, but they were on an expanse of sloping roof that seemed unbroken in both directions except for chimneys and parapets – not a good place, at least not near the edge, during a change.

The ringing of the clock quelled the fight below as everyone found a stable place to wait it out.

"What's happening?" Dom asked.

"Well," Vocho said, "you're about to find out whether it's really true about Reyes. I've never done it on a rooftop, but it's pretty easy once you get the hang of it. Scares the widdle out of newcomers first time. Best to find something to hang on to until it's done."

"But—"

"Just grab something!"

The nearest roof had some handy fretwork on a fancy parapet under a solid-looking chimney, and Vocho took hold. He'd been so used to it before, he'd barely notice it. In fact he kept waking up at midnight every third day at the farm because it *hadn't* moved.

Dom hesitated, but the first grinding sound followed by a subtle tremor had him hanging on for dear life.

Beneath them the streets unhooked themselves with a great clank and began to move along hidden rails. Vocho and Dom moved with the building they were on. A whirr, as of a city-sized clock gearing up to chime, a slow twisting, and then the guild wasn't a far-off dark lump with tiny sparks of light to the left, it was straight ahead and so close Vocho could almost smell the spiced cabbage he'd seemed to live on for his first few years there, the smell of which permeated the whole place.

The Clockwork God in the square where Soot Town met the road to the docks lit up, turned his head three hundred and sixty degrees and settled down for the next three days. Everything shuddered as it settled into place, and the great clock chimed again.

Vocho stood up, checked the street – no one about, good – and headed for a drainpipe. That hadn't been too bad.

Oddly, Dom didn't seem too perturbed. Vocho had seen newcomers faint at their first change, and that was even without going through it high up on a roof, but Dom had breezed through it annoyingly easily. He stood up straight, composed himself and flicked an imaginary bit of dust off his shoulder. "Shall we get on?"

For a bumbling fool, Dom was proving to be a surprising companion.

They made their way down to the street, Dom stamping on it as though to make sure it was safe, his only visible reaction to a movement that had many visitors swearing never to visit Reyes ever again. "I wonder what in the world it's *for*," Dom said.

Vocho shrugged. "No one knows for sure. Only that two massive waterwheels under the river power it, that it's as old as the city, older still than records. And that it doesn't affect the guild or the Shrive. My old tutor thought it was something for defence – you know, if the enemy can't work out how to get to the castle, how can they attack? Or if they get there, and then get lost on the way back . . . And they're pretty sure the guild used to be the main castle before the Castans came. The movement does a few other things too. Reveals or hides arrow slots, secret passages, that sort of thing. There's more up in the guild too, later ones that run on a different mechanism. Waterwheels under the river, the prelate says, power the clockwork duellist and all the defences. But no one knows for sure why. Too old, and the prelate won't say much about what he knows."

"And they don't think to turn it off?"

"What, and offend the Clockwork God? Unlikely."

"Ah yes, the Clockwork God. He's really taken off again in Reyes, hasn't he? Made my professors in Ikaras laugh themselves silly. Clockwork God indeed."

"What of it?" Bizarrely, considering that he only believed in a vague sort of way, Vocho found himself suddenly defensive about the Clockwork God. "Heard of stranger gods than that."

"Gosh, no, absolutely. Didn't mean to . . . Sorry."

They made their way carefully down dark and silent streets. Silent at least until they reached the square of the Clockwork God. Little clots of men and women huddled together, talking, shouting. None of it seemed very coherent.

Dom said, "Perhaps we should, well, find out what's going on?"

"Yeah, perhaps." Vocho suddenly lost interest in the huddles of people because across the square, in the shadow of the Clockwork God, he had seen a figure that looked all too familiar as it hurried down a little alley that Vocho remembered only existed in First Threeday. "You do that. I'll meet you back at the inn." He moved off before Dom could answer.

Dom was all very well, but Vocho wanted to be on his own for this, if the figure was who he thought. Quick, quiet. Above all, don't let the bastard know you're there. And if you get too close, don't look at his hands.

It was definitely the magician, Vocho would swear it. The same scarred face showing in the fitful light of the oil lamps that lit the alleyway. Definitely.

What in hells was a magician doing here? And this one in particular? Vocho's first thought was the papers, the gold. The bastard knew they were here, or guessed, and he wanted them back. If what had happened at the farmhouse was any indication, he wouldn't be too fussy about whether Vocho was alive to hand them over or not.

The alley ended on a street that always existed, even if not always in the same place. Heading towards the posh end of town. Made sense. You'd have to be rich to hire a magician. He reached a turning and paused to look about. Vocho ducked back into a doorway – he'd be more than happy if the magician never saw him again. When he peered back out, the magician was gone.

Vocho suppressed a shudder, told himself he wasn't at all scared of magicians and completely failed to believe it.

Kacha crept along the rooftops above a narrow street, empty now just after the change, though it'd fill again soon enough.

The two "smiths" she was following hadn't stopped for that, but Kacha's extra training had helped there – all those dark jobs she'd done for Eneko and the guild, sneaking, hiding, being as quiet as moonlight. He'd had her up on the rooftops for every change o' the clock for months, challenging her to keep moving the whole time, no holding on, making her perfect whether she wanted to be or not. She'd fallen more often than she cared to remember, knocked herself out three times and fallen into the inner workings once, where she'd almost got herself crushed between two cogs and scared herself stupid before she'd managed to get out again. There was a reason most people stayed indoors during the change, and it wasn't just because the priests said to or risk displeasing the Clockwork God.

Finally she'd got the trick of moving on surfaces that were themselves moving in contrary ways, up, down, sideways. She'd learned those movements by heart, knew which building would move where, and that had come in handy tonight.

She'd run the rooftops while her quarry had contented themselves with the safer option of the streets, which mostly stayed intact during a change except at the ends. Kacha had to jump from one building to the next as they moved past each other, changing streets and addresses, but she'd kept them in sight.

Right into Nob Hill – or more properly King's Row. The men stopped at a doorway that opened blackly for them and let them out a few moments later, and they weren't smiths now; they were councillors' men, with fancy tunics and feathered hats and lacy cuffs. The only question was, which councillor? It was too dark to see the colour of the flash on their tunic.

The answer to that came quickly enough. The men moved smoothly along the broad avenues, and Kacha had to abandon the rooftops – here the buildings were fewer and farther between. There were trees and scented gardens to hide in and creep through, but the men hadn't looked back once since they left Soot Town so she abandoned stealth for speed and took to the street herself. She didn't look too out of place. Her tunic wasn't guild but it was serviceable enough, and the sword marked her as a lady of at least a little wealth if no particular refinement – clocker ladies didn't wear swords as a rule, or breeches, but there were enough who did that she wouldn't cause much comment.

She kept back and as far in the shadows as she could. Easy enough – the moon was only a quarter full and fitful behind scudding clouds, and lamps were generally extinguished before the change and not lit again until the next morning so she had plenty to choose from. Besides, the men she was after didn't have far to go.

A large house, a newer one built after the revolt, with a dragon rampant on a pedestal by the gates. The men showed at last they were definitely more than they'd looked. Any smiths who'd tried dressing up as councillors' men would have been turned away at the gates, but these two were hailed like old friends, and as they passed beneath a rare relit lantern, she caught the flash of purple on their tunics. King's men.

That dying prelate's man hadn't been wrong.

She was about to turn away when the men reached the door, and it opened to reveal Petri Egimont, who welcomed them in with one of his restrained smiles, like he was thinking of something else. Knowing Petri, he probably was – he thought much more than he spoke. She'd always liked that about him, but it made him a dangerous opponent.

Seeing him made her careless. He glanced over and saw her, she was sure of it, and she cursed her stupidity. His whole body tensed. For a moment she thought he'd call the guard, but he did and said nothing. Only stared for long seconds as she stared back, conflicting emotions making her clamp her teeth.

Days when just a look could make her smile. Nights when no words were exchanged, the shiver of her skin when he kissed it. The smell of him on her pillow, in her bed when they were done. Him finishing her sentences, showing her other ways to think, to be. Him not expecting her to be perfect, just her. The sudden jarring shock of the note, double-checking the writing, the seal, the words. The blinding pain that had followed it, the anger. She wanted to run up and kiss him, and she wanted to kick him right in the cogs too. Petri Egimont – love him or hate him she couldn't stop thinking about him.

Finally, after it looked he might come down the steps and call out to her, he just nodded in her direction and shut the door, leaving her feeling unsettled. Which was probably exactly what he intended, so she did her best to shrug him off and left with a lot to think over.

This made things very complicated, and complications were things she'd always tried to avoid. Except perhaps for Vocho, who was a complication all by himself.

Usually after the change o' the clock the streets would stay empty for the night, everyone taking the opportunity for a little time off. Not tonight though. As Kacha made her way back towards Soot Town, doors opened and knots of people drifted back onto the streets. It wasn't long before they were followed by street traders. By the time she was halfway back to the Hammer and Tongs, the streets were as full of noise and bustle as ever, but there was something odd about them, as though everyone was trying to shout very quietly.

Under the Clockwork God a scuffle had broken out – nothing too serious yet, just a random crowd of young men and women railing against something. Or so she thought until she saw the colours pinned to their clothes. Gold and green and red and purple, the colour of the prelate versus the colours of other councillors, including the king. Only these were just lads and lasses, factory workers, smiths' apprentices, a few sailors. The fight broke up when a patrol of guards sauntered around the corner and took up station under the god, but by their black looks and gestures the lads and lasses would be back at it as soon as they'd gone.

Kacha stopped by a woman selling drinks out of a tray and bought one – a spirit for those with more desire to get drunk than taste buds. It smelled vile but familiar, and brought to mind a blurred memory of her da overlaid with another – of Eneko. She took a sip, winced at the taste and surreptitiously poured the rest away.

"What's with that lot?" she asked with a jerk of her head to indicate the mass of youngsters to one side of the god, posturing and posing and shouting insults at each other.

"Been away have you, love? Thought so. Couldn't have missed it, else. The usual," the woman said. "Prelate's men did this; king's men did something else; clockers this, ex-nobles that. Weren't much to it to start with – people do love a good moan, that's all, and the prelate always keeps the councillors in hand. But it's all got a bit strange lately, or rather he has. Just like my old da when he lost his marbles, wittering on about all sorts. Worse when it's the man in charge though, eh? Taxing petticoats and periwinkles, I ask you. So it was rumbling worse and worse what with all the rumours. Then that bloody priest getting hisself murdered kicked it all off good and proper, and it ain't really stopped since. You want to try that with some lemon in, love? Makes all the difference. Makes it bloody drinkable for a start."

"Uh? No, thanks. The priest?"

The woman shrugged, making her tray of clay bottles and cups clink. "Prelate's favourite, wasn't he? There's some who reckon that Vocho bloke were put up to it by one of the other councillors, you know, as a message or something, like a plot, or maybe it was them heathen Ikarans – devils they are. Of course there's some who reckon it was the prelate hisself what ordered it."

Kacha felt like she'd been hit between the eyes with a brick. "The prelate ordered it? Why would he do that?"

"Aye, *well*." The woman looked both ways in a manner that intimated that this was a rare and juicy piece of gossip not to be spoken to just anyone. "There's been a load of rumbling against the prelate, see. I don't know; they say maybe he didn't want the priest to talk to the Ikarans, negotiate with them just as like, about the coal and all, that he's hoarding it somewhere. Or maybe he just wanted to distract people from that we ain't got nothing to eat, or the bloody taxes. All the criers in the square are talking about it, though I ain't heard two agree yet."

"But there's always been taxes—"

"Not like this, miss. It's hard to get enough to eat, never mind pay them. Bread's hard to come by, and sugar? Can't get sugar for love nor money, which is why that drink's so sour, miss. Bloody Ikarans, sanctions they call it; blackmail *I* call it, trying to get us to hand over them mines and no trade with them until we do and where else can we get sugar that ain't from half the world away an' more expensive than gold and silks and all? But there, lots of things we can't get now, or we can if we want to pay a week's wages in tax, so lots of people are going hungry, see."

"Well yes, but I don't see why the prelate—"

"No, well, he's loopy ain't he, miss? Or so everyone says. Funny the things my old da used to do. So anyway, the priest dies, may the Clockwork God judge his soul for truth, and then, well, then it all sort of kicked off. You know how it does. Most of them don't know what they're fighting about or who to blame, they's just pissed off and hungry and ready to fight anyone. Same every spring when it starts getting warm. They'll stop come summer when it's too hot to move. Or maybe it's all a load of tosh and the real reason'll come out later. But you can't believe half what you hear, can you? Can I have me cup back now?"

Kacha handed back the empty clay cup and moved on. Everything came back to the sodding priest – and Vocho. There were days, and this was one, when she wished she didn't have a brother.

An hour later in the Hammer and Tongs, when the fighting had finished, everyone had gone back to serious drinking and the guards had left after a small bribe, Vocho sat with a smug grin in his room. Honour defended, fun had, unnoticed escape achieved. Most importantly, life kept. There was a magician about, but he wasn't here right now, so Vocho relegated him to things to worry about some other time, along with pretty much everything else. Dom chirruped quietly in the corner, apparently as pleased with the evening as Vocho. They'd managed to find him some suitable clothes, but damned if the man didn't look like a clocker playing dress-up. Vocho had come to the galling conclusion Dom would look good in sackcloth and fish guts. Even that couldn't still the pleasure of an evening well spent, with some jugs of wine to follow.

"Cospel! Mugs, please, and the wine."

Cospel was sporting a black eye and a pleased grin. "Like old times," he murmured as he poured.

Vocho eyed him. "How much did you make?"

"I don't like to brag." Maybe he didn't, but the way his tunic bulged at the hem told Vocho that he'd made enough.

Once Vocho had thought himself above all that, had rebuked Cospel every time he'd done his dipping trick during a fight. Conduct unbecoming a duellist, he'd called it. Once upon a time he'd cared about that, to a certain extent anyway. But that had been before he'd had to resort to thievery himself. Now his disregard for rules stretched beyond duelling and into everything.

"Did you see where Kass went?" he asked Cospel and Dom. Vocho had seen she was all right, seen her bent over a man with a gash to his stomach, and then things had got a bit frantic and hadn't let up till he and Dom had made the roof. He wasn't unduly worried because Kacha could take care of herself in usual circumstances. But being wanted for murder and with a magician after them wasn't what he classed as usual circumstances, and despite his outward nonchalance he was feeling a little twitchy.

"Someone attacked some prelate's men," Dom said. "I think she went to find out who."

That definitely didn't sound like usual circumstances.

"Maybe we should . . . Oh, there you are, Kass."

She came in looking thoughtful, plonked herself in a chair and took the mug Cospel gave her without a word. Vocho knew that look. Kacha had always been more of a thinker than he was, and this look meant she was thinking hard. About what would usually come after a glass or two of wine, so he let her be for now, though he couldn't resist a little dig. "I see you didn't stay around for the fight. Too much for you? Just as well. I'd have shown you up anyway. I was *magnificent*. Naturally."

"You haven't forgotten why we're here then, Voch?" She gave him an arch look over the rim of her mug. "Saving our skins, finding out what it is they want so badly. All that."

"Of course not! Only there was fighting going on anyway and . . . and . . . " He gave up in the face of her glare. Now was not the time to admit he'd got a bit carried away.

"Heard some funny things, you know. While you were off doing whatever it was," Dom said into the following silence.

"Yes?" Vocho answered, but he kept watching Kacha and the way she was staring into her mug like maybe it held all the answers.

"Well, the prelate, don't you know? I mean, man's always

been a bit of a pill, no class to him, but, well, it sounds to me like he's gone a bit odd."

"Odd?" Kacha sat forward at that. "What do you mean by 'odd'?"

"Oh, well." Dom's ears turned pink, as they had a habit of doing whenever Kacha talked to him. "Um, he's just been doing some strange things. Funny edicts – something about taxes, spices and squid and . . . What was it?" His face cleared. "Oh yes. An edict about flags. They should be purple."

"Squid? Flags? What the hells?" Vocho said.

"I don't know. Even heard one about his cats, but I don't believe it for a minute. I mean the man's an oik, or so my father says, but even I couldn't believe that about him."

Vocho suppressed a smile at the thought of Dom's father – who before the prelate came to power had been as low class as they came, even if he had made some money – describing the prelate as an oik.

"His cats?" Kacha asked.

"Something about him wanting everyone to call them sir, or something, though it wasn't actually passed. Talked out of it, they say. He doesn't even hold with calling *people* sir, or he never did anyway – everyone's equal, isn't that right? But the last couple of months apparently he's gone a bit strange. Or very strange. Lady told me that's what's behind all the ruckus on the streets, well that and taxes."

"Did she now? A lady told me much the same. You'd think he'd be more careful seeing as it was taxes that finally did for the old king, and Bakar never struck me as stupid, whatever else he is." Kacha looked more thoughtful than ever and motioned to Vocho to get the papers out.

He took them out from the packet he'd taken to keeping inside the back of his shirt. Once again they tried to make sense of them. Vocho kept thinking there was something familiar about them, something he should notice. And something, perhaps, that would interest a magician or give a clue as to why the prelate suddenly wanted people to call his cats sir.

Kacha was the one who saw it in the end. She sat forward, spilling her wine as she spotted it, and jabbed a finger at one of the perhaps-crests, perhaps-something-elses, which was somewhat charred from the paper's hasty escape from the chest.

"What does that look like to you?"

"Huh?" Vocho twisted the paper to and fro. "I don't know. Perhaps a stag? Or a horse?"

"A big dog?" Dom chimed in. "Maybe an elephant?"

Kacha rolled her eyes. "What about those bits there? What do they look like?"

They looked like bits of charring to Vocho, but he knew better than to say that. "It's not very clear."

"No, it isn't, unless you know what you're looking at."

"And I suppose you do?" he said. Did she have to always know best?

"A dragon!" Dom said.

Vocho would have ignored him except Kacha nodded. "A dragon. And yes, I knew what I was looking for. Did you see those prelate's men in the bar?"

"I was busy," Vocho said with a sniff. "You know, upholding the honour of the guild, fighting like a god, looking dashing while I did it, not skulking about or disappearing like *some* people I could mention."

Despite his tone, Kacha laughed. "You, uphold their honour? I'm sure they're very grateful, Voch; they'll probably build a statue to your integrity and bravery. So, you didn't see them get murdered? By men pretending to be smiths?"

"Murdered? Well it *was* a fight, and these things—"

She ignored him. "Murder, Voch. With intent, not just some brawl. Not just them being odd either. All very weird out on the street, didn't you notice? Clockworkers wearing purple badges, or gold. Others wearing blue and green and red. All just going for each other. King's supporters versus prelate's, a few other councillors mixed in, though it was mostly those two. But they were all working men and women, like Dom said, maybe upset about the prelate and what he's doing. I suggest we move quick as we can. I spoke to one of the prelate's men before he died and then I followed those 'smiths'. Because of what that prelate's man told me. The men disguised as smiths were councillors' men too."

Vocho had a sudden prickly feeling on the back of his head. Councillors' men, dragon crests, dragons being the symbol of the old monarchy, of their gods-given right to rule . . .

"King's men?"

"I followed two of them, like I said. Took me round the houses, but we ended up in Nob Hill. Which seemed a bit strange for smiths, don't you think, especially ones who managed to change into guards' uniform on the way?"

"More than bloody strange."

"Even stranger when finally they got to the king's house there. Let in, sweet as you please. By Egimont."

"Holy hen's teeth. What does Licio think he can gain from murdering a couple of prelate's men in a bar brawl?" Vocho asked. "The prelate's going to be pissed as hells no matter how odd he's getting, and that's good for no one, especially Licio."

"Currently all the prelate is going to know is some smiths murdered his men. The people he'll be pissed with are Soot Town. Not the king. But with all the unrest, it looks like a golden opportunity for someone, right?"

Vocho looked back down at the papers. Once you knew what it had to be, it was clear as the nose on Cospel's very plain face. A dragon rampant, the king's crest, the symbol of all that had been wrong with the monarchy: gods-blessed, only the gods had turned out to be fake, pretty much like dragons had turned out to be mythical.

"A bit of fighting in the streets isn't going to do much," he said. "He's got something else. Some new thing that might tip the balance in his favour."

"Like a magician?" Kacha said.

"That would do for a start, exactly like the one I saw heading into Nob Hill earlier," Vocho managed weakly. "But it can't be all. Can it?"

"Petri, the magician and the king. I think that's enough to know there's something going on here. We need this translated as soon as we can. And we need to be doubly careful. If this has anything to do with what went on tonight, and it looks like it might, then we're in big shit if he finds us or these papers. So no more bar brawls, fist fights or calling people out for duels. All right?"

"You spoil all my fun."

Interlude

Seventeen years earlier

Petri was bowled along with the mob. Not only was he hemmed in on every side, but Bakar had a tight grip on his arm. Without that he wouldn't have known where to go. Eneko had thrown him out of the guild – to save the guild or to save himself, Petri wasn't sure which – and shut the gates. There was his father's townhouse in King's Row, but his father . . . Petri wanted to deny everything that Bakar had said about him but found he believed it, believed that maybe there was more, worse, that Bakar hadn't told him. If nothing else, he was where he needed to be to find out, or soon would be. He stopped lagging, and Bakar no longer needed to pull on his arm, just gave Petri an appraising look and a cryptic smile, but said nothing as they approached the palace.

King's guards ran to and fro. A company of cavalry stood to one side, the horses snorting and stamping at the approach of what seemed like half the docks and Soot Town. Straight ahead the bulk of the men and women who made up the king's guard were drawn up in ranks, swordsmen at the front, crossbowmen to the rear. Petri squinted up at the roof and saw archers lurking there among the fancy fretwork.

So did everyone else, and all of a sudden the crowd slowed its pace to a crawl. In places it might have gone backwards, if not for the press of people behind. Bakar never faltered though. There seemed to be some kind of power radiating from him – Petri could feel the burn of it where Bakar's hand held his arm – but what it was, Petri couldn't say. Only that people looked at him and seemed to gain resolve. Bakar was so very single-minded, so intense, so *sure*, it was hard not to be pulled along, not to feel a bit of it yourself.

He strode forward, Petri in his wake, straight up to the young captain at the head of the guard looking very bright and brave in his smart uniform. The captain was trying – and failing – to keep his face blank. He'd do all right for a minute, and then he'd see another clump of men and women with impromptu weapons that looked every bit as lethal as his sword, and his lip would twitch or his eyebrows would try to escape into his hair. Bakar coming straight for him seemed to unnerve him even further.

Bakar pulled his hand out from where he'd hidden it inside his shirt and aimed his contraption at the captain's head.

"Someone to treat with us, now. Someone with authority."

The captain flapped his mouth open. Behind Petri a muffled clattering probably meant Bakar wasn't the only one with a weapon like this, and a quick glance confirmed it. The captain fought to compose himself, but Bakar's voice slid smoothly over all that.

"Really. I don't *want* to have to kill you. But I will. So why not turn this over to someone else? Then all this can end as peaceably as possible. What if I told you the Clockwork God lives again, and he knows who to trust and who not to?"

Petri could see it in the captain's face. He wanted to do as Bakar said, that was clear – he was outnumbered, and even if he wasn't aware of what Bakar's contraption could do, he'd noticed the blood on his face and the billhooks in the hands of the men behind him. Add to that a certain flabbergasted look – a flash of what? hope? relief? at the mention of the Clockwork God, at the thought he lived again. But Petri knew too that if the captain disobeyed whatever order he'd been given, he was as good as dead anyway. The king would have him sent down to the Shrive and his head bouncing across the cobbles by morning.

The captain wavered, and then something caught his eye and stiffened his spine at the same time as his mouth loosened its tight white line.

Bakar smiled at the captain's brief indecision. He lowered the gun and cocked his head. "I understand. I really do. And thank you."

"I . . ." the captain began, but Bakar wasn't looking at him any more. His attention was fixed on a dark figure off to one side. The gun came up, and Bakar did something complicated to it that Petri couldn't make out nor understand even if he had.

The dark figure stepped forward, and Petri realised that the woman wasn't dark, not really. Her skin was a shade more golden than her hair, and the loose robes she wore were of blue silk shot with silver, but still, when he looked at her, darkness was what he thought of. It hovered around her like a shroud.

The captain let out a breath, the men behind him seemed to relax, while at the same time the dockers, smiths and the rest behind Bakar shifted uncomfortably. One or two muttered curses under their breaths, and one fisherman with a dripping gaff hook made a sign as though to ward her off. Petri began to understand when he saw the woman's hands and what she carried. A scalpel in one hand, a small brush in the other. Blood dripped from her hands, but he couldn't tell if it was hers or not, and it didn't matter. All that mattered were the snaking black patterns that began on her hands and moved, crossed, twined before they dripped off her fingers along with the blood.

Petri had never seen a magician before, but he'd heard of them – hadn't they all? Stories of dark magic and hot coppery blood in the basement of the palace, of bodies discarded when they were done. Men made to move like puppets or mesmerised by the patterns on their hands, in the tattoos and wards they wove, into acting against their will. Worse things too, the older students had whispered to the younger in the guild dorms, trying to scare them, Petri had thought and not believed the half of them. Now, when all the king's guard stood taller at her approach, when the dockers who had seemed so aggressive, so certain, shrank back and muttered curses and entreaties to the Clockwork God, he wasn't so sure.

"Steady, young Petri," Bakar murmured. "They're dangerous and abhorrent, but they need time to prepare and a lot of blood to do all the things you've heard. You stay steady because clockwork has the measure of them and so do I."

Bakar and the magician stared at each other for a moment that seemed like an eternity to Petri. Bakar's finger tightened on a lever on his contraption, and the magician dripped blood and raised her brush.

A voice, familiar and cold, interrupted them: "I suppose you told the boy?"

His father was walking through the ranks of the king's guard. Petri felt a surge of wild hope – that Bakar had been lying, that Eneko throwing him out of the guild had been a mistake, that his father would now realise that Petri existed. That perhaps his father *was* a good man. He would save Petri from this madness, save the kingdom because he was noble, and didn't that mean good and just? No docker, not even if he was Bakar, could have more nobility in him than the Duke of Elona.

His father reached Bakar in a few easy strides. He strode the halls of his estates like one of the storks of the southern plains, black cloak flapping like wings, pale head only barely covered in wisps of grey hair, his nose long and beak-like, prying into everything and picking it apart. They called him the King's Vulture, Petri had heard, but not to his face.

Bakar spared the duke a glance but kept one eye on the magician. Petri almost couldn't breathe. His father had come for him, come to save him from this madman, come to bark out an order and have everyone obey, as always.

Hope dashed in an instant. Petri's father didn't even spare him a glance.

"What is it you want, Bakar?"

Bakar didn't answer straight away but took a minute to consider and to cast an eye over the supporters at his back, though the gun stayed pointed at the magician.

"You," he said. "You and the king and all the nobles, to lay down your power. For all the slaves you took by deception to be freed, the Shrive emptied, the magicians banished. For things to be *equal*."

The magician blanched before a slow smile graced her face. It made Petri's scalp itch, but Bakar didn't seem to notice even when she began to move her brush. A slip of paper slid out of one sleeve and she nodded to someone Petri couldn't see.

His father laughed at Bakar not with amusement – he'd never heard his father laugh like that – but in mockery. "And perhaps we should hand over all our wealth and estates too, dress ourselves in sackcloth and ashes and whip ourselves in contrition? Anything else? Do you really think trying to blackmail me by holding my son hostage will help?"

Petri knew then he should never have hoped. That his own father was abandoning him to his fate without even a glance. He felt it like a physical slap to the face.

In the deathly silence everyone held their breath, waiting

to see what would happen. Everyone except one man who moved behind the ranks of soldiers towards the magician. He was nothing like her – tall and dark, with skin the colour of walnuts and jet hair tumbling haphazardly around his face as though he'd just woken up – but there was something the same about the two of them. The look in the eyes, perhaps, as though everyone they saw was a mouse in a trap, and less worthy of notice.

Everything seemed to happen at once. The dark man drew a knife, and then there was blood everywhere, king's guards slumping to the ground with throats cut. The female magician gave a little crow of triumph and leaped on the blood. Her brush dipped in, quick as thought, quicker. At the same time Bakar moved towards Petri's father.

Petri never got to find out what Bakar was planning. One moment the magicians were huddled over the dead guards, and then they both stood as one and something shot towards Bakar and his father.

In the years that followed, when he dreamed of it, it was his father he called a warning to; it was his father who lived. Here and now it was Bakar's name that screeched past dry lips, Bakar who dropped to the ground. His father who took the full force of . . . something, and turned to dust before his eyes.

Things happened after that, important things, but Petri was only vaguely aware of them. Bakar shot the male magician, who fell screaming to the ground before a docker cut his throat – quick, before he could use his own blood to cast any more spells. The woman disappeared. The crowd surged forward in a yelling rush and overwhelmed the surviving guards, who stood reeling at what the magicians had been prepared to do to them, to the Duke of Elona even. The magicians they relied upon for intimidation had been prepared to kill them, and in any case were now dead or gone. Without them they crumbled. Through it all Petri stood and stared at where his father had been, not knowing or particularly caring what went on around him.

When Bakar came back and found him, the sun had moved far past noon and was sliding down over the city towards sunset.

"Why was it that it was me you warned?" he asked, looking genuinely puzzled.

Petri had thought on this a long time and still wasn't sure he had the answer. He felt loose and rudderless, with everything he thought true blown away – his father being noble, the guild being a substitute family he'd fallen on in desperation – and Eneko had flicked him off like an irritating tick.

"Because . . . you showed more interest in one hour than he did in a lifetime. You listened." He screwed himself up for it. "And everything's so un*fair*. Everything. My father and the guild throwing me to you and those children they sent to slavery or worse. Everything! Those guards that magician killed, just like stepping on a bug, because he could. You said you wanted to make it fair. For everyone."

Bakar nodded as though this was the most profound thing he'd ever heard. "Just so, Petri Egimont. Equality for all, that was always my goal. Now, I saved your life, and you saved mine. That links us." He put an arm around Petri's shoulders, and Petri wondered that no one, not his father nor brother nor guild mate had ever done this before. It felt strange but also good. "I shall be your father now, and you can help me make things right and fair for all, and I will never betray you. Maybe, in time, when the guild is at heel, I shall give it to you to rule. Yes. Yes, I promise you that, Petri. I can winkle out that old bastard Eneko in payment for what he's done to you and others. The guild shall be yours, and be good again."

After that Petri would have followed him anywhere.

Chapter Twelve

Egimont rose early – he'd barely slept anyway, even if the lodgings were a damned sight better than his box of a room at the prelate's palace. There had been too much to do, too many pots to stir, too many things to think on, or avoid thinking on. He dressed quickly and was out into the morning mists which blew up off the sea all the better to hide his exit from the king's house. More to do today, always more. First, he had to go to his clerking job at the old palace, pretend he was still the prelate's man.

The streets were still smoking with resentment and an occasional fire from the ruckus last night. Little knots of angry men and women stood around, muttering. The guards and various councillors' men seemed to have given up trying to control them for now. Petri had no doubt there would be repercussions – of late Bakar seemed to have forgotten the lessons he'd learned from the old king's rule, and some of the other councillors had perhaps never learned them at all.

Egimont hurried on and suppressed a smile when somebody spat at him. It all seemed to be going to plan, and Alicia from last night had been righter than she knew. Reyes wasn't as it once was. Or had been for a long time – the last time. This time was going to turn out better for Egimont, if it killed him. It could hardly turn out worse. At the small gate into the space that fronted the once grand palace he stopped. A familiar carriage – the king's. A familiar face peering from the dark folds of the curtains – Sabates. Egimont kept his gaze on the front door and ignored the magician's eyes on him as he crossed the space.

He hadn't expected the king so soon, or for him to bring the magician with him. He hadn't expected him at all for days. Sabates had said it would be best if the king wasn't in Reyes when things started getting heated, so he could distance himself from any accusations. But Egimont had come to realise that what Sabates said and what he meant were rarely the same. Whichever, this didn't bode well. He hurried up the steps and to the tiny corner that served as his office and the mark of his status, and showed just how little he had. His supervisor bore down on him, but Egimont grabbed some papers from his desk, waved them in the detestable little man's face and, declaring he needed signatures, hurried off.

Past the orrery, spinning on its axes, never turning aside, never deviating, suns and stars moving in their prescribed circles for ever. Like his life if this plan of Sabates' didn't work. Up the grand staircase that had once seen men and women in all their finery, past blank spaces where paintings of past kings had once hung, all glory wiped away as though it had never been. On towards the prelate's office, where the king had to be. On to find out what had gone wrong, whether he was in any more danger than usual.

As he neared it, raised voices filtered along the corridor. A few prelate's men stood at attention, studiously not looking anywhere, pretending they couldn't hear. A hiss from one side, a dark familiar face, the smell of coppery blood, and Egimont found himself in a side room with Sabates too close for comfort. How had the man got here before him? The smell of hot blood answered that.

"What—"

Sabates held up a bloodied hand, and Egimont shut up. The patterns on the magician's hand changed even as he watched, crown to dragon to fiery waste, then the crossed swords of the guild, finally a crest – his crest before he'd been stripped of his title now hanging over the guild's. A blade moved slowly across it, made patterned blood drip from the bottom.

"Listen," Sabates hissed. "Listen if you don't want that."

Egimont pulled himself back together and looked to where Sabates pointed. A perfect, improbable circle of shining blood on a table. Too much for a man to bleed and live. He opened his mouth to protest, to . . . what? He'd known, or thought he had at least, what he'd got into as soon as the magician had appeared in his life, and he'd said nothing. Done nothing because he thought the magic necessary if unwelcome. Too late now to back out if he wanted his life. Maybe it wasn't human blood . . .

Sabates yanked him over to the circle. It hissed and popped as though the table was hot, and under that there was a murmur, voices. The prelate, angry as hells, barking out questions, the king soothing, pretending.

"Riots!" the prelate shouted. "Riots for the god's sake. Smiths attacking my men, killing them, and why?"

A few murmurs – not just the king, Egimont thought. Probably all the councillors were in there, trying to placate the prelate. Paranoia and delusion had recently begun leaking out of him like sweat, till the corridors of the palace fairly reeked of it and everyone had begun looking over their shoulder. Egimont wondered whether that had anything to do with Sabates and thought it very likely.

"Some sort of plot, you think?" The king's voice – calm, soothing, a hint of reproach and disbelief. He could play the part so well when he had a mind to. When he was sober, as he always used to be and was so rarely now. "But who and why?"

"That's why I called you all here – to find out. If I fall, we all fall. A plot against me is a plot against all of us. I want you all to do what you can to discover what's going on. Start with Sendoa's murder. That's where it all started, I'm sure. Without him we're fatally weakened in the border dispute. The Ikaran king refuses to deal with anyone else, and now supplies of iron and coal are growing short, and we can't grow enough grain to feed ourselves. We *need* those supplies, not to mention all the things that only Ikaras can supply. With the grain shortage, if we grow much shorter of sugar as well, we'll have more than riots on our hands."

Sabates grinned darkly next to Egimont, his scarred face twisting. A stray thought came to Egimont – that Vocho had killed the priest Sendoa on orders. Everyone thought that it had been some drunken escapade gone wrong, that Vocho had lost his temper while in his cups and had got careless with his blade. Just like the ridiculous Vocho, who took almost nothing seriously, not even being a master duellist. The only thing that he kept close to his heart was his reputation. Exactly like him, except the one thing Vocho was always careful with was his blade. Even Petri had to admit that. And Petri knew more, perhaps – that Vocho killed for Eneko, that this priest was just another one of many people he'd been ordered to kill by the guild master, and it was only that he'd been caught this time, as Sabates had hoped.

Looking at Sabates' face, Egimont wondered but didn't have time to wonder long.

"We should look into the guild more thoroughly," Licio said. "The man who murdered Sendoa and his sister – I'm sure there's more to it, if you're right, Bakar. Perhaps . . ."

"Perhaps that old bastard Eneko is behind it!" the prelate said. "Wouldn't surprise me; he's never forgiven me for humiliating him. I'd never have kept the guild, except for the unrest it'd cause to disband them. Besides, I like having them at my mercy."

And because they've been useful to you, Egimont thought. Because if you'd got rid of them, you'd have had more than a revolt on your hands. The guild was as much a part of Reyes as its Clockwork God – more even, because it had survived since time out of mind whereas the Clockwork God was if not new only recently reawakened.

"You've the perfect man right here for the job," Licio went on. "Egimont used to be a duellist, correct? Didn't take his master's, but that was no fault of his, from what I hear. Well then, they'll trust him as they wouldn't trust an outsider, and he's your man, isn't he?"

Bakar laughed, and the sound sent quivers across Egimont's shoulders. Yes, he was the prelate's man all right, and he'd infiltrated the guild before on the prelate's orders, as Licio well knew. But he wasn't going to be the prelate's man for long, not if Licio and Sabates did what they promised.

The meeting broke up with the prelate exhorting everyone to do their utmost. Sabates waved his hand over the circle of blood and it was gone leaving nothing but the hint of copper in the air.

Licio came in, nodded at Egimont and turned to Sabates. "Well?"

"You did perfectly. You've planted the idea of Sendoa's murder being part of a plot rather than just a drunken duellist stabbing him at random, turned his suspicion away from us, and we've turned his beady eye onto Eneko instead." Sabates allowed himself a smile. "You see, Licio? I told you having the priest killed would be the key to getting this started."

Egimont had the feeling that he'd suddenly been pushed off a ship into deep water and had forgotten how to swim. "*You* had the priest killed?"

Sabates had had the priest killed . . . which had led in turn to Kacha being wanted, and that note and diagram.

Egimont had known something was going on and had thought
– looking back had foolishly believed Sabates when he said
– they were going to prove that Vocho was Eneko's assassin
by catching him in the act. He'd never thought they'd *ordered*
the death. And Vocho had agreed?

"It was necessary to prevent Bakar from making any kind
of treaty with Ikaras that might undermine our own, and
now war looks inevitable. The army that Ikaras is massing
makes it look like they're preparing an attack on the state,
not revolt from within. It keeps Bakar looking outwards,
not inwards, keeps him thinking of how to negotiate, not
how to protect his person. Today was a good opportunity
to deflect suspicion from us as well, onto Eneko. The priest
was the catalyst, the starting point. It shouldn't take you
long to engineer the end point."

"Take me long to do what?" Egimont said.

Sabates arched an eyebrow. "Destroy the guild, of course.
They're our biggest stumbling block. Eneko's far too canny
to entangle them with any one side, and no one can ever
be sure which way they'll jump if it comes to it. If they
oppose us, they're too powerful to stop because the popu-
lace is *always* with them, and Eneko has money on his
side too – lots of fingers in lots of pies, that one, and
canny with it. Bakar knew that last time, which is why
you ended up as his hostage to Eneko's good behaviour,
or so he thought. Eneko never cared about any of his
guildsmen, only what they could do for him, the money
they could make him, the prestige they could give him.
You think you know that, Petri, but you know not even
the half of it. I suspect that Eneko has Ikarans in his
pocket too, provides them with slaves and guns despite
the embargo, and he was using Vocho to assassinate stra-
tegic people to help his cause. He has plans of his own,
that one, and he's dangerous because of it. Yet the guild
could be of great use. Once Eneko's destroyed – making

sure of course, that no suspicion falls on us, because you're the prelate's man – and you're installed as guild master instead, we're almost there. We thought you'd like that, after what they did to you."

Chapter Thirteen

Vocho followed Cospel up a rickety stairwell that hugged the side of a steel mill. The clockwork hammers thundered underneath them so unrelentingly, Vocho's heart started to pound in time. Kacha and Dom brought up the rear as they edged out onto a rooftop thick with shacks made of anything available, homes tied to each other by washing lines full of rags. Little gaunt faces peered out to watch them as they passed, and whisper about them to their backs.

These places hadn't changed much, Vocho thought. He'd not been in one for an age, that first time always lingering in his head with the scent of blood and the screams of the crowd as they were trampled underfoot. The shacks were still as full, the faces just as thin. The prelate had promised change, but not much had happened. Vocho had got a hell of a shock the first time he'd seen the prelate and realised he was the man who'd started the riot at the execution, who he'd last seen being dragged up the steps of the Shrive.

So many rumours had flown about after Bakar had taken power, it was hard to know the truth of anything. The only thing Vocho was sure about, because he'd seen it with his own eyes from the dorm where he and the other youngest were hiding, was that the prelate had threatened to shoot Eneko, and Eneko had backed down. They talked of that in whispers after lights out, until the sergeant-at-arms caught them and gave them six lashes and a stern lecture on how Eneko had had to back down if they all wanted to live. Saving them had seemed good to him; did it seem good to them? Just to top the punishment off they'd each had to produce an essay on why the guild being flexible had meant it had managed to survive since before the Great Fall.

Things were hazy in Vocho's head after Eneko's retreat. At some point Bakar had brought the king to the square in front of the Shrive, had bounced his head across the cobbles before having him strung up by his heels from the ancient clock tower. The prelate had taken control, but not just for himself; he had proclaimed equality for all in accordance with the Clockwork God's instructions.

Only it hadn't worked out that way, had it? These poor bastards were still poor, still ate what scraps they could find. The smell of watery fish-head soup reminded Vocho painfully of his ma sobbing over a pan and the sensation of a hole in his stomach big enough to fit his head in. Vocho smelled that soup in all his worst nightmares.

He clutched the papers tighter with the hand he'd stuffed inside his tunic. He was never going to be that poor, that hungry, ever again. Neither was Kacha. These papers and what they might be worth to the right people would be enough to make sure they were never hungry.

Cospel ducked under a last washing line and pointed at a shack that looked just as tumbledown as the rest.

"Are you sure?" Vocho asked. "It doesn't look like the home of a scholar."

Cospel shrugged. "Got her flaws, like. Bit of a nutter, if you ask me. But she knows her stuff all right. I checked. Ten years teaching languages and cryptology at Ikaras University, another three working for the prelate. She works

for herself now. Fell out with him about the Clockwork God,
so I hear. He reckoned she was blasphemous."

"The university, eh?" Dom said. "Maybe I'll know her
then. Mind you, languages weren't my subject, and I'm not
sure what cryptology even is."

Vocho stifled the question – what *was* Dom's subject, exactly?
Trying not to stab himself with his own sword and apologising
to his opponent afterwards, with a minor in looking good?

"Go on then," Kacha said. "What are we waiting for?"

"It's just—"

Vocho didn't wait for Cospel to finish; he was too eager
to find out what kind of trouble he had in his hands, just
how much shit they were really in, why that magician wanted
the papers so badly and what it might take to make him
stop. Or how much they were worth. Hopefully, with this
lady's help, he could work out all these things. A perfunc-
tory knock on the door almost had it off its hinges, so he
gently moved it aside and went in.

A musty smell was the first thing he noticed, like thousands of old books had decided to curl up and die. Then a
whirring clank – clockwork under stress. Finally his eyes
got used to the gloom just as a figure stepped forward.

He couldn't see her very clearly in the murk, but he could
see enough. She didn't look like she belonged here; she
looked like she belonged in a palace somewhere, or maybe
in a temple overseeing prayers. She was tall, as tall as Vocho,
so that her head brushed the manuscripts that dangled from
the ceiling. He got a sense of a face that wasn't beautiful in
its parts – nose too strong, eyes too wide, lips too thin – but
together they gave the impression of someone who was.
Vocho had an almost overwhelming impulse to address her
as Ma'am. She looked like that sort of woman.

She smiled at him quizzically, and at the others when
they crowded the doorway before she saw Cospel. "Ah, there
you are. And you brought your friends. How lovely – it's

so rare I get visitors these days. I'm Cassalily. I understand you have some documents you want translated?"

Vocho pulled them out from where he'd hidden them but felt suddenly reluctant to hand them over to someone he'd just met.

"I'll need to see them, if you want me to tell you what they say," Cassalily said reproachfully and held out a hand.

Vocho couldn't help staring. The clockwork sound as he'd entered – who'd be able to afford clockwork here? Someone who couldn't leave it behind, that's who. A brass hand sneaked out of Cassalily's sleeve, and the fingers curled Vocho's way. A perfectly jointed beautifully polished clockwork hand. Hands, he corrected himself as he looked further. Then Cassalily stepped forward into the light of the doorway, turned to face him full on and it wasn't just her hands.

A chittering sound as her left eye irised, the components sliding over each other to narrow the aperture at the centre. Clockwork hands had been shock enough, but a clockwork eye?

"A genius made all of it for me," she said as her hands gripped the papers and tugged them from Vocho's unresisting hand. "The eye especially is very useful. Built-in magnification. I'm a work in progress, you might say."

Cospel was doing his thing with the eyebrows again, but Vocho still hadn't learned the language.

Kacha recovered first. "That's, er . . . nice. Do you think you can—"

"Of course! Everyone doubts me so. Well, it won't be long before I show them. In the meantime, this will be quite easy, I think. Looks like straightforward Ikaran for the most part. Oh, and one in Old Castan – that's from before the Great Fall. Not many people know it these days, but it's quite simple really. I was hoping for a cipher of some kind, something interesting. This shouldn't take me long. A day? Now did you bring the offering?"

Vocho pulled out his purse, wondering how much this was going to cost. It'd be worth it, whatever. "Of course. How much do you charge?"

The clockwork hands clacked indignantly. "Charge? *Charge*? I charge nothing. Cospel, didn't you . . .? No, I see not. Doubting Cospel, is that your name?" She sighed. "Everyone doubts. I require an offering. A truth."

"A truth?" Vocho asked, perplexed. "I don't . . ."

She smiled at him and laid a cold and whirring hand on his shoulder. "It's very simple. I require a truth, as you would offer to my statue down by the guild."

"The Clockwork God?"

"Of course. I'm his human incarnation. For each truth I receive, my fathers and mothers who created me will allow another part, until I ascend to become him once again in his true form. Now, please, a truth from each of you. If it's good enough, maybe a truth no one else knows, I shall get my clockwork heart next. Yes, a truth no one else knows will be a good price."

Vocho flopped into a chair and stared morosely at an empty wine jug. Kacha flopped down opposite while Dom arranged himself precisely near the empty fireplace.

Kacha looked oddly ill at ease. "What did you tell her?"

Cassalilly had taken them all in turn to a closed-off area at the back of her room and had them all tell her a truth. Just the thought of it made Vocho itch.

"Nothing much, but she seemed pleased enough. Do you think she'll do it?"

"Only the Clockwork God knows. Maybe we should ask him for a translation, seeing as they appear to be the same person. The same crazy person." Kacha glared at Cospel, who had the grace to look embarrassed. "No wonder the prelate called her a blasphemy."

"No wonder she hides away up on that roof." Vocho was

still trying to persuade himself he hadn't imagined her or her complete conviction that she was the Clockwork God in human form. He'd been lost for words, and had stumbled out some pathetic little truth to her while his brained whizzed around like clockwork of its own.

"I think she'll manage all right," Dom said. "I recall her name, vaguely. At the university. Some sort of scandal, all hushed up, and then she left."

"A scandal like she went completely insane?" Vocho asked.

"That does ring a bell. Yes, now I come to think of it. But she was highly respected in her field. I think. Until all the business with the clockwork. Obviously that would put a bit of a crimp on her reputation."

"A bit? I'm surprised she's in one piece. One human piece, that is. She's already told us one thing though," Kacha said. "Ikaran. Why would the king's crest be on a piece of paper in Ikaran or Old Castan? And has it got anything to do with last night? Or that bloody border dispute that keeps rumbling on with Ikaras?"

"Why should it?" Vocho shifted uncomfortably in his seat.

Kacha gave him a penetrating look, like she guessed what he was thinking and his reply was just a cover for it. He concentrated on making sure his eye didn't twitch.

"Because, Voch, king's men were killing prelate's men. Smiths were fighting factory workers and each other. The prelate's going soft in the head. Petri's working with the king, and so is a magician, it looks like. Now this. Something's going on, and it smells worse than fish guts."

"Good. Someone will be ever so glad to get those papers back then. Maybe even the original owner. Or someone else, if they'll pay more. Then we'll have some money, and we can tell your old pal Eggy that we've got shot of the bloody things, and he'll call off his magician and we can live happily ever after."

She snorted and shook her head but said no more about it, though she looked like she wanted to say plenty. Instead, it was Dom who blundered into exactly what Vocho didn't want to talk about.

"All something to do with that priest," he said. "They were talking about it in the pub before, well, before it all got nasty. Sendoa, I think his name was."

He didn't seem to notice how Vocho's head snapped around to look at him, or the way Kacha was staring at him like her eyes were red-hot pokers and she could burn him into silence.

"An important man, so they said, and he was murdered a couple of months ago. That's when it all started going wrong. Wrong how, I'm not sure, except that's when the prelate started going strange too. Grief perhaps. Sendoa was his favourite priest."

"I don't suppose it was anything to do with him," Vocho said, hoping like crap that was true.

"Oh, definitely was. Father has the Reyes newspapers sent up. Likes to keep an eye on steel prices and all that. They're a bit behind, but I remember something about a priest dying – killed by a duellist of all people – and then . . . What was it? He was a diplomatic something-or-other."

"Envoy," Kacha said, watching Vocho warily.

"Envoy, yes, that was it. There'd been all that kerfuffle with Ikaras. That's strange, isn't it? With the language? Yes, sorry. Anyway, the kerfuffle over steel prices and mines and which country owned what, and then Ikaras cut off most of our coal. It looked like the priest was going to get it all sorted, because the Ikarans would only deal with him or something, and then he died and it all went to pieces again. And of course that meant steel prices went up. Father was so pleased. He sold off all his surplus stock, made a tidy bit too, and the rumour of war made the price of everything else go up, and then there was all that tax business, and the prelate started getting strange – like telling people their flags should be purple – and then everyone got unhappy."

"OK, well what about we spend the day we've got to wait until our friendly goddess-in-waiting has translated everything by seeing if we can find anything out? The more we know, the better."

Bescan Square was packed to bursting, making any passage through tricky and fraught with random elbows and pickpockets. Yet, for all the people there, no one seemed to be buying much. Vocho kept his head down and his hat firmly pulled over his eyes. Especially near the storytellers.

One had a prime position near the main entrance and had a crate to stand on. At her feet a young boy had a sheaf of papers – selling the news for a copper a time. Another storyteller had set up over the way, and the two of them were competing to see who could be the loudest and most sensational, if not especially truthful if past experience was anything to go by. Rumours flew around this square like sparrows, and always had. These weren't stories they were telling, but bits of news, opinions, gossip. Anyone could pay them to say anything – and Vocho had, in the past. More than once. A name doesn't make itself, after all.

The woman was telling everyone that there was no war brewing, that the prelate was in full control. Ikaras would no doubt agree to negotiations and all rumours to the contrary were just the whinings of nay-sayers. She then moved on to the pirates that were ravaging the coast, pushing up the price of spice.

"Balls!" someone in the audience shouted. "Ain't been no pirates since I were a boy."

A general muttering seemed to agree with him.

"Only reason the price of spice is going up is that the prelate said we all got to buy it," the shouter said.

The woman ignored him and moved smoothly on to something else.

Over the way, the other teller was clearly not quite so in the prelate's pocket. "Taxes on everything," he said, "or taxes on everything the rich don't buy, but the poor need or are made to buy. When did you last see a rich man wearing clogs? Why does a poor man have to buy half a pound of spice a day and pay the same in taxes as a rich man what does the same? To support the sailors, the Reyen traders, Bakar says, but who's supporting us? And flags, we all got to have a purple flag to wave, so the flag makers put up the prices, and purple dye gets a tax on it too!"

It all sounded crazy to Vocho, but a quick look at a stall showed him that purple cloth was double the price of any other colour. At other stalls, there were plenty of people looking and plenty selling, but no one buying. Bread was scarce and expensive with an angry crowd around the baker's door, sugar almost non-existent and going for more, pound for pound, than gold. The only stall that actually looked like it was doing a brisk trade was the spice merchant's, who stamped a little booklet for every customer so they could prove they'd bought their spice for the day. A few guards were randomly checking people's booklets, and Vocho made doubly sure to stay out of their way.

He stopped by a stand selling hot drinks, took a cup of apple tea and almost fell over at the price. The stall had a bench beside it and seemed a place for gossip if the half-dozen conversations were anything to go by. Someone had left a copy of a paper on the bench, and Vocho picked it up, only to hurriedly put it down when he saw an etching of himself on the second page, right under a headline about the prospect of war with Ikaras and the rumour that its king was raising an army near the border. Great, just bloody great. Luckily most people couldn't read so they wouldn't bother with the paper, but anyone could look at a picture even if it didn't do him justice. He pulled his hat down further and scanned the front page.

A call for the prelate to resign dominated, and seemed the main topic of conversation at the stall.

"Better a sane king than an insane prelate. Licio's the best of the councillors at any rate."

"Bloody councillors are just as bad as the nobles ever were. This equality business only means nothing gets done because they're too busy arguing about it. Except taxes. They always agree on bloody taxes."

"Shrive's busy again too. Getting to be just as bad as the old king, Bakar is. At least the king didn't expect us to wave a sodding flag at him for being a tyrannical bastard."

"Be glad if the Ikarans *did* declare war, then maybe we'd get someone with a decent head on their shoulders."

"But they'd be Ikaran shoulders, and we'd be dead in our beds. And you're an idiot. I'd not be glad; I'd be down by the docks stowing away as fast as I could."

"Yeah, but—"

"But nothing, you're still an idiot. No one's glad about war excepting the rich buggers what make money off of it and don't risk their own necks. Here, does that bloke look familiar to you?"

One of the gossipers jerked his head in Vocho's direction, who didn't let them get a better look and, discretion being the better part of keeping his head attached to his shoulders, got himself good and lost in the crowds. He found Kacha and Cospel as arranged, by the bodyguard pen. Kacha in particular looked pensive.

"It's crazy," she said in answer to Vocho's question. "Or the prelate is. Taxes on everything, war looming. They had bread riots down at the docks last week. No iron or coal coming down from the mines on the border because of the whole Ikaras thing, so half the clockers' factories are just spinning their wheels. Ikarans sending more and more men to the border, and the prelate's worried about bloody flags."

"Ikaras again. That keeps cropping up," Vocho replied. "As does my name and face."

She grinned. "You always wanted to be famous, Voch, and now you are."

"I'd rather be alive and famous, thanks very much." He peered up at the sky, where the sun was sliding towards dusk. "Time to get going. Where's Dom?"

Dom was sauntering up an alley between two stalls, managing to look jaunty and smug at the same time.

Cassalily was waiting for them when they got there, half seen in the gathering gloom until she stepped forward. The whirring of her hands was very loud, and Vocho was hypnotised by the wind-ups slowly spiralling out their power.

She smiled regally at them all and picked up the papers along with some newer ones written in a bold clear script.

"Here you are." She handed them to Kacha. "Quite a find. Of course, all their plans will be useless once I become the Clockwork God again. Such blatant disregard for logical truth, such doubting." She sighed. "All shall become purified by fire and truth when I ascend."

"Er, thank you," Kacha managed.

"No, thank you. Look." Cassalily indicated a small table to one side. On it sat a brass clockwork heart, its movements mimicking the rhythmic beating of a human heart. "Thanks to your truths, all of you, I now have my heart. The rest is only a matter of time."

"I, er, I'm pleased for you," Vocho said. "Only won't fitting it hurt?"

She raised an eyebrow. "Clockwork feels no pain. Clockwork feels nothing except the fire of empirical truth and the strength of power in motion. Surely you all know your scripture?"

"Of course," Dom interrupted smoothly, cutting off Vocho's

sarcastic reply. "And I'm sure we all look forward to the Clockwork God truly being among us again. *Don't* we?"

He turned a bland and watery-eyed face to Vocho, forcing a weak "Yes, of course" from him.

Dom twittered out a few more banalities that left the proto-goddess looking giddy with pleasure while the rest of them hurriedly left. He caught up with them at the edge of the roof.

"Such an interesting woman, don't you think?"

Kacha gave him a pointed look. "If interesting means crazier than a bag of foxes, then yes, she's interesting. But not as interesting or as pertinent to our future as what she's given us. Come on, let's see what we've got."

The streets were busy, and it would take them a long time to squeeze their way back to the Hammer and Tongs at this time of day, so they found a little tavern with a courtyard garden in the back that was both quiet and not overlooked. A trellis covered in grapevines hid the last of the setting sun as they took a table set with little brass lamps and spread out what they had.

It didn't take long before the fading heat of the day seemed as cold as winter in the north to Vocho.

"What the hells is this?" he asked at last, though he could see it plain enough. He just wanted to make sure he wasn't imagining it.

Kacha looked as shaken as he felt. "Well," she said at last. "This is an agreement between the king and the Ikaran government, handing over certain Reyen mining and trade interests in return for support from the Ikaran army, and promising the death of the prelate's diplomatic envoy as a show of good faith. I suspect he wouldn't have given away nearly as much in concessions, so it was worth it to the Ikarans to have him dead. This diplomatic envoy I seem to recall being a certain priest." She cast Vocho a hard look, but all he could do was shrug and shake his head. "This is a loan agreement with the Bank of Ikaras for a staggering amount of money, and this is a message from Dom's old university stating that they'd be delighted to assist the king, and that three have been sent. Three what it doesn't specify."

"Hopefully not people who think they're the second coming of the Clockwork God."

"Voch, you plank, this is serious. If we could at least attempt to keep our wandering minds on it for more than a few seconds?"

He held up his hands. "All right, all right. Bang goes getting any money for this then."

"Oh, I know a few people who'd pay for this," Dom said. His eyes had stopped watering and he looked oddly sharp.

"We have to warn the prelate," Kacha said, "or Eneko. We have to warn *some*one."

"Do we?" Vocho said. "It was better for a while, but now the prelate's no better than the old king was."

"Voch, this is important, and the prelate is our head of state. He may be going slightly round the twist, but until recently he wasn't doing so badly. People weren't starving down on the docks, most people had jobs, and yes the clockers are a bunch of rich arseholes and it wasn't perfect, but things were better than before. *Were*. We swore an oath to protect Reyes if it came to it, and I'd say finding out whether the prelate is really cracked counts. As does preventing a bloody revolution. And this *is* revolution we're talking here; we can't just ignore it. Whose heads do you think will top the walls around the Shrive this time? Ours? All those poor buggers in the square today? Do you *want* a magician behind the ruler of Reyes? We have to warn Bakar, or someone. Eneko maybe. Look at this one."

Kacha handed over the last translation. Most of it was a lot of legal-sounding words that made little sense to Vocho even if they had been translated. But Kacha tapped a portion at the bottom, and Vocho saw what she meant: "*Lord Petri*

Egimont, Duke of Elona and Master of the Duelling Guild of Reyes". Dated the day after that bloody priest had died.

Vocho went back to the top of the paper. After a bit of squinting, he realised it was an assurance that the guild wouldn't get in the way of Ikaras mining the iron seams that were the source of the long-running border dispute, that in fact the guild would remove the duellists that currently guarded said iron seams and instead place them at Ikaras's disposal. A guild that it looked like Petri bloody Egimont was intent on taking over.

Kacha pinched the bridge of her nose. Vocho hadn't a clue what she was thinking, but Egimont co-signing this the day after it all went wrong with Kacha stank like week-old shark meat. And the guild – they may have been thrown out, but the guild was everything to Vocho. All he'd wanted from the start of all this was to get back in, get his old name back, his old *life* back. Fat chance of that with Petri in charge. Any way he sliced it, it looked like Vocho was going to end up on the block, Kacha with him. Unless, of course, they stopped a revolution.

"So, what do you want to do?" he asked faintly. Maybe she was right – maybe warning Eneko was the best thing to do. It might get the guild back on their side if nothing else, and that might be the best way to avoid being executed. Even Bakar wouldn't go openly against the guild. But they had to get to Eneko without being arrested, obviously. Warning Eneko and Bakar about this was the good thing. That didn't make it the easy thing.

There was a clink behind them, the sound of something being wound and the scrape of steel on leather.

"I'd suggest giving yourselves up," Egimont said in the cultured drawl that always made Vocho want to hit him.

How in hells had he . . .? It didn't matter. What mattered was that Egimont stood in the dark doorway that led inside the tavern, that a rattle at the little gate at the rear of the courtyard suggested he wasn't alone and that someone was definitely winding something up. A gun on closer inspection, one of the new revolving jobs that held ten shots. Something a sword wasn't much use against in most circumstances. Vocho *really* needed to get the hang of guns.

Egimont stepped forward, and he at least wasn't using a gun, though one was at his waist. A duellist at heart, always too fond of sticking to the rules. Something which might give Vocho an advantage. He flipped a quick glance at the papers and then to Kacha. A flicker of her eyelid – agreement.

"Hands off weapons would be a nice start. I see you've even got the papers with you. Good. Saves time," Egimont said. "I'd quite like my sword back too, Kacha, if it's all the same." There was something about his voice that wasn't quite right, some hitch to it when he spoke her name, an odd, almost quizzical look to his eyes.

Dom grinned knowingly at the use of Kacha's real name, and Vocho had a split second to think. *All the time he knew who we were. He knew but said nothing, didn't turn us in. Who* is *he?*

Two men came to flank Egimont as another three came through the back gate, guns wound and ready. Kacha spared them a sneer and slid the scabbard from her waist. "You can stick it up with your ring," she said.

Vocho tensed, ready for it even though he didn't know what it would be. Trouble with Kacha was it was impossible to tell.

She hefted the scabbard, and she and Egimont stared at each other for a long moment that seemed stretched to breaking before he inclined his head in an if-you-please manner and held out his spare hand for it. Vocho wasn't surprised to see a scrap of blood-marked paper tucked into his glove.

Kacha bounced the blade in one hand, threw it at Egimont

– he knew her well enough to flinch back – and grabbed for the hilt as it went, neatly pulling it from the scabbard, which despite Egimont's efforts bounced off his shoulder.

Vocho had moved as soon as Kacha threw. He leaped up, grabbed for the overhanging trellis and, using his momentum, swung at Egimont. Eggy, already off balance, caught a solid boot on one shoulder, which twisted him round and sent him crashing into one of his men.

Dom seemed to have moved fast too. Vocho could already hear his apologies as he used his sword on the men by the gate, but at least he hadn't stabbed himself. A shot pinged off the wall by Vocho's ear. Egimont's second flank man brought his gun to bear on Vocho, but he was too slow – a smack in the mouth made him stagger back into another group of Egimont's men. Who didn't look too happy about it.

Vocho took two great steps back out of the door and around to the side, out of their line of sight. Kacha had swept up the papers and shoved them inside her shirt, and Cospel was giving her a leg up over the wall – always the plan if they needed to get something away. Even when Vocho had grown bigger than her, she could still outrun him. He didn't plan to be long following her either.

Dom was swatting men with his sword, then ran one through the shoulder – accidentally by the looks of it – with a cry of "Sorry!" and turned towards Vocho, before his eyebrows pretty much went through his hairline and he dived to one side. A bullet cracked from the doorway by Vocho and smacked into the back wall of the courtyard in a puff of terracotta paint and brick dust. It was probably very petty of Vocho to notice that, at last, Dom had a crease in his shirt.

Vocho nodded towards Cospel, where he still waited, hands clasped. Dom shook his head and bounced back up, sword at the ready, cloak swept back, looking every inch the dapper duellist. Vocho shrugged and grabbed for a chair. Brute force was going to work best here. Another shot flew out of the doorway, but the man reached out just too far and got the chair across his wrist for his trouble. Vocho followed that up with a roundhouse smack into the doorway, was rewarded with a crunch and a lot of swearing, dropped the chair and pulled out his sword.

Using the distraction, Dom had managed to get to the other side of the door. They looked at each other, and all the twittering idiocy was gone from Dom's face. Instead he winked at Vocho, put up his sword like a professional, grabbed a chair and inclined his head. "After you."

"If you insist."

They swung through the doorway within half a second of each other and were faced with three guns and a seriously pissed-off Egimont.

"An impasse, perhaps, gentlemen?" Egimont said.

"A fuck-up for you, you mean. Kass has taken your papers. And we know what they say too."

A strange sort of smile from Egimont, somewhat sly and cold and hot at the same time. It made a shudder weave its way through Vocho's balls.

"That doesn't matter," Egimont said. "See, you forget I know you and your sister. Quite well, for my sins. I had people all around the walls. She may have got away from me; she won't have got away from them."

A moment of panic but then Dom stepped in, and he sounded nothing like his usual self – his voice was firm and decisive. "Funny that. Because I heard a lot of swearing behind that wall, and none of it was her. How sure are you of those people?"

Egimont laughed under his breath. "Found someone with as much idiotic bravado as yourself then, Vocho? Weapons *down* now, please. I won't ask again." He indicated the piece of blood-marked paper from his glove. "I don't know what this does. I only know I'm to use it in an emergency, and to make sure I'm not standing too close." A strange look came to his eyes, as though remembering something long past. "They can vaporise a man where he stands, you know that? I saw it once. A spell almost as deadly for the magician as the victim because it needs so much blood, so they don't do it often. Unless the blood isn't theirs, obviously. And the Prelate's put a lot of people in the Shrive just lately. No one misses one or two."

Vocho flicked his gaze about – a man and a woman, both holding guns, wound up and ready. Egimont with a spell at hand. Three more men on the floor groaning – it wouldn't be long before they were up.

This called for special measures. Vocho would have preferred Kacha to be there – she'd have known what he was doing – but Dom was looking sharp. Had to be worth a go.

His sword was up before he knew it. Even against a gun, a good swordsman stood a chance. If he was quick, if he took them by surprise.

He did.

His sword arrowed for Egimont's face, and Dom was half a second behind, his sword slashing at a hand holding a gun, his boot kicking out at another.

The trouble with guns was that people came to rely on them. They forgot about speed or strength or a plan. Like a sword, a gun was only as good as the person holding it.

Still, numbers counted for a lot too. He and Dom were outnumbered, and at least one of the people opposite them – Eggy – was no slouch with his blade, and he had a gun too. He used both to good effect almost immediately. Vocho only barely managed to duck the vicious slash, and was pretty sure he lost some hair, but had no time to consider it as the barrel of Eggy's gun came into contact with his neck.

He was already rolling away, looking for his best chance before Petri blew his brains out when he saw another barrel pointing his way, and another. There was nowhere left to go. He stood up slowly with his hands out, though he kept hold of his blade and all the while he was looking for a gap, a chance. Somewhere over to his left Dom was engaged in a battle of apologies with two more of Eggy's men.

"I'm rather glad Kacha isn't here," Eggy said as he moved forward, wary as a kicked cat. "It makes it so much easier."

"Easier to do what?" Vocho had a rough idea what Eggy intended, and it wasn't to shake hands and let bygones be bygones.

Eggy smiled, and it was no warmer than before. "I'm supposed to keep you alive, but . . . Well, I have this little piece of paper, you see, and it's most tempting to use it. Most tempting to say that I had to, that I had no other choice and get you out of my life for good. Out of Kacha's life, which can only be good after all the ways you've screwed things up for her."

"You're very considerate. I'm sure she'll thank you," Vocho said, still looking for a way out. "Though if I were you I'd also consider that she's a vengeful woman, and killing her brother might set her off."

"You might consider, brother dearest, all you've done to her over the years. When I bring her back into the guild, she probably will thank me."

Vocho had to concede he had a point.

Petri slid the paper out of his glove, leaving a dark red smear behind it. How long did it take for the blood to dry? Vocho wondered. Did they do something to it to keep it damp longer? It didn't matter because this blood was still gleaming wetly.

That piece of paper loomed large in Vocho's mind, made his back itch and burn in some half-remembered nightmare. He wanted to run – anywhere, didn't matter, just not be here – and that thought was so strange it left him speechless for perhaps the first time in his life. He'd never run from a fair fight – from an arrest warrant for murder or an unfair fight, yes, but from a fair fight, never. He wanted to now. Quite badly.

Eggy tipped his head to one side as though he could see the thought running through Vocho's head. Such a self-possessed bastard, always had been. Eggy looked at the paper for a moment and then stepped forward smartly, dropped it in front of Vocho and stepped back at a much faster pace. The paper fluttered one way and another, and Eggy said a word.

There was nothing to hide behind, no place to go because even though Eggy's companions were retreating, they still had him in their sights. Vocho watched that piece of paper as it flapped down in front of him like it was the end of the world. Vaporised – not the way he'd expected to go.

A strange noise came from his left, and Dom's sword arrowed through the air in front of Vocho and neatly pinned the paper to one of Eggy's cohorts. Eggy didn't stop, and neither did Vocho – they ran out of the tavern like the Clockwork God would grind them in his gears if they stayed. A faint boom followed, along with a sizzle and the odour of freshly cooked meat. It fair made Vocho's stomach turn. Vocho didn't stop running either. He'd accidentally – perhaps – killed a priest, had run and hid and tried to keep his head down. Consequences were bound to follow, but this was getting ridiculous.

He pounded down the street in the opposite direction to a certainly unnerved Eggy and considered himself lucky when, after some twists, turns and doubling back, he found he was on his own.

Interlude

Twelve years earlier

Vocho swore under his breath and wiped sweat from his eyes. No matter what he did, Kacha was always one step ahead. Her face was set now, focused on making sure she won, and he tried to do the same, but the thought of Da and the way he always looked to Kacha first kept popping up. Now Eneko, the guild master, was doing the same, playing favourites. All these years at the guild and Kacha could *still* beat him. At reading, at writing, at everything, and especially the thing that had Vocho ready to spit, at swordplay. Always she got the praise, the smile, the pat on the back from Eneko if not from their guild mates, and he got the "Never mind, son." Even now, the little group of other lessers in the guild – boys and a few girls all about turning into their teens who'd not yet taken their journeyman's test – were rooting for her, not him. They crowded onto a green area in a quiet part of the little strip of land over the river that separated the guild from the rest of Reyes. Technically none of them should be there, but it was an old tradition, this unofficial sparring in sight of the Shrive.

He was getting close, he could feel it. They were of a height now, at last, and that helped. He tried another attack, tried sneaking round on her off side, where she'd be part blinded by the setting sun, but she caught it at the last second and turned his blade.

He recovered well, but that wasn't enough. He wanted to beat her, just once. Just so he could say he had. OK, once probably wouldn't be enough, but it would do to be going on with. Besides, he'd bet a fair sum that he'd win today, money he couldn't afford to lose.

Screw it – screw all the proprieties. Screw all the etiquette of formal sparring and Ruffelo's rules for gentlefolk. The clockwork duellist, unofficial goddess to the Clockwork God, who watched over the guild, wasn't overseeing this fight so the rules could get stuffed. He changed his stance slightly, subtly, to the more free-form Icthian style, where rules were what other people kept to and impulse, speed and brute force were the order of the day. They'd only just started learning it – Eneko insisted that this style wasn't for duelling or sparring but for working – but Vocho had known it was more his sort of style from the off.

She noticed his move – no matter how subtle he thought he'd been – and made to counter it, but not quickly enough. He went for her, three quick thrusts to the face that would have had him kicked out of the arena in a heartbeat. She skipped back. The little crowd cheered and Vocho ground his teeth as they called her name, exhorted her to just beat him and get it over with.

Kacha allowed herself a small grin at his expense, and that's when he lost it. *Always* she won. *Always* she was the favourite. *Always* she was one step ahead, leaving him second best. Kacha the golden, Kacha who'd never known the end of Da's belt, who'd had all his attention and praise. Perfect bloody Kacha. Afterwards he was never sure, not really. He always told her it was an accident, and maybe it was. Or maybe it was his first really big lie.

He thrust and thrust again followed by a flurry of brutal

overhand blows that forced her back. His first bit of luck
– he caught her blade with his and they struggled, faces an
inch apart before he managed to shove her back. And was
his foot in the way on purpose? Did he yank it back against
her leg, too quick to see, making her overbalance? If he did,
well, that was the Icthian style for you. Never use only your
sword; use anything and everything you've got.

He told himself afterwards that he'd not realised how
close to the edge she was. He told himself that he'd not
meant it, but he was lying, and inside the darkest part of
him he knew it. His greatest lies were always those he told
his inner self.

That part of him crowed when she fell and didn't stop
when her stumbling recovery pitched her over the edge and
into the darkly rushing waters of the Reyes river. He stared
at the spot where she'd gone over for long seconds by the
ticking of the nearby Clockwork God before he scrambled
after the rest down the steep bank to where thick green
reeds clogged the water. Panic rose like a tide when he
realised she wasn't sitting up, spluttering in the shallows,
wasn't cursing his name as she clambered ashore. When he
realised that the waters had closed over her like she'd never
been.

Yet still he hadn't been the first in the water. That had
been Petri Egimont, naturally. He'd left the guild – no one
would say why – so he wasn't allowed within the walls, but
he liked to come and see the sparring on the bridge sometimes, sitting silent and watchful and somehow reproachful,
as though his leaving was their fault. Petri dived in as soon
as he reached the shore, searching among the reeds and
trawling the riverbed, coming up for breath and then diving
again. Vocho stood staring at the spot where Kacha had
disappeared before a splash of water revived him and he
joined in, wading into the deeper parts by the bridge stan-
chions, calling Kacha's name. He thrashed around for what

felt like hours but couldn't have been more than a minute before he felt something on his leg. A hand.

When he pulled her out, she was coughing up lungfuls of water, cold as a week-dead fish but alive, and that was almost all that mattered. Almost, because he might not want her dead – there was that long-ago promise to Da, if nothing else, and he did love his sister when he remembered to – but he couldn't still that dark little voice in his heart, telling him he had to beat her, had to be better, whatever it took, if he wanted Da to see him over the glow of the perfect Kacha.

She lay on the grass, coughing up water for a long time. Petri hovered at Vocho's elbow, but he ignored the fool.

"You saved me," Kacha said in the end, sounding surprised.

"What happened?" someone else asked, Vocho didn't know who, but he cursed them in his head.

Kacha shook her head, sending water flying from her hair. "Tripped, I think, and too close to the edge. Should have been more careful. That'll teach me, right?"

Vocho laughed with the rest of them, relief flowing from them all like the rush of the river. All except Petri, who watched Vocho with a care that made his heart miss a beat. He said nothing, did nothing overt, but it was plain all the same. Petri knew.

Chapter Fourteen

Kacha kept her head down in the tailor's shop where she was hiding as two swordsmen went past. She worked her way further into the shop – it was the perfect place to hide for a little while, until any pursuit was gone. Rack upon rack of shirts in every imaginable colour were crammed against breeches, tunics, cloaks, dresses, scarves so there was barely room to pass between. She almost felt if she pushed far enough, she'd walk out into a different city under a different sun, and wished that she could. Maybe under another sun she could be another person: one who didn't have to be perfect, didn't get betrayed, wasn't forced into being the sensible one whether she wanted it or not.

The shopkeeper came, shoving his way through his merchandise with practised ease, but she waved him away and pretended to browse, keeping an eye on the doorway and the street outside as much as she could.

What the hells was Petri about? It didn't seem like him at all, not the man she knew. She needed to look at the papers again, somewhere quiet, and she needed some answers.

When Eneko had given her and Vocho that last job, he'd said the priest had "important business" to attend to and needed a small discreet escort. She hadn't asked much more

— for a long time she'd been doing as Eneko asked without question because she trusted him. While she'd lately had her suspicions about the dark jobs he gave her, she had no reason to wonder about a normal job like this. Vocho had just been happy with the price.

They hadn't asked questions then, but it was time to start now. She pushed her way back to the front of the shop, cast a careful eye over the street, saw nothing to alarm her, no Petri or his men, and hurried to the one place that might be able to tell her what she needed to know.

The streets were quiet, eerily so, as though the population could feel some storm coming and had shuttered themselves away. She kept her hood up against a chill evening breeze dragging wisps of scrawny fog through the streets, and against any chance of being seen. The streets were empty but the church was crowded — it always was.

The church was a marvel, everyone said so, built soon after the prelate came to power on the ruins of a Castan temple to the Clockwork God, resurrecting his worship along with the god himself. The huge main doors ran on clockwork, linked to the same great waterwheels that powered the change o' the clock, the bronze duellist at the guild and the Clockwork God that sat between the guild and the palace. Above the church door was inscribed "the only comfort is truth".

Inside there was no representation of him — the statue by the guild *was* the Clockwork God in people's minds. He moved and clanked and took people's truths to his metal heart to power him, so they said. Instead, inside the church were a hundred, thousand, other things. Offerings to him, and some to the duellist, who people said was his age-old consort back when Reyes was part of an empire. Since the Great Fall the Clockwork God had been sleeping, waiting for people to be able to understand him. They might have said that he forgave them for believing in other gods while he slept, but the Clockwork God didn't forgive or condemn, he collected truth and made sure the world carried on in its prescribed motions.

The church whirred and whizzed with the sound of clock-work under the light of a thousand lamps. Toys, hammers, grinders, buzzing trinkets of all shapes and sizes. Skittering around the edge were uncountable numbers of the little votives the smaller clockers sold, intricate and shining, like golden spiders scurrying to build their webs.

At the centre of the church was a marvel that still, even now, amazed her: the tree. Made of beaten gold and silver, it shone in the flickering light, the leaves moving in a non-existent breeze. Bronze birds sang in the branches, and one, a tiny little thing all decked out in brilliant blue lapis lazuli to mimic a real trunkwalker, pattered up and down the golden bole of the tree, taking people's truths, they said. Taking them from the roots of the tree to the crown, where the Clockwork God could find them.

The rest of the church was just as fine. The walls were covered in moving murals that depicted the Clockwork God's rise all that time ago and how he'd died when the Castans no longer understood his purpose, how he caused their empire to fall for their arrogance; how he'd chosen Bakar, shown him the way to work the gears and read the truth in his movements. Kacha wasn't so sure, but it seemed as good a thing to believe in as any, and plenty of people did believe, or wanted to at any rate. A few kept to the gods she'd been brought up with, the false gods the priests now called them, invented by man to fill the void after the Clockwork God died. Only a few, and they did it in secret.

She stepped over the spidery votives as they scuttled across the floor, and went to find a priest. There were several about, winding up offerings, taking votives and truths, dispensing advice. A younger priest turned towards her with a smile when she approached. "Can I help you?"

"I was wondering, could I talk to you for a minute?"

She was staring at Kacha's face oddly, especially at the scar under her eye. Kacha ducked her head, but perhaps too late. Still, the priest said nothing about it. "Certainly. Over here perhaps, where it's more private."

The priest was young, too young to have had to make the choice between the old gods and the resurrected Clockwork God, a choice that had led to a revolt among the clergy and a few of them joining the king and nobles in the bloody square before the Shrive. It had only taken one or two executions for the rest to see which way the wind blew. Some embraced the Clockwork God like he had never been away, others doubtless merely pretended and the rest made themselves scarce or found a new profession.

This priest had ochre skin with a flush of sombre pink on her cheeks, inky hair that kinked all ways and was barely held in check by a white band, dark eyes lidded against the light or perhaps only against troublesome thoughts and a mouth that looked like it could keep secrets. She exuded calm and the impression that whatever you told her would be shared with no one but the Clockwork God. She led Kacha to a cubicle set aside for just this sort of thing. Two chairs, a small table with a jug of water and some glasses. The priest sat down, fiddling with the mark of her profession which dangled from a chain around her neck, a ball that moved and clicked and slid and wound so that if you looked too long your eyes went strange.

Kacha sat too, and the priest didn't wait for her to start. "I know who you are. Kacha. Your brother killed Sendoa."

She sat very still, waiting. No point denying it, after all. If she had to, Kacha could get out of here with no problem.

A sudden smile from the priest. "You aren't your brother though. While the guild still wants you found, the church has no quarrel with you even if the prelate does. All your truths are well kept here; nothing goes beyond these walls except to the Clockwork God. What is it you were wanting?"

"Sendoa. I . . . I'm not sure whether Vocho killed him."
The priest raised an eyebrow. "Not sure?"

Something about this priest, with her calm smile and attentive look, made Kacha want to spill it all out, every last thing. It'd been inside too long, and she'd no one to tell it to. "I don't think . . . OK, maybe he did." The first time she'd really admitted the possibility to herself. "Maybe he did, but that's not Vocho. He's not a killing sort of man, unless he has to on guild business. Only then, I swear. But . . ."

"But you aren't sure?"

She sat in silence for a long moment. Vocho was her brother, and she loved the annoying little sod, but . . . It always came back to *but*. Still, there was something more to this. Something Vocho hadn't told her, perhaps didn't know himself.

"You know they held a trial in his absence?" The priest offered her some water, but she declined with a shake of her head.

"They did?"

The priest reached out and patted her hand like she was about to tell Kacha someone was dead and was sorry about it. "Your brother killed him, there can be no doubt. For money, it looks like. Did you know about the gambling debts?"

"*What?*"

And then the priest told her the rest.

Interlude

Twelve years earlier

Kacha knocked on the door and waited.

She'd been in Guild Master Eneko's rooms often enough before, but there was something about his note that had set her senses on edge. He'd used a note for starters, when it was more usual to send one of the first years, who took turns being messengers when they weren't drilling basics or learning to read. Yet today a note via a boy she knew could hardly read yet. The note hadn't said much – a summons to Eneko's quarters with an aside that she tell no one where she was going. She'd folded the paper into little squares, hidden it in the pocket of her breeches and made for Eneko's just past the dinner bell, when everyone would be in the mess.

It was probably nothing, but her hands were jittery as she answered the soft "Come in." Maybe nothing – and maybe something.

Eneko stood watching out of his window, his back to her. Beyond him the sun was setting and faint cries wound up from the harbour along with the smell of salt and fish. The smell of home, though she'd tried to forget it. But it seemed that Eneko always smelled of the harbour, and of rich pipe smoke, even though he never smoked it.

She stood waiting quietly and at last Eneko turned with a faint smile. "Sit," he said. "You aren't in trouble."

One reason for her jitters left, to be replaced by another, happier reason. The final test, when a journeyman became a master. They said it sometimes came like this — the test was different for everyone. But she was only fifteen, had only passed her journeyman's a year ago. Still, she knew she was good, maybe even good enough. Eneko kept an eye out for her, watched her practise, gave her advice and praise, and she strove to be perfect for him and for Da. She had to be. If she wasn't perfect, she was nothing.

She sat and tried not to jiggle her legs. Eneko sat down behind his desk and looked at her long and hard, in a way he never had before. She'd been in here so often that the other masters had commented, whispering she was Eneko's favourite. She'd had a few barbed comments to that effect in the halls, but nothing she couldn't handle — years of sparring and duelling, ignoring their taunts as they tried to unnerve her, had left her almost impervious. But all those times he'd never looked at her like this.

Eneko picked up a little statue and turned it, over and over, in one hand, an exercise to loosen the muscles in his wrist after a long-ago injury and something he did when he thought.

"Do you trust me, Kacha?"

She frowned, and her legs stopped jiggling. This wasn't how a test should go. "Yes," she said finally.

"Really? Why is that?"

The answer came smoothly enough. "Because you've always looked after me. Always."

"Because you miss your da?"

The knife edge of it, dulled by years, still surprised her. She wanted to lie, to say no, but Eneko always knew her lies, just like she always knew Vocho's. "Yes."

He nodded, still thinking perhaps. "Do you think I keep secrets? Think closely."

She didn't need to. "Of course. You run the guild. There must be secrets – jobs not meant for all ears, the real identity of some clients. Some things are only for masters to know."

He smiled as though his faith in her had been tested, and she'd passed. "Many secrets. And what do you know of debt?"

She didn't need to think on that at all. "To pay it."

"Would you like to know a secret and help me pay a debt?"

She restrained herself from an outburst, barely. "I'd be honoured, Guild Master."

"Eneko, if you like. I think you've earned it. Or are about to."

The jitters were back, worse than ever. Only masters got to call the guild master by his given name. She was good with a blade, and she knew it, but was she ready for this? She was honest with herself about that doubt and how Vocho would howl unfair but knew she wanted it anyway.

Eneko kept his eyes on hers as he spoke, and she couldn't have torn herself away if she tried.

"You remember the day – your birthday – on the wall? A bad day for the guild. Meant I had to ask a few favours. From people I shouldn't have, and didn't want to, though I was left little choice. A magician."

That made her catch her breath. They'd all heard about what had happened that day up at the palace, how many had died trying to rid the place of magicians. Men vaporised where they stood, women dying, children screaming. They'd heard, but Kacha didn't know anyone who'd seen it, and so part of her – the hard part Vocho called it because he didn't understand – wouldn't believe it.

"The magician saved my life that day, all our lives perhaps, by telling me what was coming so I could prepare. And in return I helped him escape. But I still owe him. And now

I have notice he wants to collect on that debt." Eneko's lips twisted like he'd just bitten into a lemon. "This is a job I'd rather never take, but a job I have to do, and yet is almost impossible for me now. And if I don't pay . . ."

She started to protest, but he waved it away. "I'm getting old. Not too old to be guild master but too slow for this kind of job. So I need someone I can trust. Someone I've been thinking might take over from me when it's time. Will you do it? Remember – only if it seems good to you."

She almost couldn't breathe – to be guild master after Eneko . . . "Of course."

"You can't tell anyone. Not even Vocho. Everyone has secrets as they pass into adulthood. Now so have you. Here, let me show you the job."

He spread out detailed plans for an assassination. Not unheard of but not usual either and something she'd hoped to avoid for as long as she could. But . . . master. *Guild master*.

All the training, the drills, the lessons, had been leading to this one thought. Could she kill a man, not accidentally in a fight but in cold blood? Could she show Eneko just how perfect she was? She had no idea, but she knew the thought of it made sweat sting her eyes. Especially if it was for her own ambition. If she couldn't, she didn't belong in the guild. If she could, what did that make her? The endless struggle, Eneko had called it once, and had also said that the battle was only lost when you stopped struggling – anyone who killed without question was lost.

Eneko showed her the point far above a factory where she could wait, could hide for her mark to come. Showed her just how easy it would be. And he told her who the man was: a clocker, owner of a sweatshop down by Soot Town, a hellish place that Kacha and Vocho always hurried past on their rare days out. And a father, brother, husband, son, though not a good one from what Eneko laid out here

– mistresses galore, a dying mother left in poverty when he was rich. Other things too – the slaves that passed through his hands, got from no-one-knew-where, sold on to no-one-was-sure-who, though Ikaras seemed a fair bet – their sugar plantations, the trade the whole country depended upon, couldn't operate without slaves. One reason the prelate always baulked at negotiating with them. She wondered whether these things were true, or if they were, whether Eneko laid them out because he thought she wouldn't do the job otherwise. She wondered how little he knew her – or how much.

"I know it's a lot to ask," Eneko said quietly. "A lot, and if you do it this won't be the last one I ask of you. You'll need extra training, but we can arrange that. There's time enough. But there's no one else I trust to do it, and I must pay my debt. In return, I'll pay my debt to you by making you my acknowledged apprentice. Does that seem good to you?"

She stared down at the plans for a long while. A job – she'd always known it would be a job they'd task her with for her master's test. Not a guarding job either, or an escort, or anything straightforward. An assassination. A cold-blooded killing, even of a man such as this, a slaver. Was a master's title worth that?

She looked up, ready to say no, it didn't look good to her, to receive the small frown that would be his only reproof – jobs were theirs to take or leave, their morals their own past duty to the guild. If she said no, someone else would do it, someone else would get their master's title. Vocho perhaps, with his lusting ambition and lack of scruples. Eneko would invite someone else to share his chamber of an evening, someone else to play cards with and laugh with, teach all his little tricks with the blade to. Someone else for him to be father to, as he'd been to her.

It wasn't for the guild she said it, nor fear of the magician and what he'd do to Eneko if this job wasn't done, though that was part of it, she told herself. But not just that, nor that this clocker was as bad as the nobles had been before the revolt, nor Eneko's debt, or hers to him for taking her into the guild in the first place. It was because he smelled of pipe smoke and salt, like Da, because he was all the da she'd had for a long time, and she wanted that to continue. Because she wanted to bask in his approval as she had in Da's, and life had been cold without it. Because to refuse the job was to refuse to be a master, become a duellist when that's all she'd ever wanted. To refuse her test was to leave the guild, her home, and know that she could have had it all if she'd had the nerve.

"It seems good to me."

She swallowed back the spurt of acid in her throat and told herself it was only the truth.

Later, much later, after weeks of extra training, longer weeks of watching her mark, of seeing that he was exactly the kind of man Eneko said he was, she sat in her room and stared at the blood on her shaking hands, on her blades. The acid was back in her throat worse than ever, but she swallowed it down.

"Perfect. You were perfect." Eneko put a hand on her shoulder, and that, and his words, his voice sounding just like Da's, were enough to stop the shakes. For now. She was pretty sure she'd be shaking in her dreams later.

"But I—"

"Got the job done. It's always hard, especially like this. Always a fight in yourself. Worry when you don't have to fight it any more. Look at me. Look. That's it. There'll be other jobs, but I promise I'll never ask you to kill anyone who doesn't fully deserve it. Put your trust in me and I'll look after you. You saw the man he was, saw what he did, didn't you? Saw what needed to be done and did it. You handled it well, and I'm proud of you."

She blinked hard, took a deep breath and nodded. That was all she wanted: him to be proud, so she could imagine that Da was proud too.

As if reading her mind he said, "I'm your father. I have been since the day I brought you here. I'm father to everyone in this guild, but now most especially you. Because you and I have a little secret now, and both of us is depending on the other to say nothing. A *breath* of this, and the prelate will have us, have the whole guild. He tries hard enough anyway, all the time, trying to find ways to bring me down." He smiled, and there was a hint of sadness to it, she thought. "But I can rely on you, trust you. That I know. And you can trust me, with anything. Now go on, get the blood off those blades before they rust."

He left her to clean her blades and her hands, but no matter how she scrubbed it seemed like they'd never be clean, and she was still there when dawn came, thinking about dead men and trust.

Chapter Fifteen

Vocho was on his own. Dom had disappeared into one of the nooks and crannies of the city. Gods only knew where Cospel was. He had to get back to the Hammer and Tongs, find Kacha and work out what they were going to do with the papers, if anything. Maybe just get out of the city, a prospect that was looking more and more tempting, no matter what his heart told him was the good and right thing to do.

He popped his head out from the shadowy doorway. The alley was cluttered with barrels but otherwise reasonably clear and dark enough now the sun had set. Still, didn't do to be careless. Just a shame no one would see.

The barrels helped. By the time the clocks started chiming the next quarter-hour, he was up on the roofs, picking his careful way through the thickets of shanties. He doubted Egimont knew these sorts of places existed, never mind actually thought of looking for Vocho there. He was safe, for now.

He made his way as quick and quiet as he knew how to be, which in fairness wasn't all that quiet because he could never resist an opportunity to show off even if no one was watching. The few gaunt faces he saw paid him little attention – they'd learned up here the hard way not to see too much. Another few minutes and he was on the roof of an old-fashioned blacksmith's forge opposite the Hammer and Tongs.

No clockwork hammer or bellows in this smith's, just honest-to-goodness sweat and muscle. Probably explained why the place was falling down. By the look of it, all the smith could offer was craftsmanship. He didn't look up from his anvil as Vocho dropped silently through a gaping hole in one corner of the roof, but carried on hammering a cherry-red tongue of metal by the light of the forge and a mean lamp.

"Hope you ain't bringing the guards with you," he said between blows. "They play merry hells with my work. I don't got no automatons to do it for me while they piss about asking stupid questions and waiting for a bribe."

"Not this time," Vocho said. I hope, he added in his head, but he was pretty sure no one had followed him. Pretty sure. He dug out a coin, flicked it towards the smith's apprentice and peeked out of the doorway.

"Looking for anything special?" The smith doused the metal in a barrel of water, sending steam up in a cloud. "I see a lot for men with silver in their pockets."

The street was quiet, and so was the inn. "Just my sister," he said. "Fair hair, scar under one eye. Blue shirt today, I think."

The smith appeared to ponder for a moment. "Nice sword. Nothing fancy, but looked like it could do the job. Duellist's sword, looked like to me. Had one of them twisty hilts they all love so much. Like yours. Stupid if you ask me, but no one asks me much these days."

Vocho gave him a sharp look, but the man's face was all innocence. "Sounds like her. Not a duellist though."

The smith raised an eyebrow, but another dig in Vocho's pockets stopped that.

"Went in at the top o' the clock. Looked flustered. Maybe because her brother's watching her?"

Vocho ignored that, took a deep breath of relief, checked the street again to find it quiet under the lamplight and left the smith to his work. The plan was simple – get in, get Kacha, get out. It had all seemed straightforward when they'd found the chest. Just find out what the papers said and find out who wanted them enough to pay for them so they could buy their old lives back. Now things were complicated and far too dangerous. The guild and prelate after them on the one hand, which was bad enough, Egimont and a magician on the other. All wanting them dead. Dumping the papers probably wouldn't work either – Egimont had a grudge to settle if nothing else, and he was a methodical man. A nice quiet life in the country was looking more appealing every second.

The inn was almost empty – it wouldn't fill up until the whistle went to signal the end of the working day in the clocker factories in perhaps half an hour. A couple of older men sat in one corner, playing some game that seemed to involve lots of little clacking tiles, copious amounts of beer and some hefty betting. The betting made Vocho fingers itch, but he didn't have time. Maybe later. Definitely later.

Two lads were cleaning tables, and the great hulk behind the bar was the same one as before, but the person sitting at the table by the fire caught his attention. She would have caught the attention of the Clockwork God himself. It wasn't that she was beautiful. It wasn't even mostly that she was dressed like a queen in silks and pearls and a shift dress that clung and revealed at the same time it hid, though it certainly made her stand out. It was the way she looked at him when he walked in, held up a glass of wine red as blood and toasted him. Like she'd been waiting for him.

He took another look around – no one unusual, certainly no Egimont or any of his friends. The woman patted the chair next to her in invitation.

He should get upstairs, out of sight, but this woman had seen him already and either recognised him from before his disgrace, in which case he had to find out what else she knew, or from since they'd returned to Reyes, in which case he still needed to find out.

Keeping a careful eye out, just in case, and with a casual hand resting on his sword hilt, also just in case, Vocho sauntered over to her and bowed.

"The very person I'm looking for." Her voice was deep for a woman, with a strange accent he couldn't quite place.

He tried on a smile. "Are you sure?" Now he was up close, she looked hauntingly familiar, but when he tried to pin down where he'd seen her all he got were cloudy memories involving a dead priest.

"Oh, certain. Do sit, Vocho."

He fell into the chair like a dropped anchor. Did he know her? He was sure he didn't, but a tug at the back of his mind said otherwise. Something about the voice, the eyes, reminded him of . . . of . . . of the magician's hands in the carriage. Which was stupid. Why would that be?

"You have the advantage of me," he said.

"You look a little shaken. Here, have some wine. It's very good. Alicia will suffice, as far as names go."

"How do you know me?" he asked, more to play for time than anything. He'd lost his hat in the kerfuffle with Egimont, and he'd forgotten to put his hood up. Half the city might have recognised him by now, even in the dark.

"Oh, I'm *such* a fan of yours. Went to all your duels, you know. Such romance in the guild, don't you think? Honourable men and women, keeping to the old ways, the old codes. And you had a certain style about you – panache. Enough to turn a girl's head."

He took a sip of the wine and studied her over the rim of the glass. She was toying with him, a soft twist of the lips as though she was playing at being a cat to his mouse.

"You don't look like a hanger-on." His voice sounded harsh next to hers, his response petulant and sullen.

A smile at that, a narrowing of the eyes. "No. I'm just a poor woman come to tell you something you should know."

"Which is?"

She stood up and let a soft hand fall on his shoulder as though she didn't want to say, but it would be for his own good. "You aren't the only one with a secret. Maybe you should ask your sister what she's been keeping from you. After all you did for her, killing that priest to save her, and she still lies to you. Do enjoy your wine."

She swept off before Vocho could even let out a bewildered "What?" only to stop before she got to the door. Her face went from serene to fake-girlish, and she fluttered her eyelashes most unconvincingly. "I shall tell *all* my friends about this. The day I met the great duellist! We sat at the same table, and *every*thing."

Vocho sat for a few moments, trying to think, but he couldn't make any sense of the encounter apart from that she'd made him uneasy.

She was dangerous, he knew that well enough. As soon as Kacha, Dom and Cospel came back, they were moving to another inn or maybe some lodgings somewhere out of the way or out of Reyes entirely while they worked out how they'd warn the prelate or whether it might be better to just cut and run. Besides he was still feeling as though someone was watching him. Ridiculous because in a city the size of Reyes Egimont would never find them if he searched all year, except he'd found them at the tavern, and how had he managed that? Vocho fought the urge to look over his shoulder every other step as he went up the stairs and only barely won.

It didn't get much better when he got into his room, because Kacha was there pacing up and down by the lamp, and as soon as he entered she launched into him.

"What in seven hells did you think you were doing?"

He was feeling a bit fragile as it was, and her question

only confused him more. "Well, I thought if I dealt with Eggy, you could get away and—"

"Not that, you idiot." That stung. It was what Da had always called him instead of his name, but Kacha was his daughter in more ways than one. She stalked up to Vocho, her hand tight on the hilt of her sword, lips white with rage. That's what happened when she was *really* pissed off. At least she had no belt like Da, and he could take her in a sword fight if he had to, and it looked like he might have to.

She gave him a prod in the chest with a finger like a small dagger and he dropped into a chair. She took a step back and a deep breath, and took her hand away from her sword. It was only then Vocho realised that she'd actually thought about using it.

"Sendoa. Every time I asked, you swore, you *swore* it wasn't you. And fool that I was, I believed you, I stood up for you. But you never said exactly what *did* happen, did you? No, you skirted around it in typical Vocho fashion, and I didn't push because, well, because I thought you hadn't done it and I knew whatever you *did* say would only be a lie. Well, I'm pushing now. Tell me. *Everything*. And tell it true, or I swear by the Clockwork God's mechanical heart I will tie you up and take you to Petri myself."

He looked at her for long ticks of the clock, at the doubt behind her eyes. She'd never doubted him before, not once, and it was shame that had kept his mouth clamped shut.

"I don't know everything. It's true – I swear it!"

"Then tell me what you *do* know. Like about these gambling debts of yours."

"Ah."

"Yes. 'Ah.' Well?"

Vocho turned on his considerable charm and a smile that could have felled angels at twenty paces. Not that it would get him anywhere with Kacha, who knew him far too well, but old habits died hard. "They aren't that bad, really. A few bulls here and there. I . . . Actually that's another thing I don't really recall." Which was odd. He could remember some of it, but bits were missing, big bits too. The weeks before Sendoa were a blurry mess.

"How many is 'a few bulls'? Because I heard that not only is it a lot more than a few and not only do you owe people who you really don't want to owe money to, but that's why you sold out your job, Voch, sold out the guild, your name, everything. Why you sold *us* out."

He opened his mouth to say something, though only the Clockwork God knew what, but his left eye started twitching.

"You lied to me the whole time, didn't you?" Kacha said, her voice cold and quiet now, silent ice waiting for a wrong step to send a man sprawling. "I believed you the whole *fucking* time, and you were lying. I told Petri where to shove his ring because I believed you when you told me you didn't do it. I should have known better, shouldn't I, than to trust you about anything at all. Tell me now, all of it, every last scrap, or so help me I'll scalp you."

He hesitated a long time. If he said nothing she'd leave. If he told her she'd leave. If he lied she'd leave. Him and Kacha, always the two of them even when they grated on each other like two rusty cogs. Even when he hated her, always so damned perfect and expecting him to be exactly the same *sort* of perfect. Yet they always had each other's back, always had the weight of years, of their whole lives, behind them. Just the two of them against the world.

"I owe a lot," he said in the end. "Maybe three, four thousand in total. That much is true enough, I think, though it's all hazy, that whole time. But I only owe people I know, friends. No one was calling it in. And I didn't sell anyone out. I don't think."

"What then? If not that, then exactly what did happen?"

"I . . ." He almost couldn't say it. He barely even wanted

to think it, but the look on her face told him he had to. "The magician on the coach. I saw him before, though it took me a while to remember. I didn't know what he was then, not until the coach. I saw him at the priest's house. I was there, and he came, I think, and . . . and . . . the shapes on his hands kept moving. That's all I really remember, that the shapes on his hands kept moving, and blood, lots of it. A pain on my back. Hurt a lot – still does sometimes, like in the coach when I saw him."

Now he'd started, it *spurted* out of him like springs from a broken clock. He had to tell her it all before she went and left him alone.

"Then he was gone, and everything was, I don't know, all kind of dark and fuzzy, but the stupid priest was there. Praying to a little whirring shrine, with his back to me. A woman too, I remember her . . . " He suddenly recalled who the woman in the bar downstairs had been. "I saw my sword go in, saw all the blood. God's cogs, blood everywhere, made me sick like it never had before. But I don't remember why I did it. It didn't feel like me doing it; it *wasn't* me. I'd swear it, Kass, I'd swear it on anything you like, on the clockwork duellist, even on my sword, on anything you want to name. It wasn't me even if it was."

"So you did what you always do and lied. Even to yourself this time." She stared at him for a long time, and he couldn't look back. Finally she stirred and, quick as mercury, she was spitting mad and as pissed off as he'd ever seen her. He didn't even blame her.

"I *believed* you. I lost everything because I fucking well believed you – you, you, clocking arsehole! Petri, I told Petri to shove his ring up his backside because he thought you'd done it. I lost the guild, Eneko, my blades . . . *everything*, every damned thing in my life worth anything, and what did I get to keep? An arsehole lying shit of a brother who couldn't even trust me enough to tell me the truth, who's dogged my steps my whole fucking life. Well, not any more he won't. You started this, you finish it – on your own. Because I haven't got a brother."

Before he could do anything, before he could even reach out an arm to stop her, she was gone in an echo of slammed door. He couldn't seem to move, not to run after her, not to open the window and call out, not to do anything. He deserved this. All of it.

He was still standing there staring at the shut door when the room changed from being empty but for him to having someone else in it. A soft hissing sounded behind him, a rustled movement, a silky voice that echoed around his head and made the place on his back burn.

"Hello again, Vocho. I hope we haven't come at an inopportune moment?"

He didn't want to turn, he didn't want to look at the face he knew was there, but he didn't seem to have much choice. He turned, his eyes caught on the bloody patterns on the magician's hands, the spot in his back burned like someone had struck him with a poker and everything went dark.

Interlude

Eleven years earlier

Vocho sparred against himself in the mirror, checking a thrust that left him overextended and made his new shirt stretch alarmingly. He didn't want to ruin the effect or waste the money the silk had cost him. It looked good, and so did he. His little fluff of beard, all he could yet manage, was his pride and joy.

Kacha sat and watched him, her eyes dark and unreadable. She'd been off with him – with everyone – for days, weeks, longer. She was never about either; always off somewhere, and no matter how he tried he couldn't winkle out of her what the problem was or where she was going. He'd given up trying to get a smile out of her or a rise to his insults. So instead he sparred and preened and looked forward to later. To the time when, almost certainly, he'd be called on to take his test to become a master. At fourteen too! There was no doubt in his mind either.

Eneko had called the meeting with the usual words, commanding all journeymen and lessers to present themselves at the courtyard under the clockwork duellist, all masters available to attend. A few of the smaller lessers had strung bunting around the courtyard, and the smell of roasting lamb wafted up from the kitchens. It had to be a master's test — there was nothing else it *could* be. And how many journeymen were there? Five who could take the test at present. Himself, Kacha and three others. The rest were just there for the education and would leave before taking the final test, or weren't yet up to scratch.

He couldn't help but hum a cheery little tune of battles won and glories told. That he'd get there before Kacha — maybe that's what she was sulking about. Oh, perhaps they'd give her the test too, but she wouldn't get there before Vocho, and that'd rankle like buggery with his perfect sister. He hummed louder.

A sound echoed up from the courtyard and Vocho took a look — three lessers hitching the big mechanism at the centre of the courtyard to the links and gears that ran underneath and somehow connected up to the underwater wheels that ran the change o' the clock.

They said the automaton of the duellist was as old as the guild — certainly as old as the grinding machinery that spun the city once every three nights. Vocho had watched the automaton's face every night for years, wondering what it was she wanted from them. Outside, in the city, people had cast off the old gods with something approaching glee after the revolt and now prayed to the Clockwork God the prelate told everyone had made the world. Vocho prayed too, when he remembered, but it was the duellist which caught him, which inspired his most urgent prayers, which looked over the guild, watched them, guided them. It had dimmed a little, that fervent belief, as he'd grown, but now on the cusp of everything he wanted it came back in a rush. Since he'd left home he'd cared about only two things: keeping his promise to Da, maybe earning a bit of praise, showing the old bastard that he was good for something after all, and becoming a master. What they'd drilled for, taken bruises and whacks galore for, trained and studied and sparred for, learned all the stupid rules until he could recite them in his sleep. This was it.

The clock above the entrance to the arena began to chime, sounding tinny and harsh. One, two, three – not the call to arms, that was two bells. Four, five, six – not sparring, that was four. Seven, eight, nine – not a journeyman's test, that was eight. Vocho shut his eyes as the last came. Ten.

The bells stopped, and Vocho let out a great breath. He grabbed Kacha, whirled her around until she had no choice but to laugh, and set her down again. "Come on!"

He ran out of the door, down stone steps worn by thousands of feet over hundreds of years until they had a groove in the centre, past others running, all shouting and laughing. The cloister was full of them – lessers, upper and lower, those journeymen who'd be leaving before their final test and the three others who'd be up against Vocho and perhaps Kacha. He ran up behind one, a staid and methodical boy three years older than Vocho who'd gained his journeyman's two years past, and tipped his hat over his eyes before he ran on.

By the time he reached the entrance to the courtyard and stopped to ensure he was looking his best before he entered, he was fit to burst. The clockwork duellist shone ahead of them, looking down as though weighing each one's worth. In his imagination Vocho saw her smile before the mechanism started, then her sword flew in thrusts and feints, blocks and ripostes. The perfect swordswoman, elegant and deadly, revered and famous.

The mechanism ran down, and Eneko strode onto the flagstones followed by a dozen masters. Late sunlight shone red on green and gold tunics, glinted off sword hilts and eyes. With a last thrust, the clockwork duellist put up her sword and stilled. There was no sound but the painful thud of Vocho's heart, the twist of his breath.

Kacha appeared next to him. He grabbed her hand, wanting

to kiss her and pull her with him, let her share in the moment. She didn't seem to notice. Her face was still as a carved mask, eyes dark with whatever had been bothering her. He squashed a moment's irritation. Couldn't she be happy for him? Couldn't he beat her to be the first at something? Just this *once*? He turned back to where Eneko had begun speaking.

". . . proclaim a new master. I beg all your forgivenesses, but this is a special case."

Special case. Had she heard that? No, she stood with all the animation of a stone. Maybe she was worried that for once he'd beaten her, got there first. He'd make sure not to rub it in too much. Maybe just a bit though, because he'd never been first at anything before. All right, maybe a lot.

"A service has already been performed, a service in the interests of the guild."

What was Eneko talking about?

"The masters have agreed that this service shall suffice as the test. Now it only remains for the nominee to fight, in full view of us all, and force a master to a draw, or beat them. Same rules as usual for a master's test – there are no rules, as there are none in the world outside this guild. All we ask is that you fight well and nobly. As seems good to you."

A murmur ran around the assembly. Vocho frowned, his rock-solid certainty that he was to be made a master trembling just a touch. But who else? No one. He could beat them all. His hand gripped his sword, ready for his name to be called.

"Kacha, please step forward."

Vocho was halfway through a pace before the words caught up with him and he faltered to a stop. The boy whose hat he'd tipped chuckled behind him. "Never mind, Voch. Better luck next time, eh?"

He whirled to face the boy, who shut up but didn't stop

smirking, then turned back to see Kacha advancing across the flagstones. Probably only he caught the hitch in her step, the quick glance as she sought him out. A complicated look, but he was too incensed to pay it any mind, and she was quick enough looking away, towards the duellist she was going to fight. Towards whoever had agreed to take her on, to mentor her as she negotiated the shallows of being a fully fledged duellist before she braved its depths.

Vocho's hand twisted on the hilt of his sword and he ground his teeth as he watched. A crowd stood by the gates – not unusual, because the locals knew what the bells meant as well as any duellist and sometimes came to watch, though they'd get no further. Vocho recognised one of them. Petri something-or-other his name was, Petri from the river. Vocho wouldn't have paid him any attention at all except for the way he was looking at Kacha. Like he *admired* her, like Vocho was nothing in comparison. Like Da had always looked at Kacha and not him.

Kacha stopped in the shadow of the clockwork duellist and waited for her opponent to name themselves.

Vocho wasn't the only one open-mouthed when Guild Master Eneko stepped forward. He was naming her as his potential successor, as his apprentice at the least. But Kacha had to beat him or force him to a draw, and Eneko was good, more than good; he was great. He might not be the *best* fighter – being guild master needed more than just a talent with a blade – but Vocho knew he couldn't beat him. Not yet, at least. One day, when he'd finished growing, perhaps. The question was, could Kacha?

And did Vocho want her to? The answer to that shocked him. No, *he* wanted to beat her, and not just a bit. Right now he'd happily draw blood. Perfect *fucking* Kacha, always first, always best. He looked up at the clockwork duellist, at her stern face. *Please, just this once, hear me. Make her lose, make her look stupid, make her not perfect.*

Eneko drew his sword and went through the forms. Salute, bow, come on guard. Kacha followed suit. A flick of Eneko's eye and someone set the clock's bell ringing, signalling the start.

They began at a punishing pace, one that they surely couldn't keep up for long. Thrust, block, riposte, back and forth beneath the watching eyes of the clockwork duellist. The courtyard was silent except for their breath, the clang of blade on blade and the scuff of their feet.

Because the tests weren't bound by the rules of sparring, some masters' duels were soft little affairs – the mentor taking it a little easy to ensure a pass for their student, to minimise the risk of injury – symbolic things only. Frowned upon but it happened, sometimes obviously. Not this time, and Eneko was making sure everyone knew it. He went after Kacha with an aggression that surprised Vocho. The guild master had always seemed self-contained, placid almost. Now he launched himself across the arena with the energy of a man twenty years younger. Kacha held her own, kept his blade from her skin, but it was clear she'd be hard pushed to win. Vocho couldn't decide if that pleased him or not. He wanted her to win, for her, when he thought on it, but the feelings that came before thought, that surged up without him asking, were hoping she'd lose, and lose badly. They made him feel sick, but he couldn't stop them.

It looked like those darker wishes might be satisfied as Eneko forced Kacha back and back through sheer weight, brute strength and years of experience. Vocho glanced up at the clock – five more minutes before the final bell and she could claim a draw. He looked back at the duel just in time to see Eneko get past her guard and go for a move that was illegal in sparring but fair game in a master's test, a face shot which scored a cut across one cheek, under her eye.

"Come on, come on," Petri blurted out by the gate. Vocho

spared him a look and was surprised to see the bland face scrunched into a scowl as he willed Kacha on. What was it to him?

Kacha managed to get clear, and Eneko gave her a tick of the clock to wipe the blood from her cheek. She had to go for the win now – no other way, no chance of a draw unless she blooded him back or disarmed him. Her face hardened into one Vocho knew well. She was pissed off and turning her anger into a determination to win at all costs. Vocho had been on the receiving end of that look more than once, and he'd probably deserved it at least half the time.

Eneko said something. Vocho couldn't catch it but the gist was clear – come on and beat me, girl, if you can. A taunt. *Exactly* the wrong thing to say to Kacha, if you didn't want a sword in your gut.

A sudden grin split her face under the blood, and for all she was his sister and he loved her when he remembered, Vocho was glad she wasn't grinning at him. Especially when she shifted her feet just so. He knew that shift, knew that Kacha would spar within the rules but push them as far as they went when she needed to. No Ruffelo's rules here, not in a master's test.

Eneko came on with a sudden heavy thrust to her unguarded side, a move that would break her if it caught her. She moved into it, past it so the sword tickled her ear. Eneko's face crumpled under a sharp elbow that stunned him – only for half a tick, but that was enough for Kacha to grab his sword hand with hers, twist the wrist just so and leap back with her own sword in one hand and Eneko's in the other.

A long silence, and then Eneko raised his hands and smiled. "I yield." Just before the clock struck its second sequence of bells to end the duel. A fix, no matter how good it had looked. Had to be, didn't it? Eneko taking it easy on her, letting her win, making her look good, better than she was. Had to be.

Applause deafened Vocho as the lessers behind him voiced their approval and the crowd at the gate joined in. A new master, always cause for celebration. But Vocho had nothing to celebrate except a sick pit of jealousy in his stomach and the guilt of knowing he should be happy for Kacha, should be smiling as she bent to receive her master's sword, as she took the oath to serve only herself and the guild, no other to come before, not spouse or child, for as long as she lived.

He did smile when she came towards him afterwards, nailed a grin to his face until his cheeks ached. Teased her a bit because that's what Vocho always did and if he didn't she'd guess what was under his smile. Told her Da would be proud of her, which was true enough. Da'd be so happy he'd crap bricks because his precious Kacha was apprenticed to the guild master. So he smiled and laughed, came up with a few witty comments that made her laugh in return and tried to make the dark thoughts go away. Yet that night, when the air was as dark as they were, he promised himself that of the two of them it wouldn't be Kacha's name they remembered. It wouldn't be her that Da was proudest of.

Even if it killed them both.

Chapter Sixteen

Kacha burst out of the inn with no thought of hiding her face and the giveaway scar beneath her eye. She'd no thought for anything except getting away from Vocho. Leaving her lying, betraying, back-stabbing bastard of a brother behind.

The day was dying around her, the last of the red sunlight glancing off terracotta roofs crusted with soot. A whistle blew at one of the clocker factories behind the inn, swiftly followed by another and another, until maybe a dozen were in full voice and people began to spill out onto the street. Soot-smudged and weary from their day at work, they trudged along like so many giant ants.

Kacha worked her way through them, no real idea of where she was going except away. She still had the papers, she realised after a while, rustling under her shirt. What to do with them? Once she'd have known with no hesitation. She'd have taken them to Eneko and listened to his reasoning as he decided what to do. Or Petri. Or she'd have talked it over with Voch. Now she had nothing and no one except herself. She would have to do. She realised she was already on Ratchet Street, heading towards the palace. The Clockwork God loomed up ahead at the crossroads. Today it was left to the guild, right to the palace, matching her two realistic choices.

Left to the guild, to Eneko and what had been home. Back to echoing cloisters and running feet, clashing blades and kept promises, the rhythm of her whole life. Eneko might welcome her back, might arrange a pardon, might listen to her, but just as likely not. She'd broken his trust when she threw in her lot with Vocho, and with that one action she'd burned that bridge right down to the waterline.

Right to the palace. Her first instinct had been to warn the prelate, and it still seemed the right thing, the good thing. These papers meant war, she knew that if not much else. Maybe she'd even get a pardon out of it. Still, it was risky. Too risky, especially if half the rumours about him were true.

She looked up at the Clockwork God as he clacked through his motions. People left offerings at the church, but they left them here too, of a different sort. He bent down, cogs whirring, and his jointed fingers snapped shut on a ragged piece of paper before he straightened. The plinth he stood on had its own motto etched into it – the only comfort is truth. The Clockwork God collected all the little truths so he might build a bigger one, the truth that was the answer to everything, and then everyone could live in peace, so Bakar said. So that's what people brought to him, their own little honesties, plaintive pleas for the god to change the truths of their lives. The god took the piece of paper, appeared to read it and stowed it away behind a door over his heart. The actions were familiar, repeated over and over on rails, and yet . . . She knew he ran on gears and cogs, powered by the huge waterwheels under the great river that Bakar had discovered all those years ago. She knew he was only clockwork, that he was just a representation of the real god; they all did. But this time when the eyes passed over her, she could have sworn one iris shut for a moment – that he winked at her.

The papers weighed heavily under her shirt. She had a

whole stack of truth, and Petri and others wanted her caught because of it, wanted her dead most likely, though she only knew a part of the story. She could warn the prelate, show him these papers as her proof, but she hesitated. Keep the evidence until she could warn Bakar, that's what she had to do, what seemed good to her. Except one paper perhaps. She knelt down and placed it on the little platform. The god whirred and whizzed, bent down and took it in his brass fingers. Cogs ground as his eyes ran over the words and then, yes, he winked, she was sure of it, before he folded the paper, opened the door into his whirring heart and stowed it safely there. She hoped she could get it back if she needed it.

After that she felt lost. What she needed was somewhere to hole up and think things through, somewhere where no one would think to look for her, where she could plan her next move, plan a life without her brother in it. She looked up and smiled.

The rooftop shanties had always been a fine place to hide. No one bothered with them much, not even the guards, and it only took a few coppers to make the inhabitants temporarily blind. She made her way across to the roofs that looked over the back of the palace, which was lit up like a beacon of hope. Between her and it the vast clockwork garden clanked and whirled in its course.

What seems good to you?

She might not be in the guild any more, but she'd sworn, they all had, to protect Reyes if it came to it, even if it was ruled by a madman. Reyes, *that* was the good thing, and the papers in her tunic showed one thing and one thing only. Call it what you would, it amounted to the same thing – there'd be blood on the streets, Reyen blood.

As she watched, a dark figure came out of the rear gate of the palace and headed down the broad street. He passed under a lamp, and she recognised his dark, serious face and was moving before she even thought why. He was on his own, and so was she.

She dropped to the empty street in front of Petri, sword out, unsure whether she'd use it, unsure of anything right now except that he was here. He pulled up short as she landed, his face twisted, and they stared at each other. How had they come from what they had to being on opposite sides?

He broke first, took a step towards her and stopped, hands raised, when she brought up the sword. "Kass, please. Just listen to me."

"Listen to you what? Lie to me again, tell me you love me while all the time you were spying on me? Tell me you aren't planning to get rid of Bakar. Of Eneko. Tell me you aren't planning revolution, Petri. Does that seem good to you? Does *any* of it?"

His face softened, his dark eyes pleading with her to understand, but she wasn't going to let him off that easily. "It wasn't like that. I swear, really, Kass."

He tried to move forward again, push the blade away, but she kept it steady and pointing at him, even if the tip did shake. She wanted to believe him, that was the problem. She wanted to have someone she could believe.

"You could get me in to see Bakar," she said. "Stop all this. Get me in so they don't arrest me, let me show them these papers. I'd even make sure he didn't see the one with your name on it. I swore, Petri, to protect Reyes. I have to warn him."

"And I have to stop you. Look at me, Kass. Really look. It's too late for me, and . . . and there are things that need to be done. Hard things, but that doesn't mean they shouldn't be done – for Reyes, for all of us. It's not too late for you. Give me the papers and leave. Leave Reyes, leave everything. Even Vocho. Even me."

She'd been so intent on him, on what he was saying, she

hadn't noticed him get past her guard. Now he was close enough to touch.

"It was your fault, you know." His voice had dropped, was barely more than a whisper, and a hand found her free one.

She wanted to yank it away, spit in his face, call him all the names she could think of, and she wanted to stand here and listen to him talk. Actually, she could have lived with taking him to the nearest bed as well, could have lived with listening to sweet words even if they were lies, telling herself they were true just for the night and letting the morning take care of itself. She was fed up with being the sensible one.

"If it hadn't been for you showing me, I'd never have joined Licio," Petri said. "I'd still be Bakar's little pet, my life mapped out by the clockwork, with cogs in my head and gears for a heart. Don't you see? You showed me it didn't have to be that way, that I could be free of it. If I don't do this now, I'll spend my life in that bloody palace. I'd have a life, a chained-up pathetic life doing what I'm supposed to, and it wouldn't have you in it. And that does not seem good to me at all."

Her head was swimming with how close he was, how much she wanted him to be closer, but she couldn't let him cloud her thinking, no matter how much she wanted to throw caution to the winds, and loyalty along with it. She wanted to, but a lifetime of having faithfulness ground into her was too hard to ignore. "My fault? This isn't me, this is you; you're doing it all for yourself. You aren't the Petri I remember, and if you do this I still won't be in your life." A lie, she wanted to shout. All that anger was a lie, covering up what she wanted to say, to do.

She shoved herself away, tried to get the blade back between them again, but her arms didn't seem to want to move. She wanted to say more, like how could he be so stupid, how was she supposed to believe anything he said when he'd lied from the start, but his eyes stopped her.

"Give me the papers and leave. Hide," he said at last. "I'll make sure no one comes after you. Maybe, after it's all done, you can come back. The guild will welcome you then, I promise you."

She chewed at her lip, took another two steps back and found herself hard up against a wall under a lamp. No and yes both hovered behind her teeth, both ready to say, and neither could win. The guild and Petri. Against those was herself, always her own worst enemy. Her driving need to be the best she could, to be perfect, for Da, for Eneko. For herself, because anything less than perfection wasn't good enough, left her lost. And what had that got her? Betrayed at every turn. She was adrift in a current too swift, she knew that but couldn't say it, *refused* to say it or think that of all the betrayals maybe Petri's had been the least.

He laughed then, but it was such a sad sound she almost relented. "It's no good, Kass. I have to do this. Bakar's not *sane* any more, or at least not thinking straight. You bring him those, you'll be in the Shrive an hour later, and there'll be nothing I can do about it. I'm doing this for Reyes, Kass. For us. All of us."

Shadows moved at the far end of the street, resolving into four guards, impossible to tell whose from here.

"Kass, give me the papers. Quickly."

She didn't trust herself to speak so she just shook her head and turned, quick as only she could be, for a drain-pipe, was up it in a flash. She paused at the top to look down and met Petri's gaze.

He raised a hand and tried on a smile that didn't fit. "I wasn't lying when I said I loved you." Then he turned with a swirl of his cloak and disappeared into the dark of the street.

"Well," said a voice that almost sent her tumbling back

over the edge in surprise, "that was an edifying conversation, wasn't it?"

A dark shape over by the parapet. It didn't move, didn't make a sound, but a cloud rolled away from the moon and she could make out the glint of buckles on shoes, the hilt of a sword. The shape moved, and she didn't wait any more. By the time it reached her, and she realised who it was, her sword was out and ready and she'd very nearly disembowelled Dom.

"God's cogs," she said with relief as she put her sword away. "What the hells are you doing here?"

"Looking for you."

There was something different about him – about all of him. No handkerchief waving about, no dithering. Instead he moved like oiled clockwork, coiled and ready. A quick smile sharp as daggers. And how in hells had he found her?

"Maybe you should have taken him up on his offer. It's the best one you're likely to get."

"I swore when I took my master's," she said. "I didn't unswear later."

"That's true, but what did it get you? Thrown out, exiled, not even a pretence at allowing you to explain. Eneko threw you to the wolves. Not the first time he's done that to one of his duellists either. Well, too late to take Petri up on his offer, so what are you going to do? I mean, getting inside the palace and to Bakar alive would be difficult for a magician, let alone you. And Eneko . . . do you trust him? Completely? Or would he throw you to the wolves again to save his own skin?"

Kacha looked out towards the guild, hulking and dark against the night sky. She'd looked to Eneko as her father, the guild like it was her family, and here she was, having done nothing wrong but believe in her brother and having faithfully, trustingly served Eneko all those years, and when she'd gone to him after the priest the guards had already been there and he hadn't stopped them trying to arrest her.

"They used Vocho, you know that? All of them in one way or another," Dom said. "Used Petri. Used you. Used Vocho. They forced him because they thought he was Eneko's pet assassin, but we know better, don't we?"

She said nothing. He was unnerving her, the way he moved back and forth as though he had too much energy. So unlike Dom that she wondered briefly if he was some magician's illusion.

"They thought he was you. If they'd got it right, *you'd* have killed that priest, *you'd* have ruined both your lives. Does that make you feel better or worse?"

"Dom, I don't—"

"You think he's an idiot, I gathered that. Cogs knows why, because he's not stupid. He just has different priorities. He's not so stupid he'd willingly kill a man he'd sworn to protect. Is he?"

"No." No, even she knew that, hard though it was to admit. Easier to curse Vocho for a fool, blame him, nurse her righteous anger. A sudden unwelcome thought – that Da had always called Vocho an idiot and she'd picked up the habit lately. And he wasn't, not an idiot, not how Da meant it. He was funny, careless sometimes, prone to fits of rashness, but stupid he wasn't. "Why are you—"

But, quick as he'd turned up, Dom was gone, leaving her to spend the rest of the night with new dilemmas to tangle her thoughts and stop her from sleeping.

By the time dawn came she was exhausted and no closer to an answer except thinking she should maybe go back and talk to Vocho. Maybe. A*pologising* wasn't something she made a habit of and she wasn't going to start now. Maybe Vocho wasn't an idiot, but he hadn't exactly covered himself in glory, and he had nicely fucked her entire life. It would take a lot more than Dom being cryptic and mysterious and trying to make her feel guilty for that. She held on to her anger like a blanket that could keep out the chill, even if it did have lice.

She climbed wearily down to the street and started the business of finding some breakfast. She'd just found a little stall run by a Five Islands trader that smelt irresistibly of spices and sausages when out of the corner of her eye she caught sight of Cospel coming towards her, a flustered-looking Dom – Dom as he usually was, not night-time roof-wandering Dom – in tow.

"Kass, quick." Dom took her arm and led her to the side of the street where it was less busy. He looked like he was panicking, which wasn't good. Normally he was so relaxed he looked half asleep but now he was twitching and fidgeting like a third-year student given sharps for the first time. "It's Voch."

"I don't want to know, whatever it is. He can rot in hell for all I care. You can tell him that when you next see him." Even so, she felt a pang of . . . what?

"No, you don't understand. Last night, after, well, you know, I did a bit more digging, a bit more listening. But when I got back to the inn, about an hour ago, Vocho was gone. They've found him and taken him somewhere. Egimont, that is. I got one of the pot boys to tell me."

"Don't be stupid. Voch wouldn't let Petri beat him." Not unless he wanted him to. Not unless his sister had just cut him off. Gods fuck the man, she'd only disowned him five minutes ago and here she was feeling sorry for him. She cast a glance at the Clockwork God, who loomed over the end of the street and rattled through another set of actions. *The only comfort is truth*. Well, it wasn't comforting her very much.

"I don't know," Dom said. "We managed to find someone who saw him as they were taking him away. He looked . . . dazed. Not himself. Half the guards were there too. Caused quite a ruckus when the inn found out who it was."

She tried to shake away a lifetime of making sure her little brother was safe. He wasn't so little any more. He could take care of himself; he wasn't hers to look after.

But she'd lied to Vocho just as much as he'd lied to her, hadn't she? He'd never known about all the little dark jobs she did for Eneko or how she'd got her master's before him. She'd never *lied* exactly, but there was a lot she'd never told him. And while she'd happily do something dire to him with whatever came to hand, she'd be buggered if anyone killed him before she got the chance. He was an arsehole, for sure, but he was *her* arsehole. Besides, Dom was looking at her with big eyes like a dog begging for a treat, and Cospel seemed on the verge of tears.

"I'm going to regret this until I die, or he does," she said with a sigh. "Fine. I don't want him dead unless it's me doing the killing. But how in hells do we get him out? More to the point, how do we find out where they've taken him?"

"Oh," Dom said, back to his usual twittering self. "I thought you might know."

Kacha cocked an eyebrow at him, and tried to remind herself he wasn't a Reyes man and wouldn't know. Although he'd seemed at home enough last night, savvy enough to find her in a tangle of shacks almost no one ever went to.

She sifted all the possibilities in her head. "Two alternatives. First, the king's house – after the Shrive and the prelate's palace, probably the most well guarded place in Reyes. Plus it's one of the houses that changes with the change o' the clock. Depending on which set of the clock we're on, it's got all sorts of different things. What set of the clock are we on? First? Well then, let's see. Arrow slits on the top floor, two deadfalls on the first floor, some sort of trap I never figured out by the back door, and some clockwork gizmos by the front door that look pretty damned lethal."

By now Cospel was giving her a strange look, but Dom only smiled his new sharp-dagger smile.

She shrugged in an attempt at nonchalance. "What? I checked it out just in case I ever needed to know." Or more precisely because Eneko had told her to. As she said, just in case.

"Will they take him to the Shrive?" Cospel said into the silence that followed. "I mean, it's the king that's had him taken away, right? But he's got no, what's the word? Begins with a 'j'?"

"Justice? Jeopardy?" Dom said. "Jailor?"

"Jurisdiction?" Kacha said.

"Aye, that's it. No jurisdiction here. If anyone finds out he's holding Vocho, especially if the prelate's after us, er, him, all hell will break lose. So he'll make it look official and take him straight to the Shrive."

She shook her head. "No, they've been sneaky up till now. And I think they want him for something other than just execution, which is all he'll get there. What do you think, Dom?"

"Who, me?" He tried his best at a bumble, but she'd seen through him now and only raised an eyebrow. "I think they used him to kill the priest, however they managed that. I also think you taking the papers, the threat that you might show them to the prelate, has forced their hands. They have to do something, and who better than the renowned Vocho the priest murderer as someone to pin the blame on?"

They wanted the papers back or destroyed, but Kacha had told Petri she was going to show them to the prelate. Now they had Vocho and would either force him to do something for them or offer to trade him for the papers, or both. They had her over a barrel.

Dom seemed much more, well, serious. He'd lost all his twitter, all his bumbling, seemed wound up and ready to spring. He looked about keenly. "Look, it's not safe out here on the street. I can help. My father's got a house here in Reyes, not far from the king's. I didn't want to chance it before, because, well, because my father's pissed as hell at me for disappearing and he might have come here looking for me. But I went there after I got split up from Vocho, and he's not in residence. We can use it to hole up until we do whatever it is we're going to do."

Who did she have left to trust? Dom and Cospel. She wanted to leave, leave all of them behind and just go and be herself somewhere. Maybe she would, but she had to see Vocho alive first, if only because what Dom had said last night made her feel guilty as hell, and perhaps Dom and his connections were all she had to do that with.

"All right."

He gripped her arm and smiled, and she wondered if he'd been like this from the start whether she wouldn't have minded Vocho trying to play at matchmaker so much. When he stopped all that stupid twittering and the fake manners that passed for fashionable in Reyes these days, he was quite attractive in a strange kind of way. Smart too, and she liked that in a man.

"Come on," he said now. "Cospel? Why don't you hook back to the inn, see if anyone's still there or looking out for us? If not, perhaps bring our things. Meet us at the last house on King's Row."

King's Row? Kacha shook herself. That was where all the old nobles used to live, and the last house had once belonged to Egimont's father. He'd taken her there to show her once, and the echoing frustration and anger had been clear.

Dom mistook her shudder. "Not for long, I promise. We'll get your brother back, alive and in one piece."

Interlude

Eight months earlier
"Petri! Come in, come in."

Bakar hadn't changed much, Petri thought as he sat in the chair indicated in the prelate's office. Still tall and rangy, his hair still blond and untouched by grey. Still as intense as ever, even if that intensity had been turning into oddity just lately.

It was Petri that had changed, perhaps. Not surprising, given he'd been no more than a boy when he first came into Bakar's service. He'd fallen for the prelate's ideology of equality as only a teenage boy can – with every fibre of his being. He still believed it, but doubts were starting to creep in. Maybe that was why Bakar had called for him today.

Bakar smiled expansively and poured out two cups of sweet apple tea, Petri's favourite. They both took a few sips and sat in silence before Bakar got to the point.

"You're unhappy in the office. No, don't deny it. I see that you are. Not surprising for someone of your energy, but I've been saving something for you. Something that only you can do for me, perhaps. Something that it may please you to do."

"I'm always pleased to serve the prelate," Petri answered.

"Don't give me that piffle, Petri. We've known each other too long. Aren't I the father you should have had? Haven't I always treated you as a son?"

"You have." And that had been enough for a long time. Bakar had been the one person he'd been able to rely on. Only now it wasn't enough. Restless thoughts kept him awake at nights, wondering if the rest of his life was going to be like this – all mapped out, no surprises.

"Well then! Now, you're chafing in that office, and I know it. It was necessary, I'm afraid, given who you are and who your father was. Equality sadly doesn't take into account politics, and memories linger. More's the pity. For a long time it was all I could do just to keep you in the office and not have you turfed out. But now I have something more challenging for you. And perhaps a way to exorcise some of those ghosts I know still haunt you."

Petri said nothing – from long habit he now spoke little and thought more. It was safer that way, in among the rest of the clerks, who sneered at his accent and laughed at him. He'd borne it because he knew why, because Bakar had taught him that these people had had nothing before because of men like him, and they were long on forgetting it. He'd borne it but lately found he didn't want to any more.

"Eneko," Bakar said, and Petri sat up straight. "I've been keeping an eye on him, as I'm sure you've guessed. He's always been a slippery bastard. After I took power he behaved himself for a time, but for a while now I've been sure he's slipping back into his old ways. Slaves, money, power, but it all starts with the slaves. Who he sells them to I don't know, though it's possible some are going to Ikaras, and that makes me very suspicious. I'm almost sure he's doing it. Not to mention a few people have, over the years, how shall I put this? Turned up dead, and not by natural causes either, unless you count a cut throat as natural. More lately not just slavers either. Last week one man who'd spoken out against the guild was found dead, and I think we can safely say he didn't stab himself accidentally in his sleep. A few others have died, mostly my supporters, tradesmen I rely on, people who follow my lead within the council or are otherwise important to me. No one too obvious as yet, and the deaths often look like something else, accidents or random thievery gone wrong. But I see a pattern here, a slow and subtle one, killing my support. And here's Eneko with a guild of men and women trained in fighting, and killing when they need to, and a grudge against me besides. I want to find out if it's true, and if so which of them is doing the blood work. And who better than you?"

Petri could think of any number, but Bakar barely paused for breath.

"You know many of the men and women who are now masters, or you did. I know you watch them spar on the bridge sometimes, and even join in – no, don't deny it. I never minded because you're your own man and I know I have your loyalty. But you're a face they know, perhaps trust. Eneko never told what happened to you that day, why you left. He swore the masters in attendance to secrecy. All the rest know is that sometimes you come back for a visit. I want you to visit again, and I want you to use your ears and listen. Find out what Eneko is up to and which of the masters are helping him. Wriggle your way into the guild if you can. Find out what his purpose is. I need proof, Petri, so I can string the bastard up, finally get rid of the guild for good."

Petri hesitated, but in the end he had little choice but to agree. He hesitated because his trips back to that greensward were always bittersweet. He watched the unofficial sparring, the banter, the familiarity, with something that approached jealousy. That could have been his if not for his father, if not for Eneko. If not for Bakar.

Which was how Petri found himself back sparring with

Kacha. She had a way with a blade that was elegant and simple but devastating, but it wasn't that which had him entranced. He didn't know what it was – perhaps that she didn't look at him like just another fallen noble or a prelate's man, didn't mock his accent, didn't mock him at all. She saw only an opponent. She won, as he'd thought she would, and he congratulated her and saw surprise flash across her face.

She took him to Soot Town for something to eat. It had been years since he'd set foot there – if the clerks in the palace hated him, the clockworkers and smiths down in Soot Town hated him and his accent worse. Yet somehow this time it was all right.

He wouldn't have called it a restaurant – it was someone's house with extra tables crammed into the tiny front room and the smell of fried fish lingering in the corners. He sat down, wary at first because the place was full of duellists and soot-streaked working men, but no one said a word. Kacha sat, but she wasn't still for a moment. Foot tapping, fingers playing with the tassel on her scabbard or twirling her hair.

"You don't talk much, do you?" she said.

"Not much," he agreed and wondered why she'd brought him here.

She laughed at that, but she was frowning too as though she was trying to figure him out. Any moment now she'd get it, that he was the prelate's little spy trying to winkle what he could out of her. But then she shook her head, smiled at him, really at him, and started talking about their sparring, about this move and that, just like he was any other duellist, anyone else. She didn't seem to care about his accent or who his father had been or who he worked for now. By the time the food came he'd quite forgotten that he was supposed to be spying.

When the ever-preening Vocho turned up in a blast of

raucous noise, plunked down and threw a purse full of bulls onto the table, Petri was more annoyed than he ever remembered, but Kacha only laughed at Vocho's antics.

"Where did you get all those?" she asked. "Mugging old ladies? Are they all you can manage to fight?"

"Oh please," Vocho said with a sideways glance at Petri. "If I was going to mug ladies they would at least be young and attractive."

"So where did you get them then?"

Petri remembered that smug smile, remembered hating it back then, and he hated it now.

Vocho patted the hilt of his sword. "My little secret, Kacha. My little secret."

Kacha rolled her eyes and waved him away. Thankfully Vocho took the hint, and with a last penetrating glare at Petri wandered over to some other duellists and showed off to them instead, ordering jugs of "the most expensive wine you have" then throwing them over the others, toasting himself and generally being an obnoxious sod.

Kacha started saying something but Petri didn't catch it. Vocho was an extraordinary duellist, it was true. And one with a secret income. Quite a substantial income too – that purse would be enough to feed and house a family for a month or longer.

"I'm sorry?"

"I said, Vocho's a bit of an acquired taste," Kacha said. "Would you like to go somewhere else? Your choice."

Something about the way she was looking at him, as though she was surprising herself. Something in the way her lips tilted in a half smile. His choice. He wondered if Bakar's precious clocks had predicted this. Was it really his choice or was he just playing to the mechanism of the prelate's clockwork universe? Did he care?

"I've never been to the night market," he said. Bakar couldn't have foreseen this. Not the way his heart seemed loud enough to deafen him, or how the way she looked at him made him want to grin like a fool. Free will or running on rails? There were no rails to describe what was happening to him. The clockwork that seemed to have taken up residence in his head came to a shuddering halt and he was surprised that cogs didn't fall out of his ears.

"Then it's about time you did," she said and looped her arm through his.

It was about then that his world had collapsed with a crash that should have shaken the foundations of the Shrive, and a new world had started to rise in the ruins.

Chapter Seventeen

Vocho cracked open an eye and tried not to breathe too hard. Whoever had been in here before him – wherever the hells here was – hadn't cared too much about little things like personal cleanliness. When he managed to get his eyes open properly, he figured they probably had other things on their minds. Like the rack in the corner, or the brazier full of various pokers and brands, their ends cherry red where they rested on the burning coals. Yup, they'd take a man's mind off whether he was sweating or make him a little less conscientious about where he pissed.

He scraped a hand over a day's growth of stubble, found that was the limit his hand could move in the chains he suddenly noticed, and pinched the bridge of his nose. His head felt very odd, and the patch on his back that he'd never quite been able to see, even in a mirror, burned like buggery.

He was just getting to grips with that, and the fact he seemed to be somewhere underground with thick stone walls that probably wouldn't let the screams out, when a door in a dark corner groaned open.

Egimont was first in, and Vocho tried to get himself a bit straighter. *Pompous dick.* He didn't have time to dwell on

Eggy though, much as he'd like to; for Kacha's sake, he'd have loved to kick the man in the nuts. Others appeared behind Egimont – the king swaggered in, all pomp and grandeur, perfumed kerchiefs and dripping jewels and clockwork gizmos that were probably worth ten duellists. Behind him scurried a small man, shoulders folded over a little paunch like he spent his days hunched over a desk, with ink stains on his fingers. A few wisps of grey hair, carefully arranged. A pair of spectacles that reflected the flames from the brazier, made his eyes into shifting red mirrors that hid who he was. Last came a dark figure that lurked in the shadows, leaving only the shine of his eyes and the bloody patterns on his hands in view.

Vocho's stomach shrivelled in on itself. Magician. It was only when he'd told Kacha that he'd truly remembered him, his mind not wanting to probe too deeply for what it found. He'd had an inkling in the coach, a sense that he'd met this man before and a dread of meeting him again, but it was only now that the fractured memories stitched themselves back together. Bloody patterns swirling in his head. A deep voice that followed them, saying . . . saying all sorts. That woman, Alicia she'd called herself, had been there too. He still couldn't remember much, only there'd been blood, he knew that, and . . .

"Ah, Vocho." The king came forward, kerchief held delicately over his nose against the stench from the straw. Vocho had a flash of who Dom reminded him of before the king breezed onward. "You've been such a very helpful fellow, even if you did run off to the back of beyond. And stealing those papers, well, we've had to move a little quicker than we anticipated, which may mean a slightly bloodier time of it than I wanted. But Sabates here has a new plan. I like it very much. Hopefully you will too. In fact, I'm positive you will. First things first. Sabates?"

The magician stepped forward, and Vocho had to work

very hard not to shuffle back. Something about the man's
eyes unnerved him, made more black memories come to
mind. The priest, the screams as he died and . . . and . . .
the magician watching, those shining eyes urging him on.

"Egimont, help Vocho strip, please."

"Strip? Oh now, just wait a minute. I don't think there's
any need for that. I mean, I don't swing that way or—"

"Shut up," Sabates said. "Egimont?"

Eggy grabbed him and ripped the shirt from his back,
managing to get a good wrench of his arm in while he did
it, before twisting it up behind Vocho's back. It startled Vocho,
and seemed out of character for the honourable Egimont. Of
course, he hadn't been the same since Kacha . . .

Sabates peered at Vocho's back, and the patch there burned
worse than ever, so that sweat dripped from his forehead,
slicked his arms. He tried to use it to wriggle out of Eggy's
hands but his grip just got tighter.

"Still there. Very good."

"What's still there?" Whatever it was, he didn't want it.

"A tattoo. A blood-magic tattoo." Sabates' voice was smooth
and dark and cold, like the waters of the Reyes river. "It's
lasted quite well. Should only need a top-up."

"But—"

"Shut up," Licio said. "I have a proposition for you, one
which you're in no position to refuse. I understand Sabates
can do quite nasty things through a tattoo like that."

Sabates was behind him now, and Vocho could feel even
Egimont's distaste as he edged away. A sharp pain almost
blinded him and dimly recalled another night, another time.
His back was on fire, so hot all the blood dripping from it
should evaporate.

"Now then," Licio continued. "The good news is, I can
get you pardoned. More than that, if the renowned Vocho,
exonerated from the lies and treachery that led to him being
charged with murder, leads my cause, I can give you lands,

titles, money, renown. I can give you everything your shallow little heart desires."

"That's nice," Vocho said, and then had to grit his teeth against what Sabates was doing to his back. He'd have preferred the rack, or maybe one of those red-hot pokers. Anything was preferable to the grinding pain that shot through his back as the magician ran his fingers over it.

Licio frowned at Vocho's flippancy but carried on. "Actually, you'll do it anyway. The tattoo will see to that. Correct, Sabates?"

"Oh yes. To a point."

"Well, that's fantastic. Why bother offering then?" The scream came through his gritted teeth; he couldn't stop it.

Eggy muttered something under his breath, but Vocho was past hearing it.

"Oh, the tattoo is just to be sure." Licio said. "Magic's all very well, but it's not reliable, is it? Not part of the clockwork universe, isn't that what Bakar has against it? Not orderly, not logical according to our new Clockwork God, a magician's whims too much an element of chance. No, I want you to join me of your own free will. Ha! Yes, the free will that Bakar derides so much. Think of the glory, Vocho. Think of the money, the adulation. Vocho the Great, who led the revolt against the prelate, who killed him to set his fellow men free from the tyrant Bakar has become."

"You want me to kill the prelate? You'll need more than a tattoo to make me do that. He already wants me dead; I don't want him flaying me alive first."

A sudden twist in his back, the slice of a blade, and Vocho couldn't control his legs. Someone appeared to be groaning, and it was him. Eggy pulled him back up gently enough.

"There. All done." Sabates appeared in front of Vocho's sweating face. "A tricky bit of magic. But it worked on you well enough before. Didn't it?"

Vocho couldn't seem to get his breath – his throat was dried up like a fish left out in the sun. He could barely even manage to move his head. Only Eggy's arm kept him upright rather than lying on the floor like a beaten dog, and Vocho was bizarrely grateful to him. Which meant he must be going mad.

"Very nicely," Licio agreed. "First though, I need you to persuade your sister. Poor Egimont tried, but he didn't get very far, except into her underwear."

The hand gripping his arm tightened, and Eggy's teeth clacked shut by his ear.

"Persuade her to do what?" Vocho managed in a whisper.

"Join the cause, obviously. And give us those papers back. Then, once your names are restored, the ever lovely Kacha, apprentice to the guild master, now on our side and keeping Eneko's mouth shut, will be an enormous asset to Petri when he takes over the guild."

Vocho couldn't help the little giggle that escaped. "I don't think she'll—"

Licio's voice snapped out, cutting him off. "I don't give a shit what you think. You'll persuade her, or Egimont here will have to kill her. I can't have her running loose against me. Especially if she still has those papers."

Again the tightening of the grip on his arm, a mutter from Egimont.

"Persuade her to come to us with those papers, and then perhaps she can live." Licio turned to the magician. "Sabates, that tattoo will stop him running again?"

Sabates shrugged, but the shining eye told Vocho all he needed to know. The magician wouldn't make the same mistake twice.

"Good. And don't worry, Vocho. Think of all you'll gain out of this. *Everyone* will know your name, and not just as a priest murderer. Vocho the Magnificent has a nice ring to it, doesn't it?"

Licio gave him a bright smile and left, the little folded man at his heels. Sabates lingered for a while, looking Vocho up and down. "I'd consider agreeing, if I were you. There really isn't much choice." Then he too left.

It was only Vocho and Egimont now, and when Eggy let go, Vocho sagged to his knees. Sweat pooled in the small of his back; pain sat on his shoulders.

"Eggy." He wasn't able to say it very loud, but Egimont stopped with his hand on the door. "What happened? With you and Kacha?"

"What's it to you?" The voice was cold, but Vocho thought he heard a tremor in it, as though Egimont was suppressing some emotion he daren't show.

"She's my sister. She was kind of upset." Understatement of the century. "I don't like to see her upset."

"Then surely she told you? She didn't tell me, except to send my ring back with a suggestion as to what I could do with it."

"And that makes you hate her enough for this? Are they going to put one of these bastard tattoo things on her? Will you kill her if they ask you to?"

Something very strange happened to Eggy's face. It looked like someone was trying to pull it inside out. In the end he gritted his teeth, got his face under control and slammed the door behind him without answering.

Interlude

Seven months earlier

Kacha moved warily along the wall that topped the guild buildings. It was a long drop to the river, and while she'd had plenty of practice on this wall, Eneko had plenty of guile. Even after all this time he wasn't above surprising her in the name of "experience".

The moon was up, good and full in a clear sky, which hampered her only a little. This side of the guild had been built for defence from outside, and the crenellations and lowered walkway largely concealed her. Even if they hadn't, "apprentice meets master" was hardly worthy of gossip. Still, out of habit she moved with silent care and made sure no one saw.

Eneko waited in his usual spot by one of the towers that punctuated the walls, overlooking the docks. If ever she needed him, if ever he wasn't about the grounds below or in his quarters, he was here. The shadows of the overhanging roof and battlements hid him well enough, but if you knew where to look, and he was expecting you, there he was. If not, all you'd see was darkness, pale brick and terracotta tiles.

He was expecting her, so she managed to see the pale

glint of an eye a split second before he spoke. "You're late."

"Sorry, I was—"

"Petri Egimont keeping you, was it? Don't look at me like that – do you think I'm blind?"

The tone was all too familiar from those long-ago days and nights spent doing the extra training he insisted she took – his shut-up-and-listen-or-else voice. She swallowed what she was about to say and listened. She'd known Eneko wouldn't take it well. Maybe that had been half the attraction to Petri in the first place: doing something Eneko wouldn't approve of, just this once. Being less than perfect.

"Petri Egimont," Eneko said now. "What are you doing with *him*? The prelate's little pet and worth no more than a dog, not any more. Follows him like a little dog too, never does a damned thing but what the prelate tells him to. Yet here he is, sniffing at your tail. Why is that, do you think? Well?"

She bridled at that – did Petri have to have a reason except that he liked her? "I—"

"Whatever you think, whatever you're about to say, you're wrong." Eneko stepped fully out of the shadows now, and the look on his face shocked her. She'd seen him angry before, seen him hate. She'd never seen him like this, and it was only later, when she thought on it more, that she realised he was afraid. Afraid of what?

Eneko's lips twitched, and then, taking a deep breath, he seemed to calm down. He went to stand by the parapet and looked down over the docks, where the water was silver and black in the moonlight and the ships looked as if they couldn't just sail but fly.

On nights like this, especially from up here, where you could look but not notice the smell, she missed the docks and jetties, and her da, her whole childhood, with a physical ache. Everything had been very simple then – it all boiled down to having enough to eat. Simple, but not easy.

Now she had enough to eat, she had food and clothes and a good roof. She had friends, a job she was good at, that she loved, mostly. What she also had were secrets and suspicions and a grinding fear that one day she wouldn't be good enough, that all would be lost if she strayed from perfection.

"You be careful of Petri Egimont," Eneko said then, his voice the fatherly one again, the one she craved to hear. "He's always been an odd one. If it had all turned out different, I still wouldn't have let him take his master's. As it is, he's the prelate's pet, and Bakar's been looking for ways to be rid of us for a long time. It may be that's what Petri is up to. Finding some rope to hang us with, maybe feeding you lies and misinformation. Shit-stirring, whichever way you look at it."

She turned on him, about to say, no, no it wasn't, it couldn't be, but Eneko held up a placating hand. "All I'm saying is the same I said all during your training. Never act until you're *sure*. Have all the information to hand, *then* make your move. Be careful, in other words. Be careful like this is another dark job. And tell me what he tells you, eh? So I can make sure you know the truth, not his lies." He smiled then, and it seemed to her he smelled of pipe smoke and salt, almost forgotten scents of childhood, when things were simple. Before she'd met Petri and he'd started her questioning everything. Not because of what he said, but little things that made her think she wasn't the only one with secrets. That maybe Eneko had some too.

"Why did he leave the guild?" she asked into the silence that followed.

Eneko looked away from the silvered ships below them, narrowed his eyes at her and shook his head. "Hasn't he told you?"

"I . . . It seemed impolite to ask." She'd wanted to of course. The way Petris' eyes twitched, his hands tapped a nervous rhythm whenever Eneko's name came up, or the conversation came round to the revolt that put Bakar into power made her wonder. But it was still too soon for personal questions. There had been a few dinners, sparring sometimes, an evening or two spent together. Left under a cloud was all she knew, and that was all anyone seemed to know or was willing to say. She'd tried sounding out the old sergeant-at-arms, Eneko's closest confidante, but all she'd got for her trouble was a stream of curses and a threat if she ever asked anyone, ever again.

"Impolite!" He laughed a long, rasping chuckle at that. "I suppose it is. And he's not mentioned it? Well, if he hasn't I don't think I will. Not unless you decide this is going to become a regular thing. A fling's all very well – no harm if you keep your trap shut about the dark jobs, keep your trap shut about everything inside the guild if you're having a fling outside it, but you know that. Know this too, girl. If you get to having more than a fling with him, there's all manner of things you'll be wanting to know about Petri Egimont, and I don't doubt you'll hate him as much as I do before you're halfway through because there's a streak, maybe more than a streak, in him of his father. You even think about making it regular, you come see me first, all right? Let me give you a few home truths to chew on. In the meantime think on why he might not have told you. Think on where your duty lies, and it isn't in his trousers."

Just like her da, looking out for her, a bit too much at times, but still. "All right."

"Good girl." He squeezed her shoulder. "Now, if you can spare the time away from Egimont, I've got a job for you."

Petri sat opposite Bakar in the prelate's quarters overlooking the clanking garden in the moonlight, sipping apple tea and trying to decide how to answer the question.

If he answered too truthfully, the job would be done and he'd be back at his cramped desk listening to his overseer sneering at him. He'd be trapped back within the palace, left to a lifetime of grey. Oh, he'd be able to go out sometimes, but Bakar was a watchful man. It would be noted where he went, who he spoke to. Bakar was planning to get rid of the guild and hadn't that been a shock. But he'd promised Petri the guild, though now that was forgotten along with much else. Petri spent his evenings with Kacha when he could, and his days staring at the paperwork Bakar had him do, at the strange edicts that poured from him like wine these last weeks. Yet Petri couldn't be sure that it was just that he was now looking at Bakar with different eyes.

Once this job was done seeing Kacha would become difficult, and he didn't want difficult; he wanted seeing her to be as easy as breathing. He'd been restless before, chafing at Bakar's orderly world, but now he wasn't just restless, he was itching to burst out of the gears Bakar had bound him in.

"Petri?"

"Sorry. Yes, it's going well enough." Not the whole truth, no. Bakar couldn't have seen this in his precious clockwork, and Petri was going to make the most of it. "I'm concentrating on gaining the confidence of one or two before I start to dig."

"Very wise. Do you have any inklings yet though?"

Petri put down his cup – he was so full of energy it was hard to stop it clattering on the saucer. Kacha, he was going to meet Kacha later, and that seemed all he could think about. "One or two suspicions but nothing solid yet."

Bakar nodded sagely. "Has anyone asked you why you left the guild?"

"No, not yet." They hadn't asked, but he'd heard the whispers and the not-so-quiet murmurs designed for him to hear. Oh yes, and a drunken Vocho speculating with his friends at full volume what a man would have to do to make Eneko forbid his name to be spoken in the guild, or why in hells Kacha would have anything to do with someone who'd been exiled. They'd shut up bloody quick when Kacha walked into the inn, but Vocho still muttered under his breath any time Petri was near. Just as long as Kacha didn't hear him.

He'd been expecting that, which didn't make it any easier to bear. He hadn't expected Kacha not to ask, or for himself to want to spill it all out anyway. And yet he hadn't – and why was that? Because every time she talked about Eneko, he could see it in her eyes. The way she looked up to him, trusted him. Something soft under all the wisecracking with her brother, under her smooth moves and nonchalant ease with a blade. He wanted to find out what it was, but he didn't want to have to reveal the shame of his father, cast that shame over a man she clearly thought of as her father, to do it. *Everyone has secrets*, he thought, and wished he dared speak his aloud. Maybe one day, but not yet.

No matter how he felt his whole life had just spun a full turn on the orrery, changing it beyond recognition, it'd only been a few weeks. A few weeks of hours that seemed too snatched and short to him. Maybe if he could pluck up the courage to kiss her . . .

"Petri! Have you been listening? By the God's cogs, man, you've not been right ever since you started this. Maybe it was a mistake, dredging up old memories. Maybe you should let someone else do this."

Petri forced his mind back into the room. Difficult though. Clocks everywhere, ticking and tocking until he wanted to scream. Each tick was slicing seconds off his life, each tock was nailing him to this palace, to his grey little cubicle, his grey little job.

"Absolutely not," he said as he stood up. He had to get out of this room, out of the palace. "I'm just starting to get somewhere. I promise you. Now, if you'll excuse me, I've arranged to meet some of the masters."

He shut the door behind him with a great wash of relief which he didn't fully appreciate until he was out of the palace, out of the gardens, away from the constant noise of his life ticking away. Out into Reyes proper, for once feeling part of the colour and noise that surrounded him. He headed down towards the Clockwork God and the docks, to where he'd arranged to meet Kacha.

The streets were crowded tonight, but not so crowded they didn't make way for a prelate's man. He looked up at the god, brass all silvered by the moonlight, clicking his way through his preset ritual. Outside the guild, reminding everyone that the guild had bowed to Bakar, that the Clockwork God watched over even them and demanded their truth. Oh, the guild still had respect, still had admiration, but since that day it didn't have *quite* as much as it once had, a thought that brought a small smile to Petri every time it occurred.

A smile that curdled slightly as Kacha appeared. It was the guild he'd been promised that now he'd come to destroy, the guild that was her life, and he wasn't sure he could do it. Not when she bounced up to him like that, her face losing a thoughtful frown when she found him. She stood in front of him, and a second stretched out beyond reckoning. This was what he wanted, only this. No revenge on Eneko, no destruction of the guild, no doing the prelate's work; nothing but Kacha looking up at him, and the rest of the world barely a murmur around them.

The kiss took him by surprise, even though he started it. A long kiss, full of fevered wantings and desperate wishings that things were otherwise, and then past that into not caring whether things were otherwise or not. It seemed like for ever before they parted.

"Petri." Her voice seemed very deep and breathless, and made his spine shiver. "Answer me one thing. Why are you here? Why did you come back? Start sparring again?"

Something lay behind that question, he was sure, but right at this moment, here in front of the Clockwork God, there was only truth. "Right now I'm here for you."

A breathy laugh, and then she grabbed his hand and pulled him towards the guild. He hesitated – he'd never be allowed past the gates – but she pulled him on and he couldn't resist.

"What seems good to me," she said when he hesitated again at the gates, before she glared down a journeyman who looked about to protest but was probably too young to remember Petri at any rate.

She led him past cloisters full of memories, up stone stairs, along echoing passages. He shut his eyes to everything but her, here, now. She stopped outside a door and turned the soft part of her to him, the part that seemed to need something from him. "Does it seem good to you?"

He answered her with a kiss, with more than a kiss. The door opened behind her and they fell in, and he lost all the buttons on his shirt before they made it to the bed.

Bakar could never have seen this.

Chapter Eighteen

It felt odd, going into the house that Kacha knew Petri had been born in, lived in with his father when they were in the city. He'd never talked about his father apart from an odd aside here and there, except that last night, but she knew all the same how glad he'd been to escape the ice in this house and go to the guild. The guild had been his home, and then . . . He didn't talk much about the "and then" either.

With that thought came the next, inevitable one. *We were all escaping into the guild, every one of us, even if what we were escaping was different. Only some of us got to stay escaped, and some didn't.*

She followed Dom as he paced across the cavernous hall. A thought struck her. "You said you'd never been to Reyes before."

That strange, sharp new smile and a shrug. "I lied."

He led the way past sumptuous hangings, a series of clockwork gilded eggs that each was worth what any respectable smith might earn in a year, past ranks of paintings of presumably past family members which turned out to be members of someone else's family — Petri's if the little plaques were anything to go by — through a dark wood door, and into a room that was, if possible, even more luxurious if lacking in anything that could be called taste. Gilt covered just about everything not nailed down, making Kacha squint. What wasn't gilt was gaudy, colours clashing everywhere. A vast lounger in bright blue leather which might have looked classy on its own vied for attention with another in striped blood-red and black. Under them a carpet woven with gold and silver tried to get in on the act, while the curtains seemed to be evolving a life of their own in vivid patterns of green and pink.

Dom caught her look and grimaced along with her. "My apologies, but my father's had bad taste a lot longer than he's had any money. As far as he's concerned, if it costs a lot, it must be good. Ah, Rimmen, there you are." This was to a serious-faced man dressed all in neat black who appeared silently at a door on the other side of the room. He gave Kacha an appraising glance that valued her clothes down to the nearest penny and was distinctly unimpressed.

"Sir?"

"Sorry to barge in unannounced, but we've, er, I've come to see to a few things for my father. We won't be long. Is his study unlocked?"

"Certainly. I shall bring refreshments." The man disappeared as if by magic, leaving Kacha feeling faintly disturbed though she couldn't work out why.

Dom didn't seem to feel anything and again led the way, through a set of heavy velvet curtains – deep purple with red flowers, was Dom's father colour blind? – that led to another door of heavy wood, set with an impressive lock of tooled brass. As Rimmen had said, the door wasn't locked, and Dom pushed on through.

If anything the study was even worse than the previous room. A series of small deep-set windows looking out over a riotous garden were framed with possibly the most hideous curtains Kacha had ever seen. The carpet almost took her eye out. There were fancy little tables with carved frills and gold edging, all crammed with expensive . . . tat was the word that sprang to mind, and lots of worn-looking clockwork gizmos that jerked out a few movements when activated. A bird that would flap its wings once and croak out a tune. A lady with crooked eyes sat at a desk, pen poised, ready to be wound and write a letter. A box that she couldn't work out. Without thinking she picked it up and wound it, only to drop it when a red-tongued demon leaped out on a spring.

"Careful!" Dom said from behind a massive desk that had obviously been built to impress, with at least six different woods inlaid into it and a clockwork something attached to one corner. A closer look revealed the complicated run of gears and cogs, all in etched brass and gold, to be a pencil sharpener. "Those are worth a fortune. Early examples of clocker work, you see. Quite rare some of them. My father collects them. Ah, here we are."

Where they were was never actually established because Rimmen chose that moment to return not with refreshments but a contingent of armed men. Too many. Kacha quickly realised she hadn't a hope. Four of them had guns pointed before she could even reach for her sword. Four more blocked the door. The windows might have been an option, but she'd have struggled to fit through any of the panes when she was twelve.

"I really am most dreadfully sorry," Rimmen said with apparent seriousness, "but your father sent explicit instructions."

Dom stood like a statue, two guns pointed at his face. He looked like he was contemplating escape, as Kacha had, before his shoulders slumped. "How explicit?"

A thin smile from Rimmen. "Very much so, I'm afraid. He was prepared to give you a second chance, but not a third. He has the family name to consider, after all, as it *is* a name now, much more than before. These gentlemen here are to escort you to the Shrive."

"You can let—"

"Sadly no. Kacha is also a wanted person, as you are well aware. Your father has graciously said I might keep any reward monies. Please try not to damage any of your father's things as you leave."

Dom was whey-faced with shock and when Kacha threw him a questioning look shook his head. Petri might have hesitated to shoot her when he had the chance, but these were just guards under orders from a man with a lot of money. They'd shoot first and apologise for getting blood on the carpet afterwards.

As if in answer to her thoughts, one of the gun men prodded his weapon into the side of her head. She was crap with guns, but one thing she did know – no matter how quick she might be, she wasn't going to dodge a bullet from that close, especially when there was more than one bullet to dodge. *Second rule of duelling*, Eneko's voice echoed in her head from all those years ago, *is don't go charging in when you can't win. Bide your time, watch, listen, wait until you can win*.

They were cuffed, had their swords taken and then the two of them were shoved out into the street. It wasn't far to the Shrive, and the road was dark. The door gaped open ahead of them, and Kacha recalled the time she and Vocho had watched Novatonas's execution, when Bakar had been dragged off into this doorway. It had looked then like the gate to the hells. The Clockwork God had no concept of hell or heaven, but she was old enough to remember the gods before him and it still looked like the gate to the hells.

Inside was little better. They passed through a series of clanking gates, where the guards checked they had no hidden weapons, keys or anything else likely to cause them problems, before they were herded down, always down. The walls stopped being dressed stone and became rough, ancient and running with damp. Still they went down, until Kacha was sure they must be far underground. Finally, after what seemed like miles of corridors, the guards opened a door with a heavy key, removed their cuffs and shoved them in before locking the door behind them.

Dom slumped down in the rancid straw while Kacha looked in every corner that she could – the only light came from a tiny grilled window. Sadly the Shrive was far too efficient at what it did and there was nothing to give her hope, nothing at all. Finally, she went to the window. The damp was worse out there, coating her face with its chill. It smelt earthy, and on the edge of hearing she could make out both a rushing noise and a regular clack-clack-clack. The light came from a high lamp fitfully illuminating a path that looked nothing like the corridors they'd come down.

"The river," Dom said behind her. "That's how Bakar got out. Twice he escaped, and no one else even managed once. That's where he found the waterwheels too, and figured out how the clockwork was running, found the Clockwork God's broken heart and mended it. Looked at it and thought this is the logical way. The old king always said he was gods-blessed, you see. Do you remember that? No, too young, I suppose. He said he was gods-blessed, and that's why he was king, and what he said was an order from above. People believed it too, or pretended to anyway. Made a stupid kind of sense, because of course the gods wouldn't allow anyone but their favoured to be king. Bakar changed all that. Science he called it. Observing the world and using that to determine how it worked, rather than listening to the gods. He saw those waterwheels, saw the movements of all the things they run and wondered. What if there are no gods watching us? Rational thought says that's just the human ego talking. Why would any god watch over a wretch like me, or a poor docker's kid like you? Surely they've more important people to watch over? Or more important things to do. But if the world was like the clockwork, what if whoever created us wound it, provided it with its own waterwheel, and left it to run on its prescribed rails? What if *no* god watches us, and all we have are our own observations of the truths of the universe?"

Dom was pacing now, more alive than Kacha had ever seen him. *Who the hells are you?* Now he had dropped his act he didn't seem to be able to shut up. She wondered how long he'd kept all this in.

"Of course he was smart enough to give people a god to believe in anyway, only one that was more logical. After the first time he escaped, when he first saw the wheels and realised, he went to Ikaras University, where the Great Fall wasn't as bad, and they say there are records that go back two thousand years. That's as may be – I never saw any. Anyway, that's where I met him, hanging on every word of Novatonas, helping him with all his new and exciting machines, the movements and cogs and gears, the philosophy too. Novatonas had come to it through his own observations on the world and how it worked. A brilliant man. Until Bakar came."

He paused for breath, and Kacha managed to get a word in. "That's very interesting, but what's it to us right now? We're sitting in a cell, and I know I'm probably never going to get out."

Dom held up a hand. He was smiling, something like his old, twittery self, and it had her puzzled.

"He escaped *twice* – the second time after Novatonas was executed for heresy, which I was about to get to."

"All right, he escaped twice, which would be very useful if we knew how."

"We do. Or rather, *I* do. He came to Novatonas to learn, he said. I was already there, studying. Some fellow feeling between us, or so he thought. He had had to leave the guild

– couldn't pass his master's – and it rankled no end. Still does, and one reason he pushed Eneko so, why he had him spied on after the revolt and brought in to answer for himself whenever he did anything at all out of the ordinary. When Bakar recognised me—"

"Why should he recognise you?"

"When he recognised me, he thought I'd feel the same. Being the only person ever expelled from the guild after he'd taken his master's. Until you and Vocho, that is."

Ridiculous. The only person before them to have been expelled after taking his masters had been . . . "Wait a minute. You're Jokin?"

"Sadly, that is so. My name is actually Narcis Jokin Donat Chimo Ne Farina es Domenech. Bit of a mouthful, I think you'll agree."

Kacha ran a hand through her hair. It was a hell of a lot to take in. The guild hadn't taught them much history bar the highlights, but Jokin, there had been whole lessons on him – how he'd been a brilliant student, formidable with a blade, how Eneko had taken him under his wing, made him guild master's apprentice much as Kacha had been, how he'd then betrayed the guild, betrayed Eneko personally, by changing sides midway through a job, and how they must never do the same. Eneko had spent even longer on the subject with her, afraid she'd betray him as Jokin had.

"I hope you aren't disappointed in me?" Dom said.

"What? No. Hells, how could I be? I got kicked out just the same as you did. Worse even, now I come to think about it. But how do you know how he escaped? And can *we* escape?"

"We'll save the rest for another time, but Bakar thought I felt the same about the guild as he did, that we were fellow exiles. And he talked a lot when he was drunk, and he often was in those days. So he told me how he escaped. And can *we*? Not that way. *You* can though, if things haven't changed too much. I hope perhaps you might then come back and rescue me."

"I will if you ever get around to telling me how."

His grin was really quite infectious. She told herself there was still a lot he hadn't said, that she'd need to winkle out of him later. Like what was Jokin doing pretending to be a clocker's idiot son, and why had he latched on to her and Vocho, and all manner of things. But for now she'd trust him. It didn't look like she had much choice.

Dom winked at her, scrabbled about in the straw and found the drain. The grating was locked and it looked like rust had welded it to the stone of the floor. It also smelt worse than anything she could ever recall.

She looked at it and then at Dom. "You want me to go down there?"

"If you want to get out of here."

"OK, fine. But it's rusted to buggery and locked, which makes me think they've thought of people escaping that way."

"Don't they teach lock-picking at the guild any more?"

"Well, yes. But I was never very good at it. That was Vocho's thing."

"Mine as well. Especially seeing as Bakar told me exactly how the lock works and how it can be opened. He was a locksmith before he was prelate. Bet you didn't know that."

"In which case you'd have thought they'd have changed the locks."

"The first time they didn't know how he escaped. Like he'd disappeared from a sealed box. Total mystery. Besides, Shrive guards under the king weren't noted for their forward planning, mainly because they got paid so little. Mostly they went with the 'Keep 'em in large amounts of pain; they won't think about escaping' plan, which worked for most people."

"But not Bakar?"

"He's a very unusual man. Bakar is more perceptive than the old king, for all his faults. He pays by results. "

All the while he'd been talking Dom had been searching across his tunic. "Ah! Here it is. These aren't all for show, you know." He unpinned a startlingly ugly brooch, revealing an extra-long pin with a weird twist at the end. "I knew this would come in handy. Bakar gave it to me. See the bit on the end? Best thing I've ever found for those more difficult locks. Really, he should have stayed in locksmithing; he was a genius."

With that he began probing the lock. It didn't seem to go very well because after a time he started swearing. "That should work. I don't see why it hasn't."

"Because the man who runs the Shrive is the only man ever to have escaped it." The voice startled them both. "He had all the locks remade to his own designs, and *he* keeps the keys. Not only that, he had the drains trapped. If you got through the grating, you'd only end up as mincemeat in some of the more dubious sausages down by the docks."

The shadowy face at the grille in the door moved, a key turned in a lock and the door opened. Kacha wasn't sure who she was expecting, but it wasn't a smiling Eneko. He stepped into the cell, and Kacha was shocked at the difference in him. His hair had been sprinkled with grey all the time she'd known him, but now the darkness was streaked with white. He looked like he hadn't slept in a month, and there was a tremor in his hand that had never been there before. She tried to think of something defiant to say, to show she wasn't afraid, but the only words that came to mind sounded petulant and childish, so she said nothing.

"I'm really quite pleased to see you," he said to Kacha. "Really. I'd hoped that somehow I could discover your innocence, that I could bring you back into the guild without

Bakar wanting your head. But it seems we've both discovered more than we expected."

"You certainly didn't seem too worried about my innocence when the guards came for me before, or when me and Voch had to run for our lives. In fact I seem to recall you tried to hand me over."

Eneko shrugged. "A guild master has to play a political game, I'm afraid. I couldn't be seen to support you, not with Bakar watching my every move. Especially as I knew that Vocho was guilty and couldn't be sure you weren't too."

"You could have asked?"

Eneko laughed at that. "Not so simple, Kacha. You should know that. After all the little jobs you've done for me over the years. It's never simple, is it?"

That snapped her mouth shut. All those jobs, the ones he'd persuaded her were for the good of the guild, the good of the city, the right thing to do. Legitimate jobs, he'd said, just ones that needed to be done quietly. They weren't an assassins' guild but sometimes a job required them to act like one, secretly at least, and only for certain employers. He told her he'd look after her, and he had. Until he hadn't.

"What is it you want?"

"I'm fond of you, Kacha, more than fond. Besides, you were exemplary at your work. Quick, quiet, efficient, no bragging, didn't ask awkward questions, perfect. As good as Dom ever was and like my own daughter in many ways. I want you back in the guild, if I can, but *without* your grandstanding fool of a brother. *If* you're innocent, you could be of great help to me in the coming months, which promise to be interesting if not brutal. Licio and his pet magician are out to get rid of the prelate, that much I do know. Who am I to stop them?"

He spread his hands, all innocence, and Kacha recalled all the times he'd railed against Bakar, how much he'd hated him for his humiliations.

"You're just going to let it happen? What about all your talk of the guild being for Reyes? All those lessons on ethics?"

"What's more ethical, Kacha? A prelate whose whole rule is based on the lie of a god he doesn't believe in? A boy-king under the influence of a magician? Or a guild ruling Reyes in truth for its people?"

Kacha stared at his face, so familiar but now seeming the face of someone else. "The *guild* ruling . . . You ruling, you mean."

"Naturally. All those dark jobs you did for me were to remove support for Bakar one small step at a time. Did you really think they were anything else?"

She stared at him as though she'd never seen him before, and maybe she hadn't. Not this side of him. "The dark jobs were for the good of Reyes, you said. I was killing slavers and the like. For the good of Reyes, that's what you said."

What he'd said, and she'd blindly believed him. Because he was like Da, because she needed someone to be perfect for, or what was the point? She'd believed him, made sure not to question him, ignored all the little signs that now, in a flash of understanding, had grown big as elephants. The way Petri twitched every time his name came up, how Eneko had sidestepped any questions she asked, Bakar's needling of him, hatred of him. She'd been blind to it all because she'd *wanted* to be. The last part of what she thought she'd known, thought she was, crashed around her ears. She'd been murdering people for Eneko's ambition.

He moved closer, and was that real compassion in his eyes?

"Kacha, listen to me. You were the one. Always. My Kacha, helping me make this city great again. Ridding it of everything that's weakened it since Bakar came to power. I couldn't have done any of it without my perfect Kacha."

"Funny," Dom said behind her. "You used to say that to me. And you've missed out a whole section about your own foray into slavery. Or how when I found out, you destroyed me."

A flash of irritation passed over Eneko's face. "More to it than that, wasn't there, Jokin? Don't paint yourself as blameless."

"Slavery?" Kacha backed away from Eneko, from his reaching hand, the sorrow in his eyes.

His wise voice, that patient one she craved and so at odds with his words. "Not really – though some would say otherwise. Bakar and Petri, maybe. No more slavery than a guild education. They had better lives than those I took them from."

"Who did?"

He shook his head as though he was dealing with a child who couldn't hope to understand the complexities of life outside the nursery. "Won't you take my word on it? Trust me and come back. Come home."

With every word he was crushing every dream she'd ever had of the world, so that now maybe she could see it as it was – ugly as sin under its patina of beauty – but at least this was truth. "Not this time." She'd had enough of trust turning round to bite her to last ten lifetimes. "Tell me all of it."

He seemed to crumple then, his face sagging, his eyes looking even older. He reached out a hand towards her shoulder, then seemed to think better of it. "I've loved you as a daughter. And like a father I wanted you to think well of me. That's all. I sent them to Ikaras. Without them, they could never have built such a trade in sugar, in coal and iron, never got the wealth they have now, and as for the people themselves, they'd have died down on the docks most likely, starved to death in an alley somewhere. Others serve the king, his nobles, feed me information. Some pass on information from me to the king there. Ikaras owes me, and they know it, and maybe when the time comes, I'll have an ally there. A slow, subtle move to power it was going to be, with a sudden fall of the sword at the end. For the good of Reyes. Licio has hastened things on for me, though. Using Vocho to kill the priest was inspired. Maybe I can use the coming confusion to my advantage. *Our* advantage, Kacha. When the guild comes to power, I'll need a woman with a sword at the ready. Just say the word, and you can be out of here, back in the guild, back where you belong."

Oh, it was tempting. Tempting to give in, to go back to what she knew, what was comforting. Get out of this cell with her head still on her shoulders. But this . . . He'd used her for his own revenge against Bakar. He'd sent people off to slavery in Ikaras, had her kill people for his own ends. He'd lied to her, betrayed her. She'd thought he was like her da, but he was just out for what she could give him, out for himself. Just like everyone else.

Everyone had betrayed her, *everyone*. She had nothing and no one to fight for any more, except herself. No Da, no Voch, no Petri, not even Eneko, the rock she'd built herself on, had always wanted to prove herself to, had craved praise from. She had no one to be perfect for any more, and the thought was vibrantly liberating. She owed no one anything any more either, no loyalty or perfection or obedience.

The kick in the groin caught even the experienced Eneko off guard and surprised Dom into stillness for just long enough. Long enough to wrench the knife from the hidden sheath where she knew Eneko kept it. Long enough to slash the belt that held his sword and grab it. Long enough to make for the door. Dom started forward, but he wasn't quick enough, not to catch an enraged Kacha. Neither were the two duellists waiting outside, or perhaps they might have been if Kacha hadn't surprised the first by grabbing his shirt and giving him a headbutt that spread his nose over his face, before she threw him into his companion. She didn't wait for anything, not to give anyone an extra kick to be sure, or for Dom, who was calling her name a few steps behind.

She was going to find Vocho, rescue him this one last time, and then they could all go to hell, every last one of them.

Interlude

Six months earlier

Vocho had watched Egimont sneak into the guild the previous night, wary and watchful. He watched him now, as he left at dawn, with a spring in his step and a funny little smile on his lips. For a long time Petri hadn't been allowed inside the guild for no reason that Vocho knew of except he'd left under a cloud. Now he was Kacha's guest, and she had clout, so he was permitted into her private quarters at least, if not exactly welcomed elsewhere. He made damned sure to keep out of Eneko's way, Vocho noted.

He sauntered out of his nook in the corner of a tower and followed Petri down the steps that led to the grassed-over stone arch that served as a bridge to the city. The sun was barely above the walls and everything was still dressed in grey and purple with a hint of gold. Petri seemed in no hurry and was even humming to himself as he reached the greensward where Kacha had fallen in the river all those years ago. Afterwards Eneko had built a wall, waist high and topped with a railing, so it wouldn't happen again. Petri stopped there and looked out at the mists curling about the bridge and the stretch of river that flowed down from the mill race under the Shrive.

Vocho padded silently over the grass but Petri surprised him without turning. "I knew you'd come at some point, so let's get it over with, shall we?"

"Why not?" Vocho agreed.

There'd always been something odd about Petri to Vocho's mind. A little too smooth, a touch too silent, and when he did speak, his accent was an infuriating mix of arrogance and pomposity. Always watching Kass too, and now not just watching.

Petri turned and stood easily, looking down his long nose at Vocho like he was some sort of bug. Like he was still a noble and Vocho was still a dock rat, instead of Petri actually being a pathetic little clerk for the prelate and he the most renowned duellist the guild had ever seen.

"Kacha," Vocho said. "I want you to leave her be."

"Really?" Petri raised a cool eyebrow. "And what's it to do with you?"

"She's my sister; it's everything to do with me. I've seen you, always watching her. You do it even when you think she's not looking. Not like other men look at her either. You look at her like she's an interesting specimen and you want to dissect her."

The smile almost fooled Vocho but it was too damned slick. "Dissecting wasn't what I had in mind, I have to say. And that's not what's really bothering you, is it?"

Vocho whipped his sword out and held it to Petri's cheek, the tip just touching skin. "Leave my sister alone. She can do better than some deposed little lordling like you, so leave her be."

"Or what? Or you'll push me into the river, like you did her?"

Vocho swallowed a violent urge to be sick, and his blade dropped to his side. "She tripped, that was all." He meant it too, had repeated the lie over and over to himself until he near enough believed it.

Petri's smile broadened, sure his thrust had hit home, that all that was left was to provide the finishing stroke. "That's what she thinks too, though she says she doesn't remember much. We know better, don't we?"

Vocho had no answer for that, none at all.

"I admire your sister and always have. Admire her very much. So much energy, so much enthusiasm for everything, so dedicated. You—" Petri snorted derisively. "You always wanted it all given to you on a platter. Never wanted to *work* at it. Never did anything to deserve what you've got. She had to work every step of the way, fight for everything against those who laughed at her for her efforts. The guild lets in women, trains them, pays lip service to all things being equal, but only because that ancient clockwork marionette in the courtyard is a woman and the guild follows its traditions, because the Clockwork God has spoken. But how many women ever get their master's? Five perhaps in the last ten years? How many are allowed to *try* even? They trot out all the excuses they can, and people believe it. They laughed at her behind her back, 'let' her win, made bets on when she'd fail, and I know you ran at least one book on that, dear, concerned, brotherly Vocho. Showed them, though, didn't she? Showed you too, and I bet it hurt when Eneko took her on as his apprentice. When she got her master's before you, not because she was as good as the rest but because she was *better*. Did you think about pushing her into the river again? Or maybe off the walls? Just so you could be the golden one? Is that why you started pushing the rules in the arena? Is that why you started fixing duels? Oh yes, I know all about that, and the books you run on them, and paying men to lose and skimming off the top on jobs as well, taking credit for work that's not yours, paying people to make up songs about you just to rub it in that you're better. So perhaps you'd like to fuck off, brother dearest, and let me court your sister without your petulant face in the background. And then perhaps I won't tell her about how she really ended up in that river, or how much money you lost betting against her in duels, or any of the rest of it. Perhaps I won't tell her what a shit of a brother she looks to, loves, *defends*, for god's sake. What do you say?"

Vocho gaped like a ten-pint drunk asked a simple question. He wanted to say it was all lies, that he was a good brother, like he always told himself. Lied to himself. And he was a good brother, sometimes. It's just that other times he wasn't himself. Other times he seemed to watch himself from outside, banging on the window and telling himself not to do those things. And when he came back to himself, he promised never to do them again, lied to himself that it wasn't that bad, *he* wasn't that bad . . .

"I'll take that as agreement then," Petri said, sounding a thousand miles away. "Do have a good day."

Vocho stood for a good long while, not noticing the sun come up or the other duellists staring at him as he watched the water flow under the bridge.

Chapter Nineteen

Petri tried to let nothing show on his face, but he wasn't sure he managed it. Sabates' gaze was unnerving him, along with the news. Kacha was in the Shrive by good or ill luck, and only now did he see exactly what he'd signed up to, just how far Licio was prepared to go – and expect him to go.

The king sat at his grand desk in his Reyes house. The Ikaran banker, a grey hunched sort of man here to see his investment rewarded, blinked in the dim light from a smoking lamp. Alicia was here too, ice cold in silver grey but with mischief in her twitch of a smile. And Sabates, always Petri's eyes came back to Sabates, sitting in a dark corner watching. All Petri could think of was his father, of the way he'd come apart as though made of dry sand. And a magician did it. Had he deserved it? Had *any* of it been true? Those were the thoughts that had begun to plague him – that every man and woman was false, that the only truth he had was what he'd experienced, and even then he couldn't be sure.

"Well, that saves us the trouble of finding her," Licio was saying, rubbing his hands together. "With her to use, we'll get Vocho doing what we want in no time."

"I thought the tattoo—" Petri said.

"Has its limits," Sabates interjected smoothly. "I can use it to overpower his own better instincts for ten, maybe twelve minutes, though his instincts tend to run in our direction if you're right about him being Eneko's assassin. Any longer than that, it'll burn him to a husk, though he might prove useful in the future if only as a scapegoat. The tattoo's too powerful rather than not powerful enough. So he'll do what I want, whether he likes it or not, when I need him to, but I have to get him to where he can do it first, and without bloodshed or we'll be discovered. For that we need persuasion, and there are only two things Vocho cares about – notoriety and his sister. Offer him one and threaten the other. He'll see sense soon enough."

"And after?"

Sabates smiled, and Petri didn't like the look of that smile in the least. "Then we kill her. She knows more than is good for her health. So does Vocho, but I can manage that. DUELLIST KILLED BY GUARDS AFTER ASSASSINATING PRELATE. Maybe she can be his co-conspirator."

"You could put a tattoo on her?" Licio said.

Petri was sure Sabates could see right into his heart, that the thought of that made him shudder.

"Sadly, it takes a vast amount of power, and blood, to perform the initial spell, and it has to be a certain kind for this particular tattoo. I drained four magicians for the one that Vocho wears. Do you see four magicians anywhere?"

Licio stood up and strode over to Petri. He looked more regal than ever, yet boyish and golden in the dim light, but even so there was something about his eyes that told Petri he was utterly determined to do this and maybe a little bit mad too.

"I'm sure this won't be a problem for our ever-loyal Egimont. Will it? I mean, you only used her for information about her brother. It wasn't serious. Was it?"

Petri stared straight ahead, afraid that any move would

give him away, afraid that if it did he'd end up as his father had done. "It won't be a problem." He thought he could feel the heat of Sabates' gaze on him, which was ridiculous but unnerving nonetheless.

"I can kill them both, if you like," Alicia purred from the corner. "Dom, as he styles himself now, is an old friend. More than a friend."

"And he's still alive?" Sabates asked with a flick of an amused eyebrow. "You surprise me."

She flipped a fan out of one copious sleeve and wafted it next to her pale-marble face. "We all make mistakes. That won't be one I'll repeat. It would be my pleasure to kill him, as you well know."

Petri stared at her, at the face that looked carved from angels, and thought he saw the heart that beat beneath the pretty dress, the heart that was as black as she was pale. He thought too of Vocho asking him if he would do it. Would he kill Kacha, if he had to? No, no, a hundred times no, but he couldn't say that here. Sabates would see only weakness in that, and Sabates was the man to beware of. Petri wasn't as indispensable as all that.

If it seems good to you. The motto he'd been brought up on, that lived, always, inside him, guiding everything he'd done. Each individual thing had seemed good to him: joining the king against the prelate, the thought of a new, fair society. Falling for Kacha when he was supposed to be using her, and all the rest – the lying and thieving, the betrayals, the killing when he'd had to – they had all *seemed* good, or for a good cause at least, but had led him here, to agreeing that killing the woman he'd been in love with wouldn't be a problem in order to save his own neck.

A choice then. He still believed the prelate needed to go, and his Clockwork God with him. He still believed that life didn't run on any rails, that he could change it if he wanted to. He still wanted the guild to be back among them, to lead them and have Eneko's head on a pike. Against that, Kacha, who'd opened his eyes and made the clockwork fall from his head. The choice wasn't hard at all.

"Well then," Licio said. "Let's not waste any more time. Egimont, go and get Kacha, bring her to her beloved brother, and let's get started. I'll have the guards fire up the brazier. I don't think it'll take much to break Vocho, do you?"

Petri wasn't so sure – Vocho was a contrary bastard at the best of times – but Licio's words made his choice for him. He left with a glance at Sabates, at the marks and patterns that swirled on his hands, that pulled his eyes in. Of crowns and stags and crossed swords. He looked and found he didn't care.

He went to bring Kacha, but not to Licio.

Chapter Twenty

It didn't take long for Kacha to be a dozen turns away from her cell, heart skittering in her throat, but by then other problems were starting to worry her. She had to get to wherever they might be holding Vocho, but first she had to get out, and that was going to be a problem.

The Shrive was old and massive and full of twists and turns that probably took years to learn. Some corridors were wide and well lit, and she avoided those. Others were dark and cramped, and she wanted to avoid those more for the groans and shrieks that came from some of them, but dark was her friend until she worked out how in hells to escape. They said there were two ways out of the Shrive, and both of them involved being dead.

The sound of guards, of grumbling and swearing and jangling armour, came from the left, so she went right, headed further into the guts of the prison. The walls here were dank and slimy, and the air was tangy with the scent of the river. She tried not to contemplate the thought of a long swim too closely. For all she was a dock rat by birth, she'd never got the knack of swimming more than a few yards, and the incident where she'd fallen in the Reyes river while sparring with Vocho and damn near drowned was both blurred by panic and crystal-clear with utter terror. Even training at the guild – masters were supposed to be prepared for any eventuality – hadn't changed that much.

It wasn't that she *couldn't*, more that she'd rather go out the front gates and risk the guards because it would scare her just that little bit less. Because while splashing about in a backwater was easy enough, even if it did make her knock-kneed with a fright she'd never dared to show, the Reyes river was a cold and heartless mistress. It might be warm spring in Reyes, but up in the mountains the melt was in full swing and the water would be close to freezing. Add to that the currents, which made it a treacherous way to travel even on a boat, worse around the islet that supported one end of the Shrive and . . . and she didn't want to go that way.

She tried hard to ignore a flapping white hand that came through a grille as she passed, to ignore the pleading croak. The Shrive seemed just as full as it ever had been in the days before the prelate, and worse, she was sure she'd helped put people here on her little jobs for Eneko, those she hadn't killed. And those . . . She wouldn't think on it now, but later she was going to recall who he'd had her kill. She hadn't wanted to question him, which was the thing. She'd put Eneko on a pedestal, loved him and made herself blind to everything but his praise, and now he'd shown he was just like all the others.

She hurried on, telling herself she'd come back, let these poor bastards out, all of them, and worried that it was an empty promise, that she was just as bad as Eneko, as Petri. Worse even.

The walls grew darker with damp until she was splashing through puddles. The last few corridors had been ominously silent. Down here was as deep as the Shrive seemed to go. Silent except for the rushing of water beyond the wall to her right hand and the faintest of ticking noises. The waterwheels that ran the city, that powered the gears, the mechanical duellist in the guild, the clock in the square outside the Shrive. That powered the change o' the clock.

Today was First Threeday. She'd vaguely heard some chimes go off not long before, putting the time at eleven at night. At midnight the whole city would change. At the moment the king's Reyes house was across the city, the other side of the guild and the Clockwork God. When the gears ran, when the cogs engaged, the whole city would move except the two buildings that preceded even the Castans, that came from the days before. The guild and the Shrive. And on Second Oneday that whole street and the king's Reyes house would be just to the north of the Shrive, almost within spitting distance. It would also be close enough to the prelate's palace to make getting in and giving him the papers a whole lot easier.

Or it would be as long at the change went smoothly. If it didn't, if she timed it right and shoved something in the works, the king's house would be stuck halfway. Not here, or there. Vulnerable, and likely with its guards having a collective fit rather than keeping an eye out for people sneaking about. Might make it easier getting into the palace after too.

Vulnerable but still too dangerous. Screw it. She was fed up with being the sensible one. Time to bring out the other Kacha, the one Eneko had trained to a sharp, hard point with assurances she was doing a good thing, but most of all with lots of practice running the roofs during a change when everyone was vulnerable.

Her eyes got used to the dark after a time, enough to make her way without falling over herself, and all those lessons from Eneko came flooding back, the lessons that not everyone got. How to move silently, how to use the shadows, how to balance on a point smaller than the point of her toe. She'd not seen any guards since the last lamp but that was no reason to take chances, especially as she could hear something going on up above − someone was shouting like he wanted the world to know about it, and there was a general mumble of footsteps on stone. It seemed she was being hunted.

This corridor ended not in a door but blank stone, dripping wet, set with a small, rusted grille. The oily sound of large amounts of water sliding across rock was loud, and the chill of the river flowed through the holes. When she peered through the grille she could make out moonlight far away, almost as though in another time. Closer, the water was slick and black as it rushed through the channel except for little slashes of white, the tips of waves.

The grille wouldn't present too much of a problem, she thought − she had Eneko's knife, and the damp had made the mortar holding the grille soft and easy to prise away. The gap was small, but she'd squeezed through worse.

No, getting through wasn't going to be too much of a problem. It was wanting to. Every time she looked at the water − *cold and black* − she remembered − *can't breathe* − the last time in the river − *don't inhale* − how close she'd been to drowning − *just stop struggling* − before Vocho's hand had found her. Even thinking about it was making her hold her breath till spots ran in front of her eyes. No one here to save her now. Only the sudden flare of a lamp far back past twists and turns. The echo of Eneko's voice far away.

She shut her eyes and tried to drag up some courage, but it was in short supply. Odd half-remembered sounds came back to her, of words heard through water as she sank. The feel of a hand on hers, dragging her back, up into light and air.

OK, Vocho, you annoying little bastard. I owe you. And you might be a preening, lying little snot rag, but you're my brother and you're all I've got left. At least I know when you're lying because your lips move.

She twisted her way through the gap, wriggling her shoulders to get them through. On the other side she dangled from the lip and took a deep breath. The waterwheels were under there somewhere, along with all the gears and cogs that led from them. She just hoped she found them before they chewed her to bits or she drowned, whichever came first.

Chapter Twenty-one

For Egimont entry into the Shrive was easy enough, and he didn't have to worry overmuch about how to get out again — he was still the prelate's man, still wore the little badge in his lapel and the coloured flash on his tunic. At the gate he was given a guard to escort him to where Kacha was being held.

He didn't get far before the sounds of uproar filtered along the corridors, amplified by the wails of prisoners either not knowing what was going on or joining in the hubbub for the hells of it. By the time the guard had him at the cell that was supposed to hold Kacha, it was clear she wasn't in it.

Eneko was though, and that Dom fellow that Egimont had reason to regret meeting at Kass's farmhouse hiding place and again at the taverna. Eneko was blustering and shouting, ordering guards to get lamps and follow him. He noticed Egimont standing quietly watching and strode over like he owned the Shrive.

"What do you want?"

Egimont allowed himself the superior smile of someone who knows he's in the right. "Me? I've come for the prelate's prisoner. What are you doing here? Letting her go?"

Eneko's teeth clacked shut. He had no answer. He shouldn't by rights have been let into the Shrive, and most definitely not into a cell. Dom had no such hesitation. "Hardly. She escaped."

Egimont raised an eyebrow. "A tall order, even for Kacha. No one's escaped from here except the prelate."

"Until now. At least you won't get your paws on her. Or what she's got," Dom said.

The only proof he was working for the king, if it came to it, if everything turned out badly. A thing worth having. "That remains to be seen. You, yes, that guard there. Lock this man back up. I want to ask him a few questions later."

"Wait," Dom again, casting a sharp eye on Egimont. "Wait. Why are *you* here? Come to take Kacha to the prelate? Or somewhere else?"

"The prelate, naturally," Egimont lied smoothly. "Where else would I take her?"

"To—"

"Before you say anything, do you have any proof?" Egimont asked with a cool cock of his head. "I thought not."

"I don't," Dom said. "But I know who has. Let me go, and I might consider telling you where it is."

"Wait a minute, wait a minute. Who's in charge here? Thank you." The jailer, a hulking great man who looked like he must have to duck half the time when he walked the cramped corridors of the Shrive, moved between them. "You —" he poked a finger at Dom "— are a prisoner until someone in authority says otherwise. You —" he pointed at Egimont "— are a bloody clerk, and not a very important one at that. Stable boys have more clout than you, unless you have a written slip of authority from the prelate's office. Do you?"

Egimont held back a snarl. It was people like this prick, talking to him like he was just anyone, who'd made him throw in his lot with the king. "I'm acting on behalf of the prelate."

"Without a signed chit you've got as much authority here as this prisoner. In the meantime, if you don't mind, I've got a prisoner to catch."

"I know where she's going," Egimont and Dom said together and then shared a glare.

"Good. Then between the two of you I might keep my job and you might keep yours, Mister Clerk, and you —" to Dom "— might keep your head, if the prelate decides it's a mitigating circumstance. Now tell me, where's she going?"

Petri hesitated. If this oik caught her again, there might be nothing he could do.

"He doesn't know anyway," Dom said. "She's heading up. The tower. She thinks that's how the prelate escaped last time."

"And why does she think that?" the jailer asked.

"Because I told her."

It didn't sound at all likely to Egimont, but he kept quiet for now. Something odd about the man — there was certainly something else to his swordplay, as Petri had found to his cost.

The jailer screwed up his face in thought as though it was something he didn't have to do very often and finally came to a decision. "Don't reckon she'll try it." He gave a crafty look at Dom. "Ain't nothing much up there excepting guards' quarters, and she'll be caught for sure. So down it is."

Dom covered well, but the scowl was there even if it was momentary.

The jailer got Dom locked back in his cell and turned to Eneko and Egimont. "We was warned about her when they brought her in. Your apprentice, weren't she? How good is she, really?"

Eneko sneered, though there was an undercurrent to it,

as though he'd just been deeply disappointed. He looked about a dozen years older than he had the last time Petri had seen him, and his face was pinched and hollow-looking as though with grief. The sneer was familiar though, even if it did send Egimont's stomach into knots of rage. He almost wished he had a gun. It was only with supreme discipline that he managed not to grab one off a guard.

"She'll slice your guards into ribbons," Eneko said after a pause, with real pride in his voice. "She's got my knife and sword, and she knows how to use them, none better." He slid a nasty glance Petri's way. "She killed often enough for me."

She *what*? Vocho was the assassin, wasn't he? Licio had depended on it, but now Egimont thought on it, it made a strange kind of sense that it was Kacha. He didn't have time to think on it now though.

"She'll have to get close first," the jailer said, shaking his head. "All you duellists, thinking the world stays the same. Well it don't, and I got the guns to prove it."

Eneko smiled and shook his head. "And all you non-duellists think that a gun is all you need. A gun is nothing against a proper master, and she's that all right."

The jailer snorted. "So what do you suggest?"

"That myself and young Egimont here help you. We both know her well. Petri's a fair enough swordsman, and mark my words, you'll need someone good with a blade. My Kacha is the best. I trained her, lived with her, loved her, raised her as my own near enough, and I know how she fights, how she thinks. We might be able to avoid your blood staining too many walls."

The jailer looked at them both sideways, but in the end he nodded. "All right, but you just keep out of my lads' way and remember who's in charge here, OK?" He set off, shouting orders this way and that, getting his men in order.

It had been many years since Petri had been this close

to the guild master. Bakar had forgotten his promise of the guild for Petri, but it was Eneko that Petri really wanted, Eneko who had to suffer. And here he was, outside the protection of the guild's walls, and Petri with a sword.

"You plan to kill me?" Eneko said now. He didn't seem unduly perturbed by the thought.

"Not yet," Petri replied with a shrug. He had time and most likely dark tunnels. "When you have a sword on you. The guild taught me that, at least."

Eneko's smile caught him off guard. "Well enough. I had to do it, you know that? There was no other choice, not if I wanted to save the guild. Bakar wanted nobles' sons to corrupt to his way of thinking, to give himself legitimacy among those still on the fence. He would have destroyed the guild if I hadn't given you to him. He still can, he still wants to. It was a price I had to pay, and I'd pay it again."

"You wanted to hide what you were doing, the recruits you were shipping off to slavery in Ikaras, the assassinations. You expected that I'd die. You paid nothing. I paid it all."

Eneko nodded slowly. "True enough, and yes, you did, and I'm sorry for that. But you should know I'm on your side, or at least not on the prelate's side. Ah, you thought that was secret, you working for Licio as well as Bakar? I've known for some time, and I know the price he offered you. I swear to you now, Licio will fail in his promise to give you the guild, as Bakar has. The guild is not theirs to give, it is mine, and it will stay mine until I die."

"I look forward to that day," was all Petri could think to say. The guild was to be his, *his*, under Licio's rule, and that was about to snap out of his mouth when the jailer beckoned them on. Petri followed Eneko down into the darker corridors wondering whose side anyone was on.

Interlude

Five months earlier

Petri flipped the collar of his cloak up against the chill of a damp winter wind that couldn't dampen his mood or take his mind from the warm thoughts that enclosed it.

Bakar was well pleased with how he'd managed to infiltrate the guild, but Petri had long since stopped trying to gather information except about that prick Vocho. There was plenty of that to go around because Vocho wasn't one for keeping his mouth shut, but how much of the gossip was actually true was anyone's guess. Petri no longer cared – the information kept Bakar happy, and him out of his drudging little office and, more importantly, in the company of Kacha. Away from the confines of his office, where he'd spent most of these last years, he began to see more clearly. What a fool he'd been to believe Bakar, believe in his so-called equality and that he had Petri's interests at heart. Then there was the prelate's increasingly odd behaviour. A tax on *periwinkles*? On *petticoats*? Add to that the realisation that Bakar wanted the guild destroyed rather than given to Petri, as he'd always promised, and he was perilously close to all-out rebellion.

All because of Kacha, who'd shown him things and places

and people he hadn't known existed. Rooftops where people seemed to live on shadows and dust, workers leaving the clocker factories ground down by exhaustion and ground in with soot, dock rats who scurried after them begging for scraps, scrambling after the pennies that she scattered behind her like petals. "They're like I was once," she said with a sad smile. She showed him all this and saw how it horrified him. Bakar had told him that everyone was rewarded according to merit, that those who earned more, received more, but it wasn't working. Petri wasn't sure it ever could. Then Kacha would smile, shake off the melancholy for them both. They talked – he thought that was what kept drawing him back – and listened to each other long into the night. As different as night and day, she said once, where they'd come from, but the same underneath, and she'd smiled in a way that made him want to burst.

Those thoughts, and a belly full of good wine, ensured he barely noticed that the alley he'd turned down had no lamps lit, or that it was suspiciously empty and at this stage o' the clock in the wrong end of town, especially for someone like him and even more especially for someone dressed as he was. The whirring click hit him like a bucket of ice water, and he realised where he was, and in how much danger, when three men moved in front of him with another three or four behind from the sounds of it.

They were indistinct in the wavering light of a half-moon behind scudding clouds, so all he could be sure of was that they were there and one had a gun. No longer the preserve of the rich, in recent weeks and months crude versions had flooded the city. Sadly they were just as effective at killing people as the expensive ones, though with a higher chance of the person firing being the person who died.

Two of the men came at him from behind. Something cracked into the back of his head and he fell to his knees, sword partway out of its scabbard. Feet and fists blurred past his face and registered somewhere far off in the back of his mind as they struck.

The leader snarled something that Petri only caught part of, but enough to know he wasn't getting out of this without broken bones at the least, then, more clearly, "Fucking nobles, and a prelate's man to boot. The worst of both sides. Let's see how equal he is with his head kicked in, and I'll tell the Clockwork God the truth of the gold in his pockets."

A boot came flying towards him, and that probably would have been the end of his face if not the rest of him if a searing light hadn't appeared at the end of the alley. It burned Petri's eyes so that between that and the swelling that loomed over one brow, all he could see were blurs, and all he could hear were mumbling echoes and a series of whirrs and clicks.

Then a kind hand was helping him up, the alley lit with the bright yellow light of many lamps. Guards dressed in the king's colours were dealing with some very vocal men with blood on their hands – his blood, he was horrified to see, dripping from his head and face all over the golden young man who helped him into a carriage. A young man he recognised, once he'd got over the fact he'd just ruined the man's clothes. The yellow light of the lamps reflected from golden hair; the limbs were long and loose, and he exuded charm and grace and, somehow, *rightness*.

"Some men deserve equality," King Licio drawled as his guards outside bestowed a certain form of equality on the men who'd jumped Petri. "And some don't, don't you think?" He opened a small compartment in the carriage; inside tinkled crystal glasses and a fine decanter of brandy. He sloshed a generous measure into a glass and handed it to Petri.

"Petri Egimont, isn't it? Duke of Elona, or that's who you were born to be. I often wondered why you threw that away to join Bakar. Why would anyone do that?"

Petri didn't answer for the moment – couldn't, and not

just because his mouth was swollen. He took a swig of the brandy, found it to be better than any he'd had, ever, and took another gulp to steady his hands.

Licio looked at him, and Petri couldn't help but notice the difference between him and Bakar, remembering not for the first time how Bakar's eyes had begun to jump around the room when no one was there, how his hands shook and he often couldn't quite get a grip on his words. How when he did speak the words would sometimes come out garbled nonsense before he gathered himself.

"There are some who don't deserve equality," Licio said, his voice low and soothing. "You know it, I know you do. And what equality does Bakar espouse just lately? My guards will take those men to the Shrive, and maybe Bakar will set them free in the morning on a whim because the crime wasn't great, because they are just poor men, and even poor men deserve something. But what about you? Don't you deserve justice for what they did to you? Don't you deserve the equality in justice he reserves for others? Bakar keeps *some* men and women in the Shrive for years, murderers and the like, and yes, that is what they deserve. But take a trip down to the lower levels. Find the men and women there just because they didn't agree with Bakar, because they refuse to believe in his Clockwork God. Is that equality? Or even justice?"

The carriage jerked into motion.

"What do you want?" Petri asked, because it seemed clear to him that the king wanted something, though what help a lowly clerk like him could give he had no idea.

Licio leaned back as though suddenly relieved and took a sip of brandy. "Oh, the same things as you, Petri, the same things as you, even if you don't know it yet. Our fathers were terrible men, that's true, but that doesn't make us terrible men, does it? Not as terrible as who replaced our fathers, the greedy little clockers without any propriety, any *honour* to fall back on. No sense of history, of building things to live on after them. All out for themselves, for here and now and never mind the future."

Petri's head was swimming. He couldn't be sure if it was the knock on the head, the brandy on top of the wine or whether what Licio was saying was stirring something inside. Things were wrong, he knew that; he'd known for a while even if he'd not admitted it to himself. But what Licio was hinting at . . . He felt excited and sick with guilt at the same time.

"Just a little thing to start," Licio said into these thoughts. "That's all I want. Just a little look into what has gone so badly wrong. Now, what do you know about that little tit Vocho?"

Chapter Twenty-two

It took every scrap of courage Kacha had to go into the water that surged dark and cold under the Shrive. She put it off as long as she could, dragging out the papers that were her only proof, the only hint even that something was wrong. The guards had taken her weapons but left almost everything else, including a pouch of oiled leather she used for keeping tinder dry when they travelled or at the farm. That gave her a pang. Always her and Vocho. Always, no matter where they went, what they did. He might be as unreliable as the wind, but he always had her back in a fight. All she could rely on, even when she couldn't.

She'd light the fire and see to the horses as he made up stupid stories to get her laughing while he skinned a rabbit or mended a harness. He was always *there*, and she'd hated that pretty much her whole life until now, when he wasn't.

She stuffed the papers into the pouch, hoped it would be up to the job and took a deep breath. The waters oiled past her, black and deadly, but not as deadly as what was coming behind. She could have sworn she heard Petri's voice, Eneko's with him, and it was that which decided her. She didn't dare think on why they were together.

Instead she took all her courage in both hands and let

herself drop into the water. It was colder even than she expected, cold enough to numb her hands almost straight away. She spluttered back to the surface and tried not to think about how badly she swam or the last time she'd been in the river. No Vocho here to pull her out, not this time, because she'd left him on his own, and that's why they'd got him. The water closed back over her head and she kicked to get her chin above water. She spat out a mouthful of water and tried to see where the current was taking her. Nowhere good, it looked like.

Part of the Reyes river had been diverted this way long ago, before the Great Fall, into a long, narrow channel that sped past the Shrive, through a tunnel and two sets of gates with locks that were rusted shut, and then back to the river. She was between the gates, and the fast-flowing current was hurrying her along to the lower set.

The gates themselves, a thick latticework of metal with gaps a cat would have struggled to squeeze through, were made of some sort of metal that didn't rust past a fine layer of grey powdery residue on its surface. Clockers and smiths had tried to replicate it for years to no avail. The upper gates had to be cleared regularly of rubbish, but the lower gates had no such problem. Unless she got this wrong, in which case her body would form a nice blockage for a while. Yet there had to be a way past because Bakar had come this way, and the only way she could think of was down.

The current changed almost imperceptibly. Smooth waves turned choppy, and eddies dragged at her legs, trying to pull her down, making her panic – the feeling was too familiar. A shout from where she'd wriggled through and dropped into the water got her going. It was dive or stay at the gates until she got shot.

A deep breath and she plunged, the cold trying to steal her air, trying to make her gasp. She couldn't see in the blackness, but she could hear great muffled thumps, rhythmic

and constant. The waterwheels. That *had* to be the way —
there was no other. She kicked harder, and a rush of bubbles
swam past her face, tempting her to suck at them. Eddies
swirled and swarmed, tried to pull her down, further, further
. . . Her lungs were hurting from more than just cold when
her hand brushed something moving.

It was as cold as the water — colder, smooth and slick as
new steel. It moved round with the flow of the water, seemed
to suck it in, tried to suck *her* in so she kicked away on
instinct. Then her lungs weren't just burning; they were
screaming for mercy, and she had to surface, kicking hard
to get away from the sucking. In the end she only made it
by finding the gate and dragging herself up.

The force of the current slammed her into the gate, but
she had air at last if no way out yet. Not unless she chanced
letting the waterwheels drag her under and through, and
that was a huge gamble. These days there were smaller
waterwheels all along the Reyes river. Some of them inter-
locked like cogs, and some of the other wheels and cogs
they turned were again underwater. Anyone or thing dragged
in didn't come out alive again unless they sacrificed a limb,
and these wheels must be four, five times as big, at least.
Her only consolation would be that she'd not lose just an
arm or leg; she'd be dead as soon as she hit them.

Shouts erupted behind — they'd seen her and someone
was even now wriggling through the gap. He dropped into
the water with a splash and a cry, and someone took his
place at the hole. Hard to tell in the darkness, but her eyes
were getting used to it, and she was pretty sure he had a
gun. Definitely something was being wound up. She was
glad it was dark, and sank down so only her mouth and
nose were above the water, struggling to hold her position
in the fast-flowing water.

Somewhere in the distance the warning chimes began,
sounding weird and echoey. Ten minutes to the change o'

the clock. The way the chimes wavered with her ears underwater – it sounded like it had last time she'd been in the
river. Strange, billowing noises came from everywhere, voices
saying words she couldn't understand. *Can't breathe! Yes,
you can. Get a grip.* Ten minutes till things got really bloody
crazy in this vicinity – these waterwheels powered the whole
change, along with much else. Maybe only the Clockwork
God and Bakar knew exactly what would happen, but she
could be pretty sure a lot of cogs would be whirling like
mad, axles moving, all sorts of things ready to chew her up
and spit her out. Ten minutes to find her way out or get
mangled trying.

A bullet zoomed through the water a scant few inches
away from her face. Bugger getting mangled. Bugger getting
shot as well.

She took as deep a breath as she could manage and dived
again, straight down now, to where she knew the wheels
were. There had to be a way. She felt her way down the
gate, holding on so she wouldn't lose her bearings – even
though the water was slamming her into it, the sucking
eddies kept trying to whirl her around. *Better than getting
shot*. The thought kept her going.

Her questing hand found the wheel again, which was
moving with enough speed to nearly yank her from the
gate. This close the sucking was almost too hard to fight.
She carried on down, searching with hand and foot for an
opening. All the waterwheels on the main river had sluice
gates to control the flow of water, and she was hoping to
find one here too. Preferably before her breath ran out.

No good; she had to breathe. She dragged herself up,
arms like slack rope, legs kicking feebly. There – a gap –
but she couldn't stop. She tried to be careful surfacing, but
panic as the blackness started to run in front of her eyes
spasmed her legs and she came up like a breaching dolphin.
Briefly she didn't care; she only cared that she could drag

in great clumps of the sweetest air she'd ever tasted. But only briefly. A bullet spanged off the gate next to her hand, just as she saw the man who'd dropped into the water closing in on her. Not just one, either – others must have come in while she was under. They didn't look friendly.

Even less friendly was the bullet that followed on the heels of the first, which slammed along her ribs and twisted her to hit the gate face first, sending her precious breath out in a pained rush and making spots run across her eyes. For a few seconds it was all she could do to breathe. Then the first man was on her, hands yanking her from the gate, spinning her back round. She saw the blow coming half a second too late and only dodged enough to take the worst out of it. The fist careened off her cheekbone and into the gate with a crack that brought a scream from the man. Rather than put him off, this seemed to enrage him past reason. With a kick that sent him half a pace back in the water, he drew his sword, and that's when Kacha snapped. *Really? You want to use your sword in the water. Well, OK then!*

Kacha shoved herself up so she was half out of the water, yanking Eneko's sword out of the scabbard, which she'd tied to her waist. The movement and weight of the sword in her hand dragged at the wound in her side.

The water made the man slow to move and prevented any complicated thrust so all he could try was an overhead slash, which she blocked easily. Eneko's knife was in her other hand – she didn't remember pulling it out, but that didn't matter. What mattered was it was there as she parried, ready to shove straight up into his armpit. The man stared at her in surprise, making him look stupid as his blood warmed her hand and spread out into the water. A sucking sound came from just under the surface – a punctured lung. His breathing hitched as he flailed to get away from her, dropping his sword so that he could use the arm to swim.

She let him go, partly because her ribs were hurting like buggery and it hurt to breathe, partly because she'd had her fill of killing people, but mostly because in the light of a lamp she could see three more men coming her way, plus the man holding the lamp had the gun in his other hand and looked like he was ready to use it again now his comrade was clear of her.

She had no choice. It was dive or die.

The lamp shone dimly through the water, making it a little easier. It showed up a thread of blood too, though she couldn't be sure if it was hers or her attacker's. Didn't really matter. All that mattered was holding her breath, holding on. Telling herself this wasn't like the last time; no, it was worse because she had no Vocho to pull her out.

She dragged herself down to where she'd felt the gap, water rushing through like it had nowhere else to go, trying to pull her with it. It *had* to be the way. A hand grabbed her foot, but she kicked it off, asked the Clockwork God for *some help here, please*, and let the current drag her in.

Chapter Twenty-three

Petri swam down after Kacha, his heart beating so hard he thought it might burst the air out of his lungs. He followed a trail of blood into murky depths where all colour was leached clean by darkness. The waterwheels loomed over him, cutting off the faint light of Eneko's lamp above as he was pulled ever onward by the rushing water.

What did she think she was doing? Bakar had blocked the sluice gate years ago. He'd done it himself, not trusting anyone else to know the details of his escape route. All anyone knew was that he'd found the waterwheels, figured out the clockwork, found the Clockwork God's heart and heard his words, and then, once prelate, had made sure no one else could leave this tunnel except through the grille into the Shrive. Alive at least. Only he had access to the wheels, though plenty of people had ended up in the Shrive after trying to find them from above. He came down here once a month to check the wheels and sometimes brought out the corpse of some hapless soul who'd drowned while trying to find the secret. At least he *said* that's where the corpses came from, though Petri had begun to have his doubts.

All of which meant Kacha was heading nowhere except to a watery end.

The guards with him gave up but he kicked harder, reached out and had her foot for just a second, and lost her again. The water rushed faster here, pulling him along whether he wanted it or not. Bubbles obscured everything, though the grating hum of the wheels to his left seemed far too close.

The force of the water caught him by surprise, tumbled him over and slammed him into something soft – Kacha. It took him a second to get his bearings before he realised they were hard up against the grate of the sluice that fed the wheels. This was where Bakar had escaped and what he'd blocked with dense mesh so no one else could do the same. The water felt solid here, a cold, slithering mass that held them to the mesh no matter how they tried to fight it.

Egimont could see her dimly in the bubble-lit darkness. She ignored him and thumped away at a corner of the mesh, her movements jerky, panicked. He felt the first flutterings of it himself – from here there was no way out except through that mesh. The water was too strong to fight back up to the surface, and his head was starting to buzz with the need to breathe. Kacha stopped thumping and started on the mesh with a knife, sliding it under the edge and yanking. He found a corner she'd lifted and yanked with her. He felt more than saw her surprised look, but they pulled together, and just when Egimont thought he had to breathe, *had* to or die, the mesh gave way. He was pulled through, snagging his tunic on the mesh so that he ripped it off and fell through the centre of the waterwheel.

At least there was air here among the falling water. He flailed at a strut as it passed his face, managed to grab it, and almost had his arm yanked out of its socket as it took his weight. He didn't care though because, thank any god that might be listening, clockwork or otherwise, he could breathe. Sheets of water hammered across his head, but if he angled it just right, he could take in great shuddering breaths of cold, damp air.

For long seconds that was all he could do – hold on and marvel that he was still alive.

A shift in the creaking of the wheel brought him back to the world. That, and the final warning chime somewhere far up above. The change o' the clock, not a good time to be at the centre of all the clockwork in the city. He'd no idea what would happen down here, but he was pretty sure it wouldn't be good to be in it. As if in answer to that thought, things began moving above and below him. Struts trembled, axles slid across on rails, cogs moved in various directions, gears changed. The whole city spun around this one point.

Where the hells was Kacha?

The answer came immediately with a crunching sound as some piece of machinery failed to move as it should. Cogs twice the size of a cartwheel juddered to a stop by his head. Axles screamed under stress. *Everything* seemed to come to a grinding, howling halt with him in the middle of it. Petri peered up through the falling water and found her, cold and drenched and utterly determined, hanging onto a wheel, watching the sword she'd just stuck in between two massive cogs. They strained and trembled, tried to chew the sword up, but to no avail. It bent but didn't break.

"Kacha!"

He didn't know what he expected – whether she'd try to kill him, climb down and kiss him or just send a rude gesture his way before she left him dangling. Maybe join him and try to get out of this infernal machine – which would be the sensible thing – and while she could be hotheaded, Kacha was pragmatic to her core. So he wasn't prepared for the sad smile or the way it made him twist inside.

She might have said something, but the roar of the water swallowed it. Then she didn't climb down, but up into the water-soaked shadows of the main mechanism. His gaze followed her as far as it could, past gleaming cogs, smooth rails and bobbing counterweights that seemed to waver and merge as he looked. Where was she going? Stupid question. The last place she wanted to be going but always went. She was going to find Vocho.

Interlude

Three months earlier

Petri lay back and luxuriated in the feel of Kacha as she twined one naked leg around his, laid her head on his shoulder and a soft hand on his chest. They were sweat-streaked and spent on a midwinter night in his lodgings at the prelate's offices. Freezing fog hung over the city in a fume of smoke and oily tendrils of cloud that always disappeared before they could squeeze any water out. Even the usually reliable winds from the sea had died, leaving the city gasping for breath.

They didn't say much – they'd gone past the need for that long since – but Kacha twirled her hand across his chest and fidgeted. It made him smile. She was never at rest, not even when she was asleep. Always shifting, moving, either in body or mind. By now he was used to getting woken by an errant foot or hand as she dreamed. She wasn't sleeping now though, and bar that one hand she was still, which meant her mind was working faster than a whirring cog.

He ran a hand down her back and said, "What's the matter?"

Her head came up off his shoulder and if he twisted a

little he could see the shine of her eyes in the faint lamplight that slanted through the windows.

"How do you know there's anything the matter?"

"There is though – you're thinking about asking me something." He'd known this would come tonight and welcomed it. He was playing a dangerous game, he knew it, but was too lost in this, in her, to care. Tonight he'd taken her down King's Row to where his father had lived when he was in Reyes, a painful task but one he felt he needed to perform. He wanted to show her – what? He wasn't sure, only that they'd gone past the sharing of superficial things. Dangerous it might be, all things considered, but Petri had never shied away from dangerous before, and Kacha was worth it. He wanted to tell her now, before he spilled all his suspicions about Vocho into Bakar's ear, before Vocho was arrested as he went to his latest assassination for Eneko.

She propped herself up on her elbows and considered him gravely. "All right. What am I going to ask?"

"Why did I take you there tonight? Or any night?"

"Yes. No. Perhaps. More. When Bakar came for you, why did you go with him? Why did you end up working for him? What happened?"

More to the questions than that, of course. Eneko, her guild master and friend, like a father to her. He'd been like a father to Petri once too, but it seemed a long time ago. He had to tread carefully here, but he didn't want to lie either.

"Because he was right. I mean . . ." No, don't tell her about Eneko and his betrayal. No one knew, it seemed. No one except Eneko, Bakar and Petri. Maybe some others who'd seen or heard some of it, but they'd never breathed a word. Eneko was good at invoking guild duty to keep secrets. And Petri had never told anyone because who would believe it? "Bakar was right about the nobles, about me. My father wasn't a good man by any measure, I see that now. But before . . ."

He hesitated. "My father always doted on my brother. I was an afterthought, a spare. That's why he didn't care about me being in the guild. I told him I wanted to stay, to take my master's, and he waved a hand, said all right, and that was it. That was probably the most he said to me in years. He had his heir, he had Kemen, so I didn't really matter. Only Kemen died. No, it's all right, really – we weren't close. He was a good ten years older than me, and I think I met him a handful of times, though he was probably around when I was young. He seemed nice enough. He used to bring me sweets and ruffle my hair, but I don't remember much else about him. Anyway, I joined the guild and that was it. Then he died, of the bleeding sickness, they said. Only my father grieved *before* his death. Funny, I suppose. I hated my brother then because I'd have to leave the guild, and I didn't want to. Then I found out. Bakar told me why and how my brother had died, that my father was complicit in it. His own son and heir, the only thing other than his title he cared about, and he killed him. Bakar told me what I was about to become. I was what, thirteen? Fourteen? And everything was black and white at that age, and I knew, *knew*, I wasn't going to be my father and that I hated him, that he'd betrayed me. And I knew the best way to hurt him, even after he was dead, was to take his title, his lands, take them and throw them away. A fourteen-year-old boy is a vengeful thing. And I knew Bakar was right about the rest. I saw you and Vocho the day you turned up at the guild. God alive, you couldn't have been skinnier if you tried. Others too, all beaten down and eyes to the ground, though you weren't even then."

"I've never been one for looking at the ground. Nothing interesting happens there."

"I've noticed that about you." He shifted, uneasy at what he was leaving out. He'd never been good at lies, even lies of omission, but he'd had to learn.

Kacha cocked her head. She didn't care what you were, but *who* you were inside. Just as well, or she'd not have looked twice at an ex-noble exiled from the guild with nothing but a tiny room to his name and that not truly his. It was good that he wasn't noble now; if he was he'd have to marry to continue his line, and Kacha couldn't because of the oath she'd taken for her master's.

She was smiling at him, not amused but wanting to hear the rest, maybe wanting just to hear him talk. How to tell it? How to tell her his good intentions had all turned to shit? That he'd been supposed to spy on her but couldn't? Or tell her what it was that Eneko had done – was still doing most likely – sending recruits to the guild to slavery in Ikaras, having people assassinated for some plan that Petri could only guess at.

He couldn't, any more than he could tell her why he didn't want her to leave tonight, why he'd asked her to stay. Because Licio had asked him to. The king wanted to prove that Vocho was Eneko's assassin, catch him in the act, and Petri had thought it best to keep Kacha as far away as possible. If there was one thing she was irrational about, it was that irritating tick she called her brother.

She glanced over at the clock on his washstand. "I really need to go. Vocho will be wondering where I am, and it's a long day tomorrow."

He wanted to tell her. He wanted to but couldn't. He didn't give a damn about Vocho. When he'd started on this, he hadn't cared much for Kacha either, but now that had changed, and so had he. "Don't go yet. I won't see you for a long while. Do you know how long?"

She shrugged, but her smile had widened when he'd asked her to stay. "Who knows? As long as it takes. I don't even know where we're going yet. Just that the job involves escorting and protecting this priest."

"Stay a while longer?" He shifted his arms and brought

her in closer, felt her breath quicken on his neck. He couldn't tell her, but maybe he could show her how she'd changed him, what a liability her brother was, that she was better off with Petri than him.

She didn't take much persuading in the end, and she left at dawn wearing the signet ring his father had given him when he'd joined the guild.

Chapter Twenty-four

Vocho sat and sweated. He didn't have a lot of choice chained up next to a brazier with a lot of metal sitting in it glowing a merry red.

"Honestly, if you just ask nicely, I'll do it anyway," he said. "You don't have to go to all this trouble, really. One dead prelate, and then we can all be friends, right? Murdering people, I can do it in my sleep."

"I'm sure you can, and I know you have," Sabates said smoothly from across the room. "That is, of course, the worry. By the way, do you know that your left eye twitches, just a tiny bit, when you lie?"

Shit.

Sabates slid across the room, Alicia behind watching him avidly as though he was a choice little titbit to eat and she was starving. She had her gloves off today, the markings on her hands mirroring those of Sabates.

The warning bell chimed somewhere in the distance, muffled down here, wherever here was. Ten minutes to the change o' the clock. Sabates came closer, and Vocho tried to shrink back into the wall with little success.

"As soon as your sister gets here, we can start. She won't be long because she's already in the Shrive. I think Egimont's looking forward to seeing her again, though not in the way you might imagine. All that effort getting information from her, winding her around his little finger, and *she* drops *him*. With some vigour too, I gather. I don't think he took it too well, and you know how the noble classes love their honour and revenge."

Vocho was torn between hoping Sabates was lying about Kacha being in the Shrive and feeling a certain smug satisfaction that he'd been right about Petri bloody Egimont all along.

"She'll be safe enough though, if you do as I say. She can take your place here, a guarantee that you'll behave, while we take a little trip to the palace along with our friend Alicia here. Did you know the prelate had a mistress? Ah, the weakness of the flesh. Rather sad, I always think, that men of a certain age can be tempted by the thought of recapturing their youth. Of course, a little magic always helps, isn't that so?"

This last was to Alicia. She came up behind Sabates and slid an arm around his waist. All very cosy. Explained a fair bit too.

Sabates touched her hand briefly and then moved over to where a stack of parchment waited with a scalpel and a brush.

"I don't need any special blood for this to work," he murmured. "A little bit of cosmic justice, though, to use it against him. 'Magic has no place in an ordered universe,' he said. Apparently it plays merry hell with predeterminism because it doesn't fit in with all his observed laws of the universe. Novatonas was a brilliant man, but he's got a lot to answer for. So many of us died when Bakar came to power. So many. All because Bakar twisted Novatonas's work to his own ends, to his own religious theories. Time to make amends, don't you think? Let's see if his precious clockwork predicts this."

When he turned back, he had the scalpel in his hands. Vocho saw where this was heading and tried to twist away, tried to yank his hands out of the chains while simultaneously not widdling himself. Wasn't the burning on his back enough?

"Now, now," Sabates said. "Not to worry. Just a drop."

The scalpel darted out, a quick sting, and drew back, leaving a few drops of blood on Vocho's arm. He sagged in relief, glad too he'd managed to refrain from wetting his pants.

Sabates mopped up the drops with his brush and began to draw on the parchment, lines and swirls that seemed to move and change even as Vocho watched. How could he draw so much with so little blood? Vocho didn't care, mainly because he didn't want to have to donate any more.

Another chime, the first bells of the change. Sabates carefully put down his brush and parchment and sat down. Alicia sat with him, and they twined together quite sickeningly to wait out the change. The first tremors began, a slight shaking that Vocho didn't usually even notice, followed by a series of clicks and clunks and the sensation of smooth movement. Nothing out of the ordinary for any resident of Reyes, though it seemed to put both Sabates and Alicia on edge.

What followed threw Vocho across the floor, chased by the brazier scattering coals everywhere. He rolled out of the way, at the limit of the chains that held him to the wall, and realised that he was dangling at an angle. The walls and floor didn't quite fit with where his brain said down was. Hot coals danced across the floor to what was now the bottom corner of the chamber, leaving a trail of embers and smouldering straw behind them.

A great grinding screech battered his ears, and the room juddered again as though it was trying to break free of some great hand that gripped it but couldn't quite gather the strength. Vocho dangled like a fly in some demented spider's web waiting to have his juices sucked out. His only consolation was the look on Sabates' face – of mingled horror and terror. Good.

It was a short-lived consolation.

The coals from the brazier in the corner had found something to eat, namely a heap of rancid straw. Smoke began to lick up the wall, blackening the stone and making Sabates' look of horror grow.

The two magicians scrambled to their feet, both as pale as wave tops as the shudders carried on, rumbling up through the floor so that everything blurred with the vibration. The scalpel came again, and Vocho had no chance to avoid it. A gout of blood washed out of his forearm. Sabates scrambled for his brush, found a piece of parchment and painted a hasty symbol on it.

The smoke grew, twisted, spread, little flickers of flame eating the straw and starting on a chair. The growing heat was making the tattoo on Vocho's back seem like a mild sting. Fire-tinged smoke now obscured everything, colouring the room orange-black and choking Vocho's throat, burning his lungs, streaming his eyes. The door slammed open, but Vocho couldn't tell who was there until Licio spoke: "The clockwork's stuck! Bakar – he must have . . ." Air from the open door fanned the flames gnawing hungrily at the chair.

Vocho found he suddenly didn't give a fig about the prelate or the tattoo on his back. He didn't give a fig for anything except getting out of these chains and out of the door before he burned to a crisp. Get out, find Kacha, grovel for forgiveness, promise never to lie to her – a promise even he knew he'd break in under a week – and go and live somewhere nice and quiet for the rest of his days.

Licio grabbed hold of Sabates' robe and almost yanked him off his feet. "We're stuck halfway – don't you realise what that means? Up in the bloody air, fifty feet from the street, or where the street was until the change. Only the mechanism is keeping us here, but it wasn't built for this! It won't last, it can't. You have to get us out, all of us."

"I can get you out," Vocho said. "If you set me free."

Licio turned on him with a growl and a kick that was nothing to the panic that was rising in Vocho's guts. The flames were nibbling at the plaster ceiling. It was only a matter of time before it collapsed, and then Vocho, greatest duellist the guild had ever seen, would die half naked and chained to a wall. Probably having widdled his pants.

The chains were heating up now, burning at his wrists. A sudden whumph as something in another part of the building collapsed. Vocho could barely see for sweat in his eyes, couldn't breathe for smoke choking his throat. Maybe it was time to pray? Nuts to that, but there wasn't anything else he could do except sit and roast.

Dear Clockwork God, I realise that I'm not your greatest creation, considering my rather free-form attitude to the truth you find so essential, but if you could see your way clear . . .

Chapter Twenty-five

Kacha dragged herself up through the frozen mechanisms, which groaned and squeaked with the strain, and out of the waterwheel housing. She'd had little idea of what would happen when she shoved the sword into the machinery. It had just seemed like a good idea to stop all the whirring cogs, which could crush her in a heartbeat, so that she could get out alive.

The first thing to hit her was the heat. She was dripping with freezing water, and the heat of Reyes in late spring, even at midnight, made steam rise off her in clouds and warmed her hands back to something approaching normality. Which was good because instead of coming out near the bridge to the guild she was above the Clockwork God. By many feet. She grabbed hold of the first thing that came to hand – one of the rails usually hidden under the streets but now laid bare for all to see.

Everything was laid bare – cogs, rails, counterweights, gears and springs and delicate mechanisms she didn't know the name for. They spiralled out in front of her, above her, below her, the heart and guts of Reyes still now and looking like nothing so much as a great net of metal holding everyone in, keeping them in their predetermined place, if the

Clockwork God – if Bakar – was right.

The silence that had greeted her exit gave way to whispers, cries, the odd scream. People were hanging in odd places – dangling from cogs, tangled in springs – as their world had tilted and instead of moving smoothly had upended them into a nightmare of bits of metal. Somewhere behind and below her Petri called her name, but she ignored him to concentrate on the moonlit darkness. The king's house was here somewhere, and somewhere close, but it was hard to tell the buildings and streets apart when they weren't in any one of their usual places.

She wiped water out of her eyes, shook it from her hair and tried to work out exactly where she was. Above the god, OK. The guild was away to her left, the Shrive behind and below her. The two constants in the city. Which meant, given which change this was, that the king's house had been over there, but had been stopped on its way to joining the palace, which was . . . there. Hard to miss, it was so vast with its hundreds of now wavering lamplit windows.

Which meant that the street where the king had his house – where she hoped like hells Vocho was because if not she was buggered – was the one with the fire. Smoke plumed out of it, backlit in faint and flickering orange, and while it was hard to see in the darkness, there looked to be some sort of statue by its gate. Shit.

It was going to be a hell of a climb, and it didn't help that her muscles still protested against every movement, possibly because she'd banged every single one of them on the way through the sluice gate. The burn from where the bullet had scored a line across her ribs wasn't helping either, but that was nothing compared to getting Vocho out alive. Movement beneath – Petri climbing up behind her. She had to be as quick as she could, not least because flames were beginning to leak out of the windows of the king's house.

Vocho had better bloody well appreciate this.

She took a firmer grip on the rail, which ran away at shoulder height, and moved out along another, over a gap blacker than death beneath her, a handspan of steel between her and it. She'd wondered before, that time she fell beneath the streets, what lay at the bottom and how far it would be, but decided then, as now, it was probably best not to think of it. What-ifs had never worried her; it was the right-nows that held her attention.

All that practice Eneko had made her do – running roofs, chasing up and along walls, quick and quiet even during the change – now stood her in good stead. A few steps to get the measure of it – the steel was slippery under her sodden boots, so she kept one hand on the rail by her shoulder – and she started to move more quickly, gliding over the gap.

A sudden burst of swearing behind her told her Petri had made it outside and was now not happy at the prospect before him.

"Kacha! For god's sake, will you stop?"

She ignored him and carried on, faster now as she grew more confident with her footing. Smoke was billowing out of one side of the house now, and guards were trying to get out but were hampered by the fact the street wasn't level. One fell, rolling over and over before he managed to break his fall, more by luck than judgement, by slamming into a gatepost. From the crunch of bone and his strangled scream, it didn't seem all that lucky. The rest held on or moved gingerly from handhold to handhold.

As she approached the angle got steeper. Her foot slipped off the rail. She hung on for dear life, and tried to do it quietly, which wasn't easy. The guards hadn't seen her yet, and she wanted to keep it that way, until either she could find a way around them or she decided it was time they saw her, preferably at the other end of Eneko's dagger in her belt.

The two rails converged as she approached the street, the one by her shoulder dipping and the one she stood on rising to meet it. A noise below caught her attention. A sort of muffled whimper, followed by, "Miss? Miss!"

She tried to ignore it, before she realised the voice was familiar.

"*Miss!*"

Her feet bumped into something on the rail, and she looked down. A hand gripping the rail in white-knuckled terror. A face below that, one that was as familiar as her own.

"Cospel, what are you doing?" she whispered. The guards were close enough to hear anything louder. "Stop pissing about and get up here."

"I was coming to find you, and then everything went sideways, and here I am. And I would, only I've got your bags and everything in the other hand. Could you pull me up?"

She knelt carefully on the rail, keeping one hand out to steady herself. The street was closer than it had been but far enough that a fall would mean broken bones at the least. Petri was gaining on her – she could hear his muted swearing more clearly. Not much time but enough with luck. She held on to the upper rail, which was now, as she knelt, about shoulder height. With her other hand she grabbed Cospel's wrist and heaved till her eyes popped. Cospel barely even moved.

"Are you made of lead or something?"

Sweat beaded on Cospel's forehead with the strain. "No, gold. He'll kill me if I drop the gold."

Vocho and his bloody gold – that was what had got them into this mess, his love of money. Cospel wasn't much better. She didn't have time to argue or give it another try. Petri came into view along the rail, dripping darkly in the moonlight. She didn't have time to piss about at all.

"Cospel, listen very carefully. *I* will kill you if you don't drop the bags. And bear in mind that I am here and Vocho is not."

A squeak as Cospel's fingers slipped a little on the steel.

"A valid point, miss," he said after only a second's consideration. He dropped the bags, which clanked and rolled along the tilted street sounding like a muted brass band needing a good tuning. It took about ten seconds for someone to realise what was leaking out of the bag and then there was confusion aplenty as a couple of the braver ones tried their best to grab a lifetime's worth of gold as it tumbled past.

Cospel was up on the rail in seconds. "Going to kill me," he said, looking mournfully after several years' wages as it disappeared over the edge of the street.

Kacha was already moving – no time to waste. "Depends if he manages to survive himself, really. Come on."

It was chaos underneath them, which was good. People running in and out of houses, shouting men and women, crying children, everyone at a loss. Or most of them. Even here, in Nob Town, *especially* in Nob Town, the rich clockers who'd taken over from the nobles weren't above a bit of sneaky acquisition when their neighbours' backs were turned. A little bit of anarchy was always helpful if it meant they might not look too closely at her.

She swung down from her slippery perch, Cospel close behind, and just made the edge of the street where it was bound in brass to slide smoothly along the rails. In seconds she was in the shadows one house over from the king's place. Smoke swelled out of its ground-floor windows, and the orange flickering came with a faint but ominous crackle. The scented bushes near the front door were crisping nicely. If she was going to do this, she had to be quick before Vocho burned to a cinder.

A quick look behind. Where had Petri gone? Last she'd

checked he was behind her on the rails, and now he wasn't anywhere.

"What happened?" Cospel gasped out next to her. He looked around with wide eyes, but she could see the other look too – he was a master of taking advantage of a bit of confusion, and she'd bet a bullshit to a bull he was valuing everything in sight to see if he might make a little of that money back. Some of the gold was still littering the far end of the street, but not for long.

"Cospel, wait here. Look out for Petri, and if you see him try to stop him, all right?"

"Stop him." Cospel peered up at the rails, where the dark form of Petri now appeared, now disappeared, in the smoke pouring from the house. "With what?"

She'd already gone on, trusting that Cospel would be able to look after himself, even if she doubted he'd stop Petri for long. The outer garden walls were topped with high, spiked railings that even a monkey would have trouble climbing. She worked her way around, checking for entrances, other points she might get in – there was a back gate here somewhere. The fire was working in her favour in one respect. Men poured out of the front door, which meant once she was in, with luck she'd be on her own. It worked against her too, because she could barely see the walls. Eventually, she found the back gate, and the guards were all at the front shouting at each other to make a bucket chain, find the king and mind the magician – solid advice, that last, and something Kacha fully intended to do.

Beyond the gate a white gravel path shone faintly in the smoky dark. Her clothes were still wet, so she hooked a piece of her shirt over her mouth to help keep out the smoke, took a last look around for Petri and plunged on.

Chapter Twenty-six

Petri lost sight of Kacha in the thickening smoke. What in seven hells did she think she was doing? Why rescue that little piss-stain Vocho, especially if it meant risking herself? If Petri could do one thing, it was stop her in this madness. Maybe he'd get himself out of trouble too, while he was at it, because he'd realised about Sabates, what he was truly capable of. He'd known from the start he wasn't a good man, but it was only the events of the last few days that had shown him just how far from good he was. Petri was always too late to realise, first about the prelate, then about Kacha and how he felt, and now Licio and Sabates.

He couldn't see Kacha but knew where she was heading and he didn't have to sneak. With a hand over his mouth, he ran for the front door as best he could over ground that tipped away at an alarming level.

A figure loomed out of the darkness with something in its hand, but he gave it a quick shove, heard a muffled curse and ran on. He grabbed a sword from and knocked aside a guard who tried to stop him, warn him probably, as if his eyes couldn't tell him the place was afire. The sword wasn't anything like as good as his own, but it would do. Smoke curled about his ankles in the empty hallway and obscured the vast painting of Licio that dominated the far wall. It looked like it was coming from the small door hidden under the stairs that led down to the basement where Vocho was being held.

She'd be here somewhere, had to be, but she wasn't the woman he'd thought. Not honest, straightforward Kacha, always fidgeting, never still. No, she was all that and more. For whatever reasons that he could only guess at, she was, or had been, Eneko's assassin. All that time, and he'd thought it was Vocho, that it was what made him preen so much, where all that money came from. He'd *wanted* it to be Vocho and let that blind him. So had Licio because that's what Petri had told him.

He kept as still as he could given the seep of smoke choking his throat in the shadows by the door that led where he knew she wanted to go. It wasn't long before a hint of movement caught his eye. If he hadn't been looking, he'd never have seen her. No sound of footfalls or creaking leather, just a moving shadow that separated from the rest, and there she was like one of the optical illusions the prelate's artist loved so much. Now the shadow of a statue, now Kacha.

He stepped forward and was instantly greeted with a drawn dagger. She wore the face of a woman who would not be crossed, and despite having a sword he held up his hands. It was speak or die, he knew that.

"If there's this much smoke up here, then down there's an inferno," he whispered, he didn't know why. "Vocho's dead or as good as. Why risk your life to save him?"

A twist of her face, and the knife was hard up against his chest. "Because he's my brother. Less fickle than you, for all his faults."

"Fickle? I—" The blade pressed further, and he'd learned not to push her when she wouldn't be pushed. "He tried to kill you, you know that? That and more. And yet you want to save him and perhaps kill yourself in the process. Leave him! Leave the little shit to himself and live. With me."

The smile was pained but real enough. "Kill me? Ah, the trick that sent me into the river. And not all he did, not by the longest shot of any clockwork gun. I know, Petri. I *always* knew. I knew that our da beat seven shades of snot out of him, and I know why too. I know why Da loved me more, why I was always the perfect one, but I didn't *want* to be. God's cogs, no. I *had* to be perfect, and who is that? Still I try. I have to be the best because otherwise Da'd hate me too, and I couldn't bear that, and I know it's crazy wanting two opposite things at once. I know that Vocho hates me, but he loves me too, same as I hate and love him. He's a lying son of a bastard but he never expected or wanted me to be perfect, just expected me to be me. For a time there I wanted to be perfect for you too, like I had to be perfect for Da, for Eneko. You and your bloody honour, and your lies. It was never you wanting me, was it? No, it was you poking around for the prelate or the king. It was all one big fucking lie from you, wasn't it?"

"No, Kacha, I swear—"

"I told Eneko, you know, the morning after you gave me your ring, before I found Vocho and the dead priest. Told him I didn't want to do his dark jobs any more, didn't want to be his personal killer. I told Voch I didn't like the killing part but truth was, I was sick of it. Sick of being who Eneko wanted me to be, of having to be perfect for him too. I'm finished with being perfect, you hear? I'm finished with being what everyone else wants me to be. So you can stick whatever it was you were about to say while I go and get my brother."

The dagger vanished from his chest, and Kacha disappeared.

No sign of her in the smoke so he headed for the door

under the stairs, not sure even as he did so what he was intending to do. He only knew that whatever it was, it would happen down there.

The stairs were thick with smoke, and when he set a hand to the wall, the stones were warm to the touch. He had a sudden wild urge to run back up the stairs, out of the house, out of Reyes, out of the whole damned country. But he was an Egimont, however sullied that name, and that meant no going back once you'd chosen a course or given your word. His only problem was deciding which word he'd stick with.

Voices echoed up the stairwell, distorted by distance, muffled by smoke. He couldn't mistake Licio's panicked squeak though.

"Bakar's behind this, he must be! Stopping the clockwork, who else could it be? He found out too soon. Those papers . . . This wretch —" a thud and a groan as though he'd kicked someone "— and his sister. You were supposed to be infallible. You promised me my throne, now do it!"

And I swore myself to this infant. Why? Because he seemed better than the alternative. Maybe he even was until Sabates turned up.

There was no mistaking Sabates' oily voice as he started to reply, nor the sudden *whumph!* as something in the room caught fire, drowning his words. More smoke came, thick and black, choking. He'd have left then, no matter anything else – honour, promises, the thoughts of revenge and redemption that had driven him this far – if it hadn't been for the soft sound of a footfall just ahead and the shadowed swirl of fair hair he recognised even through the smoke. In the last few hours he'd learned a lot about Kacha – that she'd been a pawn as much as he ever had, though a more deadly one – and now here she was, walking into a death trap to save a brother who was worth less than his piss.

Below, Sabates said something Egimont couldn't catch

except ". . . now or not at all". The smell of burned blood briefly overpowered everything else, making Egimont gag, and then it was gone.

So was Kacha, and Egimont followed without thought.

The room was a square box of stone, its floor once strewn with rank rushes and straw that smouldered sullenly where they hadn't burned completely away. The one small window, which was more of a slit, had been masked by both curtains and shutters. The *whumph!* Egimont had heard was them catching fire. There was plenty else left to burn – papers, a couple of chairs. Vocho, chained to a wall, eyes squeezed shut, would probably burn well enough too.

Egimont peered past the burning of his eyes and the choke in his throat, but he couldn't see Sabates anywhere.

He'd been going to save Kacha, from herself and from Vocho. From Licio and Sabates too, perhaps. It looked like he'd missed his chance. She had Licio by the front of his doublet, the dagger shoved up under his chin. The king gaped like the idiot he always had been, just that Egimont had been too stupid to see it.

"Keys," she hissed.

Licio stuttered something, so scared he looked like he might piss himself, but a shadow moved behind her in the darkest corner and he suddenly regained some sort of coherence and a modicum of courage. "Unhand me at once!" If the situation hadn't been so dire, it would have been laughable, but it was pure Licio.

The shadow resolved into Sabates, his dark hood melting into the darkness at his back. The patterns on his hands jumped and flared, wriggled and spun, turned into all manner of barbarous deaths that made Petri's stomach roil, and the smell of burning blood filled the air.

"Kacha!" Petri and Vocho shouted together.

She didn't miss a beat. Still holding Licio, she turned and threw the dagger all in one movement. A dagger was never going to be enough to kill a magician like Sabates. It dissolved in midflight, droplets of metal hissing as they fell to the smouldering rushes.

Kacha swore under her breath as Petri fumbled for the blade he'd stolen upstairs. Even now he wasn't sure he knew who he was going to use it on.

A scalpel appeared in Sabates' hand as Kacha stood nonplussed for half a heartbeat – half a heartbeat too long. A step forward, a slash of the scalpel along Vocho's upstretched arm, and the smell of burning blood grew stronger, richer, more nauseating.

The cuffs on Vocho's chains dissolved as quickly as the dagger had, sending him sprawling. Kacha dumped Licio, leaving him to fall bonelessly to the floor, and was halfway to the magician armed with nothing but her bare hands and fury when Vocho got to his feet like a badly managed puppet and all but fell in front of her.

"Looks like you were right, Vocho," Sabates said. "She'll never join Licio. So I'm afraid you'll have to kill her."

The sizzle of blood was the loudest thing in the room.

Interlude

Three months earlier
Vocho stared out of the window for a while, then paced up and down. The priest's chanting in the next room stayed just loud enough to be annoying.

He hoped Kacha would be back soon because he was bored stupid cooped up on his own playing nanny to a priest. He didn't really expect her though – she'd gone out all wreathed in smiles because Petri bloody Egimont was taking her somewhere special for their last night for however long it was going to be.

But he was going to be good and not sneak out. He'd been doing his best to be good for a while now, ever since Petri had made it clear he knew *exactly* what sort of person Vocho was. He'd tried, really tried, not to boast or crow to Kacha when he beat her sparring. He'd done his best to stop doing all the petty things that made him feel better than her, even if it was only briefly, but it came hard because it was a reflex now. He'd stopped running the books, betting against her in the courtyard when the masters practised. He hadn't stopped betting though, and right now he wished he was in a certain little den of iniquity he knew with a certain lady he'd recently become friends with. Playing cards or dice, perhaps laying a bet on some ridiculousness, like the time the owner had brought in a box of frogs and they'd wagered on which one would hop out of the place quickest.

He wanted to be there right now, even if his luck had run out these last weeks, catastrophically so. Not to worry – the pay from this job would put it right, even if he didn't skim any extra, and he'd mostly stopped doing that as well. Mostly. This job also had the advantage that he'd be out of Reyes and away from his numerous creditors for the foreseeable future.

A discreet tap on the door below caught his attention. He took a look out of the window and grinned. A certain lady was on the doorstep.

He opened the door to her, and she wafted in like a summer breeze in silk and pearls.

"Alicia." He kissed the back of one delicate gloved hand.

"Vocho. I missed you at the gaming table, then I recalled you had this dreary job so I thought I'd come and relieve the boredom for you."

Vocho led her through into the small sitting room he and Kacha had been using. The priest was still chanting upstairs, and Vocho kept half an ear open. Eneko had been very firm with his instructions, even if he couldn't or wouldn't tell them much about the job. A delicate situation he'd called it. Apparently the priest was some sort of diplomat. Which meant they were probably going to Ikaras. The two countries had been squabbling over their mutual border – not to mention the rich seams of metal that ran under it – for years, and a fair few duellists had permanent jobs up there. By all accounts, things had been rumbling towards hostilities, perhaps even war, though Vocho wasn't one for paying attention to all that when he could be enjoying himself.

Alicia sat, cool and elegant, by the small fire that warmed the room against the foggy chill of late winter in Reyes.

"Come sit by me, Vocho. Leave your silly priest to his chants."

Vocho didn't hesitate. He and Alicia had been friends for a week or two now, and although he'd never figured out if she had anyone else – a lady as beautiful as Alicia wouldn't have a shortage of offers, but she was coy about it – he'd been tempted lately to make it something a bit more. From the look on her face, Alicia was perhaps starting to think the same. Which would at least make the evening much less boring.

She smiled up at him, and her gloved hand made for his knee. Oh, that looked promising. "I was wondering if you'd do me a little favour," she said. "Just a little one."

"I'm sure I can manage," he said, and then, "Ow! God's cogs, what was that?"

A scalpel, that's what, drawing blood from his leg. Alicia looked up at him with a dreamy expression on her face. "Just a little bit. For now."

"What the hells do you—"

Alicia peeled off her gloves and ran a finger through the blood dripping off his thigh. It sizzled as she touched it. That wasn't what held his attention, but rather the smell of burned blood and the markings on her hands. They squirmed and moved like worms across her skin, looking now to be crossed swords, now a deck of cards fanned out, now a set of dice, now a woman falling in water and drowning, which made him shudder. He didn't want to look but couldn't pull his eyes away, and his head seemed fuzzy, as though the rest of the world had gone away and all that existed were him and those hands.

So he wasn't sure when the man came, never noticed much about him. Only an impression of dark eyes that made him shiver, a low, smooth voice, more patterned hands, the reek and sizzle of burned blood. The patterns showed a dagger dripping with gore.

"Just a small favour," he said into Vocho's ear. "I need you to kill someone. That's what duellists do, isn't it?"

"No! No . . . I . . . Well, if I *have* to, only . . ."

"Don't you want to be the greatest duellist who ever lived? This will have your name remembered through the ages. Or, I suppose, we could ask your sister. Perhaps she'd be a better bet anyway."

The patterns moved again, scrambling his brain. Now they were people cheering, and he could have sworn he heard them calling his name then the patterns twisted and it was Kacha's name they were calling.

"No. No, Kacha doesn't like the killing part. Never has."

A soft little laugh made Vocho want to sick up everything he'd ever eaten. "So you it is then. A small favour. Yes? Or let Kacha take all the glory, like she always has?"

Now her hands showed him the guillotine from that day when he'd been just a kid needing a pee, when he'd seen heads roll across the square, only this time he knew somehow one head was his.

"Who?" It was an effort even to say that much.

"The priest. Kill him, and your name will be known as the greatest duellist who ever lived."

That couldn't be right, could it? He couldn't seem to think clearly, but he'd promised to protect the priest, and the guild wouldn't take it well if he betrayed that promise. Alicia said something in a murmur that he couldn't catch except ". . . harder than we thought".

The man sighed. "This blood was hard to come by. I was hoping to save it, but needs must."

Then there was a blinding pain in Vocho's back as something sliced into him. After that he didn't recall much at all.

Chapter Twenty-seven

The pain in his back was excruciating. If he wanted it to go away, he had to do what the voice asked, that was all he knew. A figure wavered in front of him. Smaller than he was and vaguely familiar. "Kill her," the voice said, soft in his head. Kill first and worry about it later. Seemed sensible. Not like it'd be the first time, though hadn't that ended badly? He couldn't recall.

He blinked away the sweat from his eyes, and he could see more clearly. Kacha, wasn't that Kacha? The pain in his back twisted further, and a blade appeared in his hand. He had to kill her or . . . or . . . or something very dire would happen. "Kill her," the voice said again. Hadn't he tried to that time in the river? Didn't his dark half dream of just that, her being out of the way and leaving him all the glory? All the adulation? Hadn't he wanted it for as long as he could remember? To best her once and for all so he could say to Da, "Look at me, *I'm* the perfect one."

He could beat her, he knew that. He was stronger, had better reach, was less inclined to stick to the rules, which was his best advantage. He could beat her, but it was only his ego that told him it was his name they called. It never was, except when he paid them to. Always *her*. Even when she lost, even when he beat her fair and square, it was never him they called for.

"Not so perfect now, is she?" the whisper said. "Even less perfect when she's dead."

He rubbed at his eyes with his spare hand. She was just standing there, watching him. Waiting for him.

He couldn't. Oh, he wanted her to fail all right, he wanted her to stop being so fucking perfect, he wanted people to look at him and see something more than just her brother. But he was a guildsman through and through. Stupid though the rules were, there were some even he wouldn't break, and she didn't have a blade. Besides, she was his sister too, and he loved her when he remembered.

The voice subsided but the pain grew, blinding bright, until he couldn't see anything else. All he knew was there was someone in front of him, and he had to kill them if he wanted the pain to go away.

He lifted the blade and prepared himself. Icthian style, always the best.

Kacha hesitated – she'd been ready to go for the magician's throat, blade or not, until Vocho staggered in between with a murderous look on his face and a sword in his hand. The depth of that look, the truth of it, had her take a step back. She knew he hated her at times, just as she hated him. She knew he'd tripped her into the river, but he'd regretted it, she was sure from his panic when he'd pulled her out. He did all his petty little things to thwart her, or had done until that had all unaccountably stopped. This was more. This was all that nebulous hate hardened into a point like steel, and yet she wasn't sure it was his; more like the magician's at his back. Now a lot became clearer, like how and why Vocho had murdered that priest.

That revelation wasn't going to help her now. Now she

had Vocho in front of her, ready to kill her. Worse, Petri was at her back, and he had a sword.

Until he didn't. A flicker of movement caught her eye, and she grabbed the sword as it flew past. Longer than she was used to, heavier, but she'd make do. She didn't think then why Petri had thrown it, though it would trouble her badly later. For now she had worse things to worry about, foremost that she hadn't beaten Vocho in years. Partly because she didn't want to give away that she was Eneko's assassin, and partly because she knew how much he wanted to win, how much of him was bound up in it, that it would crush him to lose. That thought was closely followed by the realisation that she'd probably have to kill him to beat him.

She didn't have time for anything more than that because Vocho was on her, leading with a vicious slash to the face that would have killed her if it had hit home. She managed to dodge back, but speed wasn't enough against Voch, it never was. He won because he was *good*. He came at her again, a series of lunges and thrusts that came close to turning her into a pin cushion. Vocho's main advantages weren't accuracy or technique, but strength and the ability to do just what you weren't expecting. He never telegraphed a move, ever, and that was going to kill her like as not. Unless she did the same. No guild, no rules.

He came for her again, and she managed a sidestep, brought her sword around and got him a crack across the cheek with the pommel before she leaped back out of his reach. It didn't seem to affect him at all, except to bring a snarl to his lips.

This isn't Vocho. This isn't the vain, grandstanding dick I know and love. He's not fighting the way he can, the way he should if he's really trying to kill me. If he was trying, I'd be dead.

Smoke obscured his face as he circled her, trying to find another opening, but she was sure he was sweating far more than he should, and there was something wrong with his eyes. Very wrong, as though he was both here and dreaming some vile dream.

Another flurry of blows, a desperate parry by her that numbed her arm, and then she saw it – as he twisted away, ready for another round, she glimpsed his back. Between his shoulder blades was a dark pattern, some sort of tattoo that moved and writhed.

Dimly she recalled Dom wittering on about magical tattoos, about a constant blood supply to keep the magic strong.

The heavier sword was beginning to tell on her, and she still didn't know how to get out of this with both her and Vocho alive until, through the thickening smoke, she caught sight of the man behind him. A man with writhing patterns on his hands and a dark shine to his eyes. Beyond him she could dimly make out another figure, a woman with matching patterns on her hands. Controlling Vocho, like they had before, perhaps, when he'd killed that priest.

He came again, a great overhand blow that missed her by a scant inch, left him wide open, and left her in no doubt that this wasn't Vocho – he'd never have given her that opening. As if to confirm this, a whimper escaped his clenched teeth.

Behind her Petri grunted at the sound of a fist hitting flesh, followed by a high pitched gasp. Licio wasn't anyone she needed to fret about, by the sounds of it, though Petri himself remained a worry. So was the man behind Vocho – the magician, had to be. And now Vocho's moves were turning them in a slow circle, bringing her closer to him.

The smoke was making it hard to breathe, and it was getting hotter by the second. She had to finish this, quick, before the fire finished them all. The magician was focused on Vocho, on his swordplay. On controlling him, she had no doubt. The man's face had grown gaunt and grey, perhaps from some sort of strain. But he wasn't paying much attention to her, that was the thing. So when Vocho came for her again, teeth gritted and eyes wild, she stepped back out of his path and brought her sword around straight at the magician. Who suddenly wasn't there any more.

All that was left was a burning piece of paper which fell and ignited the rushes he'd been standing on. Flames leaped at her feet, joining with other smaller blazes, and heat hammered at her face and back. The fire now surrounded them on all sides.

Vocho slumped to the floor with suspiciously damp eyes.

Chapter Twenty-eight

Vocho blinked hard to clear the sweat from his eyes. The pain was ebbing as fast as it had come, and breathing was no longer white-hot agony. Red hot was bad enough, but he'd take it. He blinked again, went to scrub a hand over his eyes and found a sword in it. How had that got there? Where were the chains? And why was it so hot in here?

A hand grabbed him by the shoulder and he managed to stagger to his feet. The world didn't seem much better from up here from what he could see, which wasn't much because he appeared to be standing in the middle of a fire – a tad irresponsible even for him – and what he could see was bleary with orange-tinted smoke.

"Voch, come *on*!"

Hands pulled at him – Kacha's hands. He'd been supposed to do something, hadn't he? With the sword. Something important, but she wasn't letting him. Petri bloody Egimont's horsey face loomed out of the smoke, and Vocho had just enough time to wonder what in seven hells he was doing here before he was shoved towards a corner that seemed less smoky than the rest. Petri said something which Vocho didn't catch, and then Kacha shoved at him again and they were on some stairs heading up into more smoke.

Vocho's brain had been stirred with a big stick, or that's what it felt like. He lost track of where he was, who he was with, what he was supposed to be doing. The whole world seemed to be made of thick black smoke that made breathing into wheezing gasps. Once or twice he caught a glimpse of a face covered by a sleeve or mask. It all seemed like that dream where he was running and running and never got to where he was going. Someone said something in front of him; another replied from behind. One of them was Kacha, and that relieved him. One of her more annoying features was always knowing what to do.

Finally they were out in fresh air that stung his lungs and made him cough out smoke until his eyes almost popped. His head cleared, a bit, and he found he was sitting on some grass that felt cool under his hands, though the world looked like it was sliding sideways. Probably his head needed to clear a bit more.

Whispers behind him seemed insubstantial at first, before they turned solid in his head. Kacha and Petri. Arguing at first, but then . . . but then a long silence that seemed to echo inside him. Petri Egimont helping to save him. He'd never live it down. He turned his head, ready to give the man a piece of his mind about that and every other sodding thing that had happened over the last couple of weeks, and longer, but his mouth clicked shut on his words.

They were somewhere outside, in some sort of garden. Cospel was there, sooty faced, looking nervous, helping him up. His eyebrows were talking again, but gods knew what about. Away to the left, though not far enough away for Vocho's liking, a building was having a merry time as it burned down. None of that had shut him up.

There are some things a brother should never have to see his sister do, or even think about her doing. The way Kacha was looking at Petri bloody Egimont was one such thing.

He was saying something, too low for Vocho to hear, and she was wavering, he could see it.

"It's too late now. It's been too late for me for a while," Petri said loud enough for Vocho to hear now and put something in her hand. "But I meant this."

She opened her hand, but try as he might Vocho couldn't see what was in it.

Then it really was too late, which was a relief — for a minute he thought she was going to give in and he'd have to deal with Petri in his life again. A shout came from the smoke behind them, and there was the clicking crank of a gun being wound — two guns, three. Vocho staggered to his feet, almost fell over again and held on to a handy tree.

"Kass! If you're quite finished talking to that walking arsehole?"

Egimont held up his hands in surrender. "You'd best go."

"Who goes there?" came from the darkness.

"Now." Egimont said. "Quickly! If they find you, I can't stop them."

Kacha looked up at Petri, and Vocho *really* didn't need to see that, or worse the fleeting kiss that left Egimont looking as startled as a shying horse.

A last look, and then Egimont stepped smartly past Vocho and disappeared into the smoke. "Petri Egimont," he said to the unseen guards. "I have the king here — he's unconscious but I think he'll be fine. I need some help getting him to the surgeons. This way."

Kacha propped Vocho up, Cospel on his other side as they headed as quickly as they could in the opposite direction. Not easy when everything was still tilted and Vocho's legs weren't working properly yet, but everyone else seemed to be concentrating on what had happened to the clockwork so didn't pay them much mind.

He had no idea how much later it was that he was sitting on a jetty down by the docks, lungs heaving, eyes clearing.

He still had the sword in one sweat-slicked hand and on his back the faintest memory of pain, fading now like the night as dawn grew.

Kacha flopped down next to him, soot-streaked and sweaty, and dangled her legs over the edge of the jetty for all the world like they were children again and deciding what game they might play. She sneaked him a sidelong look, and the doubt in it panicked him a little. "Are you you again?" she asked.

"Have I ever been anyone else?"

Her sudden grin comforted him – familiar and reassuring, though it also meant tread carefully. "You *did* try to kill me. Again. I suppose that's not really an answer, but you sound like you."

He looked down at the sword in his hand, then back at her, all his old pride coming back in a rush. "Pfft. If I'd really been trying, I would have done it. You were lucky; I was having an off day."

Her laugh echoed among the ships berthed in front of them, and the echo spread, made gulls take to the air and sleepy sailors on watch look over at them. It was an odd laugh – relief but with a note of something else.

"I'm sorry," he blurted. It sounded pathetic.

Her laughter died away. "Are you? For what? Voch . . . Voch, I'd no right. Not to blow up at you like that. Not really, because you're not the only one with secrets, eh?"

"They thought I was the assassin," he said. "Eneko's personal killing machine. I don't remember much, but I do dimly recall that. I never even knew he *had* a personal assassin. And it was you, wasn't it? For what it's worth, I'd never have guessed. Not until Alicia told me, or hinted at it. You were always so touchy about the killing part."

"Eneko always made out that they were not good people, and I trusted him. Besides, guild master's apprentice, who wouldn't want that? But towards the end I was starting to get suspicious because of Petri. I was right to, it seems. Not all the children on Apprentice Day go to the guild – the man's a bloody slaver, Voch. Not only that. Eneko said all those dark jobs came from the prelate. Taking out slavers and the like. Taking out Bakar's supporters for Eneko more like, slowly getting himself more of an edge. He wanted to rule Reyes himself, still does, and he was using me to do it. And I was blind because he was . . . I missed Da when we came to the guild, missed him something awful. I wanted Eneko to be my new da, someone to be good for, strive for, so I *let* him blind me, believed every word he said. I was a fool."

Vocho shivered. "God's cogs, Kass. And you couldn't tell me?"

She laughed again, and that was more like the old Kacha he knew, the one before Petri bloody Egimont, before she'd been Eneko's apprentice. The one who laughed more than she frowned. Still, he noted that she appeared to be wearing a ring again, Petri's ring. He hoped like hells this didn't mean Petri would be any part of his life, even peripherally.

"Voch, why do you think I let you win when we sparred?"

"You did not!"

"Did too, and I'll prove it just as soon as you're up to the challenge."

They sat in silence a while, watching the city as crowds of people worked to unkink the mechanism – he had to ask her how in hells that had happened – and the streets moved back into their proper positions for the Threeday. The fallout from the jammed mechanism spilled everywhere – smoke over half the city, blank-eyed men and women milling up by the Clockwork God, the racheting sedans they used for taking clockers to the hospital working like the clappers. The word had got about that the prelate had ordered the hospital to treat any injured for free in the emergency, and the place was black with people, some of whom were after free medicine for warts or squinty eye or this funny itch they'd had just lately.

"What in hells happened, Kass? Are we safe for now?"

"I wish I knew. It should have been me, Voch. Dom said – and you'll never believe who Dom actually is. They wanted to use Eneko's assassin to murder Bakar. Maybe they were going to blame it on him, take out the guild that way. It should have been me with that tattoo, and I don't think I'd have done any better." A pleading sort of look from her, one he'd never seen before. "I'm not perfect, and I never wanted to be. I just thought it was the only reason Da and Eneko loved me."

The closest he'd ever get to an apology, but that was OK. He thought everything might be OK after this. He wasn't even *slightly* tempted to shove her off the jetty. Not today at least. "Yeah, well I never wanted to be the idiot either. We can swap places if you like – I don't mind."

A snorting laugh and they were children again sitting on the jetty working out what game to play. Those had been the best times, before they got to hating each other, before things had turned sour inside for both of them.

She reached inside her shirt – it had once been bright blue but was now more sludge grey – and pulled out a leather pouch. He recognised it as the one she used to keep kindling and tinder dry when they were on the road. It was dripping water.

"I think all those papers got a bit buggered in the river."

"Looks that way. You were in the river?" That didn't seem likely; after Vocho's little escapade she'd made sure never to get too close.

"Only way out of the Shrive."

"You escaped from the Shrive? Looks like you've got a lot to tell me. So what now? No papers, no proof, no nothing. Oh, and that magician is still alive, and he's not going to be happy with us and what we know, not to mention we're still wanted for murder."

"You are, Voch. You are. I, however, have a possible invitation to go back to the guild."

"Going to take it?"

"Not bloody likely."

He watched her carefully and couldn't decide how he wanted this conversation to end. Kacha, sister, bane of his bloody life, and she always had his back. Always that. "Why did you come and get me?" he asked. He'd not wanted to ask, but he'd always regret not knowing if he didn't. "I ruined your life – you made that perfectly clear – got you thrown out of the guild and all that business with Petri. So why did you bother?"

She raised the unfamiliar sword in her hand. "Voch, you may be a lying little shit but so am I, and we're blood. Blood is everything. Da taught me that, and you too in a different way. If anyone is going to kill you, it'll be me. But probably not today. Probably."

"Kass—"

"Did you know about Dom?" she asked. "Narcis Donat Chimo Ne Farina es Domenech. Missed one name out though, the important one. Jokin. Might be a handy man to have around."

"I'm sorry. *Dom* is Jokin?"

"Oh yes, Dom. He showed quite a different side to him after you got taken. He's in the Shrive." She sneaked a peek at his back. "Looks like it's fading. Sabates is too far away perhaps?"

"What's fading? Kass, you are being so annoying I may have to try to kill you again."

"The tattoo. Dom said, remember?"

"Not really."

"How they made you kill the priest and try to kill me."

"I told you. If I wanted to, I could kill you right now." Although he wasn't so sure all of a sudden. Fragments of memory kept coming back to him – a dark voice in his head telling him to kill her; it was for her own good and then he'd be the greatest duellist who ever lived; wanting to believe it, tempted to do it.

Another silence, a loaded one that Vocho didn't want to break, but circumstances – a phalanx of guards in the prelate's colours coming down the road – made him.

"What now? Are you going to tell me what the hells just went on?"

Kacha watched the guards as they made their way along the road, accosted every step by another person wanting to know what had happened, what was *going* to happen, and hefted the sword in her hand.

"Eventually. Most of it. First I say we get Cospel to find the horses."

Vocho eyed Cospel, who was being suspiciously quiet. "And the gold, don't forget that."

He thought he might be getting the hang of eyebrow as a language. At the moment they seemed to indicate he should ask Kacha about the gold, so he did.

"Ah. Yes. Tiny little problem about the gold," she said. "Though since the clockwork's still seized, I'm sure Cospel can find it. Somewhere. If it hasn't all been stolen. Can't you, Cospel?"

He didn't answer, merely looked at Vocho's face, slumped his shoulders and headed off.

"Then, perhaps we need to get Dom out of the Shrive."

"The Shrive?" Vocho didn't fancy that much, not least because he had a nagging fear that if he got in, he'd never get out again, except to have his head cut off.

"Yes. He did try to help me escape. Seems only fair to return the favour. I know the way out now."

She seemed so very sure, it took him aback. Then again, with the city jittering like butter on a hot griddle, maybe they could do it at that. "Then?"

"Then? Before we opened that chest, you promised me my blades back. Where are they?"

Vocho hesitated, but it was no use lying now. "Eneko has them, in the guild."

"Does he? Then I say we steal them back, and I show you just who's the best. Bet you a bull I win."

Vocho wondered just where they'd go from here. To trusting or killing each other? Each was just as likely. He put on his best Vocho voice, as much arrogance as he could manage: "You are *so* on."

extras

www.orbitbooks.net

about the author

Julia Knight is married with two children, and lives with the world's daftest dog that is shamelessly ruled by the writer's obligatory three cats. She lives in Sussex, UK and when not writing she likes motorbikes, watching wrestling or rugby, killing pixels in MMOs and is incapable of being serious for more than five minutes in a row.

Find out more about Julia Knight and other Orbit authors by registering for the free monthly newsletter at www.orbitbooks.net.

interview

What was the inspiration behind Swords and Scoundrels?
Lots of things, as per usual! I was reading a lot about post-Moorish Spain – inspiration for the Castans' fallen empire – and Renaissance Italy, with all the city states at each other's throats. Then add in a re-reading of *The Three Musketeers*, and the new series on the telly, happening across a video for an architect's design for a clockwork city and . . .

Which was your favourite character to write?
That is a really hard question! I love them all in different ways. Vocho was a blast to write because he's just so vain and unintentionally funny but he does have a heart too (when he remembers). I like Kacha because she takes no crap from anyone, especially Vocho. Petri was supposed to be the bad guy . . . but I found I rather felt for his predicament. Cospel for being so long-suffering. However, the creeper over the series is/was Dom. He really grew on me.

Who really is the better duellist – Kacha or Vocho?!
Depends on who you ask ☺. As Vocho says, she's better at technique, but he has an advantage in strength and

reach. Both are devious as required. I'd say they both have their strengths but that balances out so they are actually fairly evenly matched.

What was the most challenging thing about writing this novel?
I'd say selling the first book in a series before I'd written it! A first for me. I don't usually outline at all, and the first book is usually where I discover everything about the world, so I had to try to keep myself on the straight and narrow with regard to what I'd said the book was going to be. I did allow myself a few times of straying from the beaten path (I recall saying to my editor, 'Um, it, um, may have some clockwork in it? And it's not strictly linear . . .')

You may or may not be surprised at what this almost ended up as. I'm saving those ideas for another day!

What we can expect from the next Duellists novel, *Legends and Liars*?
Dastardly magicians, dashing duellists, warring cities and some very big Venus flytrap-style plants. It gets a bit deeper into the characters, and darker too, though it's still got plenty of light-hearted moments.

What else do you read and watch in your spare time?
I'll read anything! I like a lot of historical non-fiction – good inspiration – and of course I read all the fantasy I can get my hands on. I don't get much time to watch telly (I make exceptions for *Agents of Shield* and *The Musketeers*) but we do make time for film night once a week. It's almost always fantasy or SFF, with a sprinkle of comedy or biographies. I am almost unimaginably excited to see Hicks may be back in the next *Aliens* film . . .

if you enjoyed
SWORDS AND SCOUNDRELS

look out for

LEGENDS AND LIARS
The Duellists: Book Two

also by

Julia Knight

Chapter One

Vocho threw the dice and loudly cursed himself for a fool. Treble cat's eye, of course it was, and now he was down a hundred Ikaran bushels, or about ten bulls in Reyes money.

Kacha stood the other side of the gaming table, clothed, after something of an argument, in an Ikaran dress in the latest fashion. A silky green sheath with a split up to the thigh – Vocho had been surprised to discover his sister actually had legs – and precarious heels that made her wobble and look far more fragile than her solid frame would usually suggest. The puffed sleeves covered the fact she wasn't a soft noblewoman and that her wrists and forearms were laced with muscles and striped with old scars. Her hair had been carefully coiffed, with much swearing, to hide the scar under her eye. No sword, which had irked her the most. She'd sulked in the shadows behind the avid-eyed men and women who'd just won on betting Vocho would lose, but now Kacha raised an eyebrow and smirked.

The dice were, naturally, rigged. Not that he'd tampered with them, oh no. Conduct unbecoming to a master of the duelling guild and all that, although not being a member of the guild any longer he tended to forget that bit. It was just no fun cheating people out of their hard-earned – or as was the case in this particular den of iniquity – hard-inherited cash. So he hadn't rigged the dice, but someone certainly had. At least they were dry in here, as opposed to highway robbery which had mostly involved him being wet and cold. They had to do something for money – supplies were dangerously low. Besides, he had a plan.

A slight dark-haired man with small sharp eyes and a nose that looked like it had been thumped one too many times swept Vocho's money off the table and into his purse, which was already heavy. "Not lucky with the dice tonight, are you?" he said in Ikaran, a language Vocho could just about communicate in if he concentrated. "Perhaps you'd care to try something else?"

Vocho feigned nonchalance with an airy wave of his hand, as though the money hadn't been most of what they had left. "Such as?"

The dark-haired man – his name had never been offered, though mostly he was called Bear for some unmentioned reason – cocked his head on one side and looked Vocho up and down. Took in the slightly worn finery, the hat on the table with its jaunty if tattered feather, the mud-stained boots that had once been polished to a high shine but were now dull and cracked with constant use. Finally his gaze rested on the one thing Vocho knew he was really interested in – his sword.

It was, Vocho had to admit, a damned fine sword. Not too heavy, though heavy enough, perfectly balanced and with a devilishly handsome basket hilt that had been the envy of many a master in the guild – it had certainly saved Vocho's fingers a time or two. The hilt was a giveaway.

It was a guild duellist's sword and no mistake, and very, very illegal to be walking around with here in Ikaras. And Bear was a collector, something of a connoisseur. Vocho was banking on it.

"A duel," Bear said now, and then added, as Vocho had suspected he would, "with a twist."

"Isn't that illegal?" Vocho asked.

"No more so than gambling with dice or wearing that sword in public. Anyone doing any of those things faces the galleys or perhaps even the gallows. Well? Are you a gambling man or not?"

"What sort of twist?" Vocho was fairly sure he knew the answer because Cospel had done his research well.

"Not you or I fighting," Bear said. "You're a man who knows how to use that sword, that's clear, and as a true Ikaran I know nothing about fighting with a blade like a common mercenary. The fight would be unequal."

Common mercenary? Vocho fought hard to keep the indignation from his voice. "I could tie one hand behind my back?"

A disturbance behind him made him turn for a second – Kacha had fallen off her heels and was being helped back to her feet by an amused bystander.

"Oh no," Bear said. "I value my skin far too highly."

"Who then?"

Vocho was pretty sure he knew the answer to this as well. Bear would pick someone who looked like they didn't know one end of a sword from the other but who was actually not too shabby.

From behind him came the unmistakable sound of metal hitting flagstones.

"I'm sorry, is this your knife?" Kacha said. "What? Oh, I see. That's the sharp end, is it? How exciting."

"We each pick someone to fight for us." Bear's sly grin

made Vocho struggle to keep his own face straight. "You can pick first."

Vocho made a show of weighing it all up before he nodded slowly. "All right. What's the bet?"

Bear hefted his purse in his hands – there was enough money in there to keep Vocho and Kacha fed and housed for a month, and maybe enough to see about other things besides. "This against, well, what do you have left?"

Vocho pretended to think about it and then put his sword very deliberately on the table. "This. If your man can take it off mine, it's yours. If not, if my man takes the sword from yours then the money is mine."

"You have yourself a bet," Bear said as though he knew something Vocho didn't, giving Vocho palpitations, but there wasn't much choice by this point. They shook, and Bear's grin swelled into a full-blown smirk. "You choose first."

Vocho eyed the small crowd around the tables. Unlike Reyes, which had done away with titles and replaced its nobility with clockers who'd turned out just as feckless if not as inbred, Ikaras still had a full complement of blue-blooded young men and women with lofty titles and nothing much better to do than fritter away their time and money. Duelling had been popular for a time at least. Until too many ended up with serious holes in them or worse, and the Ikaran king had declared duels, along with the gambling that seemed to be the spur for most of them, illegal. That hadn't stopped events like this, only driven them from grand palaces to dingy little backrooms where the nobles' finery seemed incongruous in the smoke that leaked through from the rank bars that fronted them.

This particular lot didn't seem out of the ordinary, from what Vocho had gathered since they'd arrived here a few weeks previously. Ikarans were less foppish and more direct than Reyens, perhaps, but no less vicious, or devious, when it came to it. But of course he and his sister had an advantage – a duelling guild education. Not to mention that in Ikaras ladies did not duel, ever. Ladies did not pick up anything with a sharp edge, or not in public at any rate. Vocho's surprise for Bear.

"My sister, I think, could take any one of you."

Bear grinned as though that was exactly the answer he'd been expecting. He pointed to a pigeon-chested young man in the corner, wheezing over a water pipe almost as big as he was. Bear waved him over and whispered in his ear. The young man nodded as though this was no surprise and started making himself ready. This seemed to include copious draughts of what was presumably something to sober him up – the water pipes' more insidious ingredients made all sorts of things dance in front of the smoker's eyes.

"Whoops," Kacha said, and metal rang on stone again.

A few muttered about ladies not duelling, but Bear sliced a glare around the room and they all shut up.

"You're on." Vocho picked up his sword and threw it to Kacha, who caught it neatly, unsheathed it and kicked off the heels she'd sworn about so much earlier.

To Vocho's consternation, Bear didn't look the slightest bit surprised. He nodded to one of his cronies while the rest made some room, and after a few moments Bear's duellist stepped forward looking far too at home with his sword.

The duellers sized each other up, before Kacha gave a brief salute and went for the other. The pokey backroom was soon drowned in the noise of swords clashing, the feet of the crowd stamping, a flurry of side bets between Bear's cronies. Bear's man was better than he looked – the pigeon chest disappeared, the shoulders came back. He was nifty on his feet too and had a style that seemed to confound Kacha at every turn. She was fighting in the Icthian style, a time-honoured method that was loose, fast flowing and devious, using not just the sword but everything else in range too – feet, elbows, handy bits of furniture. Above all it was elegant, which was not a description you could apply to Bear's man.

His sword was of a style Vocho hadn't seen before but had heard about. A *palla* they called it, a brutal-looking thing with a thick curved blade and not much of a guard, made for quick killing via brute strength not stylish sword-play. He used it far better than his looks had led Vocho to believe too, in a style Vocho had never seen before, a series of savage chops that appeared to give no thought to defence, yet somehow Kacha never got a touch on him. The man wasn't quick as such, but he was good.

Still, Vocho had every confidence in his sister. She hadn't been the guild master's assassin all that time for nothing. She didn't like using other people's blades, but as hers were still tucked up safe at the guild where they couldn't get at them, she didn't have much choice. She looked like she was missing the dagger she often kept in her off hand though, and was hard pressed to keep her guard up. She was quick enough, but if this went on too long she'd tire against the heavier blade and then he'd have her.

Naturally, Kacha being the bloody perfect person she was, she had a plan. She grabbed a bottle of something from a low table with her off hand on the way past, smashed it so she held the neck and used the jagged end to harry her opponent even as she thrust and parried with her sword. A slash to the face, a vicious thrust to the stomach, which the man only just avoided more by luck than judgement. She got in a few kicks as well, when she had the chance, but this was no easy opponent. For every thrust he had his *palla* in the way, for every feint he was ready, for every kick to somewhere soft he just wasn't there, and all the time that heavy blade was swirling, chopping, slashing, coming a shade too close for Vocho's liking.

The crowd catcalled and jeered, telling the man – Haval they called him, an odd name – to get on with it and beat her. All in all, this was taking a lot longer than Vocho had hoped. Kass must be off form, he thought, because despite the strangeness of the man's style she should have had the bugger by now.

Then she almost did have him – a vicious slash across where his face had been a second ago with the broken bottle while her sword arrowed towards his torso ready to winkle out his liver. It probably would have gone quite badly for him if the crowd hadn't erupted in displeasure, pelting Kass with bottles and other less savoury missiles from all sides. They could have coped even with that – Kass ignored them or batted them away and Voch was ready to step in, for Kass's sake not his own glory, of course – if not for the sudden prick of a blade at Vocho's waist.

"Even if she wins, you lose," Bear said into his ear. "I mean to have that sword. The sword that once belonged to the renowned, and disgraced, Vocho of the guild, the sword that killed a priest and started a war. Correct? Thought so. Now, tell your lovely sister to stop. Haval will have no hesitation killing her, and he can, believe me. Even Kacha the noted duellist can't stop him."

Vocho looked down at the whisper-thin stiletto that had pierced his tunic, his shirt, and threatened to do the same to his navel. Just as he was about to say screw it and give it a go, two of Bear's cronies came up beside him. The rest were crowded around Haval and Kacha, and other daggers were being drawn, flickering in the dim and smoky light. Sharp blades might be illegal in Ikaras, but money bought a lot of leeway.

"It's all about the sword in Reyes, yes? Or at least it was until they got those clockwork guns. Not here though. No duelling. No swords, no guns or not many, not yet. Lots of magicians though, enforcing the laws. So here we do things secretly. Subtle, not like you Reyes pigs. No chance for Vocho the Great to show off."

"You seem to have the advantage of me," Vocho managed, trying to move without seeming to. Didn't help because the blade point followed his belly button, and Bear's cronies had theirs join in. If he wasn't careful he might lose a nipple.

"As I should, seeing how much I paid to find out," Bear said. "Although you two stick out like barbarians here. Now, your sister or your innards. Your choice."

Not much of a choice then, really.

"Er, Kass? I think we're all done here," he shouted. "Hand the nice man the sword, would you?"

A sudden stillness at the other end of the room. Vocho could feel the outraged question even if he couldn't see her face behind all the onlookers. Silence followed, and Vocho didn't need to see to know she was assessing the situation, the number of people ranged against them. Luckily for his insides, she wasn't quite as rash as he was.

Finally a clang followed by a tinkling crash as she dropped his sword and the bottle.

"Excellent," Bear said. "Now, I wonder how much we'll get for turning in two Reyes spies in this time of coming war? Get moving."

A more insistent prick of a dagger into Vocho's back. He moved but being Vocho couldn't keep his mouth shut. "I don't suppose you'll get much for us, considering we aren't spies."

Bear laughed in his ear. "Reyens in Ikaras, with all the trouble lately? What else would you be? I have to say the king was very upset with that business between you and Licio. He stood to make a great deal of money, and our king does not like losing that kind of opportunity. I'm sure he'd be most pleased to meet you, even if you aren't actually spying. I shall certainly be most pleased to spend the reward money, which I'm sure will be very generous."

Kacha stumbled in front of Vocho as someone pushed her from behind. The carefully coiffed fair hair had come unbound and now flopped against her forehead in its more usual manner. "Nice one, Voch."

As Bear shoved him on towards the door, Vocho took stock. It looked like they were in seriously big trouble here. The room only had one door, which had several of Bear's cronies loitering by it, supposedly blunted ceremonial daggers drawn. The single window was firmly shuttered, and with a half dozen men in front of it in any case. They might have more luck when they got out of there and into the inn beyond, where Cospel was waiting for them, hopefully still both sober and incognito. Vocho wasn't prepared to bet on it though.

A figure appeared in the doorway, silhouetted against the glare from the inn's lamps behind him. Vocho had the strangest feeling he should know who it was, but even when the figure stepped forward he couldn't place the man for some seconds.

He was tall and slender, older than Vocho by a decade or more, and he moved like he was on oiled springs. One hand was on a duelling sword even finer than Vocho's. He cocked an eyebrow at Bear, and his smile was as sharp as daggers. It was only when Vocho noticed all the gewgaws and trinkets adorning the man's very fine clothes – clothes with not a speck of dust or the ghost of a crease – that he realised who he was looking at.

Bear got there first. "Domenech?"

"The very same." Dom gave Vocho the sort of look that said, "Shut up and let me do the talking." He was glad to leave him to it. Sort of. The Dom he knew hadn't been that smart, but this Dom looked like he might be. It was a distraction, at least, one that he and Kacha might take advantage of. They shared a look, and he knew she was as ready as he was, if the opportunity should arise.

Then it was too late for any of the talking that Dom had in mind. Three of Bear's men lunged at him, and the room became a whirl of men and knives, one flashing duellist's sword and one heavy, chopping sort of sword as Haval decided that Dom was his for the taking.

The blade was still pricking Vocho around his kidneys and Bear had his arm twisted up behind his back as well. He obviously hadn't been paying attention elsewhere though because a sudden "Oof!" sounded by Vocho's ear, Bear's grip loosened, the blade fell away, and when Vocho turned, Kacha was standing like some sort of vengeful goddess with a high-heeled shoe in each hand. The end of one heel had blood on it, as did Bear's head down on the floor. His two cronies were too stunned to move for a second – a second too long, as Kacha aimed a vicious balls-high kick at one and Vocho used his elbows and fists to good effect on the other.

Finally they seemed unencumbered by anyone trying to kill them. Kill them right this second, at least. Vocho cocked an eyebrow at Kass and her unorthodox weapons.

"Someone had to bloody well pay for me getting dressed up like this. Be thankful it wasn't you." Kass took a swipe at a passing man with one heel, getting him a cracking shot in the stomach and bending him over, breathless. "Now stop pissing about and let's get out of here."

"That's a plan I can get behind. Where's Dom?"

Dom was by the shuttered window, having seemingly attracted the attention of just about every man with a weapon in the place. Even as they watched, Haval took out a chunk of shutter at Dom's back, missing him by a scant hair as Dom twisted away, skewering another man as he went. Another chop from that brutal blade, another chunk out of the shutter, and Vocho could see what Dom was about even if Haval was too caught up in trying to hack off his head to notice. Kass saw it at the same time.

Cospel appeared at the doorway, semaphoring desperately with his eyebrows. Vocho had been studying those eyebrows for a long time now, and was fairly sure that Cospel used them to articulate things he dare not say out loud to his employers. This time they seemed to say, "Over here, you stupid bastards."

Vocho went, though Kass hesitated. "But Dom?"

He grabbed her arm and yanked her over to the doorway and Cospel.

"Said he'd provide a distraction for you, miss." Cospel had a heavy pewter tankard in one hand and looked about ready to brain anyone who came too close. "And not to let you be stupid and stay in here."

A thundering crack came from across the room. Haval seemed to have realised what Dom was about, but too late. His heavy sword had burst open the shutter, and with a wink and a wave Dom flipped through the opening and out into the night. Haval roared after him, but the others seemed less keen to follow. Given that four of them were bleeding out onto the floor, Vocho couldn't blame them.

That said, there were eight Ikarans left upright and only three of them, armed with a tankard and some shoes, and the Ikarans seemed to like the odds of that much better. Two of the bolder ones began to advance, and the others fell in behind. Where in hells was his sword? There, half obscured by bleeding bodies where Bear had dropped it. Well, he wasn't leaving without it. Vocho gave Kass a shove through the doorway, spun and dropped, grabbed the sword and bounced back up – just in time for the lead two Ikarans to slash at his face. The rest came round, trying to flank him.

He flashed them a bright grin, saluted with his sword as though about to launch himself at them, then stepped back through the doorway. As soon as he was through Kacha slammed it shut and turned the key in the lock. Which just left them with a bar full of curious and not especially friendly-looking drunks. When the barman pulled out a thick slab of wood with some nails driven through it, followed by some of his patrons whipping out some impromptu but serious-looking weapons, Vocho made a snap decision.

"I say we run."

Kass winced – shying from a fight didn't come naturally – but said, "I don't think I ever heard you say that before, but you could be right. You've got the sword. You keep them busy while we clear a path. Make it quick, OK?"

"Thanks, I think."

"You're welcome." She was still smarting about the dress, he could tell.

Then there was no more time for talk. Two hulking great bruisers, the worse for wear but still steady enough on their feet, lumbered in front of Vocho.

"Here, ain't you that Vocho bloke?" one asked, and Vocho couldn't help but preen a little that they knew him.

"Nah, he's too little," the second one said.

"'T's him. I seen the pictures in the paper, and besides Bear said so. This here bloke caused all that ruckus in Reyes. Vocho the *Imbècil*, Bear said – that was it."

Vocho the *what*? His Ikaran wasn't up to much, but that certainly didn't sound like Vocho the Great, because he'd learned that word almost first of all. He swished the sword in front of their stupid eyes and prepared to show them that whatever *imbècil* meant, he wasn't one. Nothing like a good—

Kass yanked the back of his shirt. "God's cogs, will you come on? The guards'll be here any second, and you've got a ruddy great sword in your hand."

The two lumberers came for him brandishing a wicked set of brass knuckles and a foot-long metal spike, but a swipe of his sword kept them back. A *clonk* behind him – Cospel using the tankard to good effect – a muffled scream as Kass's shoe caught a man somewhere painful, and the doorway to the street was free. Lumberer number one looked like he'd just worked out that being a good foot taller than Vocho was probably all the advantage he needed, so Vocho didn't need any encouragement to throw himself through the door after Kass and Cospel.

Then they were running down the street as fast as they could, with a swiftly dwindling crowd after them. A few twists and turns, and they were on their own and out of breath. They stopped. Cospel bent over his knees, gasping. The multicoloured lights that shone from every building, leaked from all the stored sunlight of the glass that covered the city, made his face look like that of a demented clown.

"I could have taken them, no problem," Vocho said, leaning against the cool throbbing blue glass of an upmarket tailor's. "What does *imbècil* mean?"

Cospel hesitated, and his eyebrows didn't know where to look. "Sort of . . . renowned. Infamous? Yes, that's it." His Ikaran was far better than either Vocho's or Kass's, though none of them was fluent yet.

"Renowned? Are you sure?" The way the lumberers had said it, Vocho wasn't so certain.

"Er, yes. Pretty sure. Anyway, look what I got." Cospel held up a clinking bag. "Once Dom got started, it was easy to pick up all the winnings."

Vocho took a look in the bag. Not bad for a night's work. "Cospel, have I ever told you that you're a marvel?"

"No, but you can say it again if you like, preferably in cold hard cash."

They made their way through the pulsing lights of the foreign city to the cramped rooms above a cobbler's that were their current home. Kass was unnaturally quiet all the way, and Vocho got the feeling it wasn't just because she was wearing a dress and sulking about it.

"Two things," she said when they got home and Vocho broached the subject. "One, how did Dom know where we were? Two, if he knows, who else does, and do they want to kill us?"